Totally Bound Publishing books by L A Tavares

Single Books
Each and Every Summer

Consistently Inconsistent
One Motion More
Two Different Sides
Three Beating Hearts

I0611176

Consistently Inconsistent

THREE BEATING HEARTS

L A TAVARES

THREE
BEATING
HEARTS

Dedication

Kati,
For never letting me forget that 'the doers make it
farther than the dreamers'.
This one, once again, is for you.

Chapter One

Dom

Green signs with white text reflect the names of familiar streets as the tour bus flies underneath them.

Twelve pages, I think as I peek at the last page number of the book I hold. Only a few exits from home and I'm a dozen pages short of finishing the story.

"Did you do it?" Theo sits down in a chair nearby and sips from a beer bottle. "Did you get through all fifty?"

"Almost." I hold up the book but keep my eyes on the text, trying to finish before we reach our destination. "I'm a bit short right now, though."

"What number is this one?" He leans forward and flicks the cover.

"Forty-eight." I shrug. "But unless I can finish this one and two more in the next fifteen minutes, I'd say I'm not reaching my goal."

"Technically." He takes another sip between words. "We've still got the Boston shows. The tour isn't over yet, so you've still got time." He winks as he stands and heads toward the back of the bus. I bury my face in the text.

As the bus pulls into our drop-off spot, my bandmates holler and cheer, kicking off the usual welcome home parties they throw themselves upon arrival. They will get off this bus almost before it even comes to a full stop and hop from bar to bar until last call, then open the doors to their own homes, where they will continue to drink until the sun comes up, sleep the day away and not wake until we're required to be at the venue for our home shows.

We close every tour at home. Sometimes it's one show, sometimes it's three. The number of shows and the Boston venue we play at varies, but our traditions upon returning don't. They will launch our home stretch with their inhibitions off and their 'check liver light' on. Some things never change, no matter how much we've grown. My bandmates always revert back to their wild youth years the moment the tour bus wheels hit Boston's pothole-filled pavement.

"Planning on staying the night?" Xander hits me on the back of the head in an annoying but playful way as he passes me. "We've been parked for a few minutes now."

"I only have a few pages left. I'm surprised it's taken you this long, though. You're usually halfway down Boylston Street by now."

"I forgot my sunglasses. What is that, anyway?"

"It's a book, Xander. Ever read one?"

He smiles and shakes his head, but I can't tell if the *no* motion is sincere or sarcastic.

"I'm headed out. You sure you don't want to come?"

I'll say 'no' and he will tell me that I'm missing out. The tour bus final scene never changes.

"You ask me that every time." I peek up at him over my glasses and the top of my book. "I'm good. I have somewhere to be."

"You say that every time." He shakes his head and puts his sunglasses on.

"It's true every time."

"You're missing out."

"You say that every time."

"It's true every time."

We laugh a light sound at our exchange. It's not the first time we've had this conversation. For as long as we're touring, it won't be the last. He turns to head off the tour bus.

"Xander?" He turns and looks at me, though his gaze is hidden behind dark lenses. "Be careful. Take care of yourself and the boys. I know I don't partake in the crazy sideshow that you guys put on when we return home, but I do care. Get everyone home in one piece."

Xander pushes his sunglasses into his in-desperate-need-of-a-cut hair. "You say that every time."

"It's true every time."

He slides his sunglasses over his eyes once more and retreats from the bus.

Alone on the silent tour bus, I finish book number forty-eight on my list and I'm not impressed. The story had so much potential. For nearly four hundred pages it was perfectly executed with many memorable parts, then the story crumbled in the last ten. I sink my head back too hard into the headrest. There are few comparable disappointments than investing yourself in a story that has a bad ending. At the same time, there's no stronger parallel to life. It has its ups and downs with good and bad sections along the way. Characters are introduced that we get attached to and some who are forgettable. It's colorful, exciting and every day is like turning a page until there are none left to turn. It ends. It's over. It will happen to every single one of us. For most, our final pages will be disappointing. I wish that wasn't the hard truth, but it is. Turning the final pages of one's own story or the one of someone close is always disappointing.

I order a car service on my phone then toss the book and my cell into my bag and carry it off the bus with a goodnight wave to our remaining equipment staff. My ride arrives and the driver gets out of the car to take my bag to the trunk then open the door for me. I slide into the back seat. When the driver returns, he sets his focus on the rear-view mirror.

"Consistently Inconsistent, eh?"

"Yeah," I admit in a small voice, but I'm not exactly sure what he's asking.

"I saw the patch on your bag." He puts the car into drive and pulls away from the curb. "You ever seen them live?"

There it is. He's a fan. He used the patch as a gateway to start small talk about something we might have in common, yet failed to recognize he has the drummer of said band in his car. It's not the first time. If I had a dollar for every person who has asked me to take a photo of them with Xander or Blake, I could buy a small island.

It doesn't bother me. When I'm not on stage, I lead an incredibly quiet existence. I am different than my bandmates, and though they are closer than family to me, I've always been the black sheep. We are so close, yet so far apart. We live entirely different lifestyles. One of my biggest joys comes from watching Xander and Blake smile. There were so many years that they didn't. They are so full of life that it's contagious, and I'd confidently say ninety percent of my laughter is caused by them or at their expense. Theo, too—his favorite moments are ones he gets recognized *before* Xander or Blake. He keeps on about it for hours. Even after all these years, the celebrity never gets old for them.

I fade into the background, and nine times out of ten I'm okay with that. I get lost behind walls that I built. Though I don't let it bother me widely or outwardly, it does sting every once in a while, when people know the band but don't know I'm in it. Perhaps, somewhere along the way, I let myself get too quiet.

"You sure this is the address you meant to put in?" he asks with heavy skepticism as we arrive at my destination.

"Positive."

"It's dark out there, you know. And...kind of scary, don't you think?"

I smirk as I open the door. The judgment in his eyes and stillness in his body language makes it clear he's not getting out of the car.

"I'll be okay. Pop the trunk for me, if you don't mind."

I retrieve my bag then slam the trunk closed. "Have a nice night now." I wave as he speeds off. The light his headlights had provided dimmed more and more as he got farther away. The world gets darker—and more silent.

I walk the familiar path through the gate, passing a thick grouping of trees, and continue onward into the perpetual darkness that the cemetery offers. I turn down the dirt pathway that leads to my final destination, and in the distance, I can see the light of a single flickering candle that dances against the headstone. It seems the light winds have extinguished every other candle within a visible distance—but not hers. Hers dances in the dark.

I wonder for a moment who might have lit it and smile at its resilience. She would have liked the symmetry in that—surviving brilliantly, even when the odds were stacked against her, dancing when the time seemed the most inappropriate.

The headstone is heart-shaped—a choice I never agreed with but didn't get a say in. It's made of a brilliant blue-green marble that shines with a topcoat that's so clean it's reflective. Five years of rain and snow haven't taken its toll on the stone outwardly. Just under two thousand days of battling weather day in and day out and it gleams the same way it did when it had been placed. She would've liked that, too. She'd also smiled and glistened, though she'd battled her own elements each day of her life.

Two dates—dates that are not nearly far enough apart—are carved deep into the rock. It has always been odd to me that we focus on two particular days, when the real magic and the true memories were all of the dates in between. The ones not mentioned are the times that made up her legacy and her life. There were so many of them worth publishing throughout her twenty-seven years.

The cold from the ground seeps through my jeans as I sit, but it doesn't bother me. All my memories with her come flooding back, and those mental comforts outweigh the physical discomforts.

Starting from night one, I sit and talk out loud, recapping the tour. My voice echoes as I share everything I can remember in detail, and though I am aware there is no one within earshot listening, I know she is.

"I finished *Among Broken Clocks* today. I wish you'd annotated in the margins or something to prepare me for these garbage endings." I wrap my jacket tighter around me. "I would've loved to know your thoughts on every book you left behind."

The sun peeks through the trees, turning the midnight-black canvas to shades of pink and orange. I spent the entire night sitting and talking about the tour and the books—the same way I'd spent each night I'd returned from tour for the last five years that she's been gone and with her in person the ten years before that.

I push myself off the ground and place one hand on her headstone. "I miss you, Raya. You told me all this would get easier with time. You were wrong."

Chapter Two

Stasia

I couldn't cut it in Los Angeles.

I wish that weren't the case, but if wishful thinking was all it took, we'd all have a sold-out tour and multiple platinum albums.

The problem wasn't that I didn't have what it took. I *do* have what it takes. I *am* what it takes. The issue was that seemingly everyone lived under the thumb of my father. Somehow, he had something on everyone in this business. He said 'jump', and they jumped twice for good measure. When Victor Marquette made it well known that no one was to sign me to a label or there would be consequences, they listened.

It's true what they say in the music business. It's all about who you know. I know a lot of people. I could have made it years ago if I'd have played by the rules, but I'm not known for that. Growing up Stasia Marquette pretty much guaranteed me a long, successful run in the spotlight, but I turned it down.

Even though I'm traveling by myself with the top down in a convertible older than me three thousand miles across the country from LA to Boston, I have no regrets. My big break is out there. I can feel it. When that day comes, I'll dedicate every word I sing to the people who dared to sleep on Stasia Marquette. Again, I have no regrets — but they will.

Returning home was a tough decision, but I felt like being in LA was getting farther away from my goal rather than closing in on it. Coming home isn't a defeat. I don't wave white flags. It's a chance to start over — a fresh start to grow from where my roots are planted.

I'm so close to home that I can taste it on the wind that blows against my face. I'll be the first to admit I was that 'can't wait to leave this whole damn place in my rear-view' teen. Years ago, before I realized the value of home, I couldn't wait to jump ship. The more I tried to tell myself that I didn't miss it, the more homesick I got. I take a deep breath and a smile presses into my cheeks. I have half a mind to go twice the speed limit the rest of the way, just to see that skyline faster. I bite into my bottom lip, glancing at the speedometer, knowing that no matter how much I want to push the pedal to the metal, the car is a classic, and I, unfortunately, haven't maintained her well enough to ensure that she won't spontaneously combust.

Music blares out from the speakers in the dash that's too old to support even an aux cord, but the song changes to one of my favorites — a good omen if I ever did encounter one — as I approach a red light. I don't know what comes over me in that moment, but I felt free. Matching the beat of the song, I drum my hands against the wheel and shake my head so my hair flies wildly. In the front seat of this older-than-me Alpha Romeo Spider, I use the sun rays as a spotlight and sing into a nonexistent microphone. I look to my right and am surprised to see another car has joined me at the light.

And I don't care.

Nothing can stop me today. I haven't been in control of my life in years, and I've given too much of myself over to LA, rejection and fatigue. Now, sitting in this car, at this red light with this stranger, I'm taking a bit of myself back, if only fractionally.

The driver of the car smiles shyly in my direction with a slight head shake, and her cheeks turn a light shade of pink. I pause for a moment and she turns up her radio full blast, too. She's listening to the same station. We both laugh — though we can't hear the sound over our combined music — but our eyes and our bodies, they laugh.

I give it one last air drum solo and a shimmy for good measure and her cheeks turn as red as the paint on her car. She hesitates, and in that second, I can tell dancing in the street with a stranger is not this girl's style, but she gives in. For a few beats, she allows the song to take over and rocks her head in a way that knocks some hair in her braid loose, and she's laughing again. When I settle my gaze on the stoplight once more, it's green, and neither of us had any idea when it changed.

A horn blares from a car behind me. I run a hand through my hair and glance in the mirror. A disgruntled man in a suit shouts from behind me. With one last look over my passenger seat, I shrug toward the other driver and wink as she gives me a quick wave and drives off with a smile.

I purposefully take my sweet time, though the Spider doesn't go zero to sixty on a good day. The man swerves around me, his tires screeching against the asphalt. He holds one finger out of the window as he drives by and I do the same—a good old-fashioned Boston salute. They don't call us 'Mass Holes' for nothing.

A dozen miles from the city and a *pop hiss* sounds from the hood of my car, followed by a billow of gray-black smoke. It's not a great situation, but the silver lining, if there could ever be such a thing right now, is that there's a gas station within view up ahead. Dirt kicks up around my car, combining with the fumes coming from it, as I pull over to the side of the road and aggressively slam her into park. Most of my belongings are shoved into the trunk of the two-seater convertible, but a small pile of clothing and miscellaneous items ride shotgun under the dash, safe from the wind and open road. I rummage through it and manage to find shoes to pull onto my feet. I've always heard you're not supposed to drive barefoot. I guess this is a good reason why.

The door squeaks as I slam it behind me and walk toward the trunk. There's only one belonging I can't leave behind. If someone stole my clothes, my shoes... Hell, if they took the whole damn car I'd get over it, but my guitar—which may be worth more than the car itself—I couldn't chance leaving behind. Pulling the case from the trunk and closing it tight, my Les Paul and I make our journey toward the gas station, and I call for a tow truck as I walk. Unfortunately, there's at least a two-hour wait time between now and when they can get my car. So much for getting to the city as soon as possible.

Only one car sits outside the station, occupying the space near the closest gas pump—the same car driven by my impromptu on-road dance partner.

I rest my guitar case gently against the front of her car and look around, but she's not to be found. Just as I pick up my case to head inside, a bell chimes as the gas station door opens and she steps out. She's got a large fountain drink tucked between her chest and forearm and is fumbling in her pockets. I lean against the hood of her car and watch for a moment. I know I should announce my presence or say something to acknowledge I'm standing there. It's kind of entertaining the way she keeps looking in the same places, like whatever she's looking for will magically appear.

Her gaze finally finds mine and her pocket search ends. It takes her a minute to register who I am, but the corner of her mouth lifts when she does. I bite my teeth into my bottom lip and hold one thumb out.

"Any chance you're headed into the city?" I raise my pierced brow. She thinks on it for a moment and takes a long sip of her drink. "And if so, do you have room for one more?"

"Ah, yes" — she slurps her drink — "always room for one more hitchhiking stranger."

"We're not strangers. We go way back."

"A whole three miles." We both laugh at the sentiment, but then the moment ends and reservations fill the space between us. She looks at the ground where she stands and tucks a stray strand of reddish-brown hair behind her ear.

"You're into Consistently Inconsistent?"

Her eyes meet mine, but the way her eyebrow arches says she's confused. "Your shirt," I add, pointing to the T-shirt she wears.

"Oh, yeah, that." Her cheeks blush bright once again, for the third time in as many miles. She parts her lips like further details might spill out, but she cuts the words off and goes with, "Yeah, I guess."

"I love them," I say, my last effort at a conversation. "They're really big around these parts."

"Yeah. I mean…they're from here." It's not malicious. It's not sarcasm. I can't help but smile at her wit cloaked in hesitation. She tucks another piece of hair behind her ear, not because it's out of place, but seemingly to do anything except look at me. I'm about to leave, to walk back the way I came, when she surprises me.

"Are you? From here, that is?"

"I used to be." I push myself off the car and step toward her. "I'm Stasia." I extend my hand.

She takes my hand in hers in a firm handshake.

"Jana."

Chapter Three

Dom

Theo falls into the chair next to me backstage at The Rock Room as the openers play on the other side of the curtains.

"Book forty-nine?" He kicks his feet up on a nearby table.

"Fifty." I don't look up from the text. I'm on a clock and don't have time for distractions. Sure, it's a personal goal with no repercussions if the deadline is missed, but I started this tour with a goal of reading fifty books, and I'm too close to fall short and not kick myself for it. I had someone mailing me copies, and I've mailed them back as I've completed them. A lot of dedication went into this. Failing would be heartbreaking. Quitting would be worse.

"So, you stayed up all night? How very rock star of you."

I yawn as if on cue.

"Take a nap or drink some coffee…something." Theo stands and starts to walk away. "I need you ready to bring the damn house down in an hour."

I allow my eyes to trail from the book pages to my watch for only a moment. One hour until show time and more than half a book to go. This time I may just have to accept falling short.

Theo returns with a cup of coffee and sets it on a table beside me.

"What did you end up doing last night?" I try to stay focused on the story, but I'm curious, too.

"Just went out with Xander, Natalie, Blake, Kelly and Jana. You know. The usual faces. It was actually a fairly quiet night."

"Quiet for that lot is anyone else's rough night." He laughs at the comment, and I pick up my coffee then blow across the top to try to cool the liquid. I tend to avoid caffeine, but today, I feel the need.

"What did you end up doing?" Theo asked the question as if he knew it was wrong to do it.

"Same place I always go." I refocus on the book.

"Are you ever going to tell me where that is?" The frustration bleeds through his words. He sits on the opposite end of the couch I'm using.

"Probably not."

"We have been best friends for as long as I can remember. Well, at least, you're *my* best friend. But I'm not yours. You tell me nothing. You keep so many secrets."

He's not entirely wrong. He is *Dom's* best friend but he's not *Dominic's*. I live my life as two separate people. It's the reason people don't recognize me. It's the very foundation to those walls I've put up that separate the celebrity life from my normal one. On the road, in the spotlight, on the bus, on the stage, in the hotels and the public eye, yes, that version of Dom would call Theo his best friend.

But Dominic? He had a best friend.

She's gone now. All that's left of her is the hundreds of books and an intricate instruction to read them. As for the secrets? She was one of the only people who knew the things Dominic hides. Those secrets were buried when she was.

"I've always told you everything you needed to know, Theo." I close the book and lay it on my lap. "There's no big secret. No big reveal. I've always kept my life outside of this band and my life on stage as two totally different pieces. My style of clothing, the places I hang out, the way I live? They're opposite. You know that. There's really not that much more to the story."

Xander and Blake are laughing wildly at a joke Theo and I missed as they enter the backstage area.

"Good morning, boys." Xander plops down in the seat between us and puts one arm around each of our necks.

"It's almost nine p.m." I reopen my book to try to knock out a few more pages before we have to get ready to take the stage.

"It's morning to me. I woke up like thirty minutes ago."

I have to give Xander some credit. He has changed since his accident. He takes things more seriously, and his drinking and antics have decreased significantly, but home looks good on him. Even though his hair is a disaster and even his sunglasses can't mask the bags under his eyes, it does appear he's at his best when he's backstage at *this* venue in *this* city.

"What're we talking about?" Xander removes his arms from our shoulders.

"Trying to get Dom to tell me where he constantly sneaks off to."

Xander and Blake look at each other…then at me.

"You haven't told him?" Blake asks. Theo's face is lost between surprise, anger and jealousy.

"Jeez. I thought you two were friends." Xander shrugs and I roll my eyes, not bothering to look up from the book. I smile behind the pages, but I can't let them see. It only encourages and escalates their ridiculousness.

Xander stands and stretches.

"It took me a long time to figure it out, too, Theo."

"Same," Blake adds, taking a sip of something clear. "It all made so much sense once we put it all together."

I close the book with a snap. It's a futile effort to try to read now. I've read the same line forty times and still haven't absorbed the material. Besides, I'm curious as to what scenario they could have concocted.

Theo's eyes are darting between the three of us, waiting for one of us to let the cat out of the bag.

"He's clearly a werewolf." Xander takes Blake's drink from his hand and chugs the remaining liquid. "It's the only sensible answer. Now, let's go play a goddamn show!" He slams the glass down and howls an absurd sound. Blake joins in, the two of them emitting a painful wolf impression. I shake my head. They are exhausting. Incredibly inventive, but exhausting. We stand and Theo runs forward, hopping into the space between them and wrapping his arms around their shoulders. We all laugh and head toward the wings of the stage.

They're just out of sight, and I pull my T-shirt off and replace it with one that's so ripped at the sides I'm not sure it deserves to be called a shirt. I tie a bandana around my head and catch up to them. Xander places both his hands in my hair, ruffling it up to a messy masterpiece that has become somewhat of an odd pregame tradition for us. He places his forehead against mine and his hand at the back of my neck.

"You ready?" His voice hardly competes with the music that plays beyond the stage. He slaps a hand against my back between my shoulder blades then pushes me away from him, heading toward the rest of the band for their own various hype-ups. I put my ear plugs in and pull drumsticks from my back pocket before rattling them off the wall closest to me in an even beat.

"Let's go!" Theo yells to me, grabbing my sticks mid-strike. He spins one poorly and it falls to the floor. He kicks it back to me and I pick it up, twirling it perfectly between my fingers and replacing them in my back pocket.

I catch my reflection in a nearby glass pane. The bandana. The overgrown messy hair. The five o'clock shadow. The amount of skin that shows through the tears in my shirt and jeans. I'm still *Dom*.

At least, for the next few hours.

But tomorrow morning when the sun rises and the tour window is officially closed, I'll be Dominic once more. I stretch my neck and shoulders. The night after night of drumming hard and fast for long stretches, paired with long bus rides and hotel mattresses, leave my body stiff and achy by this point every tour, but the noise beyond the stage offers a temporary relief. There's no sound quite like the one from our home crowd.

If I'm being honest, I had never planned to be a musician. Drumming was supposed to be a hobby, not a career. I tested well, graduated top of our class. Multiple acceptance letters came in from prestigious colleges with hefty scholarships attached to them — scholarships for my brain, not my hands. None of those schools cared that I could keep time for a rock band. I always figured the music was in front of me and I might as well enjoy it while it lasted, because the truth is, in this business, it usually doesn't.

Much to my surprise, this career has carried us through platinum records and award-winning hit songs for almost fifteen years. The sound beyond the crowd is louder now. Everything backstage moves in slow motion. Xander bounces up and down in the wings, jump starting the energy he is required to pour out all over the stage. Blake downs a drink, and Theo leans into our band manager Cooper's shoulder, discussing something on the set list. Everyone is smiling. They're behaving like this is the first time we've ever taken the stage, and I smile too. I'm lucky — beyond lucky. In that moment, more than usual, I acknowledge I'm so grateful I still have this life, even if it has lasted longer than I thought it would.

Xander takes the stage first, as he always does. Blake follows him out and arrives at his spot where he picks up his guitar and paces around his area. The crowd screams and chants our name. Theo finds his place by the keyboard and the stage lights start brightening in a teasing manner. They shut off all together, leaving the crowd in a midnight-black blanket, then abruptly turn on to the brightest they can be with a strobe effect and a variety of flashing colors. As Xander addresses the crowd, my gaze falls to my electric-green drum kit where the initials RG are carved into the shell. I stare at the ceiling for a moment, run my thumb over the initials then grab my sticks and slam the loudest most intense introduction my body can muster.

Chapter Four

Stasia

A few weeks have passed since I traveled across time zones to return to Boston and restart my life. I've adjusted to the time change and the weather. I've found a quaint place to rent and call my own that I can afford for now with the money I have saved but will need to work on a long-term plan. My car has been restored and returned. Everything is going smoothly and according to plan.

The mislabeled box in front of me says 'Records and CDs' but is actually clothes and shoes. I pull out my favorite outfit and slide into it. My straightener heats on the bathroom vanity while I apply some dark eye makeup alongside a red lip stain and volumize my roots with too much aerosol hairspray before leaving the apartment.

As I near the intersection, I evaluate the street signs, trying to remember which direction I need to be headed. It's not a place I can google, not a location I could look up or GPS. I just have to remember it—but it's been *years*.

Surprising even myself, I only make one wrong turn before I recognize my surroundings. I guess it's true what they say. You can take the girl out of Boston but you can't take Boston out of the girl. My heels click against the broken sidewalk underneath the soft lit streetlights. Two revolving poles with red and white stripes bookend the store front. The door that rests between them is vintage, with a large brass handle and a foggy glass pane. 'Salem's Sweet Treats' glistens in gold letters across the glass. In contrast to the newer, updated buildings, it almost looks fake, like a decoration or a movie set.

I knock on the door—twice quick, three spaced out taps, then one hard bang.

"Password?" A voice from the other side asks, his silhouette appearing behind the cursive *S* in Salem's.

"I'm not sure anymore. It's been a while since I've visited."

"Come back with a password." His shadow is almost completely faded from view as he retreats.

"Wait." I reach into my purse for my plan B. "I really have been here before. I have these, from last time." I slide an old pack of matches under the door. They're faded. Some of the gold has worn down. But they distinctively say Salem's. I only could've gotten them here. There is no noise on the other side. I've almost given up hope, assuming the bouncer took my matches and ran or ignored them altogether, but the latch clicks and the door opens, revealing a dark blue hue and the man belonging to the voice on the other side.

"These matches are almost five years old." He hands them back to me. "Impressive. Next time, come with the password."

"Yes, sir." I tuck the matchbook into my bra and head toward the descending staircase.

This bar is a favorite of mine. When I lived in Boston, I could often be found here, if, that is, one knew where to look. It's a small bar with a dark atmosphere, dimly lit in between windowless walls and an absence of modern lighting. It's the kind of place that's somewhat unheard of, purposely hard to find, with a doorman and a password and a descent down a staircase so rickety you'd think there's no way there would be a fully functional bar at the bottom. Over the years, its unstable bar stools and lingering tobacco smell have become a second home to the regulars. The tight knit, select company atmosphere drew them in, but it's the Frank Sinatra impersonator who keeps them coming back.

His voice is like velvet, booming as loud as any rock song while relaxing the nerves like a classical piece and breaking your heart the way country music does.

Throw in a dash of a limitlessly talented live band for a hint of jazz and all that in one voice, one band, so seamlessly that it's like Sinatra himself reincarnated and found the password for my favorite spot. The act never changes—the same set list, the same impersonator. He swears to whatever higher being he believes in that his name is Frank, but the truth in that remains to be seen.

The company the owner keeps is always the same bartenders, and for the most part, the same crowd. Sometimes a newcomer joins, but you can usually tell the ones who stick around from the ones who will never be seen again. It's not everyone's scene. Frank croons *The Way You Look Tonight* into the microphone as the unmistakable sounds of my high heels versus aging stairs matches the tempo of the tune—slow, but distinct—and Frank loses his patron's attention. Suddenly, they're all staring at me—the only girl in the room. The blue-tinted lights change my entirely white outfit to a UV glow.

"Miss Marquette," a man in a suit says with an Italian accent, approaching me. "It's been so long. Too long." He leans in and kisses both my cheeks.

"Marco! You still work here?" My voice raises in surprise.

"I own it now, *amore mio!*"

"Wow, they finally sold Salem's? What else have I missed?"

"Too much, Miss Marquette. And your father, is he well?"

I swallow hard and adjust my purse in my hand. "I'm sure he's doing just fine."

"Come, come." He places his hand under my elbow. "Let's get you a seat and a drink."

As we walk toward the bar, I catch a glimpse of a man sitting straight ahead. He has a black dress shirt on, buttoned up, his sleeves rolled up to mid-forearm and black dress pants. His hair is on the longer side but styled, almost too perfectly, in a wave that resembles a faux hawk in style. Black glasses sit perched on his nose, and for one second, one fraction of a glance, he looks at me over the dark rims then returns his attention to whatever he's drinking.

I pause and place my hand on Marco's.

"Marco...who is that?" He looks familiar. The chances of me knowing him are slim. He looks too much like a businessman to be somebody I would have recognized. Perhaps someone my father knew? I can't put my finger on it.

"Ahh, yes." Marco nods and sweat beads at his brown. "I cannot say."

I raise my eyebrow and part my lips to ask more, but Marco holds up one hand and keeps talking.

"I can't say who he is. But I can tell you that when you came in, he noticed."

I smile the direction of the familiar yet unfamiliar man, but he's swirling ice cubes in the clear liquid in his glass. "Shall we?" Marco leads me to a seat near the well-dressed patron. I take the seat to his left.

"You look semi-familiar," I say to my bar neighbor as Marco slides a drink in front of me—a martini, extra dirty. Apparently, he hasn't forgotten my drink of choice. "Do we know each other?"

His lips slide into a smile against the rim of his glass. He takes a sip then shakes his head no.

"Sorry." I pull an olive off the cocktail pick between my teeth. "Marco said you noticed me walk in, and you look like I've seen you before. I thought maybe we'd crossed paths in a previous life."

He lets out a light laugh, one that barely leaves his throat. "There wasn't a person in here that didn't notice you."

The back of my neck grows warm, and I take a sip of my perfectly made drink. "Is that so?"

"Well, Salem's doesn't see too many women, especially ones that look like... You know what? Never mind."

"No, it's okay." I press my teeth into my bottom lip. "I want to know."

"It's the all-white thing. The white heels. The white pants, white shirt. The almost-white-blonde hair." He lifts a finger and almost brushes my face but doesn't. "This piercing here."

"What of it?" I ask, trying to piece his descriptions together.

"It's like a modern-day Marilyn Monroe waltzed down those stairs to see Ol' Blue Eyes up there sing his tunes."

His comment makes me grin in this giddy way that hurts my jaw and ears. He's handsome, for sure, but the most noticeable thing about him is that he hasn't taken his eyes off me once, and not in a frightening way — in this attentive, respectful way that makes it seem like this conversation is the only thing that matters. His mind isn't elsewhere, and he's not distracted.

"Would either of you like another drink?" Marco asks quietly, tiptoeing as if he's hesitant to interrupt.

"I'll take another martini," I say, emptying my glass. I always did drink them much too quickly. "And you're drinking?"

"Water." He winks and raises of his glass.

"You're drinking water at a bar?"

"I come for the music. I'm not a drinker."

I nod. Handsome, attentive and marches to the beat of his own drum. I'm intrigued.

"So, what's the big secret?" I ask, and his tender green eyes shift into an inquisitive grin. "Why won't Marco tell me who you are?"

He laughs, a sort of snort, and places his glass back down. "Did he say that?"

"He did." I'm laughing too, a bit, but I'm not sure what we're giggling at.

"He's just doing me a favor." The grin doesn't fade from his face. "Tell you what. I'll tell you my name if you tell me yours first."

I think, long and hard at first, take the last sip of my second martini and say, "My friends call me Marilyn."

He nods, slow and distinct, one corner of his lip pulling up into his cheek.

"Mine call me Arthur."

I know it's a lie. His smooth, silky voice both calls me out on my alias and raises his own. He's somebody. I know he's somebody, but I'm not ready to find that out yet. I won't push. The game is much too fun to call it quits so soon.

"Arthur," I repeat, and he clinks the rim of his glass off mine.

Chapter Five

Dominic

The sun shines too brightly across her face. She presses her hands over her eyes and shimmies down farther under the blankets to try to escape the light. After a few moments, she shoves the covers off and is more than awake, jolted abruptly conscious by panic and confusion.

She rotates her head to one side and looks around at my walls and the art hung on them. The way she presses her fingers to her temples allows me to assume that for her, the room is spinning. As she turns her head toward me, her focus settles on me sitting in the chair in the corner of the room.

"Good morning." I close the book I was reading and drop it in my lap. "Did you sleep well?"

"I... I..."

She looks me over from head to toe, assessing my hair and my clothes.

"Did we...?" She starts but presses her hands against her lips. I lean forward and pass a cup of water to the bedside table.

"No." I answer her question. "Drink that."

"Nothing?" she asks again. "If I'm being honest, it's not that I don't trust you. It's me. I tend not to err on the side of caution when it comes to the person I leave with."

I smile slightly at her honesty.

"You let me sleep in this bed...and you slept—"

"In this chair." Her eyes follow my movements as I place my book on the bedside table.

"You could've slept in the bed." Her voice is quiet, laced with embarrassed.

"No, I couldn't have."

"Why?"

"Because you drink martinis and I drink water."

Her mouth falls open for a moment like she has something to say but changes her mind. Then, a light smile crosses her lips that still have a faded red stain on them.

"Thank you" — she sips the water — "for letting me stay here."

"I just wanted you to get home safe. I would've sent you to your own house in an Uber, but it would be an expensive ride back to California, Stasia."

Her whole body perks up at the sound of her name and most recent place of residency.

"You looked at my ID."

"Oh, you told me your name after martini number four." My smile grows and I rub a finger and thumb at the skin on my chin—stubble free, clean-cut. "But yes, in an attempt to get you back to where you belong, I looked at your ID."

"So, you know my name, now do I get to know yours?"

"I told you mine last night." My face melts into an expression that's both playful in nature and competitive, telling her I don't plan to forfeit the game we've been playing. "Anyway, *Stasia*," I say in a slightly mocking tone, "not to be rude, but I do have somewhere I need to be getting to."

I stand up and her eyes trace my body once more.

"Headed to the gym?"

"Yoga. Sundays are recovery days. Harder training during the week. Stretch and core strength on Sundays."

She tilts her head to one side, looking me over without trying to be subtle about it.

"Okay. I'll call for an Uber." She brushes her hair with her fingers. As she pulls up the map and sees our location, she turns her phone toward me. "Well, would you look at that. I'm just a few streets over."

"In that case, I'll walk you there." I hold out one hand and she takes it, allowing me to pull her into a standing position.

Chapter Six

Stasia

"I'm telling you, it was *mortifying*." I lean my head into the window of Jana's car. Being the only person I've met since my return and becoming a great friend incredibly quick, naturally she was my first text message. She was headed into work, and I demanded that she pick me up so I could spill every humiliating detail and also become introduced to the alleged best cup of coffee in Massachusetts.

"He sounds like a really nice guy." She takes a quick left without using her directional.

"Nice. Handsome. Incredibly intelligent. It's the eye contact that does it for me. When you talk, he truly listens. It was almost intimidating at first."

"I'm failing to see the problem."

"The problem *is* that he is literally everything I'm not. Clearly. He probably thinks I'm messy and dysfunctional.

"Are you messy and dysfunctional?"

"Yes." I laugh and so does she. "I guess I don't see why I suddenly care. I've always been of the mindset that people shouldn't behave differently when they meet someone. All the crazy comes out eventually, might as well prepare people for what they're getting. They're going to like you or they're not. But I don't know. He was just…different."

"I knew I would get along with you, first impression and all. You didn't scare me away." She stops under a red light.

"What was your first impression of me?" A genuine curiosity drapes the words.

"You really want to know?" She giggles to herself as she watches the light. "You want me to be honest?"

"That's the only way to be." I lean my head into the seat and watch her smile and hesitate to answer the question.

"My first impression of you was that you looked like someone borrowed you from one of the calendars my father used to hang in his automotive shop." She bursts out laughing at her own joke. "Sorry," she says, retracting what she said and waiting to figure out if I'm offended.

"Don't be. I can totally see it." I laugh right alongside her.

"Sitting there with your guitar and the wind blowing through your hair…" She flicks the end of her braid so it flies over her shoulder. "That's all I could think of."

"That technically was your *second* impression of me. Your first impression…that would have been when you pulled up next to me at the light."

She thinks on it for a moment, as if the memory were light years away and not only a few weeks back. "I bet you were horrified, pulling up next to me having an impromptu mid-road dance sesh."

"I wasn't." Her voice is quiet, a distinct comparison to her previous laughter and playfulness. "You want the truth?"

"That's the only way." I wink as I repeat the sentiment.

"I was jealous." The sentence is quieter than the music we have playing, but I don't miss it. "It takes a lot for me to come out of my shell like that...even by myself. You just... I don't know. You don't seem to have any insecurities."

"I have insecurities." I turn my head the opposite direction so I'm staring out of the window. "I just don't really let them control me, except when it comes to my music. Trust me. My songs, my guitar playing— I have *all* the insecurities. I think all musicians do."

"Oh, I know. My friend Xan—" she starts but cuts her sentence off. "I have a close friend who's a musician. He's his own worst critic. Speaking of that," Jana continues, "you play the guitar?"

"Nah, I just carry it around as a conversation starter."

I turn back toward her, and she narrows her glare and glances at me out of the corner of her eye. "I've played since I was a kid. Just trying to make something of it for real now."

"Seems counterintuitive to leave LA. Why return to Boston?"

"I'm not sure I ever truly left," I say. "I'm a musician. I know myself as a musician, but I want other people to know me that way, too."

"I get that." She nods as she listens but not following it up with a personal parallel. "So, you're a musician. Anything else I should know about you? Interests, hobbies, criminal record perhaps?" She presses her teeth into her bottom lip, trying to fight a smile, but the grin prevails.

"If you're trying to size me up as a serial killer or something, you're a little too late."

"If it's my time, it's my time." She shrugs her shoulders and looks into the side-view mirror before switching lanes. "What's your story?"

"I don't have one."

"Nothing? No background, no family, no exciting enigmas?"

"Nothing to tell, really. I'm kind of a loner at the moment. Haven't figured out who I am, who I'm going to be or who my people are."

"Do you have any shows here planned or anything?"

"Not really. Not yet, anyway." I pull the visor down and check the status of my red lip stain.

"There's an open mic night coming up you could check out. It's at The Rock Room — you know it?"

"Of course, I know it. Do you spend much time there?"

She flashes that 'I know something you don't know' grin once more and takes a harsh left-hand turn, cutting off the car across from her in true Boston fashion.

Chapter Seven

Dominic

I pull my jacket tighter as I walk through the doors of one of Boston's largest hospitals. They keep it cold on purpose, somewhere in the high sixties, which is optimal to fend off germs but not so enjoyable for those of us who spend any amount of time there.

A drawing of a drum kit and music notes decorates the name tag on the outside of the door. I lean into the doorway of the eighth-floor room and watch as a young boy with shaggy hair air jams to a song played so loudly through headphones that I can hear it from here. When he realizes I'm standing there, he removes his headphones and waves to me from his bed.

"How was the tour?"

"It went well, thank you." I smile. "I got you something."

I pull a tiny snow globe from my pocket, and he sits up with his hands out toward me.

"Where is this one from?" His excitement lights his eyes as I hand it to him.

"Chicago." He gives it a good shake and watches as the snow floats down over the tiny replica skyline. He leans over and places it on the windowsill in line with ten others just like it.

"Thank you." His voice is quiet. "I really appreciate that you bring these to me."

"You're welcome, Jackson." My voice is small too. I hate knowing that snow globes of cities are the closest he will ever get to seeing any of those places.

Jackson is eleven years old. I've been volunteering in this wing for most of his life. Over those years, he's been inpatient more than he's been outpatient. He was born with a congenital heart issue and has been the recipient of a donor heart that's now failing. Jackson will be a lifelong cardiac patient. Only advancements in modern medicine and the top doctors the city has can determine how long that life might be. He's a fighter.

"I have something else for you." I step forward toward his bed.

"Something else?" His voice is a mix of confused but curious.

I pull drumsticks from my back pocket and twirl them between my fingers before handing them over.

His eyes light up and he throws the blankets aside, revealing his hospital gown and an array of tubes and wires. He knows exactly what this means.

"I thought the doctors said no?"

"They did…when your medications weren't working properly and your heart rate was too erratic. They didn't want you overexerting yourself." I find myself eyeing the heart monitors around his bedside. All good rhythms, all good news. "They've normalized, for the most part. They gave me the go-ahead to start you on some lessons. You still have to take it easy, though. No intense drum solos yet. We can start with the basics. What do ya say?"

There are tears in his eyes as he throws his arms in the air—wires and all.

"I'll get one of the nurses to help get you upstairs, kid. You sit tight, okay?"

I turn the corner to the nurse's station and lean into the desk. A nurse I've come to know rather well over my time here returns to her computer and smiles when her eyes meet mine.

"Dominic." Her eyes light up and her voice is welcoming. "It's so good to see you. You've been in to see Jackson, I assume?"

"Nice to see you, Ivy. I have. He's been cleared to leave his room and go see the drum set I had set up. Can you make that happen?"

"Of course!" She scurries away from the desk and returns with a wheelchair. "He has to be transported, though. Hospital policy."

"I'm sure he will travel any way he has to, as long as he gets to leave his room."

She winks and we head down the hall. As we reach his doorway, she turns and puts her hand on my arm.

"It's incredible...what you've done for him." She whispers so Jackson doesn't hear. "Truly amazing."

"It's a snow globe and some drum lessons. It's not a big deal."

She shakes her head, and a bigger smile invades her cheeks.

"He doesn't know, though, does he?"

I watch from the doorway as Jackson strikes the air with his shiny new drumsticks, and I shake my head. "He doesn't need to."

"It's nice what you do for him—what you've done for some of the kids on this floor in general." She puts her hand on my arm once more. "I'm not sure you even know how many lives you've saved with your contributions. Some of them wouldn't have survived without you."

"Some of them didn't survive anyway."

"They made it a lot longer and a lot more comfortably because of you. And even so, you changed their families lives, too."

I nod, watching as Jackson tries to spin the sticks between his small fingers.

"Why do you do it?" she asks. "Why this floor? Why these kids?"

I look around. The hospital has changed considerably over the years, but it mostly looks the same.

"I see a lot of my younger self in Jackson. I spent a lot of time here myself, growing up. Just trying to give back a bit. This hospital was my home too, once."

"Amazing." She squeezes my biceps before entering the room and heading toward Jackson's bed.

"You ready, rock star?" she asks, placing machines and wires on the pole attached to the wheelchair.

Jackson sticks his pinky and pointer fingers to the sky and sticks out his tongue.

The three of us laugh, and I follow them out of the door to the elevator that is set to take us to the room I've redesigned and soundproofed so I can start taking Jackson and others for some music therapy.

There is a space in the hospital dedicated to the long-term-care children. The area is outfitted with toys and games, TVs and even adjacent rooms available for families to stay close by. I've been given a space on this floor and permission to soundproof it and set it up with musical instruments. Patients who find themselves living in a hospital can get music lessons or just make noise on an otherwise-bad day. Theo, Blake, Xander and other musician friends of mine have agreed to be part of the program I'm so desperately trying to make successful. Who knows? If it works out here, perhaps it will catch on and I can set up shop in multiple major hospitals.

As a child, I would have done anything to have drumsticks in my hands. Pain and recovery, constantly being hovered over by my parents and the hospital staff and watching and rewatching the same old movies on TV over and over again made the already-long days seem to drag on. It wasn't the failing heart that was killing me. It was the quiet. I hated the stillness. Hospitals are no place for a drummer. Admittedly, I was obsessed with the heart monitor. I was always incredibly in tune with even beats, both as a drummer and a cardiac patient. I knew what a normal rhythm sounded like and what an uneven beat sounded like. Beyond that, I knew what they felt like—sometimes even before the machine registered it.

That's what I do now—watch the monitors that sit near the IV pole beside Jackson. The sound he produces is mostly noise. There is no pattern, no even rhythm and no attempt to play the drums correctly. He slams and thumps every drum, tom and cymbal his arms can reach in an erratic and less-than-poetic way that has me laughing and smiling on the outside, while on the inside, the beat he was producing wasn't the one I was worried about. The monitor remained in an even-paced reading—a bit tachycardic, an elevated rate to match the exertion—but no pauses, no abnormal spikes. Nothing indicating any kind of concern.

"Are you going to teach me something or are you just going to stand there?" Jackson yells over his turbulent solo.

I nod my head and smile as I do my best to ignore the monitors and enjoy the moment. He certainly is.

After only an hour passes, Ivy returns to collect Jackson.

"Five more minutes," he pleads, but she shakes her head and gives me a sympathetic look.

"We will do this again soon, bud. I have to go, too." I hold out one palm, and he slaps his against mine before Ivy wheels him away.

* * * *

Hours later I sit on the floor of Theo's garage and hand him tools as he lies half under the body of a '66 Mustang.

"Hand me one of those hose clamps," he mumbles from under the car. I place the small stainless-steel loop in his hand. "How's Jackson?"

"Still waiting on a miracle." I flick a flashlight on and off as I speak. "Really good, all things considered, though."

Theo slides the dolly out and sits up once his head clears the undercarriage of the car.

"You let him know when he's ready to learn a real instrument, I'd be happy to help." Theo grabs the flashlight from my hand and lies on his side, further inspecting his work.

"You're practically a decoration." I laugh as I say the words. "Drums are the heart of music. You're an appendix, at best."

Theo flicks off the flashlight and brings himself to his knees then a standing position before heading to the fridge where he pulls out a beer and tosses me a water.

"I think someone has been spending too much time at the hospital." He pops the top to his bottle and tosses it aside.

"I was only there for a few hours."

"Eleven years old and he's spent more time in the hospital than out of it." Theo places his bottle down and puts two pumps of liquid from an orange container in his hand then rubs them together. "Imagine having to go through that."

I can imagine it. I did it. Most of my hospital stays, surgeries and cardiac issues happened well before I started hanging around the band. They don't know anything about it. I do my best every day to keep it that way.

It's not that I don't trust them or that they don't deserve to know. In high school I had already been playing the drums for years. *Everything* was a drum set when you had a desire to play. I drummed on desks, on buckets, on tables. My family was fortunate enough to put me in lessons but not quite fortunate enough for me to own a nice set at home. My medical bills didn't help our financial situation. We weren't rich by any means, but we weren't poor. My parents would have been far more well off if half the money coming in didn't go directly toward medications and lengthy stays. They never complained, and I do my best to make up for it now. I drummed at school frequently, before or after school — really any time they were available.

One day I left my last class and went straight toward the auditorium. A handwritten note was taped to a cymbal that read, "Band for the talent show looking for a drummer. You in?"

There was no name or contact information. The only additional markings were on the back with the time and place for the talent show rehearsal. It was that day.

I skipped an incredibly important doctor's appointment to take my chances on an unheard-of band.

I remember getting home and my parents frantically yelling at me for not returning sooner and making the appointment. It had taken them weeks to get that spot. The next available date with that particular doctor was months away. They asked me if I valued my life at all.

I *did* value my life, but I wanted to make the most of what was left of it. At that point, I knew the reality was that I was closer to death than most sixteen-year-olds. So, I played. I fell in love with music, and I made the best friends I had ever had. I was advised, many times in my life, not to partake in strenuous activity. Don't do anything that alters or increases my heart rate. I didn't play intense sports or drink caffeine. But I never once took it easy on the drums. I played as hard and fast as I could until it hurt — sometimes it did. The music might have killed me, but it saved me, too.

Miraculously, I made it to that next doctor's appointment. I never told the guys because I was enjoying my life and the music way too much to let anything ruin it but also because I never thought we would go anywhere. I was looking for fun, not an overnight success story. We got both.

The medication combination that doctor recommended was life changing — life saving. I had many more years of regular rhythms and a more normal lifestyle. More so than that, I had more years of music.

At that point, backtracking was hard. How do you tell your best friends you've been hiding a large and possibly dangerous part of yourself for years?

Then I realized that I liked living two different lives. I enjoyed the drummer side of me — the intense, hardened version who lives in bright lights and thrives on loud noise, but I liked that other part of me more, the quiet side that reads books and does yoga and is almost never recognized. I needed both parts to survive. Not only do I not wish to live the lifestyle my bandmates do, but I probably also wouldn't survive it.

"You okay?" Theo asks.

"Hmm?" I nod my chin toward him.

"You seemed far away. Where'd you go?"

"High school," I say with a light laugh.

"Ahh, the good ole days." He sits back in a camping chair and puts his feet on a cooler. "Anything particular?"

"Just where we started. All the way back to the very first note Blake left on my drum kit."

Theo takes a sip of his beer and places it on the nearby tool bench with a smile on his face.

"That wasn't Blake. It was me."

"I never knew that."

"You never asked. And it didn't really matter. We all ended up exactly where we were meant to be."

Chapter Eight

Stasia

Most of the day is gone when I wake up for the second time, but beauty sleep is essential today. Tonight, I get back on stage for the first time since my return to Boston, and I can't do it looking like I had three too many martinis while unpacking and organizing my apartment. There was too much martini and not nearly enough progress.

The clippers buzz in my hand as I touch up the undercut part of my hair. The other side is longer—angled at my chin, straight ironed and hair sprayed, then teased at the root then sprayed some more. Leaning toward the mirror, I apply dark eyeshadow and a thick line of charcoal black across each lid. The deep hues of my makeup accentuate my eye color, though I've placed vibrant green-colored lenses in for an extra pop.

When I arrive at The Rock Room, the music in the venue is booming so loudly that the walls vibrate. The lighting flashes dark blues and purples. I've heard The Rock Room had come a long way over the last few years — that it was *the* music destination to have a chance of being noticed, whether it be on a small scale or large. It's not like the open mic night advertised at your local coffee shop where every once in a while a strong voice would highlight the evening among a room full of otherwise-mediocre karaoke acts. The Rock Room hosted what could better be described as a full-on concert, with a house band, a light show and a roster of the area's most promising up-and-coming acts.

The acts that have performed so far were all varying levels of great — men, women, bands, solo acts, adults, teens, quiet acoustics and thunderous anthems. There was even a band that featured two drummers. That's not unheard of but it's been a decade or more since I've seen it done.

As I wait my turn at the side of the room, I scan the place, assessing the onlookers and musicians, crowd and staff. My search pauses at the bar, and though my stomach turns at the idea of anything resembling alcohol, my eyes widen in surprise at two of the people sitting there — Xander Varro and Blake Mathews of Consistently Inconsistent.

There's *no* way. It can't be them — but of course it is. There isn't any mistaking Xander Varro. Besides, from what I've heard, they're an institution at The Rock Room. His hair is practically trademarked, and his tattoos aren't ink one would forget. Blake claps a hand on Xander's shoulder, but Xander doesn't look up at him. I imagine, for a moment, what it would be like to be on this stage with them, what it must feel like to be part of something that is so successful and doesn't seem to be slowing down. Then I think, *why not?* If I walk up to them, if I ask them to sing one song, what's the worst that would happen?

I don't shy away from things easily. If I want it, I take it. Growing up, my father always said 'the doers make it farther than the dreamers'. Sitting around hoping hasn't gotten me as far as I would've liked at this point, so now I'll take my father's advice — maybe for the first time in years — and do something about it.

As I walk toward them, I think back on what I've heard. Xander can apparently be a little rough around the edges, a little bit of bite to him if you catch him on a bad day, though from what I've heard he's like, reformed or whatever. I've never heard or read a bad word about Blake Mathews. Everyone says he fun, easy going and approachable. For my sake, I hope that last one is true. I step in between the stools they sit on, leaving one of them on each side of me.

"Hey." Suddenly, I wish I'd rehearsed this. "Are you guys busy?"

Neither of them answer.

"I'll take that as a no." I bite into my pierced bottom lip. "I'm Stasia." I stick one hand out to Blake first.

"I'm Bla —"

"Blake Mathews, I know." I shake his hand and tuck the longer strands of my hair behind my ear, then turn the opposite direction. "And Xander Varro."

Xander keeps his body still, his mind elsewhere and eyes fixed straight ahead. "What can we do for you, Stasia?"

Rumors confirmed. Xander is definitely hard to read, but I've made it this far. I see my opportunity, and I'm taking it.

"I'm up next after the break." I throw one thumb over my shoulder toward the stage. "You two want to join me?"

Xander looks at Blake, somehow through me, like I'm not there at all and the two deliberate silently, having an entire conversation without any dialogue.

"Why the hell not?" Xander downs the remains of his drink in one gulp and pushes himself off his barstool. I look at Blake, who looks just as surprised as I do.

The walk from the bar to backstage is nonexistent in my memories. I don't recall doing it. It's as if I floated from the front of the stage to the back on adrenaline alone. At my core, I am not a nervous person, but right now, I'm unraveling. *This is really happening.*

My hands are trembling as I pull my Les Paul from its case. Xander's eyes bulge out of his head like a cartoon character at the sight of it. It was exactly the lighthearted expression I needed to break my nerves. It made him less celebrity and more human.

"Now *that* is a guitar. That's gorgeous." He steps toward me with one hand out. "May I?"

The only answer is yes. If a musician like Xander Varro asks to play your guitar, the answer is always yes. It's like the Pope asking if he can baptize your baby. You don't say no to the Pope. I hand over *my* baby to be christened, so to speak.

"Very nice." He hands it back…but with tension. For a moment I think he may not let go.

"Thank you. It was a gift from my father." I tousle my hair just a bit and slide the strap over my shoulders. "What do you want to play? Something of yours, of course."

"What do you know best?" Blake asks, tuning the house guitar to his liking.

The only three things my father ever gave me was the advice about doers, the guitar I hold and a lineage chock full of people with gambling problems. The guitar got me into the mic night. His slogan encouraged me to take a chance on asking Xander and Blake. Why leave the third out? So far, tonight, all my risks have paid off. So, I take a deep breath and go all in, all my chips on the table and play the most intricate riff of any of their songs I can think of off the top of my head.

"Uhh. Well. Yeah, that works," Blake says, at first, shocked, then visibly impressed.

The voice of the host sounds over the speaker system, introducing me.

"Now or never," Blake says, elbowing me lightly. As I step onto the stage, everything moves into slow motion. The lights are dazzling, the music they chose to play us in beats in a way I can feel in soles of my feet—in my soul in general. The microphone at center stage waits for me. I step into it, but the crowd is going crazy since the moment Xander and Blake took the stage. I wonder if they ever get used to this, if hearing the crowd scream your name and applaud your every move is something you become accustomed to. Even in a small crowd, a fraction of the thousands they usually bring in, I can *feel* the adoration, the unwavering amount of regard these fans have for the men on either side of me.

"Ladies and gentlemen, thank you for having me. My name is Stasia and these poor gents I conned into performing with me are Xander and Blake."

The small crowd emits even bigger noises. They are getting a free show from local, well-known artists.

Surely they're texting and tagging anyone and everyone, ensuring their friends know what they're missing out on.

Blake adjusts the strap on his guitar and leans forward toward where I stand at center stage. "You playing us in?" he asks.

"No, you do it so much better." I nod toward him.

Without hesitation, Blake strums the intro to one of Consistently Inconsistent's more popular songs. Xander joins him, adding depth to the instrumental.

And I *feel* it — the moment I become a real musician. It wasn't the time I picked up a guitar. It wasn't the first song I ever poured my heart into. It was *this* moment. I've seen concerts, many of them. Thanks to my father's job, I grew up in the wings of venues watching artists make it or break it. But nothing — and I mean nothing — compares to sharing the stage with someone who commands it the way Xander does. Blake plays so effortlessly, so magically, that it's as if he's not even trying. I have to work for every note I play. I must focus and think. He doesn't work for it. It just exists.

I'm so caught up in their energy, so in awe of the intensity of the moment that I almost wait for Xander to start singing. He strums the guitar and steps clear away from his microphone and nods toward mine.

The lyrics to their song flow out, but I do my best to put a personal spin on it. When Xander joins in, I harmonize. When the lyrics come to a pause, Blake plays an impressive, impromptu guitar solo that's not part of the original tune. As he plays it to a close, he brings it down, slower, quieter, until he's almost not playing at all. I see Xander flick two fingers in a downward motion toward the stage director, and before I know it, most of the lights dip to almost unlit, one solitary dark blue light focuses on me, and Xander and Blake fade into the darkness. I sing the bridge to their song, singing every word as if it's my last, knowing this is the epitome of a once-in-a-lifetime chance, and mine is coming to an end. I finish the lyrics, strumming my guitar so passionately that the strings threaten to snap under my fingers, and they both play themselves back in, joining me at either side and finishing the song in an energetic, blaring finale.

Xander and Blake flank me on either side, grabbing my hands and taking a quick bow before stepping aside, holding their hands out toward me then clapping loudly themselves, their instructions reinforcing the small but boisterous crowds' applause. I wave one last time and head to the back of the stage.

The show was over, but the dream continues. Blake Mathews and I sit backstage, messing around with riffs and lyrics, like I've known him for years. He's easy to mesh with, so simple and accepting that I almost forget he's a celebrity. He doesn't act like it. There isn't even one moment of holier-than-thou attitude. Nothing about him comes off as anything but human—other than his music skills. They aren't human. They aren't even legendary. They're mythic.

Blake strums a pattern for the millionth time, and I lean into a mirror to fix my post-show hair.

"You want a drink?" I ask, and he nods and mumbles, "Anything with whiskey in it," through the guitar pick he holds between his lips. We spend the remaining hours of the night making music, reconfiguring old riffs and chord progressions and laughing in a way I didn't expect.

Chapter Nine

Dominic

Theo and I carry a large box down the hallway of the hospital and into the elevator.

"Thank you for doing this. The music room is really coming along." We place the box down between us while we wait for the elevator to move.

"It's the least I can do. They're just kids. They deserve so much more than the hand they were dealt."

I nod and the elevator doors close.

We pick up the box once more and head toward our designated music-room area.

Theo tears the cardboard and goes to work on setting up the electric keyboard the box once held.

"Dominic," I hear from behind me, turning to see Dr. Anderson lean into the doorway in a white coat and a serious look plastered on his face. "Got a minute?"

I follow Dr. Anderson into the hallway and my heart rate picks up its pace.

"Is it Jackson? Is he okay?" I shove my hands into my pockets.

"Jackson is fine." He lifts both hands and pats the air. "Are you?"

I allow myself to unwind from my temporary anxiety of Jackson's health and look into Dr. Anderson's eyes.

"I'm fine."

"You can be sure of that?" He crosses his arms over his chest. "You need to come see me one of these days, Dominic. You're overdue for testing. You know, and have known for years, that the medications you are on were never a permanent solution to your problem."

I nod. He's not telling me anything I don't already know, but I'm not having any problems, so why bother? If it ain't broke, don't fix it, right? The more I think on it, the more I wonder if that one bout of heartburn from late-night take-out with the guys was really heartburn. And was that muscle pull after the Atlanta show actually lingering muscle pain?

"I am lenient with you when you're on the road. I do my best to accommodate your care while you're out of town. But I can't take care of you if you don't take care of yourself."

"I know. You've been very good to me. I do appreciate it."

"Act like it," he says in a stern voice that I've never heard him use before. "Are you not experiencing any symptoms—or are you ignoring the ones you *are* having?"

Doc reads me like an open book. There's got to be something about the way my expression changes when he asks about my health, because I can never lie to him. I hide this part of me on almost a pathological level, with success, but never from him. Somewhere, my subconscious knows I shouldn't be lying to him in the first place, and it surfaces to call my bluff.

"I'll come in. I'll get caught up on my testing. I promise."

"Good man." He reaches out a hand and I take it in mine in a hard shake.

Theo turns toward me as I return to the room.

"What was that about?" He turns a knob on the X-shaped keyboard stand to lock it in place.

"Nothing important," I lie — again — and start sifting through the contents of the box.

* * * *

It's almost unfair that Theo and I are allowed to team up for trivia night at any bar within reasonable distance. We hardly ever lose. We have strong points in separate categories, making us a rather unbeatable duo. For me it's science, history and literature, but Theo? He's smarter than he lets anyone know. Pop culture, automobiles, sports and food are just some of the things he's incredibly well read on, and he can answer questions on any of the topics rapid fire.

The first time we partnered up, it was accidental. We were at a small bar in a town outside of Dallas, and as we ate dinner, the DJ announced trivia would be starting. The waitress assumed we were participating and left us with a blank sheet.

At the end, we didn't leave one slot blank, and we didn't have one wrong answer. That was more than a decade ago, and at the time, the prize was a free meal. Being young and still figuring out our finances, a free meal was welcomed. Now, when the prizes are a gift card or paid tab, we casually leave it on someone's else's table on the way out of the door.

We come to play and we play to win, but we play to pay it forward, too.

We've found bars hosting trivia night in every city we've traveled in. It's what we do, at least a few times a month on every tour, and every other week when we're home.

"Those are from that table over there." Our waitress places two drinks on the table, points to a group across the way and they wave. This is a fairly frequent occurrence. I lift the cup so they can see it and smile in their direction, then casually slide across the tabletop to Theo and he downs both, back-to-back.

"I ordered some chairs and decorations for the music room at the hospital." He lifts the paper the DJ gave us and reads over the category list.

"Thank you. I appreciate you wanting to get involved with this."

"Any time, man. If it's important to you, it's important to me. Let me know what else I can do. And give me a call next time you go see Jackson. I'd love to come with."

I nod my head and take the sheet of paper from him.

80s Cinema Classic Quotes is listed first. Theo will be all over that. *All About Astrology* is second. I'd be shocked if we get even one right. I'm not even sure what my own zodiac sign is. The third category reads *Kitchen Sink,* which is always a fun one, as it's an assortment of questions. The last category on the list is *Matters of the Heart.*

"You'll be on your own on that last one," Theo says, reading my mind or perhaps, my expression.

"Hmm?" I look up from the page. I've gone far out of my way to keep my own health issues under wraps, it alarms me to hear him reference them.

"You are always hitting the mark on the medical and science questions."

"Oh, right."

As we snack on appetizers and fill out our sheet, a familiar voice joins us at our table.

"Dominic, Theo," Marco says, nodding as he addresses us. "How are you doing tonight?"

"Doing well, Marco. How's things at Salem's?" Theo asks.

"You would know if you came by once in a while," Marco says with an Italian accented laugh tacked onto the end.

"I know, I know," Theo says, patting the air with his hands. "We've just been so busy."

"Dominic isn't too busy." Marco elbows me and waves his bushy eyebrows as he speaks. "Dominic came in just the other night. He even left with a girl. *Bellissima!*"

Theo narrows his eyes and tilts his head, dozens of questions passing behind glare.

"I'm picking up take-out," Marco says, stepping back from the table. "I just saw you and wanted to say hello, but I'll let you get back to your game."

"Always a pleasure, Marco." Theo picks up his glass and tilts it Marco's direction before taking a sip. "We will come see you at Salem's soon."

"A beautiful woman, huh?" Theo says as Marco retreats.

"Trust me. It's not what you're thinking. Or what *he's* thinking. It wasn't like that."

"Sure."

As if on cue, the DJ introduces himself and starts reading off our questions in a way that changes the subject before I have the chance to.

As expected, we fill our sheet with almost entirely correct answers, even pulling a few lucky responses out in the astrology category. We sit at the bar through the last call. I sip on some mock-jito contraption the bartender whipped up for me and Theo finishes his rum and Coke.

"Hey," he says, pointing above the bar. "What they hell are *they* doing?"

I turn my attention to the TV where an entertainment network airs cell phone recorded footage of Blake and Xander singing on stage at The Rock Room. It's not that we weren't invited that surprises me the most. It's not even that they're on stage when they don't need to be. It's who is between them in the spotlight, stealing their thunder, that has all my attention.

Stasia.

She's incredible. Incredible might be an insult. It doesn't fit her the way the adjective 'flawless' does.

Theo must tune into the full attention I'm giving the screen because he calls me out on it.

"You know her?"

I shake my head. "Nope."

And, for a minute, I can play it casual. For one moment, I continue to hide behind the walls I've spent almost a decade and half building, but it's the next story the TV shows that starts chipping away at them.

The headline reads "*The Band Is Back Together.*" And I slam my glass down, accidentally, in a way that causes it to spill over the top. I disregard the mess, though

Theo starts cleaning it up. My eyes are trained on the face that stares back at me on the screen.

"Sources say former band Save Me, Save You has taken to the recording studio after a five-year hiatus to bring their fans a comeback album. The musical group, who had broken up previously, has rebanded and announced their return with the promise of new music and an upcoming tour. The lead singer, fan favorite Ames Gaherty, posted this collage photo of the group in different stages of recording in the studio with the caption 'There's no place like home'."

"Dom?" Theo nudges his elbow into mine.

"Yeah?" I force my attention to him while still trying to catch the end of the story.

"Everything okay?"

I nod my head and focus on the TV once more, though the story has changed. "Yeah. Sorry. Just got distracted for a second."

"That's not like you. You're the most focused person I know."

Usually, it's the truth. Almost any other time, I stay in tune with the task at hand and don't allow anything to get in my way. Every day that Ames Gaherty was irrelevant was a good day for me. He knows all my secrets. The day he faded out from the music scene, the threat of those stories spilling did, too. Now that he has resurfaced, I'm afraid the things he knows about me will also.

* * * *

I spent almost the entire night staring at the ceiling with my mind replaying the news clip then, as much as

I willed myself not to, falling down a black hole of social media posts and comments about Save Me, Save You's return.

Admittedly, there isn't much information. There's a lot of buzz and excitement but not any interviews or announcements that give a full backstory. Why now? Why after all these years?

Since I'm not getting any sleep and I need to distance myself from anything with an Internet connection, I roll out of bed and do something I haven't done in a long time. I lace up my running shoes, stretch outside my apartment building and run through Boston's streets.

I know I should take it easy. I've always maintained a healthy lifestyle without overexerting. The marathons I've participated in were well planned, and I had Dr. Anderson in my corner clearing me and watching me every step of the way. I stay hydrated and avoid anything that could alter the health I've worked so hard to achieve. My sugar is limited. I drink coffee, but even that I do in serious moderation. Energy drinks could throw me into an uneven heart rate I might not be able to come out of, so I've never even cracked a can.

Whether Dr. Anderson thinks I do or not, I take my condition seriously. I lift weights well within my means. I do yoga and core strength. I pass on high-intensity training and excessive levels of cardio because I know the risks. I avoid all the things that could heighten my heart rate, because of the one thing that does—drumming. I risk it every day with my career. Every time I sit behind that drum kit, I know that physical exertion of keeping an even beat for the band could be the very thing that causes my own necessary beats to get out of sorts.

But right now, all I can think about is running. So, I do. I don't slow down when my body tells me to. I don't stop to think about my breathing or my speed. I just commit myself to the fastest pace my body allows and run. People and cars pass, and I don't even notice them. I turn a corner and almost collide with a bicyclist, but it doesn't faze me, I just keep going.

A searing pain pierces through my chest and I have no choice but to stop. I halt in my tracks, skidding across the cement sidewalk. I lean into the brick building nearest me and clutch my hand against my chest. My breathing is hard and uneven as I try to settle myself and my heart rate.

My smartwatch lights up as I turn its face toward me and change the app to the heart rate monitor. It's not reading a number, just flashing a red warning symbol that indicates an erratic heartbeat. I slide down the wall and sit on the ground with my knees up and my head hung forward. Eventually, my heart rate settles, and my breathing lightens. I'm lucky, because many people in my position end up hospitalized or worse. Not every erratic beat normalizes on its own. That's what internal defibrillators are for. That's what mine would be for, if I hadn't declined it when it was suggested.

I stand and walk, slowly, down the street with regret weighing me down. I have to wonder if this particular episode was physical or mental. If it's anxiety that caused that particular bout, I'd have nothing to compare it to. I've never been this rattled before. Ames hasn't even stepped back on a stage yet, and he's already under my skin.

After turning down multiple streets and taking many steps I don't even remember, I find myself at the only place I want to be.

Today, the candle that sits on the edge of her headstone isn't lit, but there are fresh flowers left behind. This time, I don't have to wonder who had been here. I already know.

Chapter Ten

Stasia

Two nights had passed since the most unbelievable night of my life, and I still didn't buy it. It didn't happen. It was just a dream. Only, it wasn't. In a world full of tech-savvy, social media junkies, I should have known I'd be Internet famous within hours of singing with Xander and Blake. They go viral every time they get haircuts, never mind an unplanned performance. Now the video was everywhere, a welcome reminder that the moment was real, and it was mine.

I had performed a million times on stage for the better part of my young life, but usually by myself for small crowd. I had a good following in LA, people who supported me on my best and worst nights, but they get bored of the small venues and the same acts. They move on to bigger and better things, and unfortunately, I had a huge roadblock in the way of bigger and better.

I pull on a white dress covered in dark-red and black roses that zips up the front, tease my roots and apply a layer of the red lip color that makes me feel the most me. Salem's is only a few blocks from my house, and a date with the musical stylings of Frank is calling my name.

There are less people on the Boston streets than I'd expect, though I suppose it is a Tuesday. The sound echoes as I bang the usual pattern on Salem's door.

"Password?" the bouncer asks.

"Lucky elephant." My reflection reveals a light smile crossing my lips as I say it. I'm not sure I remember the moment I asked for or was told the password, but there's only one person who could've told it to me.

The door creaks as it opens. "Welcome back, Stasia."

I nod my head toward the gentleman and take the blue-lit stairs to the bar.

Marco waves enthusiastically and I return the hello, but my attention shifts from my favorite bartender to the patron seated in the same spot he was last time I visited.

The perfectly styled hair, the business-style attire, the black-rimmed glasses... I don't know his name, but I do know he has an affinity for high-end clothing, specifically the dark-colored, neatly pressed and pleated type. Color me odd, but it's the forearms that do it for me, all bold and rigid, extending from under where he rolls his cuffs.

I take the stool next to him and watch as Frank snaps his fingers to the opening notes of his next tune.

"So, you sing." He spins his glass on the bar top. I wonder for a moment if he was there, but then I remember that video has been posted over and over again, viewed and shared by hundreds of thousands of people, more to Xander and Blake's appearance than my own, but I like to believe my voice, my contribution, has something to do with the viral status.

"I have a few secrets myself." I wink one false-lash-adorned lid.

"In this area, your last name doesn't allow for you to keep too much to yourself, I'd imagine."

Any semblance of a smile I had once disappears.

"So, you know my father." It's not a question.

"Not well," he says. "But I know of him."

Everyone does. Everybody knows him or *of* him, and most people, I've come to find, somehow *owe* him.

"I'm jealous of people who have any kind of anonymity. People who don't have a reputation that proceeds them, who don't have a name that's known." I shake my head and breathe out a hefty sigh.

"I know a thing or two about that," he says as he slides his glass across the bar. It's comforting, oddly, because I can tell it's genuine. Whoever he is, whatever he is, there's a reason he has only given me an alias. I'm not sure who he is behind those emerald-green eyes or under the collared, button-up shirts he wears so well — but I want to.

"A martini, Miss Marquette?" Marco asks. I glance toward my bar neighbor and he stares back. He never released his eye contact the whole time I spoke and still hasn't, one hundred percent of his attention on me.

"Water, please." I say, still sharing a long gaze with the man I only know as Arthur, and he smiles.

* * * *

At first, it was innocent. His hand on my thigh, my fingers grazing the back of his. Tiny, stolen moments of contact.

"You want to get out of here?" he asked. That question was the gear shift, the fuel that left the twenty mile per hour back roads in the rear-view as we barreled toward the freeway. He walks close behind me under the blue lights in the stairwell of Salem's. We haven't even reached the top, but as I walk ahead of him, he grabs my hand and when I turn, he pulls me into him so our chests touch. He takes my palms into his, the rough, calloused skin on hands rubbing against my palms and the feeling surprises me. I wouldn't have pegged him as someone who worked with his hands. He tucks a stray piece of hair behind my ear, the light friction between his fingers and the side of my neck causing a shiver to cascade down my back.

"I'd like to kiss you," he whispers so quiet that it was almost lost in Frank's music.

"I'd like that, too." I tilted my head upward, closer to him.

"If I'm going to kiss you, I really should tell you my name." He runs his hands down my arms, stopping when his fingers interlace in mine. "That would be the right thing to do, I think."

"I don't." It takes him by surprise. He raises his eyebrows and swallows back the revelation he was about to speak. "What's in a name, really?" I shrug, and he twists his face into a puzzled but intrigued expression. "We agreed that there's no better feeling than having the opportunity to get to know someone with no preconceived ideals, no rumors or reputation to taint this part of the process. I know you are *someone*. I have a feeling I'll figure it out eventually. But right now...the guessing...the mystery? That's my favorite part."

He moves one hand to the back of my neck and pulls me into him. He finds my mouth and our tongues discover a rhythm and waltz as Frank sings his cover of *Strangers in the Night*.

One moment, we were in the stairwell at Salem's, and the next, we were back in the bedroom I have faint but fond memories of. We walked the streets from there to here, pausing to kiss under each streetlamp that lit the way. We did take the elevator — slow dancing to its sweet, swing-style music that floated through the air while we did the same — floating, up and up until the bell chimed and the doors opened. We kissed in the hallway, and at the door and while he fumbled to find his keys. He took my hand, pulling me with him as we crossed the threshold. The apartment was pristine. *Sterile*, practically. In that moment, I start to think maybe he's a doctor. His intelligence is as obvious as the love of high-end dress clothes he wears. Surgery could be performed in this apartment, and he certainly has the bedside manner. But doctor wouldn't explain the one thing I keep circling back around to. I *know* I've seen him before. If he were a doctor, especially here in Boston, why would he look so familiar to me?

"Can I get you anything?" He opens the refrigerator, which is stocked full of protein shakes, fruits and vegetables — all healthy, no junk food and, as far as I can tell, no meat.

"Wine? Tea? Water?" His lip picks up at the corner as he says the last word.

Behind him, a large granite bar top holds gorgeous whiskey decanters, a collection of clearly expensive glasses and more bottles than I can count, and though it is a gorgeous setup, it leaves me confused.

"That's quite a collection for someone who doesn't drink." It's harsher than I mean it to sound. It's none of my business that he doesn't drink, and it's none of my business why.

"I like to host—friends, family." He laughs, a light, quick sound and scratches his chin. "Besides, the ba—"

He trails off and as his eyes scan over me from the ground up, his mouth breaks into a full grin. "My *coworkers* tend to make short work of expensive whiskey, so I keep it around."

My gaze travels along the walls, over the expensive art, across the carved crown molding that's too intricate to be anything but custom. There are multiple doors within view of where we stand, all closed. I know the one farthest away on the right is the bedroom. I've been there before. That walk I do remember, but everything else, all the other rooms, remain classified, just like the man they belong to.

I'm torn equally between wanting to know his name, his identity, and not knowing it at all. It's thrilling, playing this constant guessing game. But the more I get to know him, the more I want to know real him. The more I get to know him, the less I want to play games.

"How about a tour?" I ask, thinking there may be clues about his lifestyle, occupation or, well, anything really that could trigger my brain into realizing why he looks so familiar.

"I'll tell you what." He pours two glasses of some intricate bubbling drink that looks like a mixed beverage but I believe is just some kind of fancy lemonade. "Behind one of those three doors is exactly everything you need to know about me. It would answer every question. No stone unturned. No need for me to tell you my name because you'd figure it out. It's a minefield of clues."

Heat crawls up my spine and settles at the back of my neck. Excitement makes me smile in a way that starts behind my ears and takes my mouth with it. This is the part that enlivens me. I like this part of the game.

"So," he says, stepping in close to me, handing me a drink, then tapping the rim of his glass against the rim of mine with an echoing ping, "pick one. Pick a door."

I take a sip of my drink and gaze at him, and he stares down at me over the rims of his glasses.

The doors are all the same, all stained a dark-brown, almost-black color with intricate handles and a light gold color lining the panels. I reach my free hand forward toward door number three and press the lever, which clicks under the weight of my thumb.

"You sure that's the one you want?" I turn over my shoulder to glare at him. "You only get one. Better be confident you're making the right choice."

My fingers slide off the brass doorknob with hesitation. He could be messing with me, but now I'm not sure which to pick. I change my choice and step toward door two, pulling it open.

"Are you kidding me?" I ask, letting my hand fall from the door and slap against my thigh. "You tricked me into changing my mind to the *closet*?"

He laughs, and though on the outside I'm maintaining my feigned annoyed state, on the inside I melt. He's *fun*, he's easy going and he's…neat. There's hardly anything in the damn closet.

"Do you actually even live here?" I playfully slam the door.

"I do." He takes a seat. "I do actually live here. A closet can say a lot about a person."

"A closet can say a lot about a *normal* person." I walk toward him, slowly. His eyes follow my every move. "Your closet barely has anything in it."

"I don't find the need for a whole lot of *things*." He places his drink down on a coaster and reaches forward to take my glass too. "I live a pretty simple life. I travel often, so I'm not home much. I have no need to pour money into belongings."

"The extremely expensive clothing you wear and the museum-caliber art in here says that's not all true." I put my hands out, guiding his attention to a large, somewhat heinous black-and-gold vase on his table.

"We all have our vices," he says, that small, barely-there smile crossing his face.

"You don't strike me as a person who has a lot of vices." I didn't mean to say it out loud, but it's out there now. "I mean. You don't smoke. You don't drink. I haven't heard you swear yet. I'm guessing you're a vegetarian, but that's an educated guess based on a thirty-second look of your refrigerator."

"Well, that's a mostly valid assessment." He leans forward and places his hand lightly around mine. "Right about the vegetarian thing."

"What did I get wrong?" I take a step forward, closing the gap between us.

"Vices." He pulls my hand, guiding me toward him. I straddle over him in the chair. "I have a few."

He leans his face upward and our lips lock. He traces my spine with his fingertips, running his hand the length of my back and stopping under my thighs. He stands, lifting me with him. I wrap my legs around his waist, both arms around his neck. He carries me effortlessly to the bedroom I've been to before and drops me gently to the bed. He finds my throat with his lips and kisses each inch of my neck, my jawline.

I run my fingers down the front of his shirt, stopping to undo each button as I go. He wraps his around both of my wrists firmly, effectively pressing pause on the undressing portion of the episode. The look in his eyes is unlike anything I've seen before.

"I…" He starts but cuts himself off. He parts his lips like he's going to speak, to explain something or admit something, but he doesn't. "You're sure?" he finally asks, holding his body weight above me.

"About this?" I ask. "Absolutely."

"No." He smiles, slow, coy. "You're sure you don't want to know my name first?"

There's a second, just a fraction of time, where I think about this game we've been playing. The anonymity I crave, the mask I hide behind, it's to hide from my name. My name comes with an assumption of riches, of success, of status. That's why I hide. I've been played like a drum by people I thought were my friends who only wanted to be close to me to be close to my father. We've had family members steal from us. I realize that the things I'm hiding from are mostly positive in nature, but I don't know this man. All this time I thought the same—maybe he's hiding the fact that he has money. Perhaps he's hiding some kind of celebrity. I've always assumed the *someone* or *something* he's hiding from was something good, something positive, something desirable.

But I don't know him. And in that fleeting moment I wondered—what if what he's hiding from, what if the name he goes by is associated with something different? Something bad…dangerous.

He shifts backward, almost removing his weight from me entirely, sensing my reservation. I hesitated, even for a millisecond and he paused, and I know without a shadow of a doubt that he doesn't have a dangerous fiber in his being.

I reach forward and grab the collar of his partially opened shirt, pulling him toward me once more. "I'm sure."

* * * *

Later, when the world is dark and the room is unlit except for a soft glow of two large, column-shaped salt lamps that provide an orange hue and a perfect ambiance, we lay under the silk bedsheets and take turns playing each other songs from our favorite playlists. When each song ends, we dissect it—our favorite line, why we chose it, where we were standing when we first heard it.

There is, in my opinion, no better way to get to know a person than to allow them to share the music that matters most to them.

"There is something I'd like you to know about me, and I know I probably should've said something sooner."

I tense at the sound of the warning, wondering, once again, what I've gotten myself into.

"I don't do relationships. So, wherever this goes, however long it takes us to exchange names and true identities, it won't amount to anything."

I smile as he says the words, and I'll be honest. He looks a bit frightened by my laugh.

"I just moved here. I'm just looking for a bit of fun. I don't even know how long I'll stick around. Physical is fine with me."

He nods in agreement.

"Can I ask you something, though?" I hit the pause button and the music cuts out.

He props himself up on his elbow and rests his head in his hand. "Of course."

I reach my hand forward and run my fingers lightly down his chest, which is decorated in a handful of small, thin scars that vary in size and are slightly lighter in some places and raised in others. "Tell me about these."

He hesitates in the same way he did when I started unbuttoning his shirt. The blankness that comes across his eyes, that breath that he cuts off before he allows himself to speak. It's déjà vu, and I get it. These marks are why he hesitated in the first place.

"I'm sorry." I pull my hand away from his chest and my eyes away from him, distracting myself by using my finger to trace the design on his bedding. "You don't have to tell me."

He reaches for my hand, linking his fingers in mine. "They're just scars. But they're old. Healed. Nothing to worry about now."

I allow my gaze to find his once more, and he smiles. Then he lets go of my hand, reaches forward and runs his fingers across my skin in the same manner, only his fingers find color and shading and lines that I chose. "Tell me about these."

"Which one?"

"All of them."

"We could be here all night."

"That was my intention."

And so, we were.

* * * *

The next morning the sun shines brightly through the blinds, lighting the room and kissing my face. My eyes fight the glow, blinking to shield themselves from the unapologetic rays. Eventually, I adapt. My vision adjusts and I scan the room to find that I'm alone. A piece of paper rests on the pillow next to me. His handwriting is pristine—a perfect, legible cursive that looks more like calligraphy than scrawl.

Stasia,
I didn't want to wake you, but I had something I had to do for work. Stay as long as you'd like. Hope to see you again soon.

The ceiling fan pumps down cold air that casts goosebumps across my skin as I slide out of the bed, and the cold floor sends a jolt through my feet. I dress quickly, lean into the mirror above the dresser and fix my hair just enough to attempt to rid myself of that 'walk of shame' look. As I tiptoe through the apartment I look around, fully aware that I could cheat at my own game and he'd never know. I could ask him who he is— his name and any stories that come along with it—and he would tell me. This is a challenge of self-control. This is me wondering how long I can go without asking or snooping. The thought crossed my mind. How easy would it be to strut to the other side of the room, open the remaining doors and dive in to the pool of information on the other side. As I look the direction of the doors, allowing myself to consider opening them, a small, white square grabs my attention.

A piece of paper is taped to the outside of door three, the door he tricked me into not opening. "*You wouldn't dare*" is written in that same perfect penmanship. The corners of my mouth dip deep into my cheeks in a mischievous grin. I pull the paper down and hold it in my fingers, thinking of something clever to write back, but the sun shines through the window and against the paper, casting small shadows of dark circles and long lines across the page, under the memo. I analyzed them for a moment, wondering where they may have come from. It doesn't take me long to realize they're on the other side of the page. I flip it over and look at the back of the page. It's not just any old scrap. It's not a piece of plain white paper.

It's sheet music.

Chapter Eleven

Dom

Cooper sits at the end of the table, leaning into his elbows with his hands folded. The four band members sit across from him waiting to see what he has to say. This is the longest we have ever sat with a wordless Cooper, so I'd imagine my curiosity mixed with apprehension is shared among my bandmates. Whatever Cooper is about to hit us with, it's not good news.

"Coop?" Xander finally asks. "You want to tell us why we are here, or should we start guessing?"

Cooper shifts his position, but his eyes and mouth stay stern. "I need you four to tell me what we are doing. What the plan is. What *your* plan going forward is."

The band members look at each other, searching for the answer, though I'm not sure any of us understood the question.

"What's going on, Cooper?" I ask.

"We didn't record an album last year. We recorded a few songs, but we really need to put together a full album before we tour again." Cooper flips through a few pages of paper and drops his glasses from the top of his head to his eyes. "This was our least productive tour yet."

The way he fumbles the words suggests that it hurt to say them as much as they hurt to hear.

"Now, that's not to say the tour was *unsuccessful*," he continues. "It just was subpar to anything we have ever done before. We only sold-out eighty-three percent of our shows."

"What was our percentage before this tour?" I know the guys don't care about the business side, but I do. I like numbers and charts. I enjoy knowing where we stand.

Cooper stares back at me like I should know what he's thinking without him having to say it.

"One hundred percent?" I ask. "We've sold out one hundred percent of the shows we've toured on?"

"As long as you have been headliners, you've sold out every show, every tour — until this one."

"I feel like that doesn't make sense," Xander says, though everyone knows math isn't his thing. "Why the sudden drop-off? Wouldn't you think this would be a gradual-type thing?"

"Actually, yes," Cooper says, flipping back farther in his book and pressing one finger toward the bottom of one of the pages. "Three years ago, we dropped just a bit. Nothing considerable. I figured we would start to see a bigger decline, but the tour before this one, we actually had a considerable upswing."

Xander scratches his head. "What changed?"

"Julian," I say, still staring at Cooper like I'm trying to read his mind, and he nods.

"People wanted to see if we were going to sink or soar without him. So, they bought tickets to see whether it was the beginning of something new or the end of something old."

"We've seen some lower numbers before, though, Coop. Even during that first tour without Julian, you and I stood outside these doors and you said this same thing. We bounced back. We always do."

"I don't know if that's true this time, boys." He swallows hard and pushes his glasses onto his head. "You're not recording—not consistently, at least. You're all in your thirties. Your lives are going in different directions. So, I ask you again, what are we doing next?"

"I still want to make music," Blake chimes in, rocking back and forth in his chair.

"I think that's the consensus for all of us," Theo says, looking at each of us as we offer an agreeable nod.

"That's the problem." Cooper shakes his head and closes the book. "We aren't *making* music anymore."

"Some of that is on me," Blake interjects with a solemn edge in his voice. "I've been a bit distracted, I guess."

"It's not all on you." Xander leans forward in his chair. "I hadn't contributed much lately. I submitted a couple of ideas to Cooper the other day but they're half-baked, nowhere near ready."

The room goes quiet for too many minutes.

"What do you suggest?" Theo breaks our awkward silence. We're not a group known for having too many wordless moments between us.

"Guys," Cooper says as he wipes his fingers over his brows, his apprehensive voice returning again. "Look... Touring is expensive. The travel, hotels, venues, marketing, merchandise...it's a lot."

"We know that." The room holds a collective breath.

"I don't think we should tour this upcoming year." Cooper takes a deep breath and lets it out. "Or any time until we have some new material."

Since we started this, we tour internationally in alternating years. We spend a lot of time on the road. When there was demand, we supplied it. We have toured every year, except for one. Five years ago, we decided as a band to regroup, work on some music and focus on some albums and music videos. The guys were anxious to get back on the road. They missed touring. For me? It was a blessing in disguise. That was the year Raya had died. I spent every one of the moments I should've been on stage at her side. I wouldn't change it for anything. But now? Hearing the words, out loud, 'no touring', it's different. We all know this is what happens in this business, and this very well could be the beginning of the end for us.

"What about the stuff Xander gave you? Can we look at that, see if we can spin anything off it?" Theo asks, eager not to let our touring days slip.

Cooper reopens the book, stands, licks his fingertip and scans through the pages, offering no real dialogue, just a few grunts and hmm-ms as he paces back and forth. He tosses the binder back on the table with a slam and crosses his arms. After reviewing it and telling us he just doesn't see how it's different enough from our old stuff to warrant spending time and money on turning it into a new album, Theo asks what we could do to make splash.

I drum two pens on the table's edge and Xander leans over and grabs them from me, ending my solo.

"Got any lyrics rolling around in that genius head of yours?"

"I don't do lyrics." I steal the pens back and return to my makeshift beat.

The band is clearly not ready to agree to Cooper's 'no tour' terms. In fact, the threat of not leaving seems to have lit a fire under us, everyone suddenly feeling the need to make progress here and now. Unfortunately, nothing sticks. Cooper cuts us loose and says his goodbyes, encouraging us to find inspiration somewhere.

"Oh, and Blake…Xander…I saw your little gig in a video online. No more impromptu shows at The Rock Room or anywhere else. Got it?"

"That's it!"

"How are spontaneous free shows going to help us at all?"

"No, no, the girl. Pull up the video."

I have seen that video—purposely gone out of my way to watch that video—more than I can to admit. She's perfect up there. It's mesmerizing in a way I haven't gotten tired of. Cooper and the band deliberate while I'm too distracted by her to add to the conversation.

"Dom?" Cooper places his hand on my shoulder and I jump, then play it off like I was focused the whole time. "What do you say? I'll only go for it with the unanimous vote here."

Saying yes means getting to see her soon, and frequently. Saying yes means being in close quarters with her. Saying yes means getting to know her.

And her getting to know me.

"I think it's a bad idea." Every eye in the room is on me simultaneously. "I do. I'm sorry. She's talented, don't get me wrong. But what if too big of a change has the opposite effect? What if we lose the fans' interest rather than gain it?"

My stomach turns. So much of me wants to say yes. I want to see her again, but not associated with this part of my life. What if things don't go as planned—for her and me or the band?

Cooper lists off a series of valid points, and I can't argue—not without admitting I have a secondary agenda. Blake tacks on his yes vote, and I add in mine.

Chapter Twelve

Stasia

The light across from me flashes *Don't Walk* while two lanes of traffic zip by. The aroma of coffee and bakery treats fills my nostrils as I inhale while waiting for the light to turn across from Chance's on the Corner. As the light shifts from its original command to the pedestrian man, the cars come to a halt and I walk across — still looking both ways for cars, of course. This is Boston after all. Bells jingle as I open the door. I went from having never heard of Chance's to becoming a daily, if not twice-a-day customer.

A loud crash beyond the door that separates the service area from the back room causes me to jump. "Damn it, Roy!" a female voice yells shortly after the commotion, then she slams her body through the door, and it swings aggressively on its hinges.

"Can I help—?" she starts, but cuts herself off once her focus finds my face. "Oh, hey!" Her voice changes from utterly annoyed to pleasantly surprised.

"Everything okay back there?" I lean to the side, peeking through the square window in the door.

"It's fine. Perfect. It's like a daily occurrence around here." She rolls her eyes. "Your usual?"

"Please."

"Size?"

"The largest you have." I place both hands on the counter and jump up so I'm sitting on it. "I'm going to need it."

She looks shocked at first, like she can't possibly believe I'd dare to be so bold as to sit on the counter of the café, but then she just shakes her head and laughs. I think she came to terms with my eccentricity the first time we met.

"Long night with the mystery man or another live show at The Rock Room?"

"Ah, you saw that?" I try to play it off cool, like it isn't the most amazing thing that's ever happened to *anyone,* but I can't.

"I heard about it." She picks a cup and pours steaming liquid into it, then seals the lid and slides it across the counter. "So much for nothing major or professional, eh?"

"Trust me…it wasn't planned." I blow across the small opening on the lid and take a sip. "I almost backed out right before I walked up to them. I've heard more bad stories than good about Xander, so I second-guessed myself but I'm glad I did it. He was great. I would've missed out."

"Xander is completely harmless." She reaches for an empty cup and fills it with ice and water, inserts a straw and takes a sip. "Especially now. Married. Trying to start a family. The media paints him worse than he is. In person he's pretty mellow."

I turn my body from sideways to full-on cross-legged on the counter, wide-eyed and wanting more. "What do you know?"

"Everything." She leans into the side of the counter and stirs her straw around her drink. "He's my best friend."

"That would've been helpful to know! Why didn't you say anything before?"

"I sent you to The Rock Room, didn't I?" She shrugs her shoulders and turns her Chance's baseball cap backward. "Besides, it didn't matter before. He's not a celebrity to me. He's not a hand I play to impress people. He's just Xander."

I can see how she would be a good fit for him — for any person trying to avoid the spotlight, someone like me. My whole life my last name has been attached to me in more ways than one. She's a person who can look past that. She's a person I know I want in my corner. The bells chime as a group of people enter the shop. She places one hand on my thigh and pushes me toward the edge in a gentle nudge. I pop off the counter and place my feet back on the floor, then slide cash across the countertop.

We exchange a wave as I head out of the door toward the crosswalk, coffee in hand. My phone vibrates in my pocket. An unknown number flashes across the screen.

"Hello?"

"Good morning, is this Stasia?" A man's voice sounds on the other end.

"It sure is. What can I do for you?"

"Stasia, my name is Gary Cooper. I'm the manager for the band Consistently Inconsistent. Do you have a moment?"

* * * *

My palms sweat as I stand outside the recording studio doors. Usually when I'm excited or anxious my heart beats a million times a minute, like a drum in a fast-moving song. This is different. This is the only time I've ever felt this way. It's as if my heart has stopped beating altogether. Paused — just waiting for someone to come and shock me back to life, because there is no way this is real.

The door opens and I jump in surprise. It's the shock that brings me back to the real world — restarts my heart, so to speak.

"Stasia," an older but handsome gentleman with light brown hair and kind eyes says as he holds the door open and one hand out toward me, "I'm Gary Cooper. The boys, they just call me Cooper or Coop. It's up to you, really."

The boys. Internationally known, bestselling artists that sit on the other side of this door and Gary Cooper calls them 'the boys', as if they're just anyone, as if they're normal. Maybe they are.

"Come on in. We're excited to have you here." Cooper holds the door as I cross the threshold and places a hand on my upper back, guiding me through the building and talking as we walk.

"I saw your open mic night performance with Xander and Blake. You are... Well, you must know how talented you are."

"Xander and Blake can make anybody sound good, I'd think." I try my hardest to play it cool and usually I wear that look quite well, but I'm only human. "It was a really great performance. I'm very grateful to have had the opportunity."

Cooper stops outside a door in the hallway and turns to face me.

"You don't have to answer today. We only have a practice room. We don't have actual studio time for a few more days, but we're looking to go a different direction, add a new tweak." Cooper's hand muscles do more work than his mouth, moving consistently as he speaks. "We love your vibe, your sound. We think having you work on a few songs with us over the next few months could open us up to a whole new level."

"The band? They're on board for adding a new person? They don't even know me."

"One of them was a little on the fence, if I'm honest."

My bet is Xander. I don't know why, but he strikes me as someone who wouldn't volunteer to share the stage with another vocalist.

"None of them can deny your talent, and after weighing in all the pros, everyone was on board. I know it's unorthodox and a big ask, but at least think about it."

"Yes." It's quick, falling out of my mouth before I give myself permission to speak, but I wouldn't say no. I don't need time to think. This is the break I returned to Boston for. Sure, everything is happening much faster than I dreamed, but I'm not about to sleep through the chance. It is unorthodox. Musicians work tirelessly to get noticed, sacrifice time, energy and wellbeing to keep their name on the tips of listener's tongues. This is not an opportunity that knocks often and here it is, breaking down my door.

"Think about it," he reiterates, squeezing my shoulder. "Give it ten minutes. You could meet them and hate them." He chuckles as he opens the door. "I'm stuck with them now. You still have a chance to run."

Xander leans back in a chair, grapes flying across the room as the other band members throw them to him — or at him. He catches one in his mouth and they all cheer like it's a championship winning touchdown. It relaxes me. They seem so…human. Blake and Xander were kind the first time around but this is different. I never thought I'd see them after that. Now, I'm not meeting them as a girl who got them on stage for one song and they never have to deal with me again. I'm practically auditioning to become the only female musician in a band who has only ever known men. I'm the change, the variable, and I know I like them, but I need them to like me.

Cooper clears his throat and the band stops fooling around. "Gentlemen, I give you Stasia Marquette."

"Like the owner of MLA records Marquette?" Xander asks. He stands and he and Blake step toward me, blocking the rest of the band members from view.

"My father owns it but we're not…close." I think Blake senses my hesitation because he steps past Xander, wrapping me in a hug like we're old friends, though we only spent one night messing around with some music arrangements.

"It's good to see you again. I'm glad you could make it."

"Glad to be here."

We part and he steps behind me, both hands on my shoulders, guiding me into the room. "This is Theo." Theo reaches one hand out toward mine.

"On the keyboard," I say, and he nods his head. "It's so nice to meet you."

"He doesn't actually play the keyboard," Xander chimes in. "It's all prerecorded. We just play something that sounds great over the system and let him stand there pretending, because we feel bad for him."

Blake laughs and Xander grins.

"Hey now." Theo holds one hand up. "Coop brought in a new vocalist, not a new keyboardist. You're slipping, Varro. Had to bring someone with real talent in to up the vocals game."

The room let's out a collective *oooohhhh*. A *buh dum tskkkk* sounds from the drum set at the back of the practice space.

"Last, but never least," Blake says, directing me toward the drummer, but his voice fades. Suddenly I'm moving in slow motion toward the drum set.

He wears a raggedy T-shirt with both sleeves torn off, a bandana tied around his head with tufts of unstyled hair sticking out wildly from the top. I'd recognize those emerald-green eyes with or without the glasses he usually wears over them. I know him. I've *known* him. I slept in his bed the previous night.

"Stasia," the drummer says, flipping a drumstick in his fingers and shoving it in a back pocket before placing his hand out for me to take. I place my hand in his and we stay there too long. I say nothing.

"Allow me to introduce myself." His overly perfect teeth show behind a bright smile. "I'm Dom."

* * * *

"I knew you looked familiar." I shake my head as Dom and I walk the city streets from the recording space to his apartment. "You are *so* different in your daily life than you are on stage—the dress clothes, the hair, the glasses. You're...two totally different people."

He smiles as he pulls the bandana from his head and tousles his hair. "I don't really do it on purpose. It's not supposed to be a costume or hiding in plain sight. I like dressing that way. I like my hair done. My glasses never bothered me. That style, I enjoy it. I know it's not very rock star of me, but that's the most comfortable I feel." He wraps the bandana around his knuckles, fiddling with the black fabric. "I don't see the harm in being both people. On stage, I like the loose-fitting shirts. There's really no rhyme or reason to it except that I like being *Dom* when I'm on stage—the rock-star image, the type that fits in with Xander, Blake and Theo. But that's only a percentage of me. A small percentage. The rest of the band? They say they're musicians first. That's not really...me."

For the first time ever—literally ever—I'm speechless. It wasn't knowing his name that made me feel like I finally knew him. It was knowing more than one side of him.

"When you said you didn't want to know my name, I know you were enjoying the guessing game, but it was nice for me, too. For a little while, there was someone getting to know things about me *before* they knew I was a famous musician. It's been a while since I got to let someone meet Dominic the person and not Dom the drummer for Xander Varro and Blake Mathews."

It surprises me that he'd choose his bandmates' names specifically rather than the band name, but I recognize the undertones. He's always in the background.

"I get that. I get that more than you know." I think back to my first day in Boston, trying to start over and separate myself from the reputation that precedes me. It was hard for any friend I ever had to understand my desire to be anyone but myself, even just for a minute. But Dom? Or *Dominic?* He gets it. He understands the need to be his own person and not be respected because of the people he's attached to. For him, it's his bandmates, but for me, it's my father.

"Tell me more about this *Dominic* the person and not the drummer."

He looks toward me and nods. "I'd rather show you."

We take the lengthy elevator ride to the top floor of the building, and he unlocks the door, then invites me inside. He takes my hand and leads me across the open space to the three doors and places his hand on the knob of number three. My body heats with excitement. He said everything there was to know about him lies beyond that door.

He nods toward the room, encouraging me to enter. I cross the threshold and my mouth parts in awe. I look around, high and low, left and right, taking in the room. Every wall is covered in shelves holding what must be hundreds — no *thousands,* of books. The main layout of the apartment is deceiving. At first, it looks standard size for a penthouse-style apartment, but this side of the apartment extends much farther than I would have guessed, wallpapered by endless book bindings, floor-to-ceiling, wall-to-wall.

"This is breathtaking." It's all I can offer. I have no words. It's funny... I can picture 'Mr.-button-down-shirt' sitting in here all day in a high-back plush chair getting lost in any world that's not this one, but right now, leaning into the door frame in ripped clothing with his hair doing this overgrowth-meets-bed-head thing, he looks out of place. That's how we're groomed. Outward appearances tend to dictate the depth of our knowledge, but he's the living definition of not judging a book by the cover. He can be two opposing people, two diverse styles — and he wears both well.

The books have been kept in pristine condition. As I run my fingers across the perfectly kept, dust-free shelf, I notice the bindings don't have any marks, no creases, like they've never been read at all. The only indication that they've ever been touched is the intricately placed gold numbers on each binding, number one to who knows how high, numerically ordered on the top of the binding.

"They're numbered?" I turn over my shoulder with a smile.

"A friend of mine left them to me. She'd numbered each one of her collection."

"And they're all here?"

"All but one." He holds up one finger as he says the words, and I turn around completely to face him. "She kept a log that has each book listed. So, when I put them all on the shelves and noticed an area that skipped over a number, I looked in the ledger to see what book it was and, sure enough, it wasn't in any of the boxes."

"You're sure it's not here? There's like, two thousand books in here."

"Two thousand six hundred and nine." My eyes widen and I look around. "Besides," he says, "this isn't a book that would be easily missed. It's black leather, and the pages are red."

"Sounds gorgeous. What is it called?"

"Doesn't matter." He pushes his hair off his forehead and smiles like he has a secret. "It's a book of poetry you wouldn't have heard of."

"Do you think I'm not cultured enough to be familiar with poetry?" I raise an eyebrow.

"Not this kind." He winks at me as he speaks. "I wrote it."

"You...wrote a book of poems?"

He claps his hands together once, then places them on my shoulders, turning me away from the shelves. "And that's enough for that part of the tour."

"I like this part of the tour!" I laugh as he propels me forward.

"Keep going." He flicks a wrist and points an inviting finger beyond the shelves. In the farthest part of the room, a gorgeous drum kit sits, looking more like a decoration than an instrument. Musical awards, records in cases and Consistently Inconsistent's greatest accomplishments plaster the wall behind the drum kit. The label TAMA glares at me from the front of the bass drum. The set is a glossy black with silver hoops, rods and casings—an antique set that appears old yet untouched.

"You can play it if you want," he says from behind me. His chest touches my back, and he places both hands on my hips.

"No, I really can't." I shake my head with a laugh. "I was practically born in a recording studio, and I've never even attempted the drums."

"Now is as good a time as any." He nudges me toward the set. I take a seat and immediately reach for the drumsticks.

"Hey now." He intercepts the sticks, twirls one mesmerizingly between his fingers and places the pair off to the side. "Patience."

"Show-off," I scoff with my lips pursed but my eyes and voice stay playful.

"You don't get in someone else's car and just drive away, right?"

"Is this a trick question?"

"No. You have to adjust the seats and mirrors. You have to make sure you know where you're going and, of course, you have to pick the right song." He gets down on one knee beside me. "Once you're ready, once all of those things are in place, then you pull out of the driveway and onto the road."

I look over my shoulder, my face dropped downward to look at him.

"Stand up for one second." He spins a winged screw on the stool and adjusts it, tightening the piece again when he's done. "All right, that should better."

I sit once more, cautiously, waiting for him to tell me what to do next.

He walks around to the front of the drum set and looks me up and down, his eyes trailing every inch of my body. Somehow, I feel extra sultry sitting behind these drums. For a second, I wonder if he finds it alluring, me sitting here where he should be. His face transforms to a mischievous expression.

"What?" I wonder if he's thinking about me the way I'm thinking about him.

"You have *terrible* posture."

Guess not. Damn it, add in a drum set and suddenly he's all business and no pleasure.

He positions himself behind me once again and runs his fingers up my arms and shoulders, stopping at my collar bones. He pulls back gently, and my spine follows his lead. "Here." He keeps one hand at my shoulder. His fingertips glide against the skin at the side of my neck as he moves his hand upward, stopping at my chin. He lifts, gently, and I extend my neck. "Head up. Straighten all this out."

I do as I'm told, but it's hard to concentrate on anything but the way his hands feel on my body. I tilt my head all the way back, ignoring his instruction, staring straight up at him. He looks down at me, my eyes reflecting in his. He moves one hand from my shoulder to my neck, resting his fingertips against my throat, tracing my jaw with his thumbs. He lowers himself to me, pressing his lips against mine, working his tongue against my own. We part, only for a moment, and I stand, guiding him to sit instead. Positioned in front of him, I pull my shirt over my head, then place my legs on either side of him, my chest against his, my arms wrapped at the back of his neck.

"How's my posture now?" I place my forehead against his and he leans up so his word kisses my lips.

"Perfect."

He runs his fingers down my abdomen and chills follow down my back.

What started at the stool ended on the floorboards in intimate moments that couldn't be described using the words in all the books that surround us. He pulled on the ripped jeans he was wearing and I slid into his tattered T-shirt. We stayed on floor, my head resting against his chest.

"Have you thought about what you're doing to do?" He lightly strokes my hair as he speaks.

"About?"

"Cooper asked you to record a few new songs with us, yeah?"

"There isn't much to think about, is there? It's the opportunity of a lifetime."

"Yeah, sure. Just know what you're getting in to."

I roll over, resting my body weight on my elbows. "What's that supposed to mean?"

"You moved to Boston to record your own music, not be a backup singer."

"Yeah, that's true. But plenty of people get noticed, and it helps kick-start their own career."

"I just don't want you to get your hopes up then have this not work out for you." He shifts his position so both hands rest behind his head and he looks toward the ceiling. "Just remember that you don't have to say yes."

I sit up, sliding away enough to create distance between us. I don't know a lot about him, but avoiding eye contact isn't his style. It's the very thing I find the most compelling about him. "Oh my God…"

"What?" He turns toward me, shifting his upper body so he's propped up on one elbow.

"It was you." His face contorts in confusion. "Cooper said one of you wasn't sure adding me in was a good idea. It was *you*."

I'd give anything to dive headfirst into one of these books and appear on the other side in a fiction world, to be anywhere but there.

I stand and head toward my collection of clothes strewn across the floor, pulling on enough to keep me modest but not bothering to stay any longer than I have to.

"Stasia." He gets up and follows me across the room.

"You were right, Dom," I say from the threshold of the door. "You do have vices." I head to the elevator, which thankfully opens as I press the button. I step inside and Dom appears at the doors, still wearing only his ripped jeans that are falling perfectly over the V in his hips.

"I'll see you in the recording studio." I wave my perfectly manicured red fingernails his direction as the doors close.

I wasted no time that day. I called Cooper from the corner of the street directly outside Dom's building and verbalized my commitment to singing on a few tracks for Consistently Inconsistent's upcoming album. The days between that one and now dragged by. I was so eager to get in front of a recording mic that I couldn't think of anything else for the five-day wait. Now, I stand in the recording studio, pacing, an hour earlier than I needed to arrive.

The door creaks on its hinges as someone opens it, their footsteps growing louder as they get closer.

Dom steps into view and pauses where he stands. He slides both hands into the pockets of his ripped jeans. I have to wonder if he has a specific set he wears when he plays, because I know he owns multitudes of dress pants and yet, this is the only pair of jeans I've seen him in.

"You ready for this?" He turns so his back is against the wall and crosses his arms.

"Of course." I take seat on the leather couch nearest me. "I was born for this."

"I know." His words are a blend of confident and assertive. "You're going to do great."

My confidence fades fast. "But you —"

He shakes his head.

"It was never about your talent, Stasia." He pushes himself off the wall and meanders over to me, taking a seat to my left. "I know you can do this. I know adding you is a positive thing. It's going to do great things for our music and take us places we've never been before."

He leaves me wordless and confused.

"You didn't want me to be a part of this album." The words are quiet, and for the first time, I pull off the bandages and allow him to see that what he said did hurt me. "You voted no."

"Stasia," he says, and it melts me. He says my name this way only he does, and any spine I have disintegrates. "If you become a part of this, if you join this band, we can't…"

As his voice fades out, my ultimate confusion turns to utter regret. *It was never about the music.* I understand it. I only wish I'd heard him out sooner.

"It's just a few songs, Dom." I reach one hand forward and place it on his knee. "It's not like I'm an official member of the band."

He stares deep into my eyes and sighs. "You really don't know how talented you are, do you?"

I've never considered myself a particularly humble person, but it's evident I don't see what he sees.

"Listen…" He places his hand on mine. "Before Cooper even called you in, we had a lengthy discussion about bringing a girl into the mix. That having a female involved was a new dynamic and any chaos or lines crossed would be bad for all of us. We made a pact that this kind of change wouldn't interfere with the success we've garnered over the last decade plus. Maybe *you're* not looking at this as a long-term thing, but they…*we* are."

I'm processing, searching for words that seem miles away.

"Whatever this is, whatever it is we are doing, I wasn't ready to give it up yet. I know that's selfish. I'm not too proud to admit it was self-serving. But once you're part of this band, what happens to *this*?" He wags one finger from his free hand between our bodies, enclosing us in an imaginary circle.

We stare into each other's eyes for too long, the distance between us getting closer unintentionally, like two magnets finding the other across an opens space.

"This? I'm not sure what you mean by *this*?" My voice is velvet smooth, with as much enchantment as possible. "You mean this?"

My mouth is pressed to his, and his tongue finds mine.

"Mhmm-mm." He moans in a low sound.

I pull his shirt over his head, then kiss down his ear, his neck, his chest.

"This?"

He nods, slow. I place his hands at my shoulders, inviting him to remove the straps of the lace tank top I wear. He glides the fabric against my skin, exposing my chest and abdomen.

I lean forward so my torso is against his, lean into his ear and nibble, gently at first, then with more bite. His chest rises and falls in exaggerated motions. He drops his head back, and I pull my teeth away from the ridge of his ear. "I know we can't keep on with this. I know the right thing to do would be to stop. I'm not sure what happens next," I whisper, keeping my cheek close to his for a moment before pulling away. "The way I see it, we can waste our time with the 'what ifs?' 'What happens?' We can play those mental games." I lean toward him and leave my lips close to ear once more. "Or we can play physical ones."

He chooses option number two, but I'm the one who wins a prize.

Chapter Thirteen

Dominic

It's true what they say — six months flies when you're having fun. Things have started to come together. Stasia has recorded a few songs with us, and though we haven't pulled enough lyrics together to record a full-length album, the singles she has been on are doing okay on the charts and sales — not as well as we would like, but fine, all the same. We even got to see her on stage at a show in Miami, and the buzz from that was all good. She's a born performer. Truthfully, having her around has brought about a bit of internal competition. The band seems to be overexerting themselves every time she's around. She has lit a fire under them that they didn't even know they needed.

That's not to say we haven't had our ups and downs — especially Blake and Stasia. They were hit with life-changing news. Stasia watched her father — well, I guess they watched *their* father — be hauled away with a lengthy list of crimes to pay for. Their mother came through like a tornado, uprooting everything in their path, just long enough to leave her mark, create a mess then fade into the wind with no indication of when she would return.

In the months that have passed since Stasia started working with us, she'd lost a father, a brother and, well…*me,* kind of. There had been instances — too many of them — when we let our inhibitions go and ended up together in ways we shouldn't be, but they're becoming fewer and further between — for several reasons. We both know it's for the good of the band, even if it isn't good for us.

As for what's good for me? Having enough free time to get myself in to see Dr. Anderson and no remaining excuses not to. Over the last few weeks, I've been poked and prodded, blood drawn, wires stuck to my chest and several other tests that will hopefully tell Dr. Anderson what I already know. I'm *fine.* I sit in a chair waiting on the results of those collective tests for what seems like hours. There is a knock before he opens the door.

"I don't know how you do it." He shakes his head. "Your case is such an anomaly. You had problems for so many years. I can't think of any medical reason that your heart seems to be holding out and getting you by."

"The medications are working."

"They shouldn't be…not for this long."

"It's like you're rooting against me, Doc." I raise my eyebrow at him. "You act like you want there to be something wrong with me."

"Not at all. I'm happy you're still stable. I worry, though. When this therapy stops maintaining its effectiveness—and it will—I'm not sure how long you'll have to decide to commit to the next step."

"Well, we are clear for today, right?" I stand from my chair. "I can go?"

"Sure. See you soon, Dominic."

"Not if I can help it, Doc." We both smile and I wave from the hallway as I head down it. All's well that ends well. Now that I've done some good for myself, it's time to do some good for some others.

Celebrity bartending became an annual thing that has evolved over time. We did it once a few years ago for fun, and it stuck. Now we do it for charity. This year, it's a road race we were invited to attend. At the end of the race, those of us who have signed up to volunteer will hand out beers, sell T-shirt's, pretzels, snacks. Some of the bands take turns playing live music, both original songs and covers.

I wear an apron and a baseball cap and use tongs to pick up a pretzel for an attendee. Theo stands to my right, filling bags of popcorn. Xander and Blake are a few tents away from us, filling plastic cups with beer, though I'm not sure if that's truly their assigned tent. Stasia, looking as flawless as ever, waves to us from the T-shirt table across the way.

"Well, well," I hear a familiar, and yet unfamiliar, voice say. It's been years since I've heard it. "If it isn't Dominic Trudell. It's been a while, stranger."

"It sure has," is what I say, but '*not long enough*' is what I mean. "How's the album coming?" I wonder if we're keeping things civil or picking up where we left off.

"It's coming along." He offers a prideful smile. "It's Theo, yeah?" He turns his attention elsewhere.

"Yeah." Theo waves a plastic gloved hand his direction. "Save Me, Save You, right? You're the lead singer."

"Ames Gaherty," he introduces himself. "Anyway, it was good to see you, Dom. You look good. Happy. Healthy."

He says the last word in a way that makes the back of my neck hot., almost like he wishes I wasn't. He turns and walks away

"You know him?" Theo asks. "When we were at the bar a few months back and they made headlines, you said you didn't."

"I don't." I tear my gloves and apron off and throw them in the nearby trash bin. "Not really. I'll be right back."

Ames stands in the beer line chatting up Xander like they're best friends.

"Hey," Xander says as he sees me approaching, "have you met Ames? He's the lead singer of Save Me, Save You."

I nod and they return to their animated conversation.

Blake steps in at my side with a beer in each hand.

"I don't like him," he says, and I smile as I turn to look at him under the brim of my hat.

"Do you know him?"

"No." He gulps down one cup. "But the look on your face says *you* don't like him, and you're practically canonized. Therefore, I don't like him." He slides the full cup into the empty one.

"Hey, Blake," Ames says, turning back to us again. "I'm Ames."

"Neat." Blake downs his second cup as he turns and walks away. I stifle a laugh.

Xander turns to serve a customer, and Ames steps toward me.

"Turning all your friends against me already?"

"Maybe they're just incredibly good judges of character."

"Obviously not." His eyes narrow as he speaks. "They keep you around, after all."

I nod and think of a response, but I don't want to go there with Ames. Not today.

"Why now, Ames?" I try to stay calm. "What's the deal with the comeback?"

"An idea for an album" — he drags out his words as he speaks — "fell into my hands, so to speak. I didn't want to let the opportunity pass me by." Ames stands about six foot four on a good day, but the arrogance his words are laced with make him seem so much taller. "You'll hear it soon, I'm sure. I have to go, though. That T-shirt table is calling my name." He winks and steps past me. I watch as he waltzes over to the booth, and my heart drops to my stomach. Stasia is the last person I want him talking to. Fortunately for me, Stasia steps away from the table and disappears behind the back of the tent just as Ames arrives at the booth. Kelly takes his order — all smiles, as she always is. Ames lays the flirting on thick. I can see it from here.

Blake passes me in more of a stomp than a walk.

"What are you doing?" I call to him.

He turns and raises both arms at his sides. "I had a change of heart. I think I want to meet our new friend after all."

I shake my head and laugh at his antics. I've wondered, for a while now, what my first meeting with Ames would be like. It's been years since I had seen him last. Then I think, maybe I'm the person holding the age-old grudge. What if I'm the one stirring the pot? Perhaps time does heal all wounds, and while I'm prepared to be defensive, maybe he's grown, changed. Perhaps I should dismiss my own reservations and give him a fresh start—one I hope he will reciprocate.

There was a time we had been friends. In that timeframe, he'd been privy to information about me in a way that allowed him to collect secrets about me, secrets that he had assured me all those years ago would be safe with him. Maybe they still are.

A host for the event takes the stage and taps on the microphone.

"We have an *incredible* act coming up to kick off our live music portion of the event for you all," she says, adorned in a hat and T-shirt with the charity logo on it. "Every person here is in for a huge treat, because right here, on this stage, Save Me, Save You has agreed to debut one song from their soon-to-be-released album."

Another indication Ames has changed. The Ames I knew never would have done charity work.

He takes the stage in a leather vest that is open in the front, revealing the multitude of tattoos he is covered in. His band takes their respective places, and he addresses the crowd.

"Wow," he says, overlooking the crowd that is small compared to a concert venue, but fairly large for a charity event. "It is good to be back on stage." The crowd applauds as he speaks.

"We've got something for you, Boston." He paces back and forth across the stage and looks around at all the faces staring back at him, but he settles on mine.

"This one has never been played live. You'll be the first people to hear it. Totally unreleased, unheard."

The crowd cheers in a shared excitement, but he doesn't take his eyes off me.

"We hope you like it." He takes a few steps back and his guitarist plays a few opening notes. "This one is called *The Heart and Other Torture Devices*."

The world around me fades away. Suddenly I'm standing in my apartment, tearing apart boxes, ripping items off shelves, looking everywhere for a missing book of poems I wrote—a book I was never going to find.

The band plays loud, energetic music and Ames performs in a way that makes it seem like we're in a full venue with a sold-out crowd. He's captivating, entertaining. He puts on an effortless show. It's always been that way. That's why the world was so shocked when he faded from the scene.

Ames starts with the lyrics—lyrics that I know every word to.

I wrote them.

They were never meant to be a song, never meant to be revealed to anyone except the person I'd written them for.

Now the world will hear them.

Adrenaline floods my body. My muscles tighten, my heart rate and respirations spike. I can feel every part of me tense to the point I get lightheaded. I lose my focus for a moment, unable to decipher if these systemic reactions are physical or mental. Maybe both.

Any fraction of benefit of the doubt I gave him disintegrated. He hasn't changed for the better. He's worse.

I stand at the bottom of the stairs in the wing of the outdoor stage. Time ticks by and I register nothing. I listened to the rest of the song but didn't absorb it. If there was applause at the end, I didn't hear it. My mind is on one track, and I can't swerve off it.

As soon as Ames' boots hit the grass, I grab him by the front of his vest and pull him to the back of the stage, then push him into the wall.

"Where is the book, Ames?" I grit my teeth. He lightly pushes my hands away and brushes himself off.

"I don't know what you're talking about." His confidence is as prominent as ever.

"What was your plan? You can't have thought I'd just casually allow you to plagiarize my work and break back through to the big time."

"What are you going to do about it?" His words are still eerily calm. There is something I'm not seeing. Some trick up his sleeve – if he were wearing any.

"What is going on here?" Cooper's voice cuts through the tension.

"Nothing at all." Ames steps forward and wraps his arm around my shoulder as I turn toward Cooper. "Dom and I are old friends. We go way back. Just catching up."

"Oh, I didn't realize you knew each other well." Cooper buys Ames' innocent act. He won't be the first or the last. "Welcome back, Ames," Cooper says over his shoulder as he turns to leave.

"Happy to be back," Ames calls. He pats me hard on the back. "Happy to be back," he reiterates, this time pointed at me with a sadistic undertone lacing the words.

Chapter Fourteen

Stasia

The night at the open mic feels like yesterday, though a turbulent but exciting few months have passed. Don't get me wrong... I know the opportunity I received was almost unfairly given to me, and that odds are, I'd have a better chance of hitting the lottery or getting struck by lightning twice than to be gifted the chance to sing with an already-established band. But it did. That being said, nothing worth having comes without a massive price tag.

It took me returning home to start over, break *up* the band before I really got to join it, even if only temporarily, and try to figure out how to revive a business with a criminal history to get these nights on stage and those hours in the recording studio. Among all that, I orchestrated and watched my own father be hauled away in handcuffs. Truth be told, in a moment that should have hurt, I'd finally found relief —

More than that, I'd found freedom. He had made it clear that if I didn't record for him, I wouldn't record for anyone, and for a long time, he'd succeeded. After years of self-doubt and loads of imposter syndrome, I had the upper hand. I was free to do whatever I wanted, pursue any number of dreams, free of his shadows. Though I feel I owe him nothing, in many ways, I owe him everything.

Believe it or not, it was the violin that had started it all.

My father had dragged me along to yet another work-related event when I was young. Music was his work and work was his life, so in turn, music was the be-all, end-all of our entire relationship. Me? I would have been fine if I'd never heard another song again. It wasn't a passion we shared. I hated music because it took him away from me—because he loved it more than he loved me.

He offered to sign me up for lessons for voice or an instrument any time I had his attention, which was infrequent at best but frequent enough to annoy me. Yet, one night I stood backstage. It was a night my father had claimed he'd cleared his schedule to come see my art on display at school, but his phone rang and he instructed the driver to turn in the direction opposite my art show. My heart crumbled in the backseat of that limo. All I wanted was to show him what was important to me, but it didn't matter. What he loved and valued always had trumped what I loved and valued.

I sat in a dark corner of the wings of the stage, my arms wrapped around my legs with a scowl plastered on my tearstained face and headphones plugged into my ears, not to produce music, but to drown it out. The effort was wasted, though, as the bass from the speaker vibrated the pieces of my broken heart deep in my chest, the words to the song the singer belted out cutting through the plastic buds shoved in my ears like a knife through butter.

The sound that came next? I'll never forget it. It was different. Unique. What felt like one hundred thousand shows with one hundred thousand stars signed to my dad's label had come and gone across the stages he forced me to sit behind, yet I had forgotten all of them.

Except for one.

I'd stood and tiptoed toward the edge of the stage with caution, as if danger loomed on the other side. Maybe it did. With each tiny step closer, I'd second-guessed myself, my curiosity entangled with anxiety that made my heartbeat pick up speed and volume at the same rate of her intensifying solo.

The hem of the curtain felt heavy in my hands. I paused for a moment, running my fingers down the fabric. These curtains kept me separate from this lifestyle I swore I'd never be a part of. They kept me distant from my father, because so long as I stood behind them rather than in front of them, I would always play second fiddle—always in the background, behind the scenes. Never in the spotlight. Never good enough for him.

I knew approaching the stage might equal admitting I was enjoying the show, thus admitting defeat once and for all—waving the white flag and bowing down to the ideals my father has been filling my ears with since the day I was born—probably even before.

But I pulled the curtain back. I surrendered.

The violin rested between her chin and shoulder, her long, pink and purple curls thrashing wildly around her as she slid the bow across the strings, her whole body moving with each pass of her arm, the artwork and tattoos across them a blurred motion as she forced the instrument to hum a tune unlike anything I'd ever witnessed. A girl. A violinist. A rock star.

In the time it took for an anything but simple violin solo, I loved music more. I loved my father more.

I loved myself more.

I wasn't even a teenager yet. So many years have passed, so many changes—for me anyway. The performances have changed from scarce crowds at hole-in-the-wall bars to sold-out crowds at well-known venues, but my routine is the same. My legs are crossed, my arms wrapped tightly around them, holding my knees close to my chest. Headphones that play no music sit pressed against my ears, the same way I did the night I fell in love for the first time. On that stage, in that moment, one musician sparked a flame in me that burns brighter every day. The violinist who changed my life gave me the ability to get on stage and fuel that passion further. It started with her, and it continues through me. Every time I take the stage, I light the room on fire.

But this is a completely different type of stage and a whole new kind of crowd.

"You okay?" Blake kicks me gently with the toe of his untied sneaker. I pull one headphone out.

"I'm fine." I raise one eyebrow and look up at him. "Why wouldn't I be?"

"I don't know." He sips beer out of a plastic cup between words. "You seem nervous."

He offers me one hand and pulls me to a standing position, and I wipe my black ripped jeans free of the dust they've collected. "I don't get nervous." I wink with the eye under my double brow piercings.

"I would be. Better you than me. Do you know how many celebrities mess up the National Anthem?"

"I'm not a celebrity." I contemplate putting my ear bud back in but with the music full blast to drown out my relentless brother. I turn away from him and face the ice. Fans are still filing in, finding their seats before the anthem is sung and the puck is dropped for the night's game. "And I've been practicing for weeks."

"I think I'd be fine with our National Anthem." He takes a bite of a soft pretzel. "But the Canadian Anthem? Good luck with that…"

"The *what*?" I whip toward him in a way that makes the arena spin around me.

"When the opponent is a Canadian team, you have to sing both anthems. I thought you knew…"

I turn away from him, stepping toward the ice, an attempt at keeping far enough away from him that he can't see the sweat bead above my brow. I move forward and stare through the glass, marked up and scarred by bodies and pucks hitting it time and time again. As I step toward the boards that line the ice, the opposing team steps out, too—a resounding *boo* resonating from the forming crowd.

"Hey." I place both hands on my hips and turn toward him. "They're playing New Jersey tonight."

Blake laughs, I glare at him through smokey-eyed, narrowed lids.

"Sorry, I had to," he says. "You'll be fine."

"Gee, thanks." I turn to the crowd again. "There's a lot of them, huh?"

"More than seventeen thousand." He joins me at the glass. "You should've seen this place during the championship run. The walls were shaking. The crowd volume could've brought this building down. Nothing quite like a Boston sports team's fan base."

I watch as the players take turns shooting at their goaltender, others stretch and skate to prepare for the game.

I shove my hands in my pockets. "Why didn't they ask Xander? Or the whole band?"

"Xander's good." Blake shovels something new in his mouth. Where is he even getting all this damn concession food? My stomach turns. "But he's not that kind of good. Not everyone can do the anthem. You have it. He doesn't. That's really all there is to it."

I smile, enough for me to feel it, but not enough for him to see it.

"We're almost ready," a man says from behind us, and I nod.

"I'm going to go to the box." Blake adds, "You'll be great." He claps his hand on my shoulder then starts to walk away.

As the moment approaches, I feel slightly more on edge than I typically do. It's a mix of excitement and anxiety. It has been a while since I've performed by myself. I'm used to the band backing me now.

"Hey, Stasia?" Blake calls, his voice echoing through the hallway that separates us.

"Yeah?"

"It's okay to be nervous."

"I don't get nervous," I yell back, but he's already retreated around the corner.

Guess he's just making up for all the years he missed getting to be the annoying older brother. *Brother.* Even after having months to process, I'm still not used to it.

A quick, light whistle from behind me captures my attention. I turn to find Cooper standing at the railing that separates the seats from the area I wait in. He kneels down, leaning into the bottom of the railing.

"How're you feeling?"

Suddenly, my mouth dries. I hold it together around the guys, but Cooper has already been more supportive and comforting in these few months than my father has been my whole life. It's hard not to be honest with him.

"If I get out there and totally blow it, do I get fired from the band, too?" I smile, but it's forced.

Cooper shakes his head, slow, his eye downcast.

"If recording with a bestselling, chart-topping band can't fix your self-doubt, I genuinely don't know what will."

I bite my lip. He's right. The bold, confident exterior version of me is just protecting the me that I am at my core — anxious, especially in regards to my music.

"Stasia," Cooper says, his voice calm and eyes kind, "the only person controlling you now is *you*. *You* make the choices. *You* call the shots. *You* get to figure out who you are going to be in this world. Only you."

"All right, Miss Marquette," a man with a headset says, interrupting us. "We will be introducing you in just a moment."

"Excellent," I say, loud enough for him to hear me, but I'm still looking at Cooper, his words playing on repeat in my head. "But can I ask a favor? For the introduction?"

Cooper nods like he knows exactly what I'm thinking. He stands and heads back up the arena stairs. I turn toward the employee, and he slides his headset back, exposing both his ears to my request.

"Drop the last name." My dark-red painted lips form a smile I can't fight. It feels right to cut the name in that moment, like a weight has been lifted—a weight I've dragged behind me for years. "It's just Stasia."

* * * *

Kelly sits against the headboard on one side of her bed, and I lie on my stomach, flipping through an old magazine I found on their shelf.

"Look at them." The magazine slides across the bedding as I push it her direction. "They look like children."

"This is so old." Kelly laughs as she picks it up. "They weren't even twenty-one yet when this was taken."

All five band members stand in various positions with tough-guy, no-emotion expressions plastered on their faces—except maybe Blake. He's clearly trying, but not even a stern photographer and a photo shoot for a high-end magazine can hide his goofy grin.

"I'm pretty sure Xander still has this jacket, though." I turn the page toward her once more and she lets out a loud laugh. "He stole that from another band's bass guitarist. Literally, on like their first or second show, he swiped it from the backstage area." She leans over and grabs a bottle of red nail polish from her bedside table. "His moral compass didn't always point north."

While she's skipping down memory lane and opening the bottle to apply to her toes, I see an opening to jump in and get some insight on my new recording partners.

"So…" I try to keep my voice calm and casual, like I don't truly care about any of their back stories. And really, I don't. Except for one. "Give me all the good gossip. What are these guys like? What should I know about them?"

Kelly lets out a sound that's a mix of scoff and laugh. "Jeez," she says, applying the first coat of nail polish. "I've known these boys most of my life. Where would I even begin?"

"Well." I readjust my position and go from lying to sitting. "Start with Xander. I'm sure he's got all kinds of crazy stories."

"Oh, Xander." She shakes her head with a fond smile on her face. "He's a complicated guy — or at least, he was. I've never seen someone change the way he has. I can't even tell you how many times over their early years he was in the newspaper — usually not for anything good, but never anything *bad*, either, really. He always walked right on that thin line where you couldn't classify him as a *bad* person, but he certainly wasn't a good role model."

"It's odd, sometimes, to know them this way. I remember reading some of those articles." We both shake our heads and laugh.

I'm about to try to shyly ask about Dom, as if it's just a casual curiosity, but the sound of a door opening and the jingling of keys in the distance distracts us both.

"Kelly, I'm home," Blake yells in a sing-song tone from the front door.

Blake slams open the bedroom door with his shirt off his body but draped over his shoulder and his hands on the button of his jeans. "Ready or not, here I — "

"Please, for the love of all things, don't." I put my hands over my eyes and Kelly laughs so hard that she snorts.

"What are you even doing here?"

"Just get dressed before I have to dig my own eyes out."

"I'm working on it."

I pull my hand off my eyes as he pulls his shirt back over his head. "Why are you in my bed?"

"We were trying to watch a movie, and I couldn't get the TV in the living room to work." Kelly uses the magazine we were flipping through as a fan over her freshly painted toes. "Instead, we ended up telling old band stories."

"Ahh." Blake leans into the wall near the door frame. "Come grab a beer, and I'll tell you all the best ones."

"Really?"

I'm excited because Blake opening up the vault on all of the cherished secrets makes me feel like 'one of the guys', but more so because I have to wonder how many of them will feature Dom. I don't know him — not like I want to — but Blake does.

Blake pulls two beers from the fridge and hands me one, then pours Kelly a glass of red wine.

"How far did you dig in?" he asks Kelly as he takes his first sip.

"Barely scratched the surface." Kelly lifts her glass and I tip my bottle toward her. Our glasses clink. "I started with Xander but—"

"There's some bags to unpack on that one," Blake says. "But you can google anything you want about Xander. He was never quiet. He didn't care what people thought about him. Anything you want to know about him is public knowledge, down to how many times he's been handcuffed or hospitalized."

My eyes widen, but after thinking about it, I'm not that surprised. The lockups I've read about. The hospitalizations? I guess I didn't realize there was more than one.

"Anyhoo, I digress." Blake walks around the kitchen like a teacher in a classroom. "Xander and I are boring, really. Old news. Everyone knows everything about us, so the stories attached aren't all that exciting. The good stuff is with the other two."

I straighten and hope he doesn't notice.

"Dom is painfully quiet." Kelly swirls her wine in her glass. "I've known him most of my life and I really don't know him at all."

"He's an interesting guy in that way, where he's not all that interesting at all." Blake shrugs.

"Does he have family around?" I ask.

"He has parents and they're great, but they live down South. But family around here? No. He keeps to himself. He has us and seems pretty content with that. He really has the loner thing down pat."

"Blake," Kelly says with a bit of a scold in her voice.

"What?" Blake leans into the counter across from us. "It's true. He has never dated—never married and never will."

I shift my position and put my bottle down.

"Why do you say that?"

Blake tips his bottle back so the bottom faces the ceiling and chugs the remainder of his drink.

"It's just how he is. He has literally never said 'I love you' to anyone, not even once."

"That can't be true," I say, disbelief seeping through the words.

"Actually, I think it is." It's Kelly who interjects. "The guys have kind of an ongoing thing about him being a terminal bachelor."

I have so many questions, but I can't ask them — not without sounding too invested.

"And Theo?" I pick at the label on the bottle. "Is he a terminal bachelor?"

Kelly tilts her head and looks at Blake like she's passing the question off to him to answer.

"Nah." Blake presses his lips together and shakes his head. "He's married."

"What?" I ask, louder than I meant to and knocking my bottle over in the process. Kelly stands to grab some napkins and lets out a light laugh.

"He *was* married." She turns over her shoulder.

"He's still technically married." Blake takes a paper towel roll from Kelly and starts cleaning up my beer puddle.

"I've got it," I say, taking over. "I'm surprised…on both accounts. Dom seems like a really caring guy. I'm surprised he doesn't have someone. And Theo? I guess I really haven't spent all that much time with him."

"He really doesn't talk about it much." Blake turns and pulls out shot glasses from the cabinet behind him. *Here we go.* I know that's it for the serious conversation. If Blake's breaking out tequila, we're going straight for the ridiculous tales. The raw, uncut version where he gets drunk enough to spill everyone's darkest stories. There aren't any secrets safe with a drunk Blake.

Chapter Fifteen

Dom

Ever since Xander and Natalie—mostly Natalie, if we're being honest—took over The Rock Room, it was the facility of choice for our meet-ups, both for business and pleasure. Today's agenda, though, is business.

The 'no touring until we have an album' rule apparently doesn't apply to music festivals. Granted, there are multiple stages, merch booths and more shared among many bands and musicians, so, in turn, we share the cost. Cooper invited us all here today to iron out some details, though we've done this festival for ten of our fifteen years, and I'm certain not much has changed. I sip a cup of coffee—decaf, I've been indulging in a bit too much caffeine these days—and as I turn the corner, what had started out as a normal, decent day didn't last long. Ames Gaherty exits through the doors of The Rock Room as I'm about to enter.

"Lovely day we're having!" he calls in a giddy, exaggerated voice. I try to walk past him, to not fall into his traps this early in the morning, but it's impossible. He's a sinkhole.

"Bet you want to know why I'm here."

I take a sip of my coffee, suddenly wishing I'd opted for caffeine.

"Nope."

"I'll take that as a yes. I—"

"It's a music venue. You're a musician—*kind of*. It's not all that surprising. Goodbye now." I step past him and walk toward the door, but he, as usual, keeps running his mouth.

"The owner here is a hell of a guy."

I almost choke on the sip but swallow and turn toward him. "Just talked to him about adding this venue to my tour."

"Xander's going to let you play a show here?" I ask, though I don't know why. Of course, he is. The entire music industry is alive with buzz of Ames' return. It would be irresponsible of Xander to *not* take advantage of it.

"Of course not."

I breathe a sigh of relief.

"He's letting me play three."

Ames holds up three fingers but might as well have slapped me in the face with all five. I'm not going to be able to get rid of him easily. I thought, maybe, he would play his little head game and move on, but it's becoming more and more evident that he's here for the long haul.

"What do you want from me?" I allow my voice to get louder, but I'm not much of a yeller.

"You like books, right?" He struts toward me. "I mean, that's a ridiculous question. Of course, you do. Anyhoo, I digress." Ames talks with his hands and a grin plastered to his face. "What kind of person would I be if I ruined the end for you? This is a story, Dom. Buckle up, drummer boy. We're just getting started." He winks and pats his palm against my cheek in a way that makes me want to lunge at him. But I don't. I stand here and watch him walk away with another win.

When I finally enter the room, all eyes are on me. They stare at me with expressions that are a mix of confused and shocked.

"What?" I ask, keeping things casual. What has he already told them?

"Are you sick?" Cooper asks, and I take a physical step back.

"What? Me? How do you mean?" My neck grows hot, my palms sweat.

"You've never been late a day since I've known you." I breathe a sigh of relief when I realize I've misunderstood the scenario. "Jeez, even Xander is here before you."

"Yeah." I step forward and pull out a chair. "Sorry… I just got caught up with something."

I sit and instantly fall into a deep level of distraction. *How did I get into this mess? More importantly, how do I get out of it?*

Cooper stands at the head of the table we all sit around. He does his usual spiels, complete with hand motions and all. He reviews our studio time, our numbers—which, admittedly, still aren't where they should be—and our plans going forward.

"We have our music festival series coming up. It's quick. Five weekends, fairly close to home. We're home during the week and perform on the weekends. All about the same except this time we will have Stasia in tow. You feeling ready?"

"I'm excited," she says. "Ready to be on stage again." I was so distracted I hadn't even made eye contact with her yet—which I try to limit. We keep our distance from each other, no matter how hard that may be.

"So, we all know how this goes. There will be multiple stages across the chosen area, usually fair grounds or stadiums, something to that extent, with various acts performing."

"Do we know who we are sharing a stage with?" Theo asks.

"I have good news on that front. We'll be sharing a stage with a handful of other bands but most notably Save Me, Save You as they promote their new album.

"You're joking, right?" The words come out before I give them permission to.

"I can't figure out if that excitement or disappointment I hear in your voice." Cooper peers at me over his glasses.

"Their performance was incredible," Theo adds in. "Often times a comeback album doesn't hold a candle to the original releases but in their case, they came back stronger. Also unfortunate for us. They're our biggest competitor right now."

"Whose brilliant idea was it to put us on the same stage?" I let me annoyance get the best of me.

"Mine," Cooper says. "We could all be good for each other. Having two major headliners on one stage is going to attract a lot of traffic. Play nice. This could benefit both bands."

I pride myself on being an attentive person. Eye contact and awareness are two things I do well. If someone is talking to me, they get my full concentration—no cell phone, no distractions. My parents raised me to focus on who or what was in front of me, and that lesson stuck. But since Ames stepped back into the scene, I'm a different version of myself. My composure is collapsing.

It wasn't always this way for me and Ames. He wasn't always the villain in my story. Besides music, Ames and I had one major thing in common—in one way or another, we both grew up within hospital walls.

As a child, I spent a significant amount of time inpatient at one of Boston's finest hospitals. They did their job. They kept me alive. At a time I wasn't guaranteed to see my teen years, my parents agreed to a risky surgery that was still in its trial phases, but it was successful, and it bought me time, but the fix for one problem had adverse outcomes all of its own.

I had a few good years, a streak of a semi-normal life, complete with a clean bill of health. When I turned sixteen, things turned. I found myself experiencing excessive dizziness and blacking out. It was usually a sudden onset with very little warning. The first time it happened, I was sitting in the driver's seat for my license test. Needless to say, I failed.

Dr. Anderson, who had been the doctor on my case for years, had an idea of what was going on but called on a friend—an electrophysiologist from LA—to verify.

Many strings had to be pulled, and the wait time for an appointment was astronomical.

I missed the appointment with that doctor for a drum audition for a school talent show. It was the best and worst decision I ever made.

The best, because, well, it worked out for me. But shortly after the talent show, before we really started to take off, I blacked out, and when I opened my eyes again, I was in the hospital. I got that appointment with the electrophysiologist after all. They inserted a device called an internal defibrillator. I was told I couldn't do anything that involved using my upper body in excess or anything that raised my heart rate.

I was a drummer in a band. Telling me not to exert myself or use my arms was basically telling me my life was over. Dramatic? Sure. But I was sixteen with a dream that they were putting a DNR on.

The device worked for two years. For twenty-four months I never had a problem. Then, I did. I could tell something was wrong and I knew I had to get it checked out, but I equally knew I didn't want my parents to come. I was eighteen, so I had that right. But the band was finally getting recognized. We had a small summer tour planned. I didn't know what the outcome would be of that appointment, but I knew if my parents had a say, they'd tell me to put music aside and focus on my health. I couldn't ask them to come. I couldn't ask any of my band members. I'd left them in the dark on purpose. So, I'd asked Ames.

The device I had implanted was only supposed to send electrical currents when my heart was erratic, to normalize them. The doctor explained that the specific device I had was recalled for a malfunction that caused the device to fire at varying intervals—whether the heart rate was abnormal or not.

Ames stood next to me as I weighed my options.

If I got one taken out and got a replacement, that meant no tour. The recovery time would be weeks. With the placement of new leads, I'd be back in the same boat — no exertion, no major arm movement. The first time, it had worked out. We were still just messing around with instruments, so I could make that recovery work. I hardly knew my bandmates at that time. I was just the quiet kid with skilled hands and an intricately developed sense of rhythm. Now, they know me — or they think they do. We're close. And though people were learning my band's name more so than my own, they still knew I was a part of it. Taking time off then was nearly impossible.

"It's a *tour*," Ames said. "You can't miss it. You'll regret it for the rest of your life."

"Or" — I kicked back in a chair in the exam room — "and hear me out here, I die. And I'm not alive to regret anything."

"You do realize there is only one option here, right?" Ames paced the room then stopped in front of me. "You heard the man. If they just take it out, it's only a few days of recovery. If they place a new device, it's *weeks*. You don't have *weeks*, Dom. This tour is once in a lifetime."

"I know," I had said, looking down at the AMA sheet in my hands — the sheet designed to refuse a new device against medical advice if I chose to sign it. "What do I tell my parents?"

And Ames? He was the devil on my shoulder.

"You tell them nothing. You don't tell *anybody* anything. You're eighteen years old. You're not living with them. You sign the damn AMA, get the old device taken out and stay with me for a few days. Lord knows my parents are never in town — and go. On. Tour."

He looked me over as he lectured me, grabbed the sheet of paper out of my hand and forged my signature at the bottom. I allowed it.

I had one device removed and several new medications started in its place. The day Ames signed a very convincing signature to an AMA form was the day all my lies and secrets, every fraction of my double life, started.

That summer tour was canceled. I had risked my life for a tour that had never happened. We almost quit music. I nearly took a spot at a university. And just when I thought I could walk away with a clean slate — separate myself from the band member's I had told so many lies to, Kelly got us on stage with a major artist. Of course, Ames had landed a tour of his own just a handful of years later. I'd helped get him there. Our bands had never truly crossed paths. We'd toured at different times and appealed to different audiences. Both of our names were frequently spoken, but they'd only ever had one album truly take off, and while we'd continued to soar, they had faded out until they were gone altogether.

Our fame grew more and more each day. People wanted to know everything about us. The further we got into this, the more I knew I couldn't turn back. I couldn't unravel the web I had already weaved. And so, I kept my bandmates in the dark. The longer it went on, the more I cultivated the *lie* into a *lifestyle*, the harder it was to turn back. How would I come to them after all the years and tell them I hadn't been honest with them? That I had *never* been honest with them. They'd never look at me the same way again. The bond we'd forged would be damaged in an irreparable way.

"So, anyway," Cooper continues, bringing me out of my head and back to the table with no idea what I missed, "I'll see you all later this week at the recording studio. Might as well work on the material we do have."

Chapter Sixteen

Stasia

As usual, I'm the first one at the recording studio. The typical order is my too-punctual arrival, followed by Dom's early appearance, then Cooper and Theo at scheduled time, Blake a few minutes late and Xander? Well, better late than never, I guess.

Today I tried to busy myself, to give myself a reason to not be there early. Truthfully, I didn't want to be alone with Dom, not in the current state of things. The intensity between us, the passion, the draw — it's all there, all day, every day, incessantly. And we can't do a damn thing about it. I can't talk to him. If we are within three feet of each other, it's not talking our mouths want to be doing.

And we can't. We can't participate in the thing we crave most. It's for the good of the band. I want the music more than I want him. At least, that's what I tell myself every time I step into this studio.

"Stasia," he whispers from behind me. I was so lost in thoughts of him, of us, that I hadn't heard him enter.

"Dom," I whisper back to him. That's it. That's as far as we ever get these days. It's been like this for weeks. Around the band, we handle ourselves well. We interact, joke, make everyone think there's nothing between us at all. We are performers, after all. We put on a show. The others don't even know they are a buffer between us. But when we're alone, it's harder to pretend we aren't wishing we were more than bandmates.

Today, though, was different. He steps behind me, his chest brushing against my back. He places both hands at my shoulders, gripping and releasing, using his thumbs to rub small circles into the muscles that surround my neck.

"You're tense." His voice is filled with heat.

I'm not. Not usually. I'm typically relaxed and loose—but not around him. I'm tense *because* of him. He simultaneously relaxes me and makes it harder to breathe.

I tilt my head back into his touch, and he applies more pressure. Turning toward him, I reach up and place one hand at the back of his neck. He leans his forehead into mine. The beginnings of facial scruff lines his cheeks and jaw. His hair sticks out of place from the bandana he wears, and his eyes aren't covered by their dark-rimmed glasses. He's in music mode full time these days, the Dom the fans and the magazines know, but I know who he is when they're not looking. He leans in and his lips just brush mine—so quick, so light that it barely counts as a kiss. He stops there and waits, our eyes locked in to each other.

"We shouldn't." It's a whisper. He closes his eyes as he says the words.

"I know."

He grasps the fabric at the back of my shirt — part passion, part frustration. I step away first. "It's for the good of the band."

I have repeated the mantra, said the words to myself on repeat for weeks. I know it's what he's thinking.

He sits on the couch — more falling into it than gracefully taking a seat. He shakes his head and stares at the floor. "It's more than that."

I'm surprised by his words. I thought we were in agreement.

"It's exactly that." I cross my arms. "We can't be together because we are in the same band. We are recording together. If I'm lucky, I'll tour with you. If this ends badly, that all will likely also go badly. We can't be together because of the band."

"We can't be together, Stasia, because you're — "

The door opens and footsteps stomp down the hallway.

"Because I'm what?" I rush the question before someone else joins us. He returns his gaze to the floor.

"Good morning, Stasia, Dom." To my surprise, it's Blake who joins us first. He hands out coffees and puts one arm around me, giving me a tight squeeze. "Dom, I have some stuff outside we need to bring in. Give me a hand?"

Blake retreats down the hall, and as Dom follows his lead I grab his arm, stopping him in his tracks.

"I'm what?" I ask again, my grip remaining tight.

"Because you're his *sister*. It just…changes things."

My fingers fall loose at his wrist, and he continues down the hall, leaving me alone and frustrated in more ways than one.

During a break between songs, I step outside. Blake leans against the wall of the recording studio with a lit cigarette. I hold one hand out and he gives me a dirty look.

"Just one pull," I promise, and he hands it over begrudgingly. Leave it to Blake to judge my every-once-in-a-while habit while he's a pack per day *at least* kind of guy. He never missed a beat stepping into the brother role. I'm an adult—full grown and doing just fine—but he started treating me like his little sister the moment we found out about our shared lineage.

It never bothered me. Never once. In fact, I found it endearing.

Until today.

"These things will kill ya, ya know," Blake says, taking the cigarette back and filling his own lungs with toxins.

"Don't lecture me," I snap, narrowing my eyes at him. "You don't have to protect me from everything. I survived twenty-six years without you."

Blake flicks the cigarette to the cement and puts his hands out, flat palmed, patting the air. "Whoa, what's going on?"

"Nothing." The word comes out more in a yell than I meant it to, the kind of growl in the word that indicated *everything*, though that's not what I said. "Ever since Dad left, you've taken it upon yourself to be him. I don't need another—"

"You did not just compare me to *Victor*, of all people."

His voice gains volume, the same way mine did. "You know what? This kind of drama and outbursts is exactly the reason we didn't want a female around to begin with. Dom had the right idea when he voted no."

My heart falls into my stomach.

"What is going on out here?" Coopers appears in the doorway.

"Nothing." We both snap at the same time.

"Can you two get your sibling rivalry crap under control for a minute?" His voice stays calm, sucking the anger out of the area and keeping our attention on him. It's the most Cooperish thing he does, this ability to be calm and inflict tranquility on everyone else. It's his superpower. "We have to go to Xander's."

Cooper turns on his heel and retreats back down the hall, giving us no further information. Blake leans against the wall, or rather, the wall holds Blake upright. His eyes close, he takes a deep breath and lets it out with sound before reaching into his pocket for another cigarette.

"Blake?" I step closer to him. ""What is it?"

"I'm sure it's nothing, you know?" A puff of smoke leaves his mouth and nose as he speaks. "It's just that a few years ago he had this accident. A *bad* accident. And seeing him lying there... I don't know. Never mind. It doesn't matter now."

"If it's bothering you, it does matter now."

"There was a long time, a lot of years, where he was the only family I had—him and his mom. That was it. I just never truly got over the way I felt the day I got the call about his motorcycle accident."

I remember hearing about that. It was all over the news.

"Every time something happens with one of the guys or Cooper says something like he just did, my mind just goes *there*."

Sparks fall to the ground as he flicks ash from the lit cigarette. His voice is sullen, shaken.

"You worry. That's normal, I think. It's nice that you worry about them like that." I trace circles on the sidewalk with my shoe.

"I worry about you like that."

"You don't have to."

"Somebody's got to."

I roll my eyes, but I smile. Sometimes the older brother protection routine is nice, I guess.

* * * *

Xander and Natalie's apartment is so high up in the building that it seems their only neighbor is the sun. Cooper gently knocks on the door, but there's no answer. Blake reaches into his pocket and pulls out his keys, selecting one and reaching toward the door. He has almost inserted the key into the lock when the knob turns and Xander pulls it slowly open. I can sense Blake's muscles unwind once he finally lays eyes on a vertical, seemingly healthy Xander. Though, I'll be honest, he looks terrible. I've seen drunk Xander, hungover Xander and even gone-too-long-without-a-shower Xander. This was a brutal combination of all three. Xander presses one finger to his mouth and a light *shh-hh* escapes from his lips. He motions with his hand for us to follow him inside the house, and we practically tiptoe in unison behind him.

We all follow Xander to a room down the hall where he carefully opens another door and nods for Blake to take a peek.

"What?" Blake asks, confusion smothering his words. "Who?"

"So long as all continues to go as planned…" Xander pushes the door open wide enough for the rest of us to see what is on the other side. A small white bassinet sits in the middle of the room, and a tiny, brand-new baby girl swaddled in a cloud of pink sleeps at its center. "That, Blake, will be your goddaughter. Her name is Cadence."

Blake stares at Xander for a moment, then, it isn't his mouth that responds, but his eyes. They fill with tears. Real, glistening happy tears puddle in Blake's lids, and damn, they just might be contagious, because as Blake wraps his arms around Xander's shoulders and they pat each other's backs, whispering some of their weird brotherly love language that none of the rest of us ever understood. Water drips from my eyes to my cheeks, too. And Cooper? He's a faucet. He did just practically become a grandpa, after all.

"How did this happen?" Blake asks, his eyes trained on the bassinet at the center of the room.

"It was very last-minute," Xander explains, sharing the space in the doorway. "She was left at the doors of the hospital a few weeks ago. You know we have been trying to adopt. There is a lot that goes into the process when a baby is voluntarily… Umm…" He stalls.

"Abandoned." A voice sounds from behind us. We turn to find that Jana has joined us in the hallway. "You can say it, Xander. Voluntarily abandoned."

"It just sounds so harsh." His voice is the softest I've ever heard it.

"They *left* her there." Jana crosses her arms. "It *is* harsh." She walks across the living room and opens the sliding door to step onto the balcony.

Xander continues. "We got a phone call. They asked where we were at with the adoption process and if we were still interested in a newborn—and here we are. For now, technically, we are fostering. With any luck, the temporary part will be...well...temporary. We hope to adopt her when we reach that part of the process."

The band *oohs*, *ahhs* and marvels at Xander finding his softer side, while I sneak out of the group and followed Jana to the balcony.

"Everything okay?"

She doesn't look back as she nods, but she does shift her position so she's leaning into the wall, her arms wrapped tightly around herself in a way that seems protective, like she's not okay at all.

"You can talk to me, you know." I reach forward and place my hand at her shoulder, but she turns away.

"Do you need space, or do you need me?" I say the question into the air, but I don't look at her directly.

"What?" She turns her attention to me for the first time since I joined her on the balcony.

"When I was a kid, I used to have these—I don't know—episodes. The whole world got loud but quiet. I was really overwhelmed but bored. I wanted to be alone, but I hated *feeling* lonely. Depression. Anxiety. It does things to you. It makes you feel like everything is wrong, when nothing is wrong at all."

Jana's shoulders and neck loosen as her arms fall at her sides, as if the words I'm saying are the very key to what's keeping her locked up, like someone finally guessed the password to a club she thought she was in by herself.

"Anyway," I continue, "my stepmother used to ask me that. '*Do you want me or do you want space?*'"

138

She swallows hard and closes her eyes. "What was the answer?"

"There wasn't one." I reach my hand out, palm up, resting on the banister, leaving the choice for contact up to her. She places hers on mine. "Sometimes the answer was both. Sometimes it was neither. Sometimes it just depended on the day. But I always knew I had the option."

She smiles lightly but enough for me to notice. We stand there for a few minutes while she ponders her answer — me trying not to pry, her seemingly trying to keep the dam solid so waterworks didn't break through and flood her eyes.

"I just don't know how anyone can make a child, bring a human into this world and just…change their mind." She breathes in deep, looks toward the sky and lets it out. "They were supposed to protect her. They were supposed to love her and keep her safe."

Her voice cracks and her eyes dampen. I realize, in that moment, she's not talking about Xander's baby at all.

I'm not good at 'the shoulder to lean on' thing. I mask all my own insecurities behind bold lipsticks and solve all my problems with retail therapy and expensive items I usually can't afford. So, I change the subject.

"Godfather, huh? Blake never struck me as the religious type." I lean into the railing of the porch area, and she looks toward me, a laugh pressing into the corners of her lips.

"And *Xander Varro* does?"

We both laugh. She has a point. The idea was probably more engrained in sentiment than actual meaning. Lord knows, the whole church would burn if this band and its ring leader stepped inside.

Jana turns and looks at me, her eyes soften, her shoulders relax.

"Thank you." Her lip turns up at the corner. "I have to work. I appreciate the chat."

"Anytime." I wink as she steps away from the balcony banister and pushes the sliding door open.

Chapter Seventeen

Dom

Stasia leans against the balcony banister and the sun beams down on her like even though it has to stay far away, it can't help but reach for her.

I know a thing or two about that.

"You've been out here a while." I stand next to her in a way that allows our shoulders to touch and even that, I know, is too much. She doesn't pull away.

"I got lost in this view." She rests her head in one hand with her elbow on the railing. "Where's everyone else?"

"Theo and Cooper left a bit ago. The baby woke up, Blake held her and hasn't let go, so Natalie and Xander took advantage of the extra hands and are getting some rest. I was getting ready to go and thought you might want some company on the walk home."

Stasia runs her hand through her short hair and lets out a frustrated exhale.

"No."

That's all she says. Her hands grip the handrail, but her voice says nothing else.

"No?"

"No." She shifts so we're face to face, and though she's inches from me, she's miles away. "I can't keep doing this back and forth with you."

"I asked you if I could walk you home…"

"If I say yes, I'm not going to want you to walk me to the door then leave and you know it. I'll ask you to stay and you will." She steps away toward the sliding door. "Walking me home is just the first step to breaking the rules we created."

"Let's just bend them, then."

I step forward and my body is against hers. She steps so her back is against the brick wall beside the door.

I reach forward, my fingertips brushing the longer portion of her hair away from her face. She rests her hand where my neck meets my shoulder. I lean toward her, put my hands on her hips and slide my thumbs into her belt loops. A smile crosses my lips, knowing they are about to be on hers, then they are. The smile? It doesn't fade.

It's a delicious kiss, a recipe that's equal parts passion and patience, topped with a dash of hesitation that makes it all-the-more sweet.

We part, but our foreheads stay close. She tucks her hair behind her ear and breathes in deeply. She pushes me back gently and walks away. Stasia turns to lean beautifully into the balcony, the cityscape backdropping her in this intricate portrait kind of way that I could only imagine as the perfect album cover.

I turn so my back is against the rail of the balcony, next to her once more.

"Still no." She steps away and slides the door open. Not only does she promptly close it behind her, but as I step forward, she also locks it. I shake my head and wait for her to unlatch it, but she doesn't. She waves her acrylic-tipped nails and leans forward to kiss the glass, leaving her lipstick there. I lean my forehead on the glass and watch as she struts through the apartment then tosses her leather jacket over her shoulder as she leaves through the door and doesn't look back.

* * * *

I was locked out almost an hour before Blake came outside. I deserved every minute of it. I'm the one who said Stasia and I shouldn't carry on our entanglement, then I kissed her. All I'm doing is making this more confusing for the both of us, and I know I shouldn't. I just can't help it. She was right about one thing. I wouldn't have been able to just leave her at her doorstep any more than she could've walked away without inviting me inside.

We're overly attracted to each other. I thought in time we would get used to each other's presence, that our continued forced proximity would void any residual feelings we might have had—that maybe, even, we'd get sick of each other. But for every day that passes, the temptation just grows more fervid.

"You know this was locked?" Blake steps out on the balcony and fiddles with the lock in a way that has his head down, completely missing the lipstick stain on the glass.

"Nope." I rub at the back of my neck and try to play it cool. "Must've slipped when I shut the door."

Blake nods as he lights a cigarette and blows a smoke into the air, the cloud he creates becoming the only one in an otherwise clear sky.

"This" — he holds up a pack of Marlboro Reds — "is my last pack."

I can feel my eyes widen then my brow raises in an expression that's both impressed and suspicious.

"Xander and I both. We're quitting together."

Now *that* is even more perplexing. Blake and Xander were practically forged in tobacco smoke and ash. They've been destroying their lungs as long as I've known them.

"So, why wait?" I ask, curious about the remaining cigarettes in his hand. "Why not just quit now? Why finish the pack?"

He takes a draw off the cigarette in a long, drawn-out way that tells me he's taking his time on each pull, savoring his waning minutes with his godawful habit.

"Listen..." Smoke trickles out of his nostrils. "I know you have something like *zero* bad habits — and I hate you for that a *little* bit." He holds up his index finger and thumb just a centimeter apart and we both laugh. "But you can't just quit a habit you've been invested in for weeks or months or years. You have to say goodbye. Mentally, you have to prepare yourself and go in knowing the last time is the last time."

I nod and allow his words to sink in.

"I wish you the best with that." I step toward the door and slide it open. "I have something I have to do, but I'll see you later." I close the door and run my fist down the glass to wipe away the lipstick mark before anyone else sees it.

The elevator lands at the lobby of Xander's building and I run through the doors, into the streets and take every turn necessary to arrive at Stasia's apartment. I knock hard on the door and she opens it, looking as brilliantly beautiful as ever even in a faded band T-shirt and ripped sweatpants.

"*You*," she says, "are not pizza."

"That was a cute little move you pulled today with the door." I smile and lean into the frame. She smiles, too, but it's got a bit of malice in it.

"Glad you liked it. Now you can watch me do it again." She starts to close the door, but I put my hand against it. My palm presses the wood enough to let her know I'd like it to stay open, but not with enough force that she couldn't close me out if she wanted to. The ball will always be in her court. If she asks me to leave, I will.

"Stasia." Her name comes out in a quiet way, a breathless but anything but weightless whisper. She opens the door once more.

"Dominic." She responds in the same manner.

I step forward and place my hands at either side of her face then lean forward. She pushes up to her tiptoes and kisses me back, slamming the door behind us.

She pushes me hard against the wall and leans into me, continuing to kiss me while grabbing the hem of my shirt in both hands and lifting it, breaking our locked lips only to pull it over my head.

"What is this, Dom?" she asks between kisses. "What're we doing?"

"We are quitting our bad habit." Her nails scratch down my back as she pulls me closer.

"I'm a bad habit now?" She tilts her head upward and shows a rogue smile.

"My favorite one." I return the same grin. "And I have a feeling you'll be the hardest one to give up."

"But we have to."

"It's for the best."

She kisses my neck, my jaw line. My heart beats sporadically in my chest. "So, this is the last time this happens?"

"It's going to have to be."

Giving each other up is the right thing to do, and we both know it. However amazing they may be, our brief sexual escapades cannot interfere with my job and her dream.

I'd say it's not worth it, but damn if it isn't close.

Chapter Eighteen

Stasia

Dom sits up against my headboard, my sheets strewn across his lap but his torso bare. I've slipped back into my worn T-shirt and lie on my stomach across my bed.

"I have a question."

He tilts his head toward me and raises one eyebrow.

"Earlier you said me being Blake's sister changes things."

Dom nods in this slow, confident motion, like he knew the question was coming.

"Why does that matter?" I finally ask. "I love Blake — don't get me wrong — but it's different. It's not like we grew up together."

Dom's focus falls downward. Eye contact is a strong suit for him, but lately, he's been more and more distracted, and I wonder what's going on deep beneath those green eyes. He avoids my gaze, and I know I've hit a sensitive spot. Just when I think he will ignore me completely and decline to answer, he speaks.

"There was this girl."

I perk up a bit at this. According to the band, Dom has never brought any girl around. They continually joke that he's a permanent bachelor, that he's never said 'I love you' and likely never will. His words are a new revelation, a deviation from the usual rumor.

"It wasn't like that." His response is well timed. He noticed my curiosity inflating like a balloon and popped it before I could even tie it off. "She was my best friend. I told her everything. I leaned on her for everything. I made…choices. And I never thought those choices would impact anyone except for me."

His voice sounds miles away and pained, almost a foreign language compared to his usually confident and unwavering tones.

"What kind of choices?" I adjust from lying to sitting. It takes everything in me to not reach for his hand, but I'm not sure what contact is against our newly written rules.

"It's a long story." He swallows hard and finally looks at me. "But I was wrong. I knew I'd made the wrong choices when I saw her brother for the first time after she'd died. There is a bond, Stasia. There is a brother-sister bond that shouldn't be messed with. I learned that the hard way already. And Blake? He's your brother, by blood. Maybe you're right, maybe he's only been your brother for a few months, but he's been *my* brother for half my life."

I hadn't thought about it like that. My mind kept circling around and coming back to him protecting my relationship with Blake, but I had never thought about what would happen to the two of them if this ended badly.

"I'm sorry for your loss." It's all I can say. He speaks of his late best friend in a way that's so injured that I can tell that he wears that wound the same way he wears the small scars that mark his chest—fading fractionally every day but never disappearing.

"You know the library from my apartment?"

"How could I forget? It's amazing." I adjust so I'm sitting next to him, back to the headboard, matching his position.

"They were hers. Well, most of them anyway. I had a collection, but it was insignificant compared to the amount she left me." He makes a noise that charades as a laugh but seems more like an attempt to avoid tears.

"What was her name?" I ask in a quiet voice.

"Raya." He smiles as he says the name out loud.

"She sounds like a beautiful person."

"She was. When she was dying, she told me that every story gets a beginning, a middle and an end. That's what makes it a story. Some people's beginnings and endings are just closer together than others." He glances out of my window and toward the sky, speaking as if he were talking to someone other than me. "I told her she didn't get enough time. That her story wasn't nearly long enough, and she told me, *'Poems are stories, too. Sometimes the most beautiful ones'.*"

Poems are stories, too. It's beautiful and painful and perfect.

"Dom?" I ask in a whisper. I've seemingly already opened old wounds, and I'm torn now between tearing one more or stopping the bleed. "How did she die?"

He pulls his gaze away from the sky and turns back toward me. His eye color is accented by a thin layer of tears that he seemingly is fighting back.

"She died while waiting on a heart transplant."

And though I spent the last few moments concerned about his emotional scars, my eyes fall to his chest where he bears his physical ones.

* * * *

Dom and I have kept our promise to ourselves and each other for two weeks. Fourteen days with no physical contact. It's been easy because we haven't had any rehearsals, any shows and no time in the recording studio. Today will be the first real test. Are we strong enough to stay away from each other? I'm not sure. Our relationship was purely physical, and though I can talk my brain into forgetting his touch, I have a hard time convincing my body to follow suit.

I return to the studio today to finish up vocals on a song we've been working on. Xander and I are putting finishing touches on the track that Blake and I worked on the first night I met them at The Rock Room after open mic night. It's odd how something can feel so nostalgic, though the memory is only a few months old. We've come so far in such a short time.

In the distance a door opens, and when the sound of footsteps follow, I assume it's Cooper or Xander. I'm surprised when it's Dom who leans into the doorway.

"I didn't know you were on the schedule for today." It comes out harsh, but that wasn't the intention.

"I'm not. Percussion for this track is done already. But I knew you'd be here."

"Dom…" I'm not quite sure what I'm going to say, but we agreed. Staying our distance from each other is for the best.

"No, no." He holds up his hands in a light surrender. "Not like that. I want to talk to you about something."

I nod my head, embarrassed at the assumption.

"I know I didn't give you all of the answers you were looking for after…well, you know. The *last* last time."

I can't help but grin as he speaks. The memories associated with our nights together are all worth grinning about.

"The conversation got kind of heavy. I understand." I lean against the wall near the door frame.

"It's more than that." He stares at me in a magnetic way that I can't pull my gaze away from. "I need you to do something for me."

I nod my head and try not to speak. The more I talk to Dom, the more I realize how much he keeps inside, and I'm fearful that if I speak, he will change his mind and keep his secrets buried.

"I've been with this band for a large portion of my life. These guys have been my brothers for years."

I'm confused, at first, because none of that is news to me.

"I've been on the road with them and in hotels with them for hundreds of nights, and you officially know more about me than they do." His eyes soften and he tilts his head to one side. "All in the few seconds it took for me to take my shirt off in front of you, you already knew more about me than the guys I call family."

"Okay?" It's the first word out of my mouth before my brain can form a more coherent reaction, but I'm still not sure we are on the same page.

"I need them to stay in the dark on that, Stasia. The things you know about me. You already know I live my life on two totally different platforms." He reaches forward and takes my hand but, for the first time, the touch feels platonic where it's usually electric. "The scars, the loss. They are part of a version of me the band doesn't know — and they don't need to."

"Why?"

"Can you just promise me that what you know about me stays between us?" He runs his thumb across the back of my hand.

"It would be pretty hard for me to explain how I know what I know — which, by the way, really isn't all that much — without blowing the whistle on our whole charade." I try to keep the mood light, but he's serious. "I promise." I hold out the pinky from the hand he's not holding. "But you have to promise me something, too."

He holds up his hand, waiting to hear my side before wrapping his pinky in mine. "Promise me you're okay now? Those scars on your chest, they're from some kind of surgery or procedure, I gather, from the limited clues you will give me. But you're okay now? I don't have to worry?"

"I'm fine now, Stasia. It's part of the reason I don't want to dredge it all up. It's in the past."

"Promise?"

His pinky connects with mine and he lifts our hands lightly to his lips then places his kiss lightly against my knuckles.

"Good luck today. You're going to do great."

He lets go of my hand and retreats through the doors.

I'm already in the recording booth with a large headset pressed to my ears listening to the prerecorded beats Dom, Theo and Blake have recorded while mentally preparing myself to record this track. The ones we have released since I joined Consistently Inconsistent are soaring, and I'm grateful for that, but my contribution was mostly just accessory. This time, this song, I split the vocals with Xander fifty-fifty. I love performing on stage, I love listening to our finished tracks, but I've never gotten used to recording in a studio. Just me and a mic, it's an odd vibe I've never been able to adjust to — especially this time, knowing that my voice will not just be a side dish but a main course.

"Ready?" Xander claps his hands as he enters the booth. At least I think that's what he said. It's hard to tell with the headphones on. He's about twenty-five minutes late, his boots are untied, his shirt is fully unbuttoned and his hair is tied into some kind of knot. I'd like to say he was in such a rush to leave his house that he didn't have time to tighten up his ensemble, but I've come to learn that this is just Xander on a daily basis. He takes no time to throw on a headset and signal to the studio crew to get us started. It's mind-blowing. As many times as I've stood in front of microphone, I have never been able to dive in the way he does.

I press my hand to one side of the headset and listen to Xander sing his piece. It's perfect, so smooth and so well done that I'd guarantee he could sing it one time and it would be the final copy. He likely never rehearsed the piece, which is both impressive and maddening. I guess that's what doing this work for a decade and half does. When it's my turn, my voice fails me. No matter how many times I practiced or run through this in my head, my voice comes out different than I had anticipated. I tried to run with it, to make it work, but Xander cuts the recording off before I get two lines out. He slides his headphones off and I free one ear.

"What was that?" He's smiling, but there's a bit of accusation on his words that frustrate me. "You're better than that, and you know it. Clear your head. You're overthinking."

I nod and we both put our headsets on once more. Xander has the crew restart the track, and he performs his part as perfectly as possible, once again.

My entrance line collided with his exit word and it's stronger this time but not perfect. Xander's shaking his head before I sing three words. I slam the headphones down from my ears to my neck.

"What was wrong that time?" I don't hide my frustration. Staying calm was never my strong suit.

"Nothing." Xander grins a stupid half smile. "It was good. But it was just *good*. You're a *great* singer without trying, Stasia. It's why we brought you on. Stop *trying*. You weren't selling it at open mic night, and you were just great. You weren't overthinking when you *wrote* this song with Blake in twenty minutes backstage at The Rock Room."

"That's when this was fun. Now it's work. You know, as a kid when you could read and love books, but the minute a book was assigned to you, you hated reading?"

"I can't say that's a feeling I've ever dealt with." We both let out a much-needed laugh.

"That's how I feel now. When I didn't have a serious career in music, I had everything to gain. I loved it, and it was fun. Now it's scary. Now I have everything to lose."

Xander looks at me then through the glass that separates us from the soundboard operators and holds up five fingers. He tosses his headset aside and walks toward the door.

"Let's go."

"Where are we going?" I put my headset aside and follow, but he doesn't answer. He walks to an office space at the back of the studio and turns on the computer without bothering to turn on any lights. He punches a few keys and motions for me to join him.

On the screen is a photo of all of us at an old diner that is hours outside of the city in a run-down, middle-of-nowhere town. I sit cross-legged on the table with my back against the wall. Blake sits next to me with his feet kicked up on the booth bench on one side with one hand in his hair. Xander sits opposite Blake with Dom sharing the space while Dom is holding a fork and a butter knife the way he'd hold drumsticks. Theo leans into the booth's edge with his hand on Blake's sneakers, ready to push his feet out of the space. No one is looking at the camera. We're all looking at each other. Everyone is smiling and laughing. I didn't even know the photo was being taken. In that picture, I look like I didn't miss out on all those years of touring. It looks like I've been there all along.

"See? We have fun." Xander places his hand on my shoulder and gives me an encouraging squeeze. "You're one of us now."

I nod and smile. It was exactly the reminder that I needed.

"You ready to rock?" Xander stood and walked away from the desk.

"As long as you never say that again..." I raise an eyebrow, and he smiles. "But yes, I'm ready to rock."

* * * *

Xander and I stand facing each other in the sound booth once more with our microphones and pop screens between us. We put our headphones on and he holds up one finger to the sound board operators. I slide one ear free.

"I know this is different. This is your first track with us where you do the heavy lifting. Just pretend we're at The Rock Room…just like the first night."

I place the headphone speaker over my ear and hold both pieces down, close my eyes tight and sing from my soul instead of my mind. I hardly recognize the voice that comes out. I added some unplanned accents and emphasis where I hadn't before planned to have them. I open my eyes and stare into Xander's as our voices collide at the climax of the duet and at a point where I'm supposed to drop out and he gets his to solo, he steps back away from his mic and twirls his finger. "*Go for it*" is the phrase I read on his lips. I do.

I nail it.

I am breathless, excited and flooded with adrenaline when the song ends.

"That was amazing!" I squeal when he removes his headset.

"It was," he agrees, but he hesitates too.

"What?" I'm waiting for him to criticize me, to kill some of the buzz I'm experiencing, but he just laughs and puts one hand on my shoulder. "Now we have to come up with twelve more, give or take, so we can get an album out."

It's hours later and I'm still buzzing with excitement. I'm all dressed up with nowhere to go and to be honest, between recording and preparing for the tour, I haven't had much time to make new friends.

I knock on the familiar door of the apartment I know I shouldn't be at.

Dom opens the door and shakes his head as he leans into the door frame. He's thinking the same thing I am. I know he is.

Chapter Nineteen

Dom

"What're you doing here?" I laugh as I ask the question. It's light, barely heard, but it's there.

"I had an amazing day in the studio." She spits out the words at an impressive rate. "I'm so excited to leave on tour I'm like a kid on Christmas Eve. I can barely sleep. I can't think of anything else. Jana spends most of her time at Xander and Natalie's. Blake is always at home with Kelly and honestly?" She shrugs her shoulders and matches my sound that's partial laugh, but mostly just a noise to fill the awkward void. "I don't want to live these moments alone, and I don't really have any other friends."

My face twists into a sarcastic expression. "You think we can be friends?"

"We are friends."

"We're not friends, Stasia."

We're each smiling a wide grin that matches the other's. I didn't say it in a malicious way, but she knows I'm not wrong, either. We are or were, at best, friends with benefits. Without the benefits, I'm not sure where we stand.

"We could try to be."

I wave my metaphorical white flag and invite her inside.

* * * *

We sit in the living room on separate couches with a pizza in between us. I hold a plastic container of salad and munch on lettuce while she inhales a masterpiece of grease and carbs.

"You're right," she says between bites. "We can't be friends if you're going to keep doing this crap."

I wipe my mouth with a napkin in one hand and put the container down with the other.

"Doing what? Being healthy?"

"Yes! You can't honestly look me in the eyes and tell me that you enjoy an underwhelming bowl of romaine and other sadness." She reaches forward and puts her plate down on the coffee table. "Life's too short to count calories."

"Life is shorter when you clog your arteries and fill your body with *empty* calories." I stand to clear the table and take our plates to the kitchen.

As I slide the dishes into the sink, I watch her. She scrolls casually through her phone, picks a song and takes over my Bluetooth speaker like she owns the place. Everything she does, she does so with confidence. She bobs her head and sways a bit, like no one is watching. Even if she knew I was, she wouldn't care.

Being *just friends* is going to be much harder than I thought.

I can't be here anymore—not with her, not in this proximity to the bedroom we have become so familiar with.

"I have an idea." I lean into the counter, and she stares at me from across the room. "Go on a walk with me?"

We walk along the empty, midnight-cloaked streets.

"Where are we going?" She nudges me with her elbow as we turn the corner. It's the most amount of contact I've allowed between us all night.

"I'm meeting you in the middle." I say the words confidently, as if they should mean something to her, but they don't. Not yet.

As we turn down one more street, a storefront sits catty-cornered across from us. It's small but well-lit with two large bay windows on either side of the door. Glass containers that seem endless sit behind the panes displaying perfect, too-good-to-be-true desserts.

"Life is too short to not enjoy *some* empty calories."

She smiles as I speak but her eyes are trained on the desserts that are so well decorated, so impeccably placed that they look more plastic than edible.

"Are they open?" She checks her watch.

"That's the best part." I run my fingers down her arm and link my fingers into hers. "Open all night."

Before she has time to react, I'm pulling her inside and introducing her to the staff behind the counter. We're old friends—and by that, I mean I've been known to frequent as a regular any time we're home. I used to come here even as a kid. It's only a few blocks from the hospital.

We sit on the sidewalk with two white cardboard boxes and a paper bag between us. "How did I not know about this place? I lived in Boston for years."

"It gets overshadowed by the touristy places that have become famous over time," I explain. "Just as good, maybe even better, but always in the background."

"So, who is the extra bag for?" She licks cannoli filling from her finger.

"A friend of mine."

"Super-vague answer, as usual."

I look at her with one brow raised. "What's that supposed to mean?"

"I don't know why I even asked. I should've known there wouldn't be a direct answer. You're not really known for being open."

I nod and run a finger and thumb over my jaw.

"Old habits…" I whisper. "I spent so long trying to keep the Consistently Inconsistent version of me from the regular version of me that the real version of me forgot how to have a life. I liked the quiet, the solitude but I relied on it too much. Now it's all I know. I'm not used to answering questions because…I'm not really used to anyone *asking* them."

"You mentioned before that you had a friend that you told everything to." She swallows hard, seemingly unsure if she's choosing the right words. "I would never try to replace her. But that go-to person? The person you cheer with on your best days and vent to when the day sucks? I can be that person."

I turn my head and look at her. A light smile breaks the straight line my lips were pressed into.

"Tomorrow," I say, unable to offer any other detail before she speaks.

"Okay," she agrees and sticks out one hand.

"You don't even know what you are committing to." I give her a moment to rethink her answer as I push off the ground and stand.

"Eh, gambling runs in the family," she says. "I'm hoping the risk is worth the reward."

I take her hand and pull her to her feet.

"I'll see you in the morning then?" I back away slowly, forcing myself away from her to be less tempted by the goodnight kiss that's calling my name.

"Tomorrow morning," she agrees. "Text me the address."

* * * *

The automatic doors open and close repeatedly as I pace back and forth at the entrance to the hospital. At the other side of the parking lot, Stasia exits a hired car, holding two coffees.

"A hospital?" she asks as she approaches and hands me a cup. "Everything okay?"

Her eyes fall to my chest, regardless of how many layers of clothing protect it from sight.

"What do I have to do to prove to you that I'm fine? Run a marathon?"

She purses her lips and narrows her eyes. "I'm surprised you haven't run one already."

"Three, actually, but that's beside the point." I link my arm into hers and lead her inside. "We're not here for me."

We take the elevator to floor eight and step through the doors when they open.

"Good morning!" Ivy waves from the nurse's station and scurries around the desk to meet us. "Wait until you see him!"

Stasia looks up at me with confusion plastered on her face. We follow Ivy down the hall to Jackson's room. Stasia and I watch from the doorway as Jackson beats his drumsticks against the air. Music streams from his headset at such a high volume that I could name the song from there. Stasia presses her fingers to her lips and stifles a light but awe-filled giggle. Jackson is dressed in his usual hospital gown, but someone has fashioned his hair in a messy way that looks like mine does when I'm on stage. They've even tied a bandana around his head for good measure.

"Jackson." I knock on the wall inside the door then wave my hand to get his attention. When he realizes we are standing there, he drops his drumsticks and pulls his headphones down.

"Hi!" he yells, flipping his blankets away and turning to get out of bed.

"Whoa there." Ivy scoots in between me and Stasia in a jog toward Jackson. "Easy. I have to help you. All this has to come with us." She adjusts a few wires and directs Jackson to the wheelchair. As he's wheeled toward us, he sticks out one hand toward Stasia.

"You're Stasia, right? I've seen you on YouTube. I'm Jackson."

"It's very nice to meet you, Jackson."

Jackson asks Stasia every question he can think of in the time it takes to reach the elevator and get to our destination. We turn the corner and Ivy pulls out a silver key, then unlocks the door to the music room.

"I have to get back to the eighth floor. Just call me if you need me." Ivy nods her head and retreats from the room.

Stasia looks around as I position Jackson behind the drums. He's banging a cymbal before I can even lock his wheels. "This is amazing." She spins around and looks at the padding against the walls. "You had it soundproofed?"

"I did."

Stasia sits in a chair in the corner and watches as I teach Jackson a few basics.

A light smile stays on her face. She never pulls her gaze away, watching us every second of our lesson, really with us, in mind and body. It's one of my favorite things about her. She never gives half of her attention to anything. When she gives you the time of day, she gives it all.

Time always moves too fast when I'm with Jackson. I wish I had more of it. I wish *he* had more of it. Time isn't something Jackson has a lot of. He knows it, but he hides it well.

When we reach his room, I sit on the edge of his bed and Stasia leans into the doorframe.

"Until next time, okay?" I hold one hand up and he high-fives it.

"Until next time."

It's never goodbye. I couldn't handle that. I've been visiting this wing as long as we've been famous, which is, give or take, right around the time Jackson was born. He's been in and out of this place the whole time. I've seen him thrive and fall behind. I've seen him at his best but more often, his worst. He's surpassed his life expectancy ten times over. Every so often a miracle comes through and prolongs his life by a few more months. He's been fortunate, but we're aware that these miracles are not infinite, but temporary.

"It was nice to meet you, Stasia." Jackson waves from his bed as I walk toward her. "He's single, ya know."

Stasia laughs too hard. "I'll keep that in mind." She winks before heading to the hallway.

"He seems like a great kid," Stasia says as we walk down the hallway. "How long have you known him?"

"Almost all his life."

"Wow." We walk in an almost in a shuffle as if we are prolonging having to go outside where we will inevitably part. "I take it you visit a lot?"

"As often as I can when we're home. He's been in foster care his entire life. It's hard, you know? Most families have a hard time caring for their own sick children. It takes a special kind of family to take in a child in Jackson's position. He hasn't found it yet."

I can see it in the way her eyes soften that she doesn't know what to say. No one ever does.

We step into the elevator, and it descends to the lobby. The doors slide open as we approach them.

My watch buzzes, and the way she reaches into her pocket at the same time leads me to assume we're getting the same message.

"What the hell does 'T.M. 2' mean?" Stasia reads the text from Cooper out loud.

"Team meeting at two." I nudge her lightly and she laughs. "You'll get used to Cooper's texting."

"Looks like we've got some time to kill then. Want to watch a movie or something?"

"Your place or mine?"

She links her elbow into mine and we walk the city sidewalks until we reach her apartment.

Chapter Twenty

Stasia

Music blares from a speaker in the bedroom as I lean into my mirror and press a dark black liner to my lids.

"I love this song!" I yell as I click up the volume. In the mirror reflection, I can see Dom perched on my bed with a book he had stolen from my bookshelf.

"You've said that about the last ten songs," Dom yells over the edge of the book. I step in the doorway.

"They were all amazing songs." I spray an unreasonable amount of hair spray into my roots and dance along as the song continues.

We sit and listen to a random playlist of today's hits and dissect each one. A familiar voice, but not a familiar song, sounds through the speakers.

I tap my phone to life. "This is Save Me, Save You's new song."

"Skip this one." Dom reaches for my phone.

"Really?" I disregard the instruction and turn it up, then concentrate on the sound and the lyrics. "Why skip it? He has a great voice and these lyrics...? They're...amazing."

"I just don't like the song, okay?" He closes the book too hard and tosses it aside, then stands up to head to the speaker to shut it off himself.

"Do you...not like them?" I type a quick search into my phone.

"Nobody likes them." The words are aggressive and pointed. He meant them to be.

"Well, somebody likes them." My eyes widen, lit by both surprise and my phone screen. "Dom," I whisper as I tilt the device toward him and he takes it, "they just knocked Consistently Inconsistent out of our spot on the charts."

"What?" He scans through the list and the articles that are a click away. The first song I recorded with Consistently Inconsistent, *If I Knew Then*, has been hovering in the ten spot for weeks. Now it's not.

"That's not possible."

But it is. Not only does the number ten spot not belong to us, none of the top twenty do. Save me, Save You, however, appears three times.

He tosses my phone back to me and I catch it, scrolling through the same info he just read.

"Did you know them or something?" I put the phone down and try to reach into him, as always, prying for answers he doesn't want to give me.

"They were a band that was up and coming right around the time we were. They broke up but apparently" — he clears his throat — "they found some inspiration and decided to regroup for a comeback album."

"I know the answer is no, but do you want to talk about it? It seems to be bothering you."

"No."

I roll my eyes.

"I just don't get along with the lead singer, okay?" It's all he offers. "It's a long story…"

"Do you have any short stories? You claim to be this guy with two lives, and you won't let me in on either of them."

"You don't have people in your life you have bad history with, Stasia?" He paces at the foot of the bed. "We had a falling out. He hates me. I'm not a fan of his. What else is there to know?"

"Since we're about to be touring with them, I'd like to know everything." I nod and return my attention to my Internet search. I was hoping some of the drama made it into the media's hands – but this is Dom, after all.

"What an odd album," I say after a while of silent scrolling. I tilt my head and keep my eyes on the screen. Dom sits at the edge of the bed. "The lyrics are so beautiful, so elegant. But the lead singer… He just seems so…aggressive. Borderline scary."

He lifts his head to watch as I analyze the information. Part of me only did it to annoy him *just a little,* but it turns to something more. I'm impressed by them.

"Say what you will about them, Dom. Or, in this case, *don't* say what you want about them, but this album cover art is amazing. It's all incredibly well done. I wanted to not like them on your behalf, but we might actually have some competition here."

Dom checks his watch and stands from the edge of my bed.

"We're going to be late." He storms out of the door before I can say another word and our walk to The Rock Room is just as silent.

Cooper slides each member of the band a packet of paper as we take our seats. "Cities, travel schedule, set list, et cetera" he says, short and sweet. I scan the text, the paper shaking in my hands as adrenaline courses through me. I'm holding my first-ever schedule for my first-ever real tour, and though I try not to let my nerves show and act like I've been doing this as long as they have, I can't help but feel like my lifelong dream is truly coming to life in my hands.

The guys all hit Cooper with requests, set-list changes and questions about the schedule. Me? I say nothing. It's perfect the way it is to me. I'm just happy to be along for the ride. At the end of the meeting, Cooper stacks pages back in his binder and closes it with a slam.

"Let's chat award shows."

My mind immediately goes to fashion. I've seen the shows on TV. The lavish outfits, the multitude of platinum-selling artists all sitting under one roof — now *that* is the dream. It's hard to picture myself sitting among them, like maybe I haven't earned that right yet.

"Of course the data isn't in yet, so I'm not sure what awards you will be nominated for, if any. I can tell you it won't be Best New Album at this juncture, since you actually have to put an album out to qualify for that." My stomach turns, as I feel like that is aimed at me. Xander and Blake, they both laugh lightly in their typical no-care-in-the-world way.

"Anyway," he says, after shooting a narrowed glance at Xander and Blake, "even if we don't win an award, it seems one of you will be taking the stage either way."

The room goes quiet as everyone looks around for an answer.

"The production company that is putting the show together has put out their list of artists they'd like to perform at the show. They thought it would be exciting for two of the hottest new artists to do a duet together."

"We're not a new artist, though..." Blake says in a slow, drawn-out way as he tries to understand the scenario.

"She is." Cooper tilts one hand toward me. "It's unconventional, pulling one member of the band. But after she did the anthem and the amount of times her performances have gone viral already, they wanted to highlight her a bit. The buzz is strong around Stasia. We're going to ride it—if, of course, you accept their invitation."

I almost don't think before I say yes. The agreement jumps out of my chest and tries to spill out before I even allow it, but it gets caught in my throat when it's Dom who speaks next.

"You said duet with the *two* hottest new artists..." Dom's shaking his head as he speaks. He's already put the pieces together. He always is the quickest person in the room.

"Yes." Cooper nods. "The show producers want her to sing with Ames Gaherty."

My eyes almost involuntarily find Dom's, but I fight it. From the corner of my view, I can see him shift from his usual upright, perfect posture to a slumped version of him that I hardly recognize.

"Okay, but why?" Blake asks, and to be honest, I'm glad he did. I'm wondering, too. "First thing, Stasia is not a solo artist, so why are they treating her like one? And also, that guy is kind of a tool."

The guys laugh, including, to my surprise, Dom.

"Enough," Cooper says, less than entertained by this group. "If I've said it once I've said it a million times. It is about what is selling. What Stasia does is good for this band. People are curious about her. A rise in her name does equal a rise in yours. This show, the magazine shoot she did recently? They are all good things for her, and in turn, are boosting us up as a unit."

"You did a magazine shoot?" Blake asks. "How did I not know about that?"

"Would you have cared? Last time I asked you to come with me for something it was a radio show, and you missed it."

"You're really going to stay hung up on that forever?" Blake leans forward in his chair. I feel bad about what I said, but he gets under my skin quickly these days.

"Only if you want to, Stasia," Cooper says over the chatter among the guys.

"Of course she doesn't want to," Dom interjects, looking at me.

Between Dom and Blake, there are times, too many of them, that this 'looking out for me' comes off as controlling. I'm not the kind of person who can be tamed.

"I'll do it," I say to Cooper. "I'll do the awards show."

I don't miss it when Dom's eyes darken in a way I've never seen before.

Chapter Twenty-One

Dom

Stasia and I haven't spoken since the meeting the previous week, but now is as good of a time as any. One, we play a show at home tomorrow to kick off our musical festival tour. Two, she specifically asked to be alone in the recording studio today, so I know no one else will be there.

For some reason, she just cannot get the hang of recording this track. This is one of her songs. She wrote it, but something is holding her back. It's almost like her body language and mood don't back the lyrics. Maybe something's changed in the time since she wrote it. Or, perhaps, the stress of it all is finally getting to her. She went from a glorified karaoke performance to a viral sensation in a matter of months. I don't blame her for being worn down.

She stands in the booth, her headset on, with only the team of employees who run the mixing console visible to her.

The first time they play the music, she misses her cue and doesn't get the lyrics right. The second time, her pitch is off, and she can't correct it. After multiple attempts, they hit the button that allows them to talk to her through the glass and suggest she call it a day.

"Let me get in there with her." I step forward behind the attendants. When she sees me, I think she might be relieved to have me there, but then her expression shifts closer to annoyed, likely because I broke her rules. "You guys can break for fifteen minutes," I say. "Come back and she will be ready."

Her mouth falls open and her eyes widen at the promise.

I lean forward and click the speakers off, then join her in the booth, walking forward and reaching up to slide the headphones off her ears and around her neck.

"What're you doing here?" Her voice sounds torn, like she's trying to sound frustrated but the hint of a smile over the words suggest she's also flattered. "I told you I didn't need you here."

"Oh, don't I know it. I'm not naive enough to think you *need* anyone. I know you can do this on your own. I just thought you might *want* a distraction." I run my fingers down her arms and link my fingers into hers.

"I didn't think you wanted to do that anymore."

"There you go with that 'want versus need' thing again."

Before I finish the sentence, she pulls the headset off and tosses it aside, then throws her arms around my neck, pulling me close so her mouth is on mine. "We can't do this here." I grab her hand and pull her out of the sound booth. We walk briskly across the room to an office space, and I slam the door behind us.

"Shh…" she says, but she's laughing through the sound. I step forward and take the hem of her shirt in both hands and pull it over her head.

"We have…approximately eleven minutes," I say as she undoes the button on my jeans.

"Better stop talking then."

I pay no mind to anything covering the desk as I pick her up and push her onto it. Picture frames fall and papers float to the floor. I don't care about knocking anything out of place or keeping the noise down. Neither of us do. I only care, in that moment, about having her close to me again, even if it's just a 'for now' fix.

I kiss her slowly as our clock runs out. I dress and a small grin appears as I watch her do the same. The door creaks when I open it and hold one hand out, allowing her to go first.

"You were right." She smooths out her somewhat unkempt hair and adjusts her clothing. "That's exactly what I needed. I'm ready to get back into the booth."

I look past her and my smile fades, the solitary moment of bliss turns to confusion. The gentlemen running the sound board are packing up, throwing some papers in a briefcase and pushing their chairs in.

"She still has an hour left." I take her hand and step toward them.

"Not according to him." One man points the opposite way, and Cooper stands with his arms crossed, his eyes on us, leaning into the wall nearest the booth.

I drop my hand, though it's too late. The secret's out. Cooper already knows.

"Stasia," he says in a soft voice, and I'm surprised he speaks to her first. "You can go. Practice your song in the sound booth or take off and get some fresh air, but I'd like to speak to Dom in private, if you don't mind."

She stands there in silence, unmoving.

"Stasia," Cooper repeats, "sound booth. Practice. Vocals." He points to the booth, and she leaves us.

Cooper doesn't have to speak to give me my next prompt. I follow as he turns toward the area the band usually hangs out in between sessions where there's a couch and some scattered chairs. Typically, I think he'd use the office space, but we've likely tainted that for him. My stomach knots with guilt.

This is what we were trying to avoid. We, as a group, had made a pact regarding two of the band members dating—or, well, whatever it is we're doing—and I broke it. Cooper's silence says it all. I can see his tensed muscles and rigid stance even while he's walking. It's intimidating. I've never been on this side of an angry Cooper.

Cooper paces back and forth in front of me with his arms crossed.

"Coop?" I ask after what seems like hours of silence.

"Shh," Cooper says, stopping his incessant shuffling for a moment. "Don't say anything else."

I do as I'm told and keep my mouth shut for a few moments longer before Cooper speaks again.

"I have this...template, of sorts. Speeches tucked away for a rainy day or for one of those occasions where somebody royally screws up. I've got it down to a science."

I nod and keep eye contact with Cooper.

"But those pre-rehearsed lectures? They've pretty much been reserved for Blake and Xander for the last fifteen years."

I crack a smile but retract it as soon as it appears. I've heard all about Cooper's infamous lectures.

"What the hell were you thinking, Dom?" Cooper's words come out harsh and fast, more frustrated than angry. "We made a pact. As a band, you all promised me, and each other, that this wouldn't happen."

"It's not what you think, Cooper."

"What's your plan?" Cooper takes a seat next to me. "How serious is this?"

"What do you mean?" I ask, though it's a filler. I'm mostly just buying time. I don't know the answer.

"Are you going to marry that girl?"

If Cooper was trying to make a splash, he'd succeeded.

"No." I laugh a little, because the idea is incomprehensible. I'm not the marriage type. Everyone knows it. They don't know *why*, but they know it's true. "Definitely not."

The door closes at the end of the hallway, reminding me there is still a world turning outside these walls. The sound can only come from one person. *Stasia.* I think about her as I share this room with Cooper. She should be here, too—not because I want her in trouble, but because I don't want her to be by herself wondering and worrying about what's going on in this conversation she was dismissed from.

He stares at me for a moment in this quiet way that invites me to elaborate, but he doesn't ask anything else.

"Why do you ask?" I finally press, trying to propel the conversation toward an end.

"I just figured since this was such a huge risk, it must be something serious, the girl you're finally ready to give your heart to. You're not the kind of guy who does things halfway. If you're willing to risk the fallout, it must be the real thing."

Cooper stands and starts pacing again, the old flooring creaks beneath his steps.

"The fallout?" I raise an eyebrow. "With the band, you mean?"

Cooper stops and crosses his arms. "All of them, yeah," he says, nodding his head, "but mostly Blake."

I run my hand through my hair and let out a sigh. "Are you going to tell him?"

"No," Cooper says, too quick, with a short laugh that almost identically matches my earlier response, "you are."

My gaze shoots upward once more and I hold my breath.

"That's what I have to offer." Cooper takes the seat next to me. "End it altogether, once and for all. *Over*, like it never even happened. An annulment, of sorts. Or tell the guys, come clean and get ahead of it."

The shock doesn't leave me, internally or externally. Where I thought he'd be furious, he's giving me the opportunity to keep this going. I could be with Stasia if I wanted to. He's giving us his blessing to try to obtain everyone else's. I hadn't thought about that before. There was always only one choice—hide this from the band. But what if it wasn't? If I come clean, I could have the chance to do something I've never done before with a person who is changing me in ways I never thought possible.

"Make a choice, Dom"—he claps a hand on my shoulder—"sooner rather than later."

We stand together and walk down the hall toward the sound booth. Sure enough, Stasia is using the booth to practice the track she's supposed to be recording. When she notices our presence, she pulls open the door, walks through it and though I smile at her, anxious because I'm holding on to the secret about Cooper giving us the choice, she ignores me like I'm not even there.

"Cooper," she says, short and sweet, "you can work this thing, right?" She points to the table with the switchboard and equipment.

"I can." He nods. "I spent a lot of years at one of these desks."

"Great." She looks at me, but only for half a second and with narrowed eyes, then looks back at him. "Let's do this."

She re-enters the booth, closes the door and slides the headphones on so they only cover one ear. There is no hesitation, no lack of confidence.

Stasia nails it. Cooper's wearing the largest smile he's ever worn, and I can see it in his eyes. This is the moment he was waiting for with her. This is the breakthrough to make this band fresh again, the thing that buffs and shines the faded parts of us and makes us brand-new.

She pulls the headset off and tosses it aside then walks out of the booth with her head high.

"That was amazing," I say as she exits the booth.

"I know." She gives me almost no direct attention as she says the words, then turns her body to Cooper, cutting me out completely.

"It truly was phenomenal." Cooper pushes away from the desk as his eyes shift from Stasia to me. "I'll give you two a minute."

"See?" I say to Stasia, trying to keep things light after Cooper has left the room. "All you needed was to let loose for a bit."

"Trust me when I tell you the breakthrough behind that song didn't come from a place of passion, Dom." She crosses her arms and looks at the floor. "It came from a place of... You know what? Never mind." She turns to walk away from me, but I step forward and place both my hands at her upper arms, then softly turn her toward me.

"Talk to me. What's going on?"

"I heard what you said to Cooper."

I swallow hard. *What part?* There were two different sides to that conversation, and I'm unsure which one has her this tense.

"I knew this was just physical, Dom. You've made it abundantly clear that you don't do relationships. It wasn't what you said. It was *how* you said it. I mean, it's one thing to not have a future, but the way you answered him made it sound like you regret that we have a past—or a present, at that." She shrugs and looks anywhere but at me. "Just forget it. I knew the rules. It's ridiculous for me to even say anything."

I place one finger at her jaw and position her face so our gazes find each other.

"Don't discount how you feel. If it's upsetting you, it's not ridiculous." She smiles only slightly and steps forward, linking her thumbs into my belt loops. "If it's important to you, it's important to me. If it bothers you, it bothers me."

"How can you be so keen on someone else's feelings, so eager to respect everyone's feelings for what they are and connect with someone in a way where you want to feel everything they're feeling, yet say you never want to be in a relationship?"

I take a deep breath and step away from her, turning and stepping toward the seat at the soundboard desk. It moves backward on its wheels as I fall into it.

"There's a lot to unpack there, Stasia."

"Great." She tosses her hands to the side then lets them fall to her thighs. "You've got baggage. Let me help you carry it."

I shake my head and think on it. All she's asking for is answers. I can't give her the whole story, but I can give her the synopsis.

"Have you ever lost someone, Stasia?" She frowns with her eyes at the question. "I mean really, truly lost someone."

She shakes her head in silence, and a few strands of hair come loose around her face.

"Everything ends—friendships, relationships. Even family bonds can be broken beyond repair."

She swallows in a way I can see, and it seems a light sprinkle of tears develops in her eyes. I realize, as I see her expression shift to sadness, that the last part pressed on the bruise that is her father.

"We, as people, open ourselves to other people. We give away pieces of ourselves and become so dependent on other people, people who intertwine themselves into our lives, then one day we wake up and they're gone." She watches me as I divulge the parts of me that are broken, the pieces of me that I usually hide away.

"Life goes a different direction, or the person moves on or—"

"Or they die." The words she chooses to finish the sentence for me come out in a whisper. "You mean your friend, right?"

"It was the worst pain I've ever dealt with, Stasia. I don't want to feel that way again, and I don't want anyone else to feel that way because of me."

Stasia tilts her head, and her expression turns to worry.

"Are you planning on going somewhere, Dom?"

"Not today."

She steps forward and takes a seat on the edge of the soundboard desk. I turn the rolling chair toward her and she puts on foot on either side of the chair, sliding me closer to her and draping her arms over my shoulders.

"You know," she says, with a sparkle in her eye that shifts the conversation from heavy to light, "I was starting to worry about you."

"I told you I'm fine—"

"No. Not because of that." She smiles but I can feel my expression turn in a confused twist. "I was really starting to believe you were perfect. Turns out you are just as screwed up as the rest of us...maybe more."

She laughs at her own joke and leans forward so her forehead rests on mine. I kiss her in a way where our lips just barely touch, then pull away only fractionally.

"You walked away too soon."

She blinks and her eyelashes tickle my face, but she doesn't pull away or speak.

"Cooper didn't say we couldn't be together."

She pulls back slightly, but leaves her arms around my neck, hanging on to every word I speak.

"He said we can be together, if we want to be. But we have to tell the guys."

She smiles and eyes brighten, but the light fades fast. "You don't do relationships, Dom. It's like, a self-made rule."

"No one had ever given me any reason to break it."

Her smile lights up the room.

"We can tell them, if it's what you want. If you want to try to make this work, I'm in. But it's up to you. I don't want to mess things up for you, either."

She nods her head in an enthusiastic yes and grabs the back of my T-shirt with both hands, keeping me close.

"Tomorrow, before the show?" She returns her forehead to its spot against mine.

"Before the show." My smile grows. In this moment, everything feels right.

"You're sure?" she asks, and though I know she's confident in her choice, I think she's second-guessing mine.

"I'm not one to do things halfway. I'm in, Stasia, all the way. My only regret is that I didn't do this sooner."

She kisses me long and hard, though neither of us can control our smiles that break through even where our lips touch. I wrap my arms around her lower back and pull her onto my lap. The chair I sit on rocks backward, the wheels give way and we fall. We both try to catch ourselves and laugh an uncontrollable, can't-catch-our-breath sound as we lie there. We try to recover, but neither of us can keep quiet long enough to speak any further. Our bout of silliness continues and worsens every time one of us looks at the other, until finally I stifle the laugh with a continued kiss, leaning my body over hers on the floor of the recording studio.

Chapter Twenty-Two

Stasia

If I was asked to recap the time between leaving the studio and arriving at my apartment, I'd be at a loss to provide the details. Even now, lying in my bed with Dom beside me, it doesn't feel real.

I understood the rules, originally. Physical only. I had been told countless times that Dom would never be fully available, but I had allowed myself to hope. I fell for him, hard and accidentally. I gave in to the idea of an 'us', and at long last, I think he has, too.

We lie together, his lips find my hairline every few moments and I trace small circles on the skin of his chest. There is stillness, quiet and nothing between us — no more rules, and soon-to-be no more secrets.

The sound of my front door opening startles me. I sit up, too fast, and whip my head toward Dom whose wide-eyed expression matches my own.

"Stasia?" the intruder calls.

Blake.

I hop out of bed and throw on a T-shirt and shorts.

"*What* are you doing?" Dom whispers as I place my palm on the doorknob. I hold one finger to my lips.

I only crack the door enough to slide through it and close it behind me.

"Hey," I say, "what're you doing here?"

He opens my refrigerator, helps himself to a beer and twists off the cap.

"I missed you." He shrugs and smiles as he puts the beer to his lips.

Seriously? Right *now* is when he feels the need to be sentimental?

"Which loosely translates to 'Xander is busy with the baby and you're bored and have no one to drink with', am I right?"

"Yes," he admits with a laugh, "but seriously. Do you ever miss the days before we found out we were related?"

His question catches me by surprise. There's even a bit of hurt in his words. I find myself reaching into the fridge to grab myself a beer, almost, for a moment, forgetting Dom is still on the other side of my bedroom door.

"Not really," I say as I pop the lid, which rattles as it hits the countertop. "We're still the same."

"I don't know," Blake says. "We used to hang out. We used to spend time together. We were friends."

"We still are friends, you goof." I lean into the counter. "Things changed. You got married, you have a wife and the newlywed stage taking up your days. Xander and Natalie have a baby, and they've relied on you and Kelly a lot. These aren't bad things, Blake. Besides, we're about to go on tour together. We will see *too much* of each other."

He takes a drink from the bottle and places it on the counter.

"What's this really about?" I sense there's more to the conversation.

"I...I'm sorry. You and I had a few words after Cooper asked you to do that performance at the awards show." He rubs his palms at the back of his neck. "I'm sorry for what I said."

"Me, too."

We stand there for a while, and though he doesn't seem to find the silence awkward, I do, because I know Dom is still on the other side of my bedroom door with no escape route.

"Anyway" — Blake downs the rest of his beer — "I figured now is just as good a time as any. We have Cooper's band bonding thing tonight. I could just hang out until then."

"No." The word comes out too quickly, with more of a bite than I mean. "I mean, I can't. I still have to shower and get ready."

"Get ready?" Blake opens the fridge once more. "We're going to a billiard hall. There will be absolutely no one there to impress."

"We live very public lives." I shrug. "There's always someone to impress."

"You're out of beer." He shuts the fridge.

"Darn." I snap my fingers for dramatic flair.

"Want to go to a bar?"

"*Goodbye*, Blake," I say, opening my front door and inviting him to leave through it. "I'll see you in a few hours."

Blake steps through the door and starts walking down the hallway.

"And, Blake?" I call after him, he turns to face me. "I miss you, too."

He disappears out of sight and I close the door, locking it this time, and skip back to my bedroom where we focus only on ourselves and where we're headed until we have to be at the pool hall.

"So, since we haven't told them yet," he says, about one block from our destination, "I'll let you go in first. I'll be in in a few minutes, okay?"

"We could just tell them now." I bat my long lashes and lay the flirting on thick.

"Tomorrow," he reiterates. "Tonight is supposed to be fun and light—a kick-off to the tour. I don't want to ruin it."

"Yes, ruining the tour sounds like a much better plan." I raise one eyebrow.

"If we tell them tomorrow," he says as he leans forward and presses his lips to mine, "they'll have less time to kick one or both of us out." He winks and places both hands on my shoulders, turning me and pushing me gently toward the building.

When I enter, Xander leans over the table, setting the billiard balls in the triangle. Natalie and Kelly sit at a high top in the corner, drinking wine and signing to each other. Dom enters and joins Theo in the corner. They stand shoulder to shoulder, having some conversation I can't hear over the music, but Dom steals glances, looking my direction and tracing my body with his eyes.

Blake comes stomping through the doors, wearing an angry expression—a vast difference from how he appeared just a few hours ago. The smoke that clouds the pool hall almost appears to come out of his ears.

"A little warning would've been nice, you know." His voice is laced with annoyance and somehow, I feel a lecture coming on.

"Well, hello to you, too." I chalk the end of my pool cue and toss the blue cube back into the bucket. I look past him at Dom, who seems to be as concerned as I am, though I'm trying to hide it. *Does he know about us?* "I haven't the slightest idea what you're talking about."

Blake pulls a rolled magazine from his back pocket and slams it to the center of the pool table.

"If you're going to pose naked for magazine covers, the least you can do is give me a heads up."

"It's just a body. Who cares?" I take the magazine and Kelly leans forward, grabbing it out of my hands.

"You look hot!" Kelly exclaims. "Besides...'naked' is an exaggeration. This barely even shows anything."

"Where did you even get that, anyway?" If I'm being honest, I'm proud of it. I stepped outside my comfort zone, and like Kelly said, it's not like anything is showing. I'm topless, sure, but I also hold a guitar so its body covers mine. The photo highlights my tattoos more than my body.

"It is *everywhere*." Blake grabs a cue stick from the rack and walks to the other side of the table, leaning forward and hitting the white ball so it breaks the triangle grouping and sends balls in multiple directions. "Every end cap at the stores...in the magazine racks on the street..."

"I stand by what I said," Kelly says, flipping through the spread. "She looks beautiful. If she wants to be confident enough in her body and skin to let everyone else see it, too, I say more power to her. What do you think, Xander?"

"I'm staying *far* away from this one." He pulls a beer from the bucket on the table and drinks half the liquid in one sip.

"Did you know about this?" Blake asks Cooper. Cooper looks at me then back again.

"I did." Cooper follows Xander's lead, reaching for a bottle off the nearby table.

"And you didn't stop her?"

"Why would I?" Cooper takes a sip of beer. "She's a grown woman. She wanted to do it. Nobody forced her to. It's not really my place to tell her what she can and can't do with her body."

"That's literally my sister." Blake tears the magazine from Kelly's hand and tries to toss it into a nearby trash can, but I intercept it. "Besides, whatever happened to 'one of the guys'?' *'Having a female in this band won't change anything'*? You don't see us posing like that for magazine covers."

All the guys look at each other. Kelly laughs and places her hand over her mouth when Blake shoots her a narrowed glare. Even Cooper joins in on this silent exchange where everyone knows the inside joke except me.

"What?" I look into each of their eyes and hope one will cave and fill me in.

"This right here," Xander says, wrapping one arm over Blake's shoulder. "This is Boston's sexiest man...what? 2015? 2017? I don't remember."

"Both." Kelly sips her wine. "I have both spreads."

And suddenly, we're all crowded around Kelly and Natalie's high top, googling pictures of throwback versions of Blake. Everyone is laughing and enjoying themselves, and even though Blake's cheeks are as red as they've ever been, he starts to laugh, too.

"You're quiet over there, boys." I address both of them, but it's Dom I'm trying to bait and hook. "What do you think of the spread?"

"I think you look beautiful," Theo says, and it's kind. There's no flirting, no alternative motive in his compliment. He's just genuine. "Congratulations.

Front cover of any magazine is huge. You rocked it."
He lifts his drink toward me, and I do the same.

"Dom?" I raise one eyebrow.

"I'm with your brother on this one." He takes a long
sip of water and stares at me over the glass, then places
it on the table. "It was supposed to be your voice that
sold the music – not your body. If our fifth member had
been another guy, he wouldn't have made the cover.
He likely wouldn't even have been interviewed."

Dom steps away from the table and walks toward
the opposite corner of the pool hall.

"I'll go talk to him," Theo says, downing the last sip
of his drink.

"Actually, maybe I should." I watch as Dom walks
away. "I know Dom had always been the one to
hesitate when it came to bringing me on. I didn't mean
to make any waves. I'll talk to him."

I hop off the bar stool and make my way to the
opposite side of the building, following Dom's path.

He steps into the small hallway between the men's
room and the women's, and as I turn the corner, he
grabs my wrist and pulls me in close to him. He moves
his hands from my arm to both sides of my jaw, gently
lifting my chin so I'm facing him.

"Are you insane?" he asks, but he's all smiles. "That
was the hardest lie I've ever told. You can't just put me
on the spot like that."

"So, why lie?" I place one of my hands on his. "You
could've just said the photos were nice and moved on."

"No, I couldn't have. Trust me. If I had said
anything… If I had tried to say even one thing about
you in that photo, they would've figured out it's not the
first time I've seen you that way."

With that, his lips are on mine. He is, as always, a
gentleman, but I'm not in the mood for slow and

steady. I grab the front of his shirt and drag him into the utility room behind us, locking the door as we enter.

Chapter Twenty-Three

Dom

"Everything okay?" Theo asks, leaning over the pool table readying for his shot as we return.

"Fine," Stasia says. "Someone was just being a little sensitive." She pouts her lips and says the words in a mocking tone. It takes everything I have not to smile at her, because, well, she's *adorable*.

I take a sip of my drink and look at her over the rim of the cup.

"I give her two months before she ditches us for a career in pop music," I say as I set the drink back down.

The bands members let out an *oooohhhh* and a light laugh, tossing in small jabs of their own as Stasia and I continue to exchange words that no one else takes for anything more than banter between friends. All except one, anyway. Cooper stares at me with questioning eyes. As everyone else is occupied watching Blake and Xander face off against Kelly and Natalie in a boys versus girls pool round and exchanging roasts and jokes of their own, I walk over and stand next to Cooper.

"You haven't told them yet." He keeps his eyes straightforward, watching over the crew as they laugh and enjoy themselves.

"I will." I nod. "Can I ask you something?"

He turns his head toward me and gives me his full attention.

"Why are you allowing this?" I slip my hands into my pockets and keep my voice quiet. "You were so against it before. That's why you made us all promise it wouldn't happen. Why the change?"

He scratches at his chin and returns his gaze to the game in front of him.

"Let's just say I've recently come to face a similar situation." He smiles as the scene in front of us, stays light and cheerful, with Xander trying some ridiculous trick shot and Blake stealing Xander's drink while he's occupied. "There is a woman in my life, too, who would create a slew of mixed reactions, should I pursue it." He sips his drink and shrugs.

Cooper has been single as long as I've known him. I wasn't sure if it was by choice or not. He was, essentially, a single dad to five boys for a dozen years. Then four, which has shifted to four boys and a girl. The family he was responsible for was ever-changing, very needy, always on the road and requiring his watchful eye, regardless of how much we've aged. I never realized, or thought about, how putting us first meant putting himself last.

"I have a feeling it will all work out." I watch as Stasia laughs at something in this way that lights up even the dimmest back room of a run-down pool hall. "It did for me."

When we all go our separate ways and everyone else is out of visibility, I catch up to Stasia and slide my fingers into hers. We walk in silence, but every once in a while she looks up at me, smiles under blushed cheeks and looks away.

"I am excited about tomorrow," she says. "I think it is best to tell everyone about us. But, I will miss the sneaking around just a little bit." She holds up her thumb and pointer finger of her free hand spaced an inch apart.

"Trust me. If Blake doesn't kill me first, we will still be sneaking around." I laugh. "You saw how he reacted to your magazine — which is gorgeous, if I haven't said so yet."

"You have, several times."

"I will continue to do so, I'm sure." We reach the doors to the lobby of her apartment and stop, turning so we're facing each other. "As I was saying. He's not going to want any single second of PDA in his line of vision. When we're traveling, on the road or on stage, we are going to have to still be just bandmates."

"I know," she whispers. "Do you want to come in?"

"Back to that 'want versus need' thing." I shake my head. "I do, *want* to, but I also *need* to be prepared for the show tomorrow. And so do *you*." I lightly tap my finger to the end of her nose and wink. She blushes a light pink that she wears so well, kisses me softly and turns away to enter the building.

"Until tomorrow then." She waves as the automatic doors close, and I watch her walk away until she's out of sight. For a moment, it was the perfect end to a perfect day, but as I turn to walk away my chest tightens. My body feels like it's overheating, sweat beads at my neck and brow. I try to steady myself against the light post nearby, but I'm seeing double and

I miss, falling awkwardly to the sidewalk. The world spins and the muscle in my chest burn.

I pull myself into a sitting position with my knees up and lean my head forward, forcing myself to take a few deep breaths. My vision starts to clear and breathing gets easier. The tightness in my chest fades. The worst of the episode isn't the physical symptoms. It's the mental ones. I know now, more than ever, that I can't deny this part of me any longer. For a few hours, for a fraction of a day, I got a glimpse of what a normal life might be like, but nothing about my life is normal. It was foolish of me to think otherwise.

For as long as I can, I avoid pulling my phone out of my pocket and making a call I know I need to make, but I can't wait anymore.

"Hey," I say, angry at both myself and my situation, "I'm sorry it's so late. I need to see you."

"Absolutely," Dr. Anderson says through a yawn. "Come see me first thing in the morning."

"Actually…" I hesitate for a moment, knowing if I don't do it now, I never will, "can you see me tonight?"

* * * *

A shiver runs the length of my spine, both from the cold temperature of the exam room and the aura of it.

"I wasn't sure you'd ever come back in to see me," Dr. Anderson says through a smile, but something tells me it's forced, like he's hiding worry behind his pearly whites.

"I wasn't sure I would either."

"What's going on?" He takes a seat on a rolling stool and pulls up my chart on the computer screen. "Must not be great if you've finally given in to coming for a visit—especially one in the middle of the night."

"I'm sorry about that." I swallow and hesitate to respond any further. If I say the words out loud, it's all real. After years of being able to hide behind my health that was only temporary, I have to admit that my borrowed time may be coming to an end.

"My heart rate fluctuates quite a bit." I take a deep breath and listen to my body. Even now, sitting here, I can feel my heart speed up, beat too many times too close together, then fade out fast, slowing down until it normalizes again. I know rhythm better than anyone, for more than one reason. "And I have frequent chest pain. It varies in duration and intensity, but it happens, and it's happening more than I'd like it to. I've mostly just ignored it, but I almost passed out earlier tonight, and the last time that happened —"

"You ended up in surgery."

"Surgery that failed," I remind him.

"Listen," he says, both in a playful and a defensive way. "The surgery was successful. The device failed."

I force a small smile, but I'm not in the mood for jokes.

"Let's run some tests," he says, getting back to business and punching in keys on the keyboard. "EKG, Holter monitor, a full spectrum of labs."

"No Holter monitor." I shake my head. "Not right now. I have a show to play, and we leave on tour from there."

"Dom" — he shakes his head, heavy with frustration — "why are you here? If you're not going to go against all my advice, why even come in?"

"You know what?" I push myself off the exam table to a standing position. "I have no idea."

"Wait," he says, holding his hands up in a surrender. "EKG and labs now. Then we will go from there to figure out exactly what is happening, but I think you and I both know that answer."

I nod my head. "The medications aren't working."

"They were never supposed to work this long. And you shouldn't play this show. You have to know that." He stands and heads toward me. I take a seat once more, and he places a stethoscope at my chest and plugs his ears to listen. It's all for show. He doesn't need to listen to know I'm right. He frees his ears and places the stethoscope back around his neck. "You knew the medications were only a temporary bandage. The question was only how long it would hold for."

"I know."

"Disappointment isn't something I'm used to hearing in your voice." Dr. Anderson switches from his cardiothoracic surgeon voice to his psychiatrist voice seamlessly. I guess in this business, you have to be both. "Is there something more going on?"

"Nope." The word comes out before I give myself permission to say it. There is more, so much more. For my entire life I have sidelined myself from love. I've never allowed anyone to get too close to me. Losing someone you share a connection with is the worst kind of pain, and I never had any intention of subjecting anyone to it—not for me. I distanced myself from friendship and intimate relationships with tight strings to ensure I prevented any bond from forming before I was forced to permanently sever it. Even by way of the band, I never thought we'd be in it this long. They, unfortunately, are collateral damage.

With every passing day of no sign of imminent cardiac danger, I allowed myself to believe I was normal. I was foolish enough to start living a blissfully ignorant life where I pretended the very clock that keeps me going could lose power at any moment. I made the conscious decision to get close to Stasia, to let her get close to me.

That changes today. No matter how hard it will be to end what we have now, I know in my heart that no matter how weak it may be, that looking in her eyes and saying goodbye now will be easier than her saying goodbye if my eyes are no longer open — and I know, every day I choose music over my health, that possibility remains very real.

Once I've arrived home, sleep evades me when I need it most. My eyes won't stay closed, no matter how much I will them to. My mind is on a loop. *When did I let this get this bad? How has it gone on this long? When is it going to end? Was the risk worth the reward?* I run this closed-loop-circuit marathon of 'what if' and 'what will' until I tire myself out completely and finally give in to sleep.

When I wake, I have dozens of texts messages and phone calls. For the first time in my career, it's me who has missed sound check.

They're not mad. Sound check for our home shows is more tradition than required. The staff knows what we want and how we like things, and we hardly rehearse our concert sets any more. It's Stasia's name on my screen that causes the most agony. I don't want to see her. I'm not sure I can.

But once again, 'want versus need'. I don't *want* to face her, but I know what I *need* to do. It's what needs to be done to protect her heart, even if I've done a terrible job at caring for my own.

* * * *

Backstage at a show is usually a sanctuary — a safe place, a place where everything is happy and everything is in place. Not tonight. Since I arrived, I've wanted to be anywhere but here. So far, I haven't found any of my bandmates. I stand in the wing of the stage and watch the openers. I look around — at the crowd, at the lights and the set — then when the opposite wing comes into vision, I stop looking.

The pain in my chest is different this time. Stasia stands at the other side of the stage, watching as the band plays. She nods her head to the music, sways a bit as she appreciates every note. Her eyes meet mine and she smiles, then waves. She figures out my response doesn't match hers before she completes the motion and she drops her hand, letting it fall to her side. I nod my head to one side, and she follows the direction, leaving the wing to meet in the center of the backstage area behind the curtain.

"Everything okay?" She pushes her hair behind her ear. I can hear it in her voice. She already knows it's not. I can't tell her the truth, no matter how much I want to. This is the first time, the only time, I've ever wanted to spill all my secrets. I could do it. I could unlock the vault and tell her the two different sides of me are not limited to appearance. That both sides of me have one thing in common — they're both liars. If I do, it's over. The covert operation I've been silently operating for years will be blown. And for half a second, I wonder, would that be the worst thing?

But I can't. This is a slope that continues to get steeper. There's more to this than her and me. What will the band say? Cooper? Even my parents live under false pretenses where their only son is safe and healthy. I want to tell her everything.

But I can't.

"We can't do this anymore."

"We've done this dance a million times, Dom." She shakes her head. "We always end up back in the same bedroom."

"It's different this time. I'm serious. We're done." I stare into her eyes and keep my lips in a tight line. I drain as much of the emotion out of my voice as I can. I don't want to give her any excess rope to hold on to. I have to cut it away completely.

If she were the kind of person who cried, tears would be filling her eyes. She's just fighting it off and winning, but I can see her shoulders tense and her breathing change.

"How is this different than any other time?"

The nice guy, clean-cut act isn't going to work. Not with her.

"It was fun in the beginning. It's not anymore. Time to find other people."

Her eyes narrow under her dark makeup and false lashes.

"You're going to do this now? Minutes before a show?" She bites her black painted lower lip and takes a deep breath. "I still need you."

I shake my head and take a step back. I pull my bandana from my pocket and wrap it around my head. She watches as I change, in front of her, from Dominic to Dom. "But I don't need you."

As I turn and walk away, hoping that that final word is enough to burn the bridge completely, she tries to salvage the engulfed pieces.

"You don't mean that. I know you don't. What changed since yesterday?"

Everything. But she doesn't know that. Yesterday I still had tomorrows, and now, I don't know how many of those I have left. I don't have it in me to let her be the saddest person in my story.

"You don't get to have your feelings hurt in this, Stasia. There was never supposed to *be* feelings. That was the deal."

"Just because I agreed to keep it simple doesn't mean I can't wonder what the hell happened when you decide you're done with me. I've at least earned that."

"The guys were right, I think." I pull my ear plugs from my pocket. "A relationship within the band was a bad idea. Hell, having a female in the band was probably a bad idea."

I turn away from her, eager to take the steps to go anywhere but here and put one ear plug in. Just as I'm about to put the other in, she takes her final stand,

"I'll give you until midnight to change your mind, Dom. This is your last chance with me. I don't know what you're going through, but you have the rest of the night to figure it out."

I turn back around, slowly, but she's already walking the opposite direction. Even in a moment where she was filled with anguish, she didn't cave. Instead, she turned the table in her favor. She made it so she took the last word and the final choice. In that second, I crave her more than I ever have. She's the strongest person I know.

Chapter Twenty-Four

Stasia

The lights are still dark on stage, and the venue plays an assortment of songs that the crowd sings along to. I pace in the wing.

I'd love to say Dom's words didn't affect me, but I'm only human.

"You okay?" Blake joins me in the wings. "You're straying from your usual pre-show rituals."

"Oh." I check my watch. Only seconds until we go on and I haven't done any of my usual routine. "I'm fine…just distracted."

I look past Blake as we speak and watch Dom as he drums his sticks off a nearby wall. He doesn't look at me. I'm so used to stolen glances and intense eye contact from across rooms that I had to wonder if he'd still be trying to make an across-the-room connection. He's not.

"I'll be fine." I force a grin and Blake squeezes my upper arm before going to finish up his own pre-show business.

We take the stage, and the crew lights up the area only fractionally. Enough that the crowd can tell there's people on it, but not enough to guarantee which one of us is which. They scream and applaud, and Dom plays a light, tempting beat while the rest of us get set. I turn my head over my shoulder to take one last, long look at him. He doesn't look up. He doesn't wink like he usually does. He didn't walk me out onto the stage and let his hand fall down my back as we part the way he has in the few shows I've done with them.

I've seen the videos of both Xander and Blake's worst shows. I wonder if this is how they felt in those moments — lost, like they don't know which way is up. Confused, like they don't know if the things they had grown used to were gone forever.

I make a choice in that moment. He doesn't deserve to cut me down at the knees or make me feel like I, in any way, have to perform poorly because of him.

He won't get my worst show. Not tonight.

So, I give him my best.

It's my most spectacular appearance to date. I usually try to let Xander take the lead and I fade into the background. I'm the extra. That's been my role, and I've accepted that. But tonight I'm feeling extra nonexpendable. I take on as much of the show as I can handle while still letting Xander claim the front and center spot. Later, he grabs my attention and waves me up to the front. We play our guitars, facing each other, sharing a mic and singing in this way where we're both competing to be heard over the other but equally complimenting each other's unique sounds.

I realize, about halfway through, that I'm not performing for the crowd. I'm performing for Dom. He'd avoided looking at me all night until now, but now he can't look away. I use the power in these songs written about missed opportunities to turn so I'm partially facing him, and even though nobody else in the sea of thousands knows I'm singing directly to him, he does.

In the final moments of our show, during a booming finale with lights and sound, my heart could burst with pride. As confetti rains down around us and the crowd screams louder than the instruments we play, I stop strumming, turn toward the drum set and tap my finger against the face of my watch.

There may even be essence of a light smile before he forces it away and beats his final, loud pattern before standing and walking to the front of the stage. He leans forward and tosses his drumsticks to the two most beautiful girls he can find in the foremost part of the crowd, then makes a hard step past me, leaving the stage completely.

* * * *

When I return home, I collapse on the bed and stare at the ceiling longer than necessary. I've dreamed of these moments my whole life—how it would feel stepping off that stage after a good show, how my name would sound when thousands of fans screamed it, what this kind of lifestyle would entail. This isn't what I pictured.

Every night, he's less than ten feet away from me and yet miles away now. I've given Dom every chance to open doors to me and he keeps adding locks.

Usually, there's an intensity between us, a magnetic pull that we both have to fight. Not tonight. He barely looked at me, and what was more noticeable was how easy it was for him to pretend that I don't exist. He meant it when he said we were done. I could see it in his eyes.

A knock at the door distracts me from my self-pity. I force myself into a standing position and head toward it. Looking into the peephole offers no help. The person on the other side of the door either isn't there any more or is out of my line of view. There's only a vacant hallway in front of me when I open the door, but I look down. A vase of what must be at least two dozen roses sits near the threshold. They're gorgeous — fully bloomed and perfectly placed in an intricate bouquet, but the sheer amount of them and the quality of the design isn't what's most striking about them. The thing that really sets them apart is their coloring.

They're black.

I lean down and run a finger and thumb gently across the petals of one of the blooms then pick up the arrangement and carry it inside. There's a small purple envelope adhered to the vase. I slide one perfectly painted acrylic nail under the seal and tear the paper away. There's no name, only an address and a time.

These roses aren't a gift, they're an invitation.

5260 Moirai - 1 a.m.

There isn't any part of me that doesn't jump at the chance of adventure. I punch in the address on my phone and hire a car to take me to it.

Maybe I was wrong about Dom after all. Perhaps he's not as done as he says he is.

* * * *

The driver looks back at me, his eyes in the rear-view mirror lighting up when we pass under streetlamps and darkening again when we're in between posts.

"Are you sure that's where you want to go?" There's hesitation in his voice.

"That's the address that was given to me."

"Okay." He shrugs. "We will be there in just a few minutes."

As we drive onward, it's hard not to notice the trend. The farther we get from my apartment, the darker it gets. The more miles we put between us and the city, the more miles it seems are between each building. The bright, brand-new builds of the city limits morph into run-down, boarded-up vacancies that look like they haven't seen humans in years.

For a moment, I allow a fraction of me to second-guess myself, but I'm too proud to admit it. We come to a stop in front of a massive building with spires and incredibly high roof peaks.

"What is this place?" I ask, before exiting the car.

"It used to be a performance theater." He leans forward so he too can see where the tapering structures on the roof reach into the sky. "Do you… Do you want me to wait for you?"

I smile. He's kind. A perfect stranger who is clearly concerned, putting his own reservations aside to protect me.

"I'll be fine." The words are confident. I exit the car, using the headlight's beam to illuminate my otherwise-dark path to the crumbling stairs. Despite my instruction, the driver of the car sticks around a bit longer than required.

The doors are barely on their hinges, hanging off in a way that allows me to enter without unlocking or opening anything. There is very little light in the building. The moon shines down through an old, faded stained-glass dome at the center of the high ceiling. Every few feet, candles have been lit. The presence of their flames indicate that I'm in the right spot, when I was starting to think otherwise.

My footsteps echo as I walk down the center aisle of the expansive space. Even only lit by small tea lights, the beauty of the place is unmissable. Years of neglect and desertion have taken their toll on the structure and decor, but there's so much left, so many stories left behind in the now-graffiti-covered walls and it's almost possible to picture what the place looked like before its fall from grace.

"I wasn't sure you'd show."

The deep voice catches me off guard and I jump at the sound, but it's dark enough in here that the owner of the words likely missed my apprehension. Maybe the driver was right. Suddenly I'm not sure I should have come.

I turn and look toward where I assume the voice traveled from, though the vaulted ceilings and remarkable acoustics make it hard to tell.

Ames Gaherty stands in one of the boxes hanging off the wall levels above me, leaning into a banister that threatens to give way at any second. He wears jeans and a leather jacket with nothing underneath but the tattoos that cover so much of him.

I have no idea what to say. Truthfully, I came with other intentions. If he had signed his name to the card, I can say with the utmost certainty that I wouldn't have come.

"Which tells me you had no idea it was me who sent the roses." Ames continues to speak out loud, practically narrating my thoughts.

"I don't really know you." It's all I've got. There is something unique and exciting about a late-night adventure to an undisclosed location that's appealing when you believe the invite came from your inner circle, but there's a darkness to an invite of the same nature when it comes from a stranger.

"You don't know me at all." He holds a long-tapered candle. The flames light his small grin only fractionally. He tilts the candle to one side and places his opposite hand underneath it. He doesn't flinch as the wax drips from the candle onto his open palm. "We could change that, though."

"You picked an interesting place. Would've been just as easy to talk at the show or get a drink, I don't know, say…somewhere that has electricity?"

"All conventional choices." He continues to twirl the candle in a way that's both alluring and alarming. It's slow and intricate, but one wrong move and this place whole will turn to ash and dust and memory. "But you don't strike me as a conventional person."

I smile at that, though I do my best to hide it. I'm impressed at the lengths he's gone to thus far.

"Do you make a habit of hanging out in abandoned buildings?" I look around, soaking in the dust-decorated art that's been left behind by visitors before us.

"Yes."

I tilt my head to one side, as if the new angle will help me decipher if he's serious.

"I find there is beauty in the broken things."

He's not wrong. Beneath the layers of dust and disarray, there's a captivating amount of enchantment to this place.

"This one is my favorite, though."

I walk slowly toward a lonely row of torn and damaged chairs and lean against one. "Is there a story in there?"

"It has to do with the street name. Are you familiar with Greek mythology?"

I shake my head no, but that's not all true. I'm hardly an expert, but I do find the limited stories I've heard interesting. The street name nags at me. *Moirai.* It sounds familiar but nothing comes to mind.

"That's a story for another time then," he says. "I have a mission to complete, and I thought you might help me."

"Is that so?" I stand from the seat and walk toward the wall to continue my assessment of the property.

"I'm here to choose my next tattoo."

His words catch my attention, and I find myself allowing my eyes to dart away from the drawings on the walls and be pulled toward the ones on his body.

"Every piece I've gotten has been inspired by the art left behind on these forgotten buildings."

Suddenly, I wish I were closer to him. For the first time, I want to be within arm's reach. Rather than step back when he's around or avoid him altogether, I want to look at the stories inked on his skin.

"I found one I like, I think, if you want to take a look."

When my eyes find his, he holds one hand out to a staircase that's just as fragmented as the rest of the building. I walk toward it with hesitation and place one foot on the first step.

I stare up at him, too long, before making another move. I'm not a person who traditionally judges a book by its cover or makes an assessment on a person based on what other people have said, and with him, I've done both. Everything about him screams he's dangerous, every tale I've heard about him is cautionary.

"Is it safe?" I grip the loose banister.

"No," he says, with confidence.

Chapter Twenty-Five

Dom

Our tour bus looks different these days—or, well, *sounds* different, I should say. It's quieter. There's no loud music, no constant party. Blake and Xander sit toward the front of the bus, using headphones to listen to demos of bands that Kelly has asked their opinion on. It benefits them all. If Blake likes them and Kelly signs them, when they start touring, Xander and Natalie will likely book them at The Rock Room. Their businesses are intertwined, and though I never thought I'd see the day, they've both grown into semi-responsible entrepreneurs.

Theo sits at the back, his headphones on, typing an email on his laptop as we make our way a few states over to continue the music festival. Stasia sits cross-legged on a long couch, facing the middle, using the next cushion as a table while she flips playing cards from a deck in her hands.

I stand and walk toward her, taking the remaining seat on the couch with the deck of cards and a heavy awkwardness between us.

"Solitaire is a one-player game." She never looks up as she speaks. "Goodbye now."

I can't help but smile. She's resilient, stubborn and so frustrating but mostly? She's gorgeous and tempting, both in mind and body. She is unique, opinionated. Being this close to her on this tour and not being able to touch her in any way will be hard, sure, but I can't go to all these cities night after night and not talk to her. It's the conversation I miss most. She explores topics beyond music, and for hours I can get lost in listening to her fight for her beliefs and offer intelligent conversation on things she's passionate about, but sit back and listen on things she wants to be educated on.

She gives in, collects all the cards from the cushion in one swipe and reunites them with the deck, shuffles, then deals us each seven cards.

"Got any sevens?" She stares at her hand, still averting her eyes from mine.

"Go fish." She takes a card from the pile. "I came by your room last night."

"Not before midnight." The words are cold, plastered with sarcasm, and if I'm not mistaken, maybe a bit of pride. I nod. It's true. I missed that deadline on purpose.

"I just wanted to make sure you got back safe." I look at my cards. "Got any threes?"

She tosses a three of hearts at me and rolls her eyes.

"So, where'd you go?" I set my matching pair aside.

"Are you fishing for numbers or information?"

"Both." I shrug. "Kings?"

"Go fish," she says, and I reach for the deck. "On both accounts. I have no King and I have no answer for you."

"I was just curious."

"You don't get to be curious about me anymore. Tens?"

I hand over a ten and our fingers touch, briefly, before she pulls away and asks for a five but I don't have one.

"How about you?" Her eyes finally meet mine over the top of the cards. "How does that work, anyway? Do you write your number on the drumstick you hand out to random groupies or…"

Only one corner of my mouth hitches into a small smile.

"Was it the blonde one? Or the brunette? Both were great options. Oh, wait, was it both? Plot twist…"

"Are you done?" I cut off her million-mile-per-hour inquisition. "I spent the night alone."

I don't miss the small movement toward a grin her mouth makes.

"So," I press, wondering if she will return the favor with an answer of her own, "what did you end up doing?"

"I…" she says, but she hesitates. "I spent the night exploring that old theater downtown on Moirai."

I stare at her over my remaining cards, and she locks her gaze on me, neither of us speaking for a few moments. I don't want to ask the question, and she likely doesn't want to admit the answer.

"Luring young girls to abandoned buildings does sound like something Ames would do."

"Young girls?" she scoffs. "He's only two years older than *you*."

"Which makes him nine years older than *you*."

"It's really not that big of a difference, and you know it. How do you know it was him, anyway?"

"Guy is practically a vampire."

She laughs but dulls the sound as soon as she makes it.

"I'm serious. He's nocturnal. Always sleeping during the day and staying up all night, hanging around in sketchy, abandoned buildings. He has little-to-no soul."

"Don't hold back now," she says, surprised by my assessment. "Besides, it's not like I'm dating the guy. We just hung out."

"I don't…" I try to skirt around it, to find a more diplomatic way to relay my concerns, but I can't. "I don't want you hanging around him."

She shakes her head and tosses her hand of cards face up onto the draw pile as she starts to stand.

"Stasia." I reach out and grab her wrist. She turns to me, slowly, but doesn't pull her hand away. "Please." I hold my free hand out toward the cushion, and she takes her seat again. "You need to be careful with him," I advise in a hushed voice. "He's…not the greatest guy. He's been arrested a handful of times. He's got a lot of secrets, a lot of bad habits and I'm afraid he will hurt you in the long run."

Stasia, in a move that completely shocks me, *laughs*.

"Dom," she says once she pulls herself together, "you do realize who you share this tour bus with, right? Xander has seen himself behind bars in record-setting numbers, Blake kept secrets for the better part of this last year, Theo spends ninety percent of his pay at strip clubs and *you* hurt me in the long run, so how about you don't throw stones in this glass house until *you* have perfect aim."

"I really am trying to look out for you," I say in a whisper, looking around. As she raises her voice, I wonder how many listening ears will catch on to the nature of our conversation.

"You don't get to do that anymore," she snaps. The words hurt me, and she can tell. Her voice softens. "Maybe if you would tell me the real reason you and Ames hate each other so much, I'd consider keeping my distance."

"I can't do that."

"Of course you can't. You can never give me a reason for *anything*, including one to stay here and continue this conversation." She stands, and she has a point. I can't make her stay, and I don't deserve to. "You might as well get used to him being around, Dom. We are sharing a stage with him, and when we're not performing, he and I will be practicing our song for the award show. He's going to be around a lot, whether you like it or not."

The bus comes to a stop outside the hotel, and while the rest of us head inside to the lobby, Stasia excuses herself, saying she will be in in a moment. Cooper hands each of us our keys. I watch as Stasia stands outside leaning into a lamppost, staring off in the distance. I can feel it. She's avoiding me, keeping her distance. She's smart and a hell of a lot stronger than I am. Her choice to go outside, to take a breath of fresh air, was to force us apart. I want to go outside, to stand next to her and offer her company, or take a walk and explore the city.

But I can't. The message she's sending me with her body language is loud and clear. And she's right. Staying away from each other, for now, is the only way.

I make my way to my room, throw my bag into the corner and stand at the window, staring out at the view of the streets below. Using the remote, I power on the TV, turn the channel to a classical music station and toss the remote onto the king-sized bed in the middle of the room.

As I stare outward and listen to the music, the lock on my door sounds, as if someone has inserted their key, and to my surprise, gained access.

I turn over my shoulder as the door opens and Stasia steps through it. The confusion that fills her expression is likely a mirror image of my own. She steps back, looks at the number on the door and the key in her hand, then back at me again.

"What are you doing here?" She holds the door open with one foot.

"This is my room." I shrug. "I could ask you the same question."

"Well…" An additional person's voice joins us, then Cooper steps into view behind Stasia. "As you can see, there has been a little bit of a mix-up with the rooms. I'm trying to get it sorted, but with the music festival, almost everywhere is booked solid. For now, I have Blake with Xander, and Theo with me, which leaves you two together. It's not my favorite plan, but I figured you two wouldn't mind, all things considered."

Stasia and I stare at each other but neither of us speak. Discomfort rains down from clouds that seem to only be following the two of us.

"Oh…" Cooper says. "*Oh!*" He mumbles a mixture of awkward backpedaling and uneasy pauses. "I could put Theo with Dom... Well, actually, that would put you with me and jeez, what would the media say about that? No, I could switch Blake and —"

"It's fine, Coop." Stasia places her hand on his forearm and smiles widely. He buys it, but I don't. "This isn't a big deal. We're all adults here. Bandmates. It's only for one night."

Cooper wipes his brow and retreats. Stasia and I stare at each other for a moment, and as the door closes, we both burst out laughing. In reality, none of this is funny. But the back and forth, the awkwardness, the forced proximity, all topped off with Cooper's rambling, has us coming apart at the seams. But then, something is different. The laughter fades, and the temporary comic relief comes to a halt. She forces her walls back up and re-enforces them, like she suddenly remembered I'm the enemy and sharing a laugh with me is equal to some form of surrender.

She rummages through her bag, pulls out enough cosmetics to do a full face of makeup on a full Broadway cast, applies color to her lips and touches up her eyes.

"Where are you going?" I look at the time on my watch.

"I already told you, Dom." She tosses her makeup back in her bag. "When we're not on stage, I'm spending my time working on my performance with Ames. I'm going to meet him. Besides, it's not like I'm going to stay here."

"But you told Cooper —"

"I thought about it. I changed my mind." She shrugs and throws her bag over her shoulder. "That happens sometimes, right?"

She has a point and it's sharp, aimed at me and hurts like hell when it connects.

* * * *

Stasia never came back to our room, and I'd say I didn't lose sleep over it, but that would be a lie just tacked onto the list of the several others I keep in rotation on a daily basis.

Hours later and I still haven't heard from her or caught sight of her. I sit in the backstage area reading a book when I hear her laugh echo from out of sight, but it's distinctively hers. She steps into view with Ames following closely behind.

"I have to go get ready," she says to him over her shoulder, "I'll see you for our practice session after the shows, though."

He nods his head and watches every step she takes as she struts away.

I purposely bury my nose back in the book I'm reading, but Ames doesn't leave the area. I look up over the pages. He stands in all black, from his hair to his outfit to his shoes, leaning into a wall nearby.

"Is it killing you?" he asks. "It's *gotta* be killing you."

"I have no idea what you're talking about." I return my attention to the book, though I've lost my place.

"I'm ten Chapters ahead of you, and you don't even know what book we're reading." He leans down on his knee, uses one finger to pull the book downward and keeps his face inches from my own, his voice in a careless whisper. "Your life as you know it could end at any second. Every lie you've told, all the secrets you've held on to for years... I could do it, you know. Sooner or later, everyone will know what I know."

I grit my teeth and toss the book to the side.

"If you planned to ruin me, you would've done it by now."

He shrugs and smiles as he stands and walks backward, allowing just a bit of room between us.

"All in good time, Dominic. All in good time."

"Besides"—I lean toward him—"you messed up. I know your secrets, too, Ames."

His smile only grows, and with it, my stomach turns.

"Whatever do you mean, Dom?"

I stand and walk toward him. With only inches between us, I breathe heavily between every word I whisper at him. "Does it bother you?"

He looks at me with a feigned curiosity.

"You're making headlines. You're regaining all this popularity and fame, and all your fans are buying it. Does it bother you at all that your entire comeback is based on a lie?"

He smiles a malicious grin and walks toward me. We stand toe to toe, and though he towers over me, he has never scared me. He didn't then, and he doesn't now.

"Does it bother you, Dom?"

I tilt my head to one side and keep my eyes trained on his.

"Does it bother you knowing your entire life revolves around a lie?" Ames' devious smile grows as he asks the question.

I grit my teeth and my hands clench to fists.

He steps back and starts to walk away, but I can't let him leave with the last word.

"Eventually everyone will find out, Ames."

He turns toward me slowly and puts his hands in his pockets.

"Find out what, Dom?" He plays dumb in an Oscar-worthy way. He knows exactly what I mean.

"Your fans, your band… They will eventually figure out that you didn't write one word on that album."

Ames runs his thumb and finger at his jawline and nods in a slow, drawn-out way.

"Who is going to tell them?" He shrugs and raises an eyebrow. "And even if you did tell them, who do you think will hurt more? My band? Or yours?"

I hate the way he makes me feel tongue-tied. I'm an intelligent guy, a quick thinker, a well-read person with a sharp mind but not with Ames. Ames gets under my skin and shuts me down in a way I can't explain.

"How do you think your band will feel, knowing they had a lyrical genius sitting behind the drums all along? While you hid from the limelight, built up these walls and lived this life as far from the fame as you could, you were sitting on a platinum-selling album's worth of lyrics for years, and you stayed quiet?"

He's not wrong. Over the last few years, we've stayed afloat, but not as effortlessly as we did in our early years. We've been fighting to get new lyrics out of Xander and Blake. We needed a new sound. We needed something fresh. It's part of the reason we brought Stasia around. And me? I was too scared to contribute. The words I wrote came with strings attached. If I'd told them about the poetry I had written, every line they turned into a song would pull me apart, healed stitch by healed stitch. My heart problems… My deceased best friend… The past I had buried would become very much present.

"I did you a favor, Dom." Ames is confident. He believes every word he speaks. "The poems were great. You're talented, but you're a coward. I won't apologize for taking a chance you weren't willing to take yourself."

"It's wrong on so many levels. The stealing is one thing—"

Ames' eyes narrow, darkening his irises even more in a way I didn't think was possible. It's a look I haven't seen in him in years. It's rage...or maybe it's resentment. Whatever it is, it's powerful, pure and he is made of it.

"You are the *last* person who gets to lecture me about morals, Trudell." He steps back once more, this time in a way that seems final. "You can weave your web and trap everyone else in it, but I know better. I know you better than they do. Our secrets are intertwined, and you know it."

I step away from him, distancing myself as much as I can before I make a choice I can't take back.

"If I go down, you're coming with me." It's not a threat. It's a promise. "You wouldn't do that to your band, would you? To the guys? To Cooper?"

I turn to walk away, but it's what he says next that turns me into a version of myself I don't recognize.

"And what about Stasia?"

I turn and stomp toward him before I even comprehend the whole thought, slamming my body weight into him in a way that sends us both backward until I have him pinned at the wall.

"Don't even say her name." The words barely come through my clenched teeth.

He laughs, and the sound alone pierces me like a knife.

"I plan to say her name—frequently, in fact."

"You—"

"Dom," he says in a calm, tranquil voice, "get your mind out of the gutter. We're practicing a song together. I meant, like, good job, *Stasia*. Well done, *Stasia*."

He bumps his shoulder hard into mine as he walks past me, his head held high, laughing like someone had just revealed the punch line of a clever joke.

I didn't throw a punch. I didn't spit angry words or comebacks. I just let go. My arms fell to my sides, my stomach turned and I gave in.

A woman with a headset leans in and gives me a two-minute warning.

I can't take my anger out on him, not publicly anyway. But I can take it out on my drum set—and I do, the entire length of our set.

Chapter Twenty-Six

Stasia

Our set was excellent. There is something about these outdoor setups I can't explain but can't get enough of. As the acts performed, the stage lights flashed, and the crowds sang along. The sound was indescribable. In an indoor setting, the bass vibrates and shakes the walls. Outside, the sound soars through the sky the way thunder would, carrying on over an expansive space. The sound can't be contained, and the music travels for miles.

But now that the performances are over and the crowds are gone, the fields the stages are set up in look abandoned. The curtains are closed, and the instruments are locked up. There are no brilliant stage lights to break up the blackness. It's the very definition of dark and silent...almost eerie.

"You're early. Thought I'd have this place to myself for a while." Ames walks across the field as he joins me under the open midnight sky. He's wearing dark jeans and, to my surprise, a shirt. His hair is damp in a way that darkens the already pitch-black hue and suggests he just got out of the shower before taking a stroll under the stars.

"Sorry to disappoint you." I lie backward and stare up at the sky.

"Quite the contrary." He hops up on the stage and sits down next to me, then lays so he's looking up at the stars, too. His face is next to mine, but his feet point the opposite direction. "I need to know something."

I turn my head so I'm looking toward him, but only slightly.

"What are we doing? Are we friends? Are we more than friends? Are we enemies?" He runs his fingers through his hair then puts both hands behind his head. "I can handle any answer, honestly, but I don't want to guess. I just want to know."

I laugh at his persistence. He is beautifully stubborn, and charming without trying to be. A mix like that could be dangerous, just like he supposedly is.

"Okay, okay. I'll take one guess." He holds his pointer finger to the sky. "You're supposed to hate me, right?"

I drop my head so I'm looking directly at him and widen my eyes. How is it that he knows all this so clearly? More so than that, how does it not bother him?

"It's okay, really." He lets his face fall so his cheek is against the stage boards, much like mine. His eyes are the very absence of color, a brown so dark the iris and the pupil are indistinguishable. "Most days I hate me, too."

He smiles as he says it, and I match him.

"Why am I supposed to hate you?" I stare at the sky once more.

"Because you're sleeping with the enemy."

I sit up and turn away, hoping to hide any indication of my cheeks blushing a bright pink.

"I'm not sleeping with him." My voice is quiet as I turn over my shoulder to peek at Ames.

"Maybe not anymore." He rolls to one side and props himself up on his elbow. "I've seen the way he looks at you."

I spin myself around and sit cross-legged in front of him.

"You called him the enemy." I run a finger across the crease in the floorboards of the stage. "Dom doesn't really seem like the type to have any of those."

"Ugh." Ames sighs dramatically and lays back again. "Not you, too."

"What's that supposed to mean?"

Ames sits up slowly then pushes himself off the stage and begins to walk away.

"Where are you going?" I follow suit, sliding off the stage and walking after him, though I'm not sure why. "Hey." I catch up to him, reaching forward and grabbing his hand. "Wait one second."

He stops and turns toward me. He towers over me. I've always been petite, but standing inches from him with him looking down at me with those dark, lightless eyes makes me feel about half his size. "Tell me what you meant by that."

Ames pushes his hair back off his forehead and stares at me.

"Dom isn't quite as perfect as he seems."

I hold my breath with a hope that he will say more, but he doesn't.

"He won't tell me why you two hate each other so much."

"He never will."

His certainty is alarming. Any inkling of a smile or expression I was wearing evaporates.

"Dom lies by omission, Stasia. His whole world... His whole life... He doesn't necessarily lie outwardly, but he just never admits the truth. He will tell you, if he hasn't already, about my own issues — that I'll hurt you, that I lie or steal or cheat."

"Do you?"

"Yes." He steps toward me and runs a hand down one of my arms. "I've been selfish. I've made bad choices. I'm not even sure I've learned from all of them. The fact of the matter is I'm not always a good guy, but I can own that. I can admit that I am just as imperfect as every other human out there. But he can't. Yet I will always come off as the bad guy while he's out there hiding in plain sight."

What he's saying can't be true. Dom is a good man.

But Ames? He's honest, sometimes too much so. He owns his shortcomings. I can't help but think for every step I take toward trying not to be his friend, there are parts of me that can't stay away from him.

"I'm not as bad of a person as he paints me to be." Ames gently pushes my hair away from my face. "You know it already. Every time we're near each other, you let me get a bit closer. You tell me a bit more. As much as you try to keep your distance, there's something there that keeps you coming back." He runs his hands down both my arms and links his fingers in mine. I stand frozen in the moment, staring up at him. I can't help it. I'm a bit unnerved by him, but it's both a positive and a negative. He interests me in a way where

I can't tell if I'm nervous to be around him because I like him or because I don't.

"The thing about me and Dom is that eventually, he will make you choose a side of a battle you're only getting one side of information from."

"I don't let other people make choices for me." The words were meant to sound final and confident, but my voice failed me.

He leans forward, his face coming toward mine in slow way that gives me enough time to think. Is this what I want from him?

Before I can make a choice, before I can decide to stand up on my tiptoes and bring myself close to him or step back and walk away altogether, another person joins us in the fields and Ames pulls away before I do.

His mouth twists into a crescent moon smile and he shakes his head.

"Dominic." Ames' greeting is forced and unfriendly, like it hurts for him to even have to says Dom's name. "Can we do something for you?"

"Stasia." Dom ignores Ames' existence like he's only visible to me. "Can we have a minute?"

"I told you," Ames whispers so only I can hear. "This town truly ain't big enough for the both of us." He nods once and steps away, slowly, growing the distance between us.

"I don't, actually. I don't have a minute." I grab the front of Ames' shirt and he steps close to me once more. "Not for you."

There's something about the grin Ames' smile breaks into that both melts and annoys me. When I established that I wasn't a prize, I meant for either of them.

"That's fine." Dom tilts his head and looks at me with eyes that are soft and sympathetic. "Do you have a minute for Cooper? Because he's been looking for you for hours."

Any confidence I had before, any reason I had to brush Dom off, is gone. I find myself stepping away from Ames and toward Dom, standing directly between the two.

"Is it Blake? Is he okay?"

"Yeah, yeah," Dom says putting both hands out toward me and patting the air. "He's looking for you, too. Cooper wants us all in for the night."

Curfew seems extreme, but I've heard the stories about these guys on the road, so I'm sure Cooper feels he needs to keep a short leash. I don't have any fight left in me tonight, so I give in and start walking.

"I'll walk you back." Dom steps toward me, but I turn toward him in a tornado of a turn.

"I can walk by myself. I don't need you to do anything for me…not anymore."

We walk near but not next to each other until we reach the hotel.

The elevator doors slide open, and we step onto it, both facing forward. I stand a few feet in front of him, both to avoid close proximity and to be able to make a quick exit.

As the numbers above the door tick by as the elevator passes each floor, I finally speak. "I told you I don't need anything from you."

When the doors open, I step off, stomp down the hall and freeze when I reach the room. I turn slowly and he smiles, laughing—just fractionally—as I put all the pieces of this puzzle together.

Not only did I forget about our unfortunate room situation, but I don't have my key.

"What was that you were saying about not needing me for anything?" He leans into the hallway wall.

I sigh and roll my eyes, starting to walk back toward the elevator.

"Stasia." He reaches forward and wraps his fingers around my wrist. "Relax. I was kidding. We used to do that, you know?"

"We used to do a lot of things, Dom."

For a moment, my heart clenches as his gaze is downcast. I have to wonder if he misses me how I miss him.

"Here." He reaches into his pocket and pulls out the key card, stepping forward and scanning it until the lock clicks open. "Have a good night, Stasia," he says as I step into the room. I backpedal just beyond the door frame, prop the door open with one hand and look at him with a curious expression.

"I'll go stay with either Theo and Coop or Blake and Xander. I'll figure it out."

As he turns to walk away, I speak.

"You're just going to leave?"

"Stasia, I will sleep on the floor of this hallway tonight before I do something that makes you upset."

"I don't know how to be around you," I admit with a shrug that is the equivalent of a forfeit. "Being friends doesn't work for us."

"It doesn't. But I don't want us to not be anything."

"Let's go," I finally say, with a sliver of confidence and a smile, "but you're buying room service."

Chapter Twenty-Seven

Dom

These kinds of music festivals — specifically the ones on the East Coast — are my favorites. We're close enough to home that we can stay in our own beds during the week and only subject ourselves to being on the road on the weekends.

The atmosphere, though, is unbeatable. The crisp fall air keeps it cool enough that fans are comfortable during the day but don't freeze at night when the headliners finally make their way to the stage. The sky is dark, but the lights are bright. The music booms and echoes. It's almost perfect, except Save Me, Save You is on stage, and in a truly perfect world, they wouldn't be here at all.

I'm leaning into an area near the wings of the stage. Across from me, Stasia leans into a wall in the opposite wing. She watches as Ames performs. With every note he sings, with every move he makes, she becomes more enamored by him.

For a moment, I think I know what heartbreak feels like. I find it hard to breathe, and there is an ache in my chest that's different than any I've ever felt before. Though I know some of it is related to watching her slip away, the room starts spinning and I know it's more than that.

I grab at the wall and finally find a hard surface to steady myself on. The air around me seems thicker, hotter and harder to breathe in. My legs feel weak, and my only choice is to turn so my back is against the wall then slide down it so I'm seated on the floor. I pull my bandana off my head and wipe it across my face and neck. It's saturated instantly. The vibrations from the speakers travel through the floor and my body, which allows me to know I'm still conscious, but barely.

I take deep, steadying breaths with as much air as my lungs will allow and let it out, trying to calm myself. My watch buzzes wildly on my wrist. I don't have to look to know it's warning of an irregular heart rate. This is what Dr. Anderson warned me about.

"If your heart rate gets too out of control, there may be a time it doesn't normalize on its own."

There isn't anything in the world that slows a clock the way fear does. Distress has this way of turning milliseconds into an eternity, and though my episode likely lasted less than a minute, I felt like hours had passed.

"Dom?" It's Stasia in front of me, down on one knee, leaning in and assessing my current state. "Dom?" She asks again, pressing something cold to the side of my head then the back of my neck. "Hey. Is everything okay? What happened?"

Her face is so pale that it's almost green. She's worried about me. And I know how wrong it is, but I can feel myself almost smile when I realize she still cares.

"I'm fine." I do my best to perk up and shake it off. "I think I just got overheated. Maybe dehydrated. I haven't had enough water today."

"I'm going to go get you some, okay? Will you be all right here for a minute?" She places her hand against mine and I wish she wouldn't leave, but she does.

By the time she has returned, I can feel the color returning to my face. My heart rate is somewhat normalizing. Though I have a tightness in my chest that is lost somewhere between a pulled muscle and heartburn, I feel better...fractionally.

I rest for as long as I can and drink as much water as I can tolerate, more to follow the dehydration front than anything. My legs hang over the arm of the chair I now sit in, and I hold the water bottle against my head. It is hot in the small, makeshift backstage area, cardiac episode or not.

"I'm fine," I reiterate as Stasia paces back and forth in front of me. Footsteps, voices and laughter can be heard, growing in volume and proximity. She and I both look at each other when we realize it's the rest of our band. "Don't make a big deal out of this, Stasia."

"Ready, Stasia?" Cooper asks, placing a gentle hand on her shoulder. She looks at me with tender, worried eyes, and I shake my head in a way that begs her not to mention anything.

"I am." Stasia leaves her eyes one me. "But he's not. He passed out during Save Me, Save You's set."

Cooper rushes toward me and kneels down in front of me, but I'm looking past him, staring at Stasia in disbelief.

"Dom?" Cooper's eyes are soft, but his body is tense like he's holding his breath. "What's going on?"

"I told her that I'm fine. Just dehydrated."

"You are one of the healthiest people I know, Dom," Theo says, stepping in next to Cooper. "People like you don't just pass out. There has to be something going on."

I stand from the chair, and though the room spins, I pretend it doesn't. "I'm fine. Look. Vertical and ready to go. Can we just get on with it already?"

Cooper stares me down. I can see it in his eyes. The gears are turning and he's trying to come up with a solution.

"Cut out the two songs before Xander and Blake's acoustic set and the one right after. We will expand the acoustic set by three songs. It'll give you a longer break."

"Absolutely not." It's the angriest I've ever allowed myself to be with anyone that involves this band. "You have to be kidding."

Cooper looks at me with a stern expression.

He's not kidding.

"Don't change the set, Coop. I want to be on stage as much as I can be."

Cooper considers my offer then looks around to each of my bandmates.

"Make the change," he says with a final, no-means-no nod.

I whip a drumstick to the corner of the backstage area in frustration. "Fucking ridiculous." The words come out mostly under my breath but my first-time-ever use of profanity has them all deciding to give me space.

I step past them and into the field behind the stages where Ames stands with no shirt on, wiping sweat from his face then the back of his neck.

"I'd hate to be you right now." He points to me and shakes his head. "That's going to be a tough act to follow."

"It was a decent set. Get used to that number two slot, though, Ames. It's where you've always been. It's where you'll always be."

"I don't know about that, Dom. This tour has been kind to us. Last I checked, we were climbing up the ladder you're falling down."

"You ready, Dom?" a woman with a headset on approaches and asks. I turn toward her.

"Buy me five minutes, will you?" I ask, and she nods.

"Where are you going?" Cooper asks as I walk by the band at the entrance to the stage.

"The bar." I don't look back as I walk past them. I lean into the bar top and yell my order to the barback, though the request isn't nearly as common as anything he's ever heard — or will likely ever hear again. He waves me over to the side and I grab an empty ice bucket. As I turn to collect a few more items, Blake appears at my side, wearing a mischievous smile.

"I know defiance when I see it," he says. "You're not sitting out any of the songs, are you?"

He watches as the barback starts bringing various items toward us.

"Nope."

"Cooper's going to be pissed." Blake shrugs.

"Yep. You going to talk me out of it?"

"Hell, no." He starts walking toward the bar. "I'll help carry some buckets."

* * * *

We take the stage, and the crowd booms an intense sound that's a mix of yelling and applause.

"Ladies and gentlemen," Xander yells into a microphone, his voice carrying over the open air, "how are we doing tonight?"

The crowd resumes their rambunctious response, and Xander paces the stage.

"We have a special show planned for you tonight..." he begins, in a way that would keep the fans on the edge of their seat if it weren't standing room only. "So special...that I don't even know what the hell we're doing."

The crowd laughs in unison and the band does, too. "But Blake says it's going to be good, so I guess we're all in for a helluva night. What do you say?"

The light in Xander has never dulled. In fact, he seems to grow more luminous every year we do this. He captivates the crowd time and time again. As impressive as Ames is on stage, this is what Xander does best. Pride swells in me, even after all these years, knowing I get to work with this group, and for as many times as I've griped about feeling unnoticed, sometimes I just have to face it. It's hard not to notice how great Xander is at what he does. All of them. All of us.

I start the show the same way every time. Get on the stage. Take in the sights. Be grateful for who and what I have. Then, I press my fingertips to the initials carved in my drum kit and give the crowd the best song opening I have in me.

And Stasia? She's phenomenal. She's the best she's ever been—better than open mic night. I smile and watch as she moves across the stage. She struts to the back toward me, never falling out of character, but leans in and yells "You okay?" over the beat I produce.

"Never better," I yell back, and like most things in my life, it's a half truth. The show is flawless, I'm content watching her be her truest, happiest self—it's all I've ever wanted for her—but I can feel myself physically slipping, and with it, wondering how much of this particular lifestyle I have left in me.

Thankfully, the main lights go dark, the spotlights produce a gentle blue hue that covers the stage. Usually, me, Theo, and as of late, Stasia, depart and Xander and Blake take the stage with their guitars for an acoustic set. As Theo and Stasia start to make their way off the stage, Blake whistles loudly and gets their attention.

"Not tonight," he says. "Tonight, everyone stays on stage."

Stasia smiles, and Theo, though confused, rolls with it and produces a simple, twinkling piece on the keyboard. Blake and I set up my makeshift percussion set as quickly as possible—an empty ice bucket, two five-gallon buckets, some various-sized glasses and a cowbell I'm pretty sure Blake borrowed from a fan. Stasia, Blake and Xander sit at the front edge of the stage, and I hang out in the background, providing a light beat that sounds different than a professional drum kit, but adds an extra layer of creativity and new sound to the songs Blake and Xander have stripped down. Theo keeps his keys airy and quiet, and Stasia throws in a few new harmonies we haven't yet tried.

By the end of the acoustic set, everyone is smiling — the band, the fans. Well, almost everyone. Coopers stands with his arms crossed and his face stern at the side of the stage when we return to our usual spots to finish up a few stronger, more upbeat songs and our finale. He doesn't move from his spot until we leave the stage after our final exit. Each band member passes, but Cooper sticks his arm straight out until his hand hits the wall, cutting me off from going forward.

"I don't know what is going on with you, but I don't like it." He drops his hand, but I don't cross the line he metaphorically drew.

"There's nothing going on with me, Cooper."

"You can lie to them, if you want." He throws his head to the backstage area where the band retreated to. "But not to me. I might not know the truth, but I know this isn't it. After fifteen years of never once having to have a conversation like this with you, this is twice in as many months. Plus, your episode before the show… Come to me when you're ready to talk about whatever it is you're dealing with."

"I told you. There's no—"

"That's not true. You know it and so do I. Don't look me in the eyes and repeat the lie, Dom." He backs up and begins to walk away. "It's insulting."

As if my post-show balloon couldn't be deflated anymore, when I finally make my way back to the band, Ames is there, too. Stasia notices my entrance and excuses herself from her conversation with Ames. I notice when she pushes one strand of hair behind her ear as she holds one finger up, like she's hesitating to step away from him to talk to me. He watches her every step of the way toward me.

"Are you sure you're okay?" she whispers. I wish, more than anything, she'd stop asking me that. I don't want to lie to her, so I just don't answer.

"Late-night take-out back at the room?"

She looks over her shoulder then back at me with sympathetic eyes. "I'm actually going out with Ames for the night."

"Where?" I ask, too quickly and unexpectedly.

"Does it matter?" She shrugs. As much as I hate him for getting close to her, I hate that she makes herself smaller around me as a result of it. Now, she tiptoes around every question I ask like one of us might break if any more pressure is put on us.

"I'm okay," I finally say. She nods and heads toward Ames, and I watch as they leave the fields.

Chapter Twenty-Eight

Stasia

Ames and I walk to a building that is too clean and modern to be abandoned but too quiet and vacant to be currently occupied.

"Pick a number, Stasia."

"Excuse me?" I ask, and he switches his position so he's leaning into the building.

"Pick a number."

I think on it for a moment but don't respond. He turns away and starts walking away, toward the other end of the street.

"Fifty-four."

He stops in his tracks, turns toward me and a victorious grin slides into his cheeks.

"Let's go."

"Where are we going?" I yell down the alleyway.

"Hop to it there, Stasia. We're wasting precious nighttime hours." He turns the corner and disappears from view.

"Can you at least try to let me keep up?" I shout after him, but he doesn't return. "Your stride is like three times mine."

I start to speed walk toward him, and though I'll never admit it, I stop and peek in a window reflection, adjusting my hair before continuing my attempt to catch up with him.

I look around, up and down each street and peeking into each alley to locate him, but he's gone. Disappointment sets in, and I allow myself exactly five seconds of pouting. Now I'm going to wonder all night what it is he wanted and where we might have gone. I waste a lot of time thinking about Ames these days. Add this to the list of things that will keep me up at night. Though, as much as I hate to admit it, I wouldn't mind if *he* was the one keeping me up at night.

"Are you coming or not?" He appears seemingly out of nowhere and emerges from a door of an older building's emergency exit door.

"You are not supposed to be using that door." As soon as I say the words, I regret it. He already knows that. It's probably the reason he did it.

"It doesn't say don't." He shrugs.

"It does. Several times, in fact."

He tears the *Emergency Use Only* sign off the door and tosses it behind him.

"I saw nothing," he says as I fight back a laugh. "Now. Let's. *Go.*"

We step through the door and travel down a brick-lined hallway lit by a faded yellow light, then exit through a door on the opposite side, which spits us out into a parking lot. I'm beginning to think he's taking the road less traveled simply to make me lose track of where we are, to keep our ultimate destination cloaked in surprise.

"I need you to do something for me." His voice is velvet and hypnotic. I nod, wondering what I'm getting myself into.

"I need you to pick a number." He returns to the stimulated quick-witted side of himself, doing away with the slow and alluring facade.

"I picked a number!" I say too loud. He shakes his head.

"One through four this time."

"What is this, Ames?" I put my hands on my hips. "What are we doing?"

He steps in close. There's almost a full foot difference in our heights, and he towers over me as he speaks.

"You are figuring out if you can trust me or not. I'm hoping that you do. That's what we're doing here."

I stare up at him, trying to read him the way he can read me, but I can't.

"One through four, this time."

"Three," I say, with confidence, and when he reaches one hand forward, I place my palm against his. He leads me forward through the parking lot, and though I have no idea where we're going, I'm not sure I care.

"What about my first number?" I ask as we walk the streets to my unknown destination.

"That was basically just a yes or no." He puts a vape pen to his lips and takes a draw off the box. My confused expression is enough to signal to him that I'm looking for more information.

"If you picked a number, any number at all, I knew you were in for the adventure. If you wouldn't pick a number, the date was over before it started. See?"

I stop in my tracks.

"Date?"

He stops and looks at me, then shoves both hands and his vape pen in his pocket. "Date." Then he turns and continues walking. "We're almost there. Keep up."

I smile when he turns his back to me. There is just *something* about him. The more I tell myself I don't want to know him, the more I do. I skip to catch up to him and we turn down another road — one I'm familiar with.

"The train station?" I try to keep up with his lengthy stride.

He holds up three fingers. "You picked three. Three was train station."

When we step into the station, Ames steps over the turnstile, then places both hands on my hips, assisting me as I do the same.

We walk up the stairs together and our footsteps and voices echo through the open stairway.

"What if I had said four?" I ask with genuine curiosity.

"Then we'd be at an airport." He keeps climbing the stairs, but I stop. He turns over his shoulder. "We could've been in Paris by morning."

I part my lips and inhale a sharp breath. "You... You're kidding, right?"

"No. But you chose three, so it doesn't matter." He takes the last few steps and I catch up. As our feet reach the top platform, a train whips into the station, screeching and echoing as it sounds its arrival, the forceful wind coming off of it sends my hair flying. The doors open and we step on, each taking a seat in the almost-empty car.

"So, where now?"

He just tilts his head, arching one pierced eyebrow. *Pick a number, Stasia.*

"What's the range this time?"

"One through thirteen," he says, and this time, I don't hesitate. I choose seven.

The doors open at the seventh stop on the route, and we step through, taking to the city streets. I've stopped asking where we are going because he's not going to answer me anyway, and I have to save my breath to keep up with him. His half-step is my jog. Besides, I'm not sure he even knows where he's going. He sells the part well, like he has every next step of this choose-your-own-adventure series down pat, but I have a feeling he's flying just as blind as I am.

Though the light has a red hand indicating we should stop, Ames doesn't. He walks into the middle of the usually busy intersection and I follow quickly behind. Then, he stops. Dead in his tracks, in the middle of a four-way intersection that could have any number of cars flying through it at any second.

"What are you doing?" I back up, allowing the soles of my shoes to find their way back to the sidewalk.

A car speeds around the corner and flies by, holding the horn down as he flies by Ames. He doesn't even flinch.

"What are you doing?" I yell as another car's headlights can be seen rounding the corner. "Are you insane?"

"I've been called worse things." He laughs and shrugs off the comment. He says something else but I miss it as the light gets closer and the car speeds by, missing him by what seems like inches.

"You're in all black, Ames! It's dark. You're going to kill yourself or someone else." My heart pounds in my chest and my hands sweat.

"I told you to pick! Pick a direction!" His voice echoes between the multi-story buildings. Everything I've heard about him, every warning hits me at the same speed as those passing cars almost hit him. Maybe he is bad news. Maybe he is trouble.

"So, what will it be?" He lifts his arms and turns in one large circle. The next sounds that fill the area are a mix of metal screeches, and the rumble of an engine that seem much larger than the previous vehicles gains volume, sounding closer until I can see the lights of the semi coming toward him. He puts one hand over his eyes and turns, slowly, with one hand up and his pointer finger extended, continuing his blind twirl as the noise grows nearer.

"Ames," I yell, unsure of what to say next. His antics cause me an anxiety I'm not used to and it's clouding my thoughts and judgment. *He's* clouding my thoughts and judgment.

"Which way are we going, Stasia?"

Before I realize I've made a decision, I run toward him, slamming my body into his and pushing him out of the way of the truck, but also guiding him down the street directly opposite where I stood.

"Good choice," he says, through that stupid, confident, no-worries grin I'm beginning to hate.

One thousand angry words, insults and fear-induced questions cross my mind, but none of them are fully formed enough to speak. I shake my head and walk away.

"Stasia, wait." He jogs up to me and turns, cutting me off and placing both hands at my upper arms. "It was just a joke. I was never in any real danger."

"How do you know?" My voice echoes between the buildings.

"I was watching the lights." He points to the traffic lamps above. "I knew what direction had the green light. I wasn't as close to their side of the road as you think. *Breathe*." He moves his hands up and down, rubbing his palms against my tense shoulders and upper arms.

"Why? What was the point?" My voice is a broken whisper.

"What's the point of any of this?" he whispers back.

"Of what?"

"Life."

His word is sharp and quick, but he means it. He's not setting me up just to see how I'll react. There's an alarming amount of truth in his word.

"A little bleak, don't you think?" I step away from him and cross my arms to block out the cold air that seeped in where his hands were.

"Or just realistic." He slides out of his leather jacket and pulls it around my shoulders. I swim in it, but I appreciate the gesture.

Ames is straightforward and complicated. He is equal parts 'live every moment like it's your last' and 'life ain't worth living'. He is driving me crazy — in more ways than one.

"Look…" He pulls the jacket tighter around me and steps in close. "I'll take you home if you want. Safely. No games. If that's what you want, just say the word."

"I've survived this long. Might as well finish the journey."

"A little bleak, don't you think?" He winks and smiles with only one corner of his mouth.

"Or just realistic."

We continue down the sidewalks until we end up in the heart of the city, an area crowded with skyscrapers and high-rises.

"This is the one." Ames turns toward the main door of a massive, mostly glass building that's lit only by the light of the moon.

"They're clearly closed." I peek through the doors where the only visible light is an exit sign at the opposite end of the lobby.

"Yes, they are. Guess we will just have to break in."

"You can't be serious."

He pulls a key card from his pocket and holds it up while he wears a mischievous grin.

"Of course you weren't serious. You hardly ever are." I roll my eyes as he swipes the card then punches in a code on the keypad.

He doesn't turn on any lights as we enter the building, but instead uses his phone to guide me toward the elevator. The doors open and we step on. He stands behind me as I look over the buttons on the elevator.

"Let me guess. *Slusia, pick a number.*"

"Not this time." He leans forward so his body grazes my back, but only long enough for him to hit the number forty-seven.

Forty-seven. It's the highest number listed on the glowing white, circular buttons—the top floor of the building. My heart and stomach drop and stay on the ground level as the elevator moves and we climb higher and higher. I don't do heights...ever. I don't even like the balcony at concerts or sporting events. Ferris Wheels? Forget it.

The ride is made even longer by the lack of elevator music. I'm too frightened to speak and my feet are planted firmly on the elevator floor, petrified to this spot, but I don't want him to know that.

When the elevator comes to a slightly abrupt stop, I jump but try to settle myself as the elevator doors open. I step out, never happier to be on solid ground, but make the mistake of looking up. The entire area is ceiling-to-floor glass that overlooks the city for miles. I step backward, instinctively, into him. He wraps his arms around me in a soft, light embrace and leans forward.

"Are you okay?"

I nod but don't speak. He slides his hand into mine and I accept, locking my fingers into his as he leads me to a white, blank door at the opposite side of the area. He uses his free hand to swipe the card once more and push the door open.

On the other side of the door is a short ladder that leads to a hatch in the ceiling.

He steps forward, pulling my hand as he reaches the ladder, but I pull away.

"Absolutely not." I cross my arms and shake my head in a forceful no that shifts my hair out of place.

"You came all this way, took all these chances, played along the whole journey to give up right when you're about to reach the destination?" He lets out a small *tsk-tsk* with his disappointed head shake. "This is the kind of thing that will keep you up at night. Maybe not tonight or tomorrow, but someday you'll waste time wondering what the view from up here looks like and you'll never know because you didn't allow yourself the opportunity." He places one foot on the bottom rung.

"You can stand here and fortune cookie me until the sun comes up. I'm not going."

He steps away from the ladder and steps toward me, taking both his hands in mine.

"You're sure? I won't force you to go. I promise. But I do think you'll regret it. If you never trust me on anything else, trust me when I tell you you'll never see a view like this one."

His voice is calm and kind and the least Ames-like I've ever heard it in this hypnotic vibe that somehow sinks into me and coerces me to do things I'd never be able to talk myself into, but he can.

I hold his hand as tight as I can as I step past him and drag him with me to the ladder before I change my mind. I'd be lying if I said I climbed the steps confidentially—my knees were shaking so forcefully I swear I could've caused an earthquake enough to bring this whole building to its foundation.

But I do it. I climb. I did it because he'd convinced me to, because he'd made me believe I could.

Chapter Twenty-Nine

Dom

Theo sits to my left sipping on bourbon at the bar of a local joint we came across.

"What's the deal with you and Ames?" he asks through sips of the amber liquid.

"I just don't like the guy." I squeeze a lemon in my glass.

"I've known you half my life. I've never once heard you say there's someone you don't like. What's the story?"

I stare into my water. He's been in my corner since we started this journey. I think about it long and hard for one moment. For sixty seconds I allow myself to believe I can open my mouth — childhood cardiac issue, dead best friend, current cardiac issue. All that and, well…Ames.

I don't get the chance before he speaks again.

"I can guess." He chews on ice and I turn toward him, face to face, to see what kind of theories he's come up with. "You can't stand that he's with her."

"I don't know what you mean." My ability to lie to the people closest to me with a natural ease is borderline disgraceful, but in this moment, that skill dissipates. The words are turbulent. Hell, I don't even believe them.

"Stasia?" He smiles as he says her name, like we're in elementary school whispering about a new crush. "It bothers you that he's with her."

"That's not why I don't like him."

That part isn't a lie. My history with Ames goes well beyond the part of the history book my band members opened to.

"I've seen the way you look at her." His eyes soften and his voice quiets, like he feels bad, though I'm certain he doesn't know what it is he's sympathetic to. "All the places we have been and all the women we've met, I've never seen you look at someone like that. I've never seen you look at anything like that."

Do I confirm his intuition? Is he the person I hand a key to? The person I unlock the vault for? But he continues on in a way that makes me grateful I didn't open my mouth.

"I think it's good — what you're doing, you know."

I raise an eyebrow and don't try to mask my confusion.

"Letting her go. I know you like her, man, but this is a good choice. Not pursuing it for the good of the band? I know it's hard, but it really is for the best."

He was only half right.

What he doesn't know is about the months of intimacy — the countless times of the *last time*, how much of myself I gave away when I agreed to let her in. He doesn't know how much of my heart she holds.

Then again, neither does she.

"I know." That's all I can manage. Somehow, as he's dredging up half-truths and inhibiting my ability to lie. I knew it would all catch up to me eventually.

"I have to get going." I take the last sip of my water and slide a cash tip across the bar. "I'll see you later."

I walk out of the door and to the city streets. Fortunately for me, a taxi sits at the end of the block and saves me the time of having to order a ride through an app.

I have the driver drop me back off at the field where the stages are set up and walk across the silent, crowdless areas until I reach our assigned stage and sit on the front of it.

"I'm not really sure what to do anymore." I talk out loud to Raya and shake my head. It's been a long while since I've felt this much at a loss, unsure of what to do next. I painted this picture for myself. I was very aware of what it would cost me to push every single person away, to keep everyone at enough of a distance that they never got close enough to see the parts of me I was determined to hide, I just never intended to do it for this long.

"He's making my life exceptionally difficult, you know. I'm not going to be able to get through to him, not the way you always did."

Lying back, I put my hands behind my head and count the stars, wondering what she would think about me in these moments. What I wouldn't give to see her roll her eyes at me when I'd suggested something she didn't agree with or stick her tongue out at me when she was being utterly ridiculous—which was more often than not. She never needed music to dance. She never needed darkness to shine. There was a time someone asked her about her bucket list. *"Since when do we have to be dying to live?"* she'd asked, and there was something beautiful in that.

Everything about her was beautiful.

"He's going to tear me apart. I'm not sure what he thinks he's going to gain by making life this hard for me. I know he's hurt. He's hurt by what we did and the choices we made and I get that. But nothing he is doing is going to fix it."

I sit up and stare at the area the crowd would be occupying if there were one.

"I need to know how to fix this, Raya."

Chapter Thirty

Stasia

He wasn't wrong.

I've never seen a view like this one.

From here, I can see more of the city than I've ever seen at one time. It's the closest to the stars and moon I've ever been. Sure, there are planes, but I'm usually a martini and several anti-anxiety meds deep anytime I step onto one.

I stand exactly in the center of the building, not brave enough to move.

Ames walks to the very edge, the toes of his boots overhanging the edge.

"How do you do that?" I ask with an exasperated exhale. "How do you just walk through life like nothing could go wrong?"

"I'm incredibly aware of all that can go wrong, Stasia." He turns toward me so his heels flirt with the edge and the city backdrops his dark silhouette. "I just don't let it dictate my days. What if it goes bad, yeah, but what if it goes great? Everyone focuses on the bad outcome. I choose not to. What are you afraid of?"

"I mean…we could die up here."

"We could die down there." He stretches one hand straight out toward me, palm up, and in a move that surprises me more than it does him, I take the slow, steady steps that get me to stand at his side, balancing what seems like miles above the streets.

The sound of a camera shutter and the flash of a light distract me, causing me to snap out of my daze.

"What are you doing?" My cheeks flush.

"Enjoying the view," he says, though his camera is on me alone, hardly catching any of the cityscape.

He steps back and takes another picture, this time surely capturing my position in front of the multitude of sky rises and gorgeous buildings.

"You'll want to remember this." He snaps one more picture. "I know I will."

I turn over my shoulder and I can't help but smile. I can't fight him anymore. He's contagious, and I'm not immune.

"Take one with me." I hold out my hand and he takes it, walking me a few steps in from the edge.

"You know what they'll say about us if you post this anywhere." He laughs as he speaks. "Can't possibly have two celebrities in one picture without a media buzz detailing dating, marriage, pregnancy. You know."

"I haven't really dealt with that. I'm not much of a celebrity, yet."

"They know your name. They know my name. As soon as we post this, they'll use them both in the same headline. Are you ready for that?"

I stare at him, too long, then I reach up, place my hand at the nape of his neck and pull him down to me in a long, slow kiss.

"I'm ready."

He hands me the phone and turns me around so he's hugging me from behind and places his pierced lip lightly against my cheek. I reach my arm as far out as I can, careful to include both of us as well as the city's most pristine backdrop and snap the picture.

I don't know what happens next, but who cares? *What if it's something great?*

Ames has this way about him that makes me throw all caution to the wind but feel good about the choice I'm making, like I'm invincible, like I'll never be hurt again. He's even convinced me to sit at the edge of the building, looking out over my new favorite view.

It's easy to forget how many stories up we are with his arm around me, making me feel safe and secure, even with my feet hanging hundreds of feet above the ground.

"How did we end up here, anyway?" I lean my head into his shoulder and close the opening of his leather jacket tighter around me. I haven't given it back, and I likely never will. "And by that, I mean how did we end up *up* here. Where's the key card from?"

Ames rubs his hand up and down my upper arm and grins. I can tell he plans to make some kind of smart remark or crack his wit, but he doesn't. For once, he actually answers me.

"My parents own it." He stares ahead and points to other large, expansive buildings. "And that one, and that one, and a handful of others just like them all over the country."

My mouth falls open, and I blink several times before composing myself.

"They own the companies?" If I'm being honest, I had no idea Ames came from money. It doesn't matter to me. I come from wealth, too, but many people who have money talk about it. He doesn't.

"They own the *buildings*. They are, essentially, commercial building real estate tycoons. The major companies rent or buy the property from them, but they do the purchasing, fixing up and leasing."

"Impressive."

I can't even begin to wonder how much work and money goes in to a business like that. I had the chance to run a large company, and I gave it up. Kelly is doing an incredible job. She was always a better fit for that kind of position than I was.

"Are you close with them?" I look up at him.

"I used to be. Growing up, my sister and my parents and I were all incredibly close. We did everything together."

"What changed?"

"Everything." He shrugs and let's go of my shoulder, tightly clasping his hands together in front of him. "My sister passed away five years ago. She was so young, so full of life. In the end, I've realized she was the one who kept us all together. Now that she's gone, we've mostly fallen apart. Sometimes, though, I think my parents can't look at me without hurting for her. There were always two of us. There's not anymore."

"I'm so sorry." I place my hand on his and he runs his thumb over the edge of my finger. "I can't imagine how hard it must be to lose someone so close to you. I've only known my brother for a year, and I can't imagine my life without him."

"It was far and wide the worst thing I've ever been through. I wasn't ready."

"It was sudden?" I try to read his eyes though he's purposely keeping his gaze angled away from mine.

"No, not really. But in some ways, yes." He finally looks at me, the tiniest, almost unnoticeable hint of tears filling his almost-black eyes. "She had a heart condition. She spent most of her life battling — procedures, surgeries, medications. She had turned a corner and was doing better, or so we thought. But her heart had other plans. Just further proof that money really can't buy happiness. She was at the top of the donor list when she died."

I drop my head back and stare at the sky, glancing from one star to the next in this way that's like trying to connect the physical dots while I connect the mental ones.

The initials carved in Dom's drum set. The incessant but seemingly uncalled for feud. And of course, what Dom had said to me early on. *"There is a brother-sister bond that shouldn't be messed with."*

"Ames," I say, out loud, about to ask a question I already know the answer to, "what was her name?"

He drops his head back and looks upward so his voice, too, is directed to the moon when he answers.

"Raya."

Chapter Thirty-One

Dom

The soundproof walls likely have little to no effect on this particular mess of a masterpiece I'm playing. No rhythm. No order. Just noise and aggression in a way that I could likely make into a song, but I haven't actually paid attention to any of the patterns. I strike, they sound. Nothing else matters. Sweat pours down my forehead, my chest and abdomen. My heart beats rapidly and I'm not wearing my watch, which is more monitor and less timepiece. I finish an intense drum solo and toss my sticks behind me as I stomp toward the kitchen and use the dish towel to wipe my head and chest. I slam it to the counter once more and stand there for a while, leaning into the granite, unsure of what to do next.

Their picture is everywhere. I can't open my phone or turn on a TV without having to deal with everyone's new favorite couple.

I only have myself to blame. I pushed her away. I could've had her here, now, in my arms, rather than being a bystander while she rests comfortably in someone else's.

After a record-setting lengthy shower, I get dressed then go for a walk to clear my head. I lost count of how many miles I've gone a while before. I stopped paying attention to what turns I was taking, allowing my subconscious to take over and direct me wherever it pleased.

I end up at Salem's, which is something of a security blanket for me. It's the place I feel most at home, other than my apartment.

"Mr. Trudell," Marco says as he hustles toward my usual spot. "A pleasure as always."

"Dominic is fine, Marco, like I've always said."

"I'll work on it." He grabs a cup and fills it with water from the soft-drink dispenser. "But I make no promises. You're by yourself tonight?"

I nod and lift my glass toward him then take the first sip.

There's no act on stage tonight. Frank must have the night off. Instead, the few patrons that Marco serves take turns at the jukebox, selecting and playing songs from various decades and genres. It's quiet tonight. Even with the songs playing, the small crowd is calm and seemingly enjoying the relaxed atmosphere.

"It's your turn to pick the music," Marco says, pointing to the jukebox at the bottom of the old staircase. I step away from my stool and take the short walk to the brightly lit machine, trying to mentally make my selections before I have to input them. My thoughts fail me, not allowing me to come up with any good choices on the spot, so I use the arrow buttons to flip through and decide what to add in.

As I'm clicking, a new sound echoes through the area over the silence, since I haven't picked a soundtrack to fill the voice. The *click clack* of high heels hitting hard against the wooden stairs distracts every person at Marco's bar. I smile, because I know exactly who it is before she turns the corner. When she does, she takes another step and tucks her almost-white hair behind her ear and I think back to the first time I saw her. The déjà vu is welcome, a memory that comforts me in a way I'm not sure anything else can.

She takes one more step, then turns over her shoulder, laughs at something out of sight, and I see another body, dressed in all black, the distinct opposite of the way she appeared that first night.

"Oh, hey!" she says, all smiles and excitement as she joins me on the floor near the jukebox, like everything is fine between us. Maybe, for her, it is.

"Hello," I manage, but it's forced, and I know she knows it.

"Dom," Ames says with a nod. I disregard him completely, and the awkwardness is only more intensified, but the silence surrounds us as I still hadn't made a music selection.

"You do know there's dozens of other bars around here you could have gone to. There's seven others on this street, in fact."

"Really, Dom?" She rolls her eyes and crosses her arms.

"This is *my* bar, and you know it."

"So weird," she says lifting one hand to the bar and twisting her voice into a sarcastic snarl. "Last time I checked, Marco owned it."

"You know what I mean."

"There's no rule that says I can't drink here just because you and I aren't seeing eye to eye. It's a public place and a free country." She looks pleased with herself, smiling a victorious grin.

"I never said I didn't want you here." I match her tone for tone and stand my ground, protecting my house. "But I don't want *him* here. Feel free to stay as long as you want, but that invite doesn't extend to him."

"You don't own the bar, Dom," Stasia bellows.

"You wouldn't even know the password to get down here if it weren't for me."

"Don't be like this."

Her voice quiets for the last words, like she's almost begging me to take some steps toward something that could be considered civil.

"You know what?" I punch in a song selection without even paying attention to the choice. It doesn't matter, anything to cut through our intense exchange. "I'll go. You two have a lovely night."

I take a step past both of them, my shoulder hitting hard into Ames arm as I try to step past. I nod to the doorman as I exit the building. I can hear the footsteps behind me, and I know I'm not going to be alone for long.

"Dom, stop!" Stasia yells as she bursts through the door.

I don't turn around. If she's alone, I can settle down and talk to her, but if I turn and he's behind her, I can't promise I know which version of myself everyone he will meet tonight. Giving in, I drop my head over my shoulder and out of the corner of my eye, it does seem she's alone, so I commit and make the full turn.

"You did this, you know." Her voice is trembling, and she's noticeably quieter than her usual confident, vibrant self. "I never walked away from you. It was always you who was running in the opposite direction. *You* always made the choices when it came to us. *You* controlled the red and green lights, not me." Her eyes are downcast as she rocks back and forth in the middle of the road under the streetlight, so she's perfectly illuminated against the otherwise-darkened street.

"I know." I shove my hands into my pockets.

"Dom, I know there's a reason. I know there is something going on with you, and it would be nice if you would just tell me what the deal is rather than give me bullshit excuses."

My mind races. She deserves an answer. I take steps toward her until we're only about a foot apart, sharing the spotlight above her. She looks up at me with pleading eyes that trance me in that's impossible to say no to. All the answers she's looking for are on the tip of my tongue. I'm about to tell her, to truly tell her everything she's asking for, everything she deserves to know — about to spill to her fifteen years or more worth of secrets that could ruin my life as I know it, but damn it, she's worth it.

And the door opens.

Ames steps outside onto the street and walks up behind Stasia, placing his hands at her shoulders.

"Everything okay here?" he asks, and though Stasia can't see him, I can. He smiles and I hate him for it. He just made her part of the cruel game we've been playing, and of all the lines he's crossed, this one is the one I find the most unforgivable.

"It would be better if you'd go back to whatever rock you were living under and leave the rest of us the hell alone." My fingernails dig into my palms as I tightly close my fists.

"Dom," she says, and the sound that comes out of her mouth, though a whisper, screams disappointment.

"You don't have to defend me, Stasia," Ames says, "but do defend yourself. Dom has a habit of only thinking about himself and destroying everyone else in the process."

His already-black eyes darken and the street light flickers overhead as the two of us take steps toward each other so we're toe to toe.

"Stop it, both of you!" Stasia screams, stepping back in between us and putting one hand at each of our chests. "Whatever is wrong between you, work it the hell out."

I breathe deep, heavy breaths, and his nostrils flair, but neither of us volunteer to take the high road.

"Dom and I are in a band together, and that's not going to change anytime soon. And Ames is part of my life now. The three of us, in many ways, are stuck together, despite how you two feel about it. All your issues, all these pent-up feelings you two have toward each other... Aren't they like five years old? Or more? It's time to move on. Both of you."

Ames looks at her then back at me and his grimace turns to a grin. "You really never told her?"

"Ames," I say, but the threatening tone I'd like to maintain dissolves. He looks at Stasia once more and her confused eyes are trained on his.

"Do you know what the last words my sister ever spoke were, Stasia?"

She shakes her head in a long, drawn-out no.

"Neither do I. I wasn't there." He shrugs as he says the words, then points one finger toward me. "But he was."

Chapter Thirty-Two

Stasia

Dom's door is unlocked when I arrive, and though he didn't answer when I knocked, I let myself in. The apartment is silent, and in most places, that would be eerie — but not with Dom. He's just quiet...soft spoken...secretive.

I turn to the three doors, and as I approach the middle one, I remember him telling me everything I needed to know about him was behind it. He lied. The things he let me in on barely scratched the surface of who he actually is. The hinges squeak a bit as I press the door open. Dominic sits at the other side of the room in an oversized chair. Though he's facing away from me, I already know he has his glasses on and his nose pressed into a book. Dominic is a person who is hyper focused, almost to a fault. Reading is one of the only times I could consider him distracted. Once he's lost in a world outside of this one, everything and anything beside him is ignored. It's odd how even then, he's so focused that he's distracted.

I walk across the room without announcing my presence. Once I reach his side of the room, I take the chair next to him and stare out of the window. We sit there wordlessly for too long. He doesn't look up at me or speak, but if I had to guess, I'd say he's just trying to finish the Chapter. I don't know everything about Dominic, but I know he hates closing a book in the middle of a chapter. I know he hates when people bend the corner of pages to mark their spot. I know he prefers hardcovers over paperbacks. I do know him...just not enough.

He closes the book and places it on the side table but still doesn't speak to me or look my direction.

"I'm sorry." I slide my palms across the thighs of my jeans. Dominic looks at me with a confused expression, trying to figure out where my apology is blooming from. "Let me be clear. I am sorry for your loss. I am sorry about everything that happened with Raya. I am sorry that whatever details are attached to that friendship pain you so much that you feel the need to punish yourself for it day in and day out and I am sorry that you're so scarred, both physically and mentally, that you cannot possibly open up the deepest parts of you to any other person on this green earth. But I am not sorry I found Ames. I will not apologize for living my life and doing it in a way you don't approve of."

"That's fair."

His answer takes me by surprise. He doesn't fight—not for me or against me. He just gives in. On some levels, I'm mad. I'd be lying if I said it wouldn't be nice to have someone argue back in a passionate way that made it, for just one moment, seem like all of the months prior weren't a figment of my imagination, but on the other hand, I'm impressed. He's not the kind of guy who tries to talk his way out of things by lying or manipulating a story. Every time he falls, he acknowledges his shortcomings. He is human, and he owns it.

"Are you going to tell me what happened, or…?"

He cocks his head to the side and raises an eyebrow. "Ames didn't tell you?"

"I haven't talked to Ames—not since you both walked away outside Salem's with no answers."

He pulls his glasses off and places them on the table.

"I met Raya in the hospital when we were kids. We both spent a lot of time there—too much. Between surgeries, treatments and experimental methods, we grew up on the floors of that medical center. Our families became very close. Ames came around frequently. Our parents bonded over the one thing they truly had in common. They were both trying to learn how to make it through every day, knowing they'd outlive their child."

My heart hurts as he speaks—in some ways, physically. Raya and Dominic grew up with pain and illness that was unfair, and discomfort sets in deep in my chest just thinking about the symptoms they lived with as chronically ill children. In other ways, mental. I can't imagine what he went through losing his best friend, and I don't want to. And what their parents went through? It's all unimaginable.

"Six years ago, Consistently Inconsistent hit this odd timeframe where we weren't touring and we weren't in a studio. We've always followed this pattern where one year we tour longer and go international, and the following year we record and release, then tour the states. But that year, for the first time in all our years together, we got a real break. Don't get me wrong... Cooper makes it so we can live our lives. But this was the first long-term, no commitment, nowhere to be for months stretch we had ever had."

One thing I've always liked about Dominic is his ability to maintain eye contact like no one I've ever met, except when it comes to talking about Raya. This is the second time he's brought her up to me, and in both instances, he kept his gaze anywhere but on me, likely so I can't see the pain in his eyes as he reopens every wound he's ever gotten.

"The guys were a little lost. *What do we do with all this free time*? Not me, though. I was grateful for it. You see, while we were finishing our last tour before that break, she'd called me. Her heart was failing. The thing is, Stasia, that the heart that was failing was a transplant to begin with. She'd had her first donated heart placed when she had been fifteen. By the time she'd turned twenty-six, it was already not functioning. So, I came home. I sat by her bedside, and I thanked my lucky stars for all the time I got to be there instead of drumming in some random city."

My eyes fill with tears because I know how this story ends. I'd known the beginning and I know the end, but the middle is the part he has to fill in, and it's killing him. Every word he speaks breaks him down a bit more, but he keeps talking.

"I sat next to her while machines beeped and she choked down hospital food that she hated. I held her hand while tears filled her eyes every time a nurse had to set an IV. She was miserable. She hated it there. And after days of being at her bedside, watching her fade out a bit more each day, the doctors came in and told us that she wouldn't qualify for another transplant. Her kidneys had been adversely affected by the medications she'd been taking since her first surgery, and her immune system was shot. She was susceptible to every infection, and somehow, she always picked them up. She was in the worst shape — and she begged me to take her home."

I close my eyes tightly, and the tears break loose and drip down my cheeks.

"There was nothing left for her there. But there was a whole world outside of its walls that she hadn't seen yet. So I helped her get packed up, and we walked out of that hospital for what she had decided would be her last ever long-term stay. She signed a DNR on the way out of the door. That was the day she decided that if she was dying, she was going to live."

I wipe under my eyes and hope he hasn't noticed my emotions, but the story is heartbreaking. "I don't understand what part of this has caused so much hate between you and Ames. From where I stand, you stood by her. You were there when she needed you most. If anything, wouldn't he respect you more for that? You took care of her."

Dom stands and walks to the window, pacing back and forth in front of it before finally turning, leaning against it and crossing his arms.

"She made me promise I wouldn't tell Ames or her parents that she was dying."

My breath catches in my throat and one tear breaks free.

"She wanted to see the world. She wanted to enjoy every happy moment she had left with them. And she did. They did family dinners, traveled and had a lot of laughs. We all did. For that handful of months, we truly lived. She thought that if they knew what she was going through, they'd try to change her mind. They'd talk her out of taking her chance and doing the things she wanted to do. Or, they'd do it — but only because they felt obligated, and they'd look at her with those worried, sympathetic eyes that would have taken the joy out of her waning days. She begged me not to tell them what was going on. I didn't."

"Oh, Dominic." I stand and walk toward him, but he steps away from me and resumes his staring contest with his own reflection in the window.

"He has never forgiven me. He blames me for her death. In his mind, it wasn't my right to keep a secret of that magnitude. He has held a grudge against me every day since, and right now, he's determined to ruin my life the way he feels I ruined his."

"You were put in an impossible position," I say at the close of his saga. "That's what she wanted."

"He doesn't see it that way. He never will."

"Have you told him? Have you explained to him that you were just doing what she wanted?" My words are pleading, and honestly, I'm not sure why I'm trying to salvage the wreckage. Perhaps because I'm stuck in the middle of two wonderful men, and on some deeper level, I wish that their reconciliation would offer me the chance to have a civil relationship with them both.

"It was never my place to tell him how to grieve or how to feel his anger. He doesn't want to talk to me about it, so the least I can do is respect that. I made the choices I made. I have to live with them every day."

I'm at a loss for words. There is too much of me that wants to run toward him, throw my arms around him and tell him everything will be okay, that if I could share his pain or take it away I would. But that's not my place anymore.

"So, this thing with Ames," he says, finding his way back to the large chair. "Is it for real? You really found something in him that's worth looking past all the anger and rage?"

"If you're going to try to talk me out of it, please, just…don't." I run my hand through my hair then let it fall to my side in frustration.

"I wasn't going to."

When my gaze finds his, his eyes are kind and genuine. He's making eye contact with me again, and his expression softens into a look that is enough to melt all my intuitions, but I can't afford to go back down the path that leads to Dom. It's also the path that leads to destruction.

"I should go." The words are awkward, and I talk with my hands, pointing to the door. "Yeah. Okay. I'm going to go."

He laughs, presumably at my embarrassment, and stands from the chair once more.

"I'll walk you out."

As we reach the door, he opens it and watches me cross the threshold, then leans into the frame.

"Stasia?"

I turn toward him.

"You know Ames started as a solo artist?"

This surprises me, and I smile. I shake my head in a tiny no.

"You should have him play some of his original songs for you. I think you'd like them."

"Since when are you on Ames' team?" I try to keep it light, but I do want to know the answer.

"I'm absolutely not on his team." His words are low and serious. "But I am on yours. If he's good to you, I'll support it."

"And if he's not?"

Dominic thinks on this for a moment then shakes his head, retreating through the door and taking his answer with him.

Chapter Thirty-Three

Dom

Dr. Anderson sits across from me with a stern look plastered on his face.

"How long did it last?"

"Not long," I respond. "It was before a set. I got dizzy, I sat down and I was fine by the time we took the stage."

"You played anyway?" I look at him, but I don't have to. I already knew what kind of disappointment his expression would hold. "Of course, you did. I don't know why I even asked."

We're silent for a while, and he paces back and forth.

"When are you back on the road?"

"Tonight."

"Dom." He shakes his head. "You *have to* finish your testing. I need a Holter monitor and stress test and ECHO. There is a good chance you'll end up with another internal defibrillator."

"I will," I say. "I only have three more shows. We have this weekend then we're home for a while. I will get this done."

"Dominic, you might not have three shows left in you. Do you understand? There is an incredibly high chance you don't have three *days* left in you, and we have no way of knowing that because you won't let us help you."

"Three shows." I hop off the table. "I promise."

"Dominic, if you are not back on this table the moment you return from these shows…"

I wait to see what kind of threat he hits me with.

"…I won't be your doctor anymore. I'm sorry. But I can't stand by and continuously let you cast your health aside. If you won't let me complete your tests, you'll have to find another physician."

I'm speechless, but on the other hand, surprised that he hasn't cut ties with me already.

"Three more shows, Dom. Not one more."

"I get it," I say, and he leaves the room.

* * * *

I haven't talked to Stasia all week. I haven't seen her or Ames in person, but their faces have flashed across my screen approximately one million times in three days.

The bus is silent for all of us. Cooper is still mad at me for the past weekend's acoustic set. Stasia and I are just better off staying away from each other in all respects. Blake hates Ames now more than ever, which has caused a special type of divide between him and Stasia. Theo has opted to give me some space, still theorizing — correctly — that I'm hung up on Stasia and pissed she's with Ames. And Xander? Well, for the first time ever, Xander is doing nothing wrong and has nothing newsworthy going on in his life.

The tension across the band is thick and worsening each day. This is not what we wanted for ourselves. We're all in bad moods that we're taking out on each other. This isn't us. It never has been. We're falling apart, and I'm not sure there's enough glue to put us back together.

I hop off the last step of the bus by myself and walk to the area where my drums are locked up. I just want to play. It's my stress relief — the sound, the feel. I just want to play. As if things couldn't get any more tense, Ames is hanging with his band directly behind our assigned stage as I approach.

"How was the trip?" He's all smiles and welcoming, as if we're friends. I walk past him, away from either of our bands, turn a corner and he follows. "Not even a hello? Pretty rude, Dom. Your parents would be so disappointed. How are your parents, by the way? They must be so thrilled about your miracle recovery and years of good health…"

"I need you, for five minutes, to be anywhere but here. You are everywhere, all the time. If that was your intention, you win. You beat me. I'm done. Can you go now, please? For the love of all things, just find somewhere else to be."

His lips curl, his shoulder muscles relax and his voice falls into a derisive whisper.

"I'm just standing back here waiting for my girl."

My hands connect with his chest, and he laughs as he stumbles backward, but the laugh turns to a snarl and he steps forward, coming face to face with me once more.

"Listen carefully, Ames. She is not part of this. Whatever you're doing, you'd better be doing it for the right reason. She sees something in you. I haven't any earthly idea how or what, but she's giving you a chance. This better be the real thing for you, 'cause if it's not—"

"You'll do what?" He emphasizes every word as he asks the questions.

"I'll out us both. I don't care anymore, Ames. I don't. If you hurt her, I will ruin you. My band? My parents? Sure, they'll find out I've lied. But the world will find out you're a fraud. Your parents. Your band. Your fans. Stasia. You'll never play music again in your life." I start to walk away, but he continues speaking, even when my back is toward him.

"You'd like that, wouldn't you?" I turn over my shoulder. "Consistently Inconsistent is drowning in the waves Save Me, Save You is making, and you know it."

"In a head-to-head battle, Ames, we will win every time. You don't want to go there."

"Let's do it then."

I turn toward him. There is about ten feet of space and an intense silence between us.

"A battle of the bands. We can put this to bed, once and for all. Truthfully, when I started all this, I didn't know where it would end up. This seems like a fitting finale. My band outplaying yours, watching you fail very publicly."

Before I can answer, Cooper steps around the corner.

"What is going on out here?" His focus darts in between us.

"Nothing at all," Ames says. "Good luck today, boys." And with that, he retreats.

I start to walk toward the backstage area, but Cooper wraps his fingers around my bicep.

"You've got to let her go, Dom. You've got to let it all go."

I nod and gently shake free from his grasp, putting my ear plugs in as I head backstage.

We take the stage, and as I look out from it, it seems the crowd spans for miles, like every person has migrated from all the other stages to ensure they are in front of ours. The show is going perfectly, the audience is spirited and Xander has reached deep inside the archives to pull out some throwback songs and display a younger version of himself all over the stage.

Stasia moves across the stage, hitting her notes and adding in her inimitable flair. She comes back toward me and sings a part of the song directly to me. She has always done it—since day one, even when we weren't seeing eye to eye. She comes to the drum kit, sings part of the song as she walks around me, then grabs a stick and slams a cymbal, right at the correct moment. The crowd loves it, and it's her way of bringing the show to me, making the background the foreground, even if just for a moment.

This time, though, it's different. Ames stands in the wings, and he doesn't like our act. I can see it in the way his eyes narrow when he looks at me, and my pride grows, until I look away. When I look back, Ames is standing face to face with Cooper. I keep the rhythm going, but my eyes are trained on Ames. Cooper's arms are crossed and his face stern. His focus skates toward me every once in a while, retaining his serious expression, and Ames? He rubs his hand at the back of his neck and talks with his hands in this way that has all of Cooper's attention and makes Ames appear to be sympathetic or nervous. Ames doesn't have a sympathetic or nervous bone in his body. So, what the hell are they talking about?

Cooper nods and retreats out of view and Ames returns his gaze to mine, a victorious grin on his face as he waves, steps backward and becomes one with the dark area beyond the stage.

My heart rate beating uneven or uncontrolled is not something I'm not used to, but hardly ever out of fear. Is this the moment all my years of fables and tales comes crashing down? When I finish the solo for this finale, when I stand from this chair and exit this stage, will it be the last time I ever do? The feelings of remorse and anxiety hit me all at once, making it harder to breathe. My solo, though passable, is distracted and weak, and my band members know it.

The lights go down and my uneven heartbeat slams in my chest. What am I walking into now? Is this it? Is this where it ends for me?

Cooper stands outside a small space at the back of the makeshift stage set ups. He doesn't speak, but he does wag a finger and indicate I follow him. I debate not going. If I don't follow, if I don't face whatever lies beyond that fence, it's not real. But it *is* real. I have known, for a long time, that this day would come. That my worlds would collide, and I would be left to clean up the mess. If today is that day, well, I had a good run. I got more time with this band and this life than I ever thought I would. So, I take a deep breath and trek forward, turning the corner to face Cooper and whatever information he has on me once and for all.

When I turn, Cooper is standing behind the fence — and so is Ames.

"What's going on?"

"Ames told me some things you've apparently been keeping to yourself." He scratches at his five o'clock shadow and waits for me to talk, but I don't volunteer. My stomach does a somersault. "I think it's an amazing idea, really. I wish I had thought of it."

I raise an eyebrow and look from Cooper to Ames and back again.

"Oh, don't be humble now, Dom," Ames says, throwing an arm around my shoulder. "The battle of the bands. I told Cooper you wanted to do a little showdown. Hype up both bands. Sell tickets. Winner gets bragging rights, and all proceeds go to charity. It's a helluva publicity stunt."

"It's smart, it's fun…" Cooper says.

"It's for a good cause." Ames still hasn't removed his arm from around my neck and I'm tempted to accidentally-on-purpose elbow him in the ribs.

"What do you say?" Cooper says. "You want to pitch it to the band?"

I nod my head as he continues to speak.

"I know we were only supposed to have three shows left for the year, but what's one more?"

"Three shows. What's one more? Three shows. Not one more." Both Cooper and Dr. Anderson's words play over and over again in my head, and once again, my thoughts are spiraling.

"I'll talk to them," Cooper says as he leaves.

"Everything all right there, Dom?" Ames digs his fingers into my collarbone as he asks the question, then he lets go and walks away, leaving me to try to figure out what the hell just happened.

Chapter Thirty-Four

Stasia

The papers scattered between us crunch under Ames' hand as he leans toward me, wrinkling all the plans we've been trying to make. His mouth is on mine, and he uses his arms to steady himself over me.

I could get lost in him for hours. I've been lost in him for hours.

"Okay, okay," I say between kisses with a smile on my face. He backs off and I smooth the paper out once more. "We have to practice this song. The award show is coming up in just a few weeks."

"We don't need to practice. Let's just wing it." He leans forward again, and I place one finger against his lips.

"Are you ever serious?"

Of course not, he hardly ever is.

"I'm serious all the time. 'Serious' is my middle name."

I shake my head.

"It's Syrus, actually, but close enough."

A large smile grows into my cheeks. *Ames Syrus*. I like it.

"What's your middle name?" he asks. I raise an eyebrow and glance toward the pages set between us — the ones we're supposed to be focused on. He grabs several of the pages and tosses them behind him. They float to the ground in disarray.

"Bethany," I say and push myself off the bed. "Now *focus*." I pick up the pages and pace the room.

"Which song are we going to pick, Ames? We get together, we practice different songs to see what sounds the best, but we never really settle on one. We can only do one. We have to pick."

"I had an idea, I think. Hear me out." He pulls a small notebook from his back pocket and hands it to me. The list includes several songs and artists, taking up most of the page.

"Way to narrow it down…"

"What if we don't pick one?" He takes the notebook back and runs his finger down the page. "What if instead of picking one eighties tribute song, we create a montage of them? We can make it our own, and no one will expect it."

I look up at him with wide eyes. He doesn't talk much about his creative side or his lyrics. This is the side of him I've been waiting to see, and here he is, displaying those secret parts of himself, just for me. I've been holding back with Ames. I know I haven't been able to clear that mental hurdle that is Dominic, but Ames is good to me. He's good *for* me. If tonight is the night he's going to let go of his reservations and let me all the way in, tonight could very well be the night I let go of mine.

"It's brilliant."

We spend time taking turns figuring out how to combine one song into the next, where to sing together and where to solo, how to make one song lyric blend seamlessly into the next. It's fun, piecing together pieces of this giant, soon-to-be-live-on-stage puzzle.

When Ames is on stage, his voice is deep and aggressive. He's passionate, and entertaining, but the words come out as more of a strategic yell than a melody. But here, as he looks over sheets of lyrics and sings bits and pieces of the songs in this 'thinking out loud' type of way, I can hear the skill, the perfect vocals.

"Dom told me you were a solo artist once." I hesitate, but the sentence tumbles out eventually. I don't like talking about one of them to the other, but we're all intertwined now. We share stages, we share awards shows, we share these three beating hearts that are full of equal parts love and hate. I wish they weren't. I'd give anything to fix the breakage between Dom and Ames, because selfishly, I need them both. Dom is my bandmate and one of my brother's best friends. And Ames? He's helping my heart heal. The blood between them, though? Well, I'm learning that not all hearts are fixable. Some are damaged beyond repair.

"I was." He smiles like he's seeing an old friend for the first time in years. "That was a different time."

"Will you sing for me?" I ask, and he nods an uncharacteristically soft, gentle yes.

"Not here though."

He's rolling off the bed and strolling out of the door before I can decide to follow.

"Can I at least put shoes on?" I yell through a laugh, pulling on one boot then the other as I stumble into the hallway, trying to keep up. Fortunately, this time Ames doesn't disappear like he's been known to do. He waits in the hallway and stretches one hand toward me as I join him. I take his hand in mine and he slows his pace, making his stride small to keep me close at his side.

We reach the hotel lobby and leave through a side exit. Beyond the door is a courtyard decorated with lush greenery, an archway drenched in vines and flowers, spiral bushes and rows of gorgeous hand-carved wooden benches.

"This place is gorgeous." I rub a rose petal between my pointer finger and thumb.

"This is where they do weddings." He stands behind me and places both hands at my shoulders, turning me slightly until I can see where he wants my focus. A stunning grand piano sits off to one side of the courtyard, lit by the moon's glowing spotlight. He guides me to the bench and we both take a seat. He runs his fingers across the keys, silently, like he's trying to remember how to play. He commits, pressing down on the keys, which emit an airy, twinkling sound. The piece seems odd coming from his fingers, like someone who's so determined to strain his vocal cords under the pressure of his aggressive tone couldn't possibly be capable of playing such a delicate melody, but he does — and it's brilliant.

It's almost unbelievable how different of a person he is in this moment, tapping into a version of himself he claims doesn't exist anymore. The tone of his voice and the lyrics of the song are a smooth, tender mixture that leans into soft rock but borrows elements of jazz and blues. He doesn't look at me as he sings the words, and truthfully, I'm glad. He's focused, astray in the words of a song he wrote before grief and loss and hurt found their way into his world.

When I heard Ames had once planned to be a solo artist, I didn't understand. I do now. He has it all—the demeanor, the range. The first time I saw him live, I fell for him the way the fans do. It's hard not to be captivated by him, the way he is so incredibly present on stage and pours his soul into the energy he leaves there. But this version? It's like a secret only I know, and so much of me wants to keep it that way.

When the song ends, it's not me whose clapping. We both turn and find that onlookers have gathered at the edge of the courtyard, leaning into and sitting on the low, cement wall that separates the courtyard from the street. Many have their phones out, videoing the performance. The video of Ames singing an old song that was meant only for me has likely already started taking its viral turns, but Ames doesn't seem to mind. He stops and takes pictures with a few of the onlookers, and dare I say it, I think I even caught a glimpse of a genuine smile.

He walks across the courtyard once more and leans down to place his lips on mine.

"What do you want to do now," he asks, a twinkle in his eye and a smirk on his lips.

"You sure you want to know?" I raise one eyebrow and he mimics the expression, surely excited for an answer he's not going to get. I move one finger in a come closer fashion and he does. When my lips meet his ear, I whisper, "Practice our song."

I step past him and run away while laughing. He shakes his head and chases me down effortlessly, wrapping his arms around me and keeping me close as

we walk back to his hotel room, where he gives in and
we finally let our voices work together.

Chapter Thirty-Five

Dom

We stand behind the stages before show three of three. Just like that, the weekend festival series is over and truthfully? I've never been happier. Suddenly my favorite tour style is a nonhealing wound, nothing more than a recurrent ailment.

Ames is everywhere — always behind or in front of our stages, always hand in hand with the person my heart aches for most, always making the headlines I can't help but see. Our fan bases aren't even separate anymore. They're connected by one common thing. Everyone is rooting for Stasia and Ames. And there's absolutely nothing I can do about it.

"You okay?" Cooper places one hand on my shoulder.

"Of course." I nod. "Why?"

"You're a quiet person, Dom. I respect that. I'm used to that. But you haven't spoken a word to anyone since right after we got off the bus. Not even one."

Has it been that long? I think back. I can't pinpoint one conversation I've had with anyone since Ames and Cooper about the bands playing a head-to-head show.

"The guys are worried about you." He squeezes his fingers gently into my collar bone. "And whether or not she will admit it, she is, too." He nods toward Stasia before releasing his grip and walking away. My gaze meets hers, but she quickly pulls her eyes away.

* * * *

Later, when it's almost time for us to be announced and take the stage, she stands next to me. We both keep our eyes fixed on the stage. There were shows, many of them, where we stood here and took the steps onto the stage together, my hand on her lower back, cloaked by the darkness and lack of stage lights until we went our separate ways at the center of the stage.

"Think we will be okay?" she asks, still staring ahead, neither of us daring to look the other's direction, like even eye contact is connection too much.

"Hmm?" I ask, and out of the corner of my eye I can see her tilt her face to the sky.

"Think we'll get through the whole show before the rain?"

I look up to a sky that's blackness is covered with angry gray clouds. I don't answer her, and my chest clenches. This is why this was a bad idea — us, being together. Things will never be the same, and with every passing day, things get worse instead of better. I can't let her go. I have to, but I can't.

Xander comes in full speed behind me, rubbing his hand aggressively at the top of my head to mess up my hair, yelling something in my ear that I miss because my mind is elsewhere. He's electrified, amped up and doing his best to get everyone else to match his level. We take the stage and the crowd cheers wildly. I hold a stick in each hand and I'm instantly more content, because there's almost nothing in the world I'd rather be doing than drumming. It's a bandage, though. As soon as the show is over, as soon as the beat dies down, the quiet sets back in.

* * * *

Xander has been keeping us all on our toes lately. He throws in songs we don't have on the set list and makes last-minute changes we don't expect, but it keeps the shows fun and the crowd loves it. For the most part, though, we don't see it coming. It doesn't truly blindside us. We've been doing this long enough to know what to expect from an excited Xander. Tonight, for the first time, he goes so far off script that the rest of us might as well be in the crowd. We're just as surprised as they are, especially Stasia. I can see it in every inch of her body language. She had no idea this was coming.

"I think you guys know a bit about Stasia by now, yeah?" He addresses the crowd. Her muscles tense and her eyes widen as she watches Xander pace back and forth at the front of the stage and tease the crowd.

"You might think you know her. But I'm going to tell you one more thing about our girl here." He holds up one finger. "Better yet, I'll just let her show you."

They both back off their microphones, and though I can't hear her, I can see the distinct lip movements form the phrase '*what the hell are you doing*' as he ventures off stage and returns with a violin.

She shakes her head in a no that is light enough for us to notice it but not enough for the crowd to see. The band groups together quickly at the center of the stage and I run toward them, joining the impromptu huddle.

"Play us in, Stasia. You're going to perform *Indecision* for them.

"Xander, no." Her voice is practically pleading. "You know how hard it was for me to even *record* that song, never mind do it live—and unprepared, nonetheless."

"Sink or swim, Stasia," he says. "You can do this."

Stasia walks to the back to get a headset microphone. She hands off her guitar to a stage worker, and I step toward her, just behind the curtain at the side of the stage. A light rain starts to fall as they get her set for the changes.

"Dom," she says as they place her guitar on a stand and get a headset ready, "I can't do this."

"Yes, you can." I wrap both my hands at her upper arms and move them gently in small up and down, reassuring motions. "This is your song, Stasia. You're the only one who *can* do this. Let's go. You've got it."

She shakes her head and lets out a frustrated sigh, but ultimately steps past me and takes the stage in front of thousands of exhilarated fans.

She turns toward me, slowly in a way no one else sees and I nod my head confidently her direction. She takes a deep breath, turns to the crowd, lifts the violin and plays in a harsh but passionate sound that takes the crowd by storm. Within seconds, she's forgotten her reservations and is playing like this had been rehearsed. I play in a light beat that doesn't overpower what she's doing. By the time the lyrics come into play, one of the stage techs runs up the side of the stage, hands her her guitar and takes the violin. She wears a large smile as the crowd continues to cheer. Xander, Theo and Blake continue to play while she switches instruments, still singing along into the headset. As she takes the front of the stage once more, Xander and Stasia sing together, a magic blend of deep and light tones.

As we play, the sky opens up and rain falls in sheets over the stage and the crowd. Xander keeps playing. Blake strums even harder, shaking his hair wildly in a way that sprays drops off the ends. Stasia leans back and sings to the open sky as the water pours over her. Theo backs up as the techs help him move the keyboard back, but he jumps right back in once he's situated. Water jumps and dances off the tops of my drums as I play.

The song comes to an end and the crowd—who mostly stayed put, despite the rain—cheers a thunderous cry fitting for the weather.

"Ladies and gentlemen," Xander yells, "that was *Indecision,* written and performed by our very own Stasia, with a special appearance by Mother Nature." The audience whistles and applauds, Xander pushes his soaked hair back off his face.

"Anybody quitting?" He looks out over the crowd. "Let me tell you something," he says, and all eyes are on him. "It's only a little bit of water. I'm not going anywhere."

The volume of the applause heightens. Xander turns and points to me and I lead us in on a heavier, more upbeat song. Stasia performs at the front of the stage, sharing a microphone with Xander, then walks back toward her own setup. She strikes a few hard chords then gives up her guitar to an employee, hops off the stage and dances with the people closest to the barrier at the front of the stage. No microphone. No instrument. Just Stasia freeing herself of the wires and dancing with strangers in a crowd.

I stop playing as I watch her spin and jump—and smile. No beat. No dynamics. I might not know what love is, but for the first time, I want to explore the possibility of it.

But I won't. I won't do that to her. The thing that bothers me the most is how much she smiles these days. I know how wrong that is, which bothers me even more, because I know it's not me who put that happiness there.

It won't be me who takes it away.

Chapter Thirty-Six

Stasia

I miss the music festival weekend already. The setup was so unique, being home for a week but gone on the weekends, it was like touring and normal life collided. It was, truly, the best of both worlds.

Now that we're home long-term again, we're settling back into our routines. Well, mostly. My routine has never included last-minute rehearsals for a quickly approaching awards ceremony with a man I'm falling hard and fast for. I'll be honest. As much as I didn't want to perform *Indecision* live and unprepared, I owe some of my new-found confidence to Xander. I'm feeling really good about the awards show. I've rehearsed, I'm prepared and I'm not doing it alone.

Ames invited me to his house for a rehearsal.

Wealth has several different levels. I grew up with money. There was almost nothing that wasn't accessible to me — except my dad. Though I had a house with all the best features and upgrades and had anything I desired at my fingertips, I never understood why people said 'you're so lucky'. I've always imagined a crowded apartment is more comfortable than an empty mansion.

But Ames? He comes from real money. He comes from wealth I can't even begin to understand. A driver opens the door to the limo, and we step out. The mansion we stand in front of is more castle than house. Built in carved stone that expands over several stories, boasts astonishing archways and columns, and has landscaping so lush that it looks fake, I feel like I'm about to enter a museum rather than a place of residence.

"This is *your* house?"

He wraps his fingers in mine.

"I mean, credit where credit is due. It's my parent's house." He pulls my hand and leads me forward, opening and stepping through the vast front doors. "None of us are ever here long enough to cross paths. I take care of it when they're gone—which is almost always—and I have traveled over the last few years. Now that I'm recording and touring again, I just hang out here when I'm not on the road."

"Makes sense." I'm listening, but I can't believe my eyes. The artwork on the walls, the marble statues that decorate the room… It's all intricate and immaculate. There's a full-sized, three-tier water fountain at the center of the foyer with staircases on either side.

"To the music room?" He places both hands on my shoulders as he stands behind me.

"There's a music *room*?" I'm not sure why I ask the question. Why wouldn't there be a music room?

"It's more like a music *wing*."

Of course it is.

He leads me up the stairs on the left and down the hall to another large door that is intricately carved. Once the door is open and I can see what awaits on the other side, his description is nothing short of perfect. It is a music *wing*. The room is large—the size of some people's houses. All the decor keeps the musical theme in play. Several instruments are placed about the room. A piano. A violin. Several guitars. Drums. A *harp*.

"Tell me you can play that," I whisper, keeping my eyes trained on the gorgeous golden instrument.

"I can play that," he says, confidentially.

"Really?" I turn over my shoulder too quickly with a smile on my face, but I force it to a feigned pout when I realize he's messing with me.

"I was just following directions." He winks at me and heads to the side of the room where the corner contains a floor-to-ceiling box.

"Is that a sound booth?" I assess the structure without stepping any closer to it.

"It is." He knocks on the side of it. "The whole room is soundproof, though. This is good for recording, but for practicing? The acoustics are better out here." He stands in front of one mic and raises his hand toward the space next to him. Though the mic is off and we won't use it, it's a nice aesthetic to help get in the mood.

"Let's get started then," I say, and he laughs.

"Let's take a break," Ames says, turning away and leaving the room.

"Don't you dare!" I yell after him, knowing he just chose me as 'it' for the impromptu games of hide and seek he likes to play, but I stumble then struggle catching up to him. When I reach the doorway, he's gone. And there's only about a million hallways and staircases to choose from. My phone pings, and I pull it from my pocket.

Find me if you can.

Ames Gaherty. As playful as ever. Now how in the hell am I supposed to find him in here?

I tiptoe down the hall and choose a room on the right. Behind it is a large game room with ping pong, an arcade-style basketball game, pinball, air hockey, and just before I'm about to close the door I notice there are three wooden strips of flooring at the far side of the room which are none other than bowling lanes. No Ames, though.

I venture to the next door, which holds a built-in movie room with a large screen, several rows of black leather couches and a full bar stocked with cold drinks and mountains of snacks.

The next room I open is smaller than the rest, dimly but romantically lit with two spa beds in the middle. A floral scent invades the hallway I stand in. There are unlit candles around the room, and a table with various oils and stones. At the back of the room, a large, carved wood door extends floor-to-ceiling with the word 'Sauna' scrawled across it in gold script.

My phone pings.

Getting warmer.

And I realize that two can play this game.

I take the complete opposite hallway, well aware that I've taken steps to a 'colder' path. Now I open random doors, somewhat being nosy because, let's face it, this place gets better with every turn, but equally because it's fun to make him wait. I don't chase guys. If he wants me, he will have to find *me*.

After opening several doors and finding everything from art rooms to bathrooms to storage rooms, I grab the handle of a door at the end of the hallway, and it doesn't budge. For the first time since I've gotten here, I've encountered a locked door. I jiggle the handle a few times, allowing curiosity to get the best of me, but give up and turn away, jumping when I see Ames leaning into the wall at the end of the hallway.

"There's nothing in there," he says with a shrug. "You can break that door down if you want. There's nothing worth seeing on the other side."

"Then why lock it?"

He shakes his head in slow motion. His eyes say he doesn't want to talk about it, but to my surprise, he steps forward to a nearby decorative table in the hallway, lifts the vase that sits on top of it and reveals a key that was hidden away. He inserts it and turns the knob. There is one second where I almost tell him to stop, where I can feel myself prying in somewhere I don't belong, but he pushes the door open, reaches inside and flicks on the lights.

He wasn't lying or hiding anything. There is almost nothing behind the locked doors. But there was, once. Now, a fleet of spectacular floor-to-ceiling bookshelves sit empty against every inch of wall space in the room. It's easy to picture what it looks like, because, well, I've seen it before—on a tour just like this one, behind doors just like these, but with a man who is not this one.

"My parents love giving tours of this house. They love telling people what island each plant came from or what lavish artist designed the pieces in each room. It never gets old to them, bragging about the price tag everything came with. But this room, and my sister's bedroom? Well, it's easier to pretend they're not there at all. Trying to explain why these rooms are empty puts a damper on their tour of absurdly priced material items. So, they lock them. Besides, there's not much here to look at anymore. She made it abundantly clear that those books never belonged on these shelves — that when she left, the books would too. They have a new home now. But you already knew that, I'm sure."

"I'm sorry," I whisper. It's weak and pointless, but I say it anyway. "I shouldn't have pushed. I was just curious. This house really is like something out of the magazines or TV shows. I can see why your parents like to show it off so much."

My attempt to change the subject is weaker than my apology, but he doesn't seem to mind. He takes the opportunity to step away from the once-locked door as soon as I present it.

"There's more to see, if you'd like." He reaches his hand out and I almost reach for it, but then step past him, looking over my shoulder.

"You'll have to find me first." I take off in a run, continuing our earlier game. My laugh echoes through the arched hallways as I sprint.

"You have a forty-five-second window, Stasia," he yells after me. "Then, ready or not, here I come."

For thirty minutes we run around, hiding from and finding each other in the never-ending rooms, texting each other clues and chasing the other around like children on a school yard in a carefree way that makes me forget there is a real world outside of these castle-like walls. We walk side by side, in a quiet that serves as a break from all the foolishness. He links his fingers into mine and our hands swing between us in unison as we walk.

"As beautiful as this house is…" I start, looking around at the art on the walls of the hallway. "I'd never get anything accomplished. That music room is amazing. The game room… The balcony over the pool with those fountains… I'd literally just be distracted twenty-four seven."

Ames lets out a light laugh and squeezes my hand.

"I haven't even shown you my favorite room."

"There's more?" I ask, and he looks down at me and nods, though his eyes glisten with a secret.

We reach the center of the home once again, where the front door stands tall in front of the split staircase. He leads me down the right side and through a long hallway, not stopping to open any of the doors. Who knows what could possibly be hiding behind them? At this point, I've seen it all.

Only…I haven't seen it all.

At the end of the hallway, large white canvas drapes hang from a golden archway. He takes a few long strides ahead of me, pulls the curtains back and nods his head toward the entry. I step through, as directed, and momentarily I'm convinced the archway is more of a portal than a door.

The entire room is shades of green. Plants, trees, flowers—every surface is wallpapered with living greenery. Whoever designed the room pulled out all the stops, essentially bringing a full rainforest indoors. No detail had been left undone. The room even *sounded* like nature. A rush of water and subsequent burble echo through the area in a soundtrack that matches the landscape. I push a palm aside and step forward to where I can see a rock formation with a waterfall running over it, meeting it in a large pool.

"My parents had this area modeled after one of their favorite resorts in Costa Rica."

I turn over my shoulder and smile at him, pull my shirt over my head and start to shimmy out of my jeans.

"What are you doing?" he asks, but the way he laughs through the question makes me think it's rhetoric.

"C'mon. You didn't bring me in here just to *look* at it."

"That's fair." He grabs the hem of his shirt and pulls it off, revealing his full body murals. "It's shallow. It's more like a faux hot spring than a pool, so no swan drives."

"Do I strike you as the kind of person who would voluntarily get her hair wet?" I sit on the edge and pop into the water in a soft plunge that doesn't result in a splash.

Ames looks down at me and shakes his head. "No. Not voluntarily."

"Don't you dare," I say, but the effort is wasted. He's splashing in my direction as soon as his body meets the water.

Ames has this personality that's contagious, this way about him that doesn't fit his exterior in the least. He's tall and tattooed with dark eyes and this mysterious aura that follows him around and almost tells you to run the other way, and yet, he's playful and childish in this manner that makes me feel young again, that makes my problems feel like they aren't really problems, a way that makes my stress evaporate and the only emotion left in the world is joy.

We screw around, splashing water and wrestling in a way where there will be no winner. If one of us gets submerged, both of us will.

It's freeing and exciting and fun. For the few moments where he ruined my hair and laughed about it and I jumped on his tattoo-covered back and tried to take him down, I forgot I was in this house for a reason.

"We should get back to practicing," he says, pulling me into a fireman's carry with both his arms underneath me while I float in the warm water.

"The acoustics are better in here." I wink at him and his eyes light up.

"You might be right about that." He lets me go and I float away on my back as he pushes himself out of the pool and connects his phone to speakers in the room. As the music begins to play, I place both feet on the floor of the pool. He walks down the steps, singing his part of the mix as he does so. Even in practice, soaking wet, with his jeans falling down around his hips, it's as if he's on stage in front of a million people. He doesn't hold back. I fall for him more in these moments where there is no background noise, because I appreciate the sound of his voice when he uses it this way. Ames can sing…well. It's mind-boggling to me that the world allowed him to fade away for five years and didn't bang down his door demanding he grace the musical world with his perfect voice. Then again, the music world doesn't know *this* side of him. They know him as a rock star, an entertainer, a musician who borderline screams the words to his heavily aggressive songs, and I wonder, how does he live in both realms?

He reaches me in the pool and holds out both hands. I place mine in his and our voices collide as I duet with him, our tones combining and bouncing off the pool area walls, competing with the sound of the waterfalls. His voice fades out, and I sing my part. He never takes his eyes off me. We take turns going back and forth then sharing lines of all the songs we chose to make up our compilation. We sing the last line loud and passionate, ringing out the final note until our voices fade and so does the music. And it was perfect.

He places his hands gently at my jaw and lifts my face upward, placing his lips against mine. I know what I came here for, but I got so much more. I saw a side of Ames I hadn't yet seen. And now, there's a *different* side of Ames I haven't yet seen...but I'd like to.

"I don't think the tour is quite over," I say between kisses. "I haven't seen your room yet."

We drop water in a trail that follows us from the pool, up the stairs, down several hallways and into his room. I couldn't even describe what it looked like. My mind was so preoccupied with thoughts of what was coming next that I never truly looked around enough to get a picture of the room. The only thing I looked for was the bed, which doesn't take much effort. It sits at the center of the room, the mattress larger than any other I've ever seen. It's covered in an onyx black comforter with a mountain of black-and-gold pillows at the headboard. He places his hands on my hips and turns me toward him. He has to lean down considerably to keep his lips on mine, but he does so as we walk backward, wrapped up in each other, pulling at the wet clothes the other wears and tossing the soaked fabric aside until we're skin to skin and falling into the satin bed set.

He takes his time with me, enjoying every moment and not rushing any part of our first time together. Again, in every sense, he displayed how he's the opposite of dangerous. He's kind and gentle in a way completely opposing his rugged appearance. The night was flawless. I couldn't have scripted it any better if I wanted to. I'm glad we waited and took our time to get to know each other, but I have no regrets about giving ourselves to each other tonight. I fell for him more in those vulnerable moments.

"Everything okay?" He wraps one arm over my abdomen and places his lips at my ear. "You're unusually quiet."

"Absolutely perfect," I lean my head back, inviting his playful bite. "I couldn't have asked for anything bett—"

As I speak, something at the other side of the room catches my attention, and the slow motion, exceptional moments we were living in come to a crashing halt.

"Stasia?" He sits up and assesses my expression. "What is it?"

I shake my head and force myself to return my attention to him. "Nothing. I just got distracted for a second." I force a fake smile. "You know what we need? Drinks. I'm sure there's champagne somewhere in this house."

Leaning forward, he presses his lips to my hair line. "You've got it. I'll be right back." He hops into a pair of jeans from the floor and leaves the room. I hesitate, because the reality is I don't want the answer to the questions I'm asking, but I know I only have a few moments to investigate before he returns.

I wrap myself in a small blanket from the end of the bed as I slide out of it and tiptoe as quietly as I can to the other side of his room, I get a better look at the item on his shelf that caught my eye.

It's a book—leather-bound, black—but its pages are red. With a shaking hand, I reach upward and place my fingers on the book. I pause, because I'd bet anything that as much as I don't want to admit it, if I flip it over, the title will be etched in red writing on the cover that reads *The Heart & Other Torture Devices*.

I pull the book down and flip it over in my hands. Why does Ames have this? What does it mean? I crack the binding and scan the words. My stomach turns. I press one hand over my mouth to hold back the gasp that escapes when I realize their familiarity.

The album that is famous and recognizable worldwide as we speak.

The album that knocked Consistently Inconsistent off the charts.

The album that ended his five-year hiatus and fueled his record-setting comeback.

The album that had me falling for him in the first place?

He didn't write it.

Dominic did.

There's nothing I'd love to do more than climb back into that bed, rewind to a better time—a time that was only a few moments ago. The seconds that were once filled with passion and joy, now, only a few beats later, are eclipsed by regret.

Ames steps inside the doorway with a bottle of champagne and two glasses in his hands. He pauses when he realizes where I'm standing and what I'm holding. He doesn't backtrack. He doesn't try to make excuses. He doesn't even speak.

He smiles.

It's a slow, almost-menacing grin. He shakes his head, places both glasses down and pops the top on the champagne bottle like it doesn't faze him at all that I'm holding irrefutable evidence in my hands. The bubbles dance as Ames pours the golden liquid into each glass.

"Why do you have this?" I finally ask. We all think we will be heroes, that our voices won't fail us and our confidence will shine when we need it the most. But I'm not a hero. My words are a whisper where I need them to be a yell. There is weakness where I need conviction.

"You are going to want to put that down and pretend you never saw it." He picks up both glasses and tries to hand me one, but I stand completely still. He shrugs and taps the two glasses together, like a cheers to himself, and he downs one glass.

"You're awfully relaxed for someone who committed the ultimate creative crime, standing across from the person holding the smoking gun."

His smile grows. His lack of compassion or remorse only darkens his black eyes. He looks at me over the rim of the glass as he takes another sip of his celebratory drink.

"Pull the trigger."

"What is that supposed to mean?" I swallow hard, unsure if I want to know the answer.

"You opened that book, read a few pages and think that you know everything—yet, you don't even know half the story." He refills a glass, twirls the stem in his hand, and holds it close to my face. "Are you sure you don't want any of this, because it's amazing. You're missing out."

I hit the flute out of his hand and the glass shatters, the contents soak the floor.

"I'll tell everyone," I threaten him. "The world will know that you plagiarized those songs. I will make sure of it."

"Just when I thought you couldn't be any more beautiful, you go and get all fierce and feisty. I like it." He steps forward and places his hand at the side of my face. "Don't you think Dom would've come forward already if he had the choice?" Ames' eyes are dark pools of anger and deceit. "He would've taken me down, dragged my name through the mud, made a scene if he wanted to. He hasn't. That doesn't strike you as odd?"

It does, actually. Dominic heard the songs months ago. I was with him. He knew they were his. So why isn't he making this a bigger deal than he is?

"What do you have on him?" My voice raises a decibel. I step away from him, forcefully removing myself from his touch.

"You'll find out soon enough, I'm sure." Ames points to the book in my hands. "But know this. This book is just the first layer of secrets Dom has buried. Dig this one up and the rest will quickly be unearthed. Ruin my life if you want. There are no words to describe how much I do not care what happens to me. But if I go down, Dom comes with me. And it will be your fingerprints on it, not mine."

He doesn't mean literally. I can see it in the way his eyes narrow and his smile widens. His warning gives me the choice to go quietly and forget what I know or start the avalanche that will take Dom out in its path. And it won't be Ames' voice or actions that are associated with the downfall. It will be mine.

"That chance might be worth taking. It's Dominic, for crying out loud. He doesn't have a bad nerve in his body. Nothing you could have on him could possibly be as bad as you plagiarizing an album."

Ames laughs a hearty, a full-bodied laugh, then leans into the small table, suddenly shifting gears and casting it aside so the remaining champagne flute and bottle slam to the floor beside the horizontal table.

"He's *lying* to you, Stasia!" Ames yells. "He's lying to everyone."

I take a deep breath and step back from him. I don't think he'd hurt me, but I don't trust him either — not when he's like this.

"You are not as good of a judge of character as you think you are. Allow me to be exhibit A. But do not for one second think he's exempt from that list."

Ames walks to the center of the room and looks up at the ceiling before letting out a long, calming breath.

"Do you remember how to get back to the pool area to get your stuff, or do you need me to show you?"

"I think I've got it." It's all I can manage as I take the steps toward the door, then run down the hallway with tears running down my face. My head is pounding. I don't know where to go or what to think.

The warm air hits my face and the rumble of the waterfall echoes through the space. After I find the pool area and open the doors, I pick up my belongings and dress as quickly as I can, the humid air making my clothes stick to my skin. Tears fall down my cheeks as I roam the hallways, only making two wrong turns before finally finding the split staircase to the foyer. Ames sits at the bottom step, facing away from me. The opposite staircase seems like the obvious choice. As I hit the last step, he stands and walks toward me.

"For what it's worth…" He reaches forward but I step away from his touch.

"You lost all your merit when you stole work from another creator. Nothing you say is worth much, if anything, now." I hold the book a bit tighter against my chest and step toward the door, leaving one palm on the handle before speaking. "Let's be clear about one thing." I can feel more tears forming in the back of my eyes, but I fight them back. "I will do the song with you because we committed to it, and I don't want to put any more attention on us than there already is. Let the world think we're still together for the good of the show. I don't care. But we are not. You and I are done. I can be civil in public, for now. But outside of work? Don't ever talk to me again."

My stomach turns when I reach the end of the driveway, and I feel like I'm going to be sick. From the beginning, I had a bad feeling about him—not because Dom warned me, not because social media told me to, but because my instincts told me. I ignored them, time and time again until I dismissed them completely. I left myself unlocked and free for the breaking in and breaking down.

For weeks, I've kept things slow. We didn't rush. I'd kept my body to myself until I was ready, and I finally had been. I'd shared every part of myself with him, and I've never wished I could take a choice back more in my life.

Chapter Thirty-Seven

Dom

The page in front of me is the brightest white — and it will stay that way since poetic ideas are a thing of the past for me. Historically, if I wasn't reading, I was writing, but I've stared at this same blank paper with this same black pen for five years, and not one word has made its way from my brain to these pages. The words used to flow. I could write a poem about anything on the spot…and now? Nothing. My former poems and ideas were mostly fueled by Raya. She read every word I ever wrote. She asked me to write them, and I did. It was as simple as that. When she died, she took that part of me with her.

The room was mostly silent — no music, no TV, so when a door slammed unexpectedly, I jumped a bit, though I'm fairly used to my band members and Cooper coming in and out of each other's homes as we pleased. It's always been that way with us. When you spend as much time in small quarters with each other as we tend to, locked doors and personal space become a thing of fiction. I turn over the arm of my chair and hear footsteps — well, more like stomps coming toward my library door.

What the he – ? I think to myself, but the door flies open and Stasia comes through.

I furrow my brow because she's clearly upset, but I can't imagine about what. We've barely spoken. I haven't been around her long enough these past few days to do anything to upset her.

"What does Ames have on you?" she says in a voice that cracks under the pressure of tears. For half a beat, my heart stops as she asks the question. What does she know? What has he told her? I swallow hard and stand from my chair, tossing my notebook and pen on to it, then leaning into the back with my arms crossed. "You let me be with him for weeks *knowing* there was an ulterior motive. You knew he wasn't a good guy. You knew what kind of person he was, and you let me be with him. You encouraged me to be with him!"

"Whoa, hold on." I lift both hands and pat the air with my palms. "I told you for *weeks* not to be with him. Since the day his name resurfaced, I have been trying to keep you away from him. You made it very clear you were going to disregard everything I said and make your own choices. I *never* encouraged you to be with him."

"You did!" She screams and points toward the front door. "You stood in that hallway, and you told me to have him sing me his old songs. You told me you supported me."

"I told you I would *never* be on his team, Stasia!" Uncharacteristic of me, I'm yelling, too. "You smiled when you talked about him. He seemed like he was treating you right, and you do deserve that. Even though every part of me was telling me not to, I gave him the benefit of the doubt." I take a deep breath and soften my voice. "I just thought maybe he'd changed. I thought maybe five years had done him some good. I didn't want my history with Ames to get in the way of your present. You seemed happy. I just wanted you to be happy."

"That plan worked out real well, Dom. Do I look happy to you?" Tears stream down her face, and though I've tried to mellow my own voice, she's still insistent on raising hers. "You should've just told me the truth. It's not just him I should've stayed away from. It was both of you."

"What is *that* supposed to mean?" I push myself away from the chair and take steps toward her.

"If I'd never gotten involved with you, I wouldn't have ever gotten involved with him either, right?" Her chest rises and falls as she takes quick, uneven breaths. "I just stepped on to the court of whatever stupid game you two are playing. Now I don't even know if the last few weeks were real or just him using me to get back at you."

"They were real," I say too quickly, closing the distance between us and placing my hands on her arms. "You were never a part of all this. Ames wasn't using you. He fell for you."

"How could you possibly know that?" she whispers, looking up at me with tear-filled eyes.

"Because I know how easy it is to fall for you. I know because I've been there." She stares at me and her lips part, like she's going to speak, but she doesn't. It's not an 'I love you', but it's the closest I've ever come to one, and she knows it.

She steps backward and slides her arms out of my hands.

"I can't do this." She shakes her head and wipes under her eyes. "With you. With him. Is anyone honest anymore?" she yells, then stares at the ceiling and takes a few deep steadying breaths. "I've spent weeks…*months*…thinking Consistently Inconsistent's problems were because of me, that you all started going downhill since I came along. But all this time while Cooper has been looking for new ideas and Xander and Blake have been struggling with lyrics, you stood by and said nothing while Ames got more and more famous by the day and wiped us of the charts by singing songs that *you* wrote!"

I'm quiet, by design, a closed-off person — never the center of attention, but this is a whole new kind of silence. There's nothing to say. I can't back out of this one, I can't lie and I'm not ready to admit she's right. I've spun a web of falsehoods that spans more than a decade, and it's not that I'm fearful that Ames may have just damaged a part of it. It's that I think this piece of information is the start of the storm that will wipe away the entire thing.

"How do you know about that?" I ask in a voice so small that it can't even count as a whisper.

She stares at me for several seconds that seem like hours and reaches into her sweatshirt's front pocket, then slowly removes a leather-bound book I haven't seen since before Raya passed away.

"I found this in Ames' bedroom," she says, her voice no louder than my own. She steps forward and presses it into my chest. I place my fingers over hers, so both our hands are on the book, exactly where my defective heart beats, but she pulls away and leaves.

* * * *

The next morning, I'm halfhearted about the awards show. On one hand, they are always a good time. The guys get spruced up, usually in something very over-the-top and noteworthy. This time, the band is going classic black but with electric-green accessories. My favorite color. It matches the drum set I tour with. Getting dressed up is more my scene than theirs, so I get more excited about the red-carpet events than the guys do. They usually groan about it for days but enjoy themselves once they are there. On the other hand, Stasia is performing with Ames tonight, and though I'm fairly certain they're only performing together and not still *together* together, having to watch them duet the love songs they've planned is going to be painful.

Before we are scheduled to arrive at the venue for our entrance, the band decides to meet in a parking lot adjacent to where the show will be held. We can see the red carpet, the abundant camera equipment set up and waiting, fans gathering at every inch of the area, awaiting the arrival of their favorite celebrities. We meet a few hundred feet across the way and the guys drink while we await our turn to enter. Tailgating for a big-name awards ceremony was originally Cooper's idea. He believed it was the only way to get Xander to show up. He was right, and the tradition carried through. We do this nearly every time now. I get out of the limo that was sent to my apartment and step out into the parking lot.

It may be our best look yet. Xander wears black tux pants with a fluorescent green button-up shirt, unbuttoned, half tucked in. And though he's kind of a mess, he's a stylish one. He even has the lime-green sunglasses to match. Theo went the opposite track—a fierce white suit with a green shirt and black underneath. I kept it simple—black tux pants, green belt, green suspenders and tie, a black shirt and, just for kicks, a highlighter-green bandana tied the way I do it for shows, with my hair sticking out wildly from it. Blake went anything but simple. He's wearing a full electric-green tux, with a black satin cummerbund and shiny black shoes. He too wears sunglasses, but his are black. He simultaneously looks like he had the outfit custom-designed but possibly also bought the entire ensemble for ten dollars or less at the local thrift.

The camera crews have found us already and are eating up the whole charade. Blake stands with his jacket held open, posing with his eyes peering over the rims of his glasses. He does a little twirl, and everyone laughs. Almost everyone—I still haven't seen Stasia.

"You okay?" Cooper says as he joins me.

"Yeah." It's the simplest lie I tell.

"I know this is hard for you, watching Stasia perform with Ames. I'm sorry that it's difficult, but it was a good choice. This is free publicity for us, too. I know you're mad at me for that. I know how you feel about her. But I have a band to promote. I have a new singer to promote. This is good for us. It's good for her."

From the sound of it, he still thinks they're still together, which means for now I can breathe, because it also means Stasia hasn't told Cooper or anyone else about the notebook that Ames turned into a platinum-selling record.

"I know, Cooper. I've been in the business a long time. I can be accepting of it and not happy about it at the same time. Besides, she and I aren't together, and that was my choice. So, in the end, it's not you I'm mad at."

He rests his hand against my shoulder and shakes his head.

"Why did you do that, anyway?"

I'm surprised for two reasons. One, he hardly ever wants to know about our love lives, and two, I figured he'd be thrilled that I chose to end it.

"That's a loaded question." I rub my fingers at the stubble I've allowed to grow in over the last few days. "It was just the right choice at the time — for both of us."

A limo pulls up outside the venue. As soon as the car comes to a stop and the door opens, every person in attendance screams and claps. *Of course they do.* America's current favorite celebrity couple sits just feet away from them. Their fan base has dubbed them 'Stames', some weird combination of their first names, but the world doesn't know that their given name is a thing of the past.

Ames steps out first, wearing deep black dress pants and only the vest portion of a tux, revealing his murals of tattoos that cover his arms, chest and abdomen.

He reaches into the limo and Stasia steps out with Ames' assistance. The heels she wears are several inches tall. Her top is a short-cropped black suit jacket, completely open in the front. Though it covers the parts that cross the line from what can be shown on TV and what can't, that's essentially *all* that is covered. Her under-breast tattoo and the designs that run up both sides of her abdomen are on full display. She finds stability on the ground with Ames' assistance and fixes her skirt, which is the same green we all wear, short in the front and long in the back. Stasia leans into Ames for a photo op. The crowd continues to cheer, and she waves at them with a large smile on her face. She sells it well, not shying away from him in any way. If I didn't know better, I'd say they're still together.

Maybe they are. My heart sinks into my stomach.

"All right, boys, we're up," Cooper says. The guys down what remains of their drinks, and we walk across the street to where hundreds of people and flashing cameras wait for our grand entrance. We pose for a few pictures and stop to sign autographs for a few fans. Stasia joins us and we continue the photo ops.

"Nice of you to join us," I say as she leans into me for a picture. "I thought you two weren't together anymore," I whisper as we smile for pictures.

"We aren't, so what's it to you?" she hisses under her breath so only I can hear it. It's a fair point.

She breaks away from me as soon as she can and smiles and waves in a perfect performance.

"All right, boys — and girl — " Cooper claps his hands together and addresses us. "Have fun but not too much. We are contenders for Song of the Year in the Rock category and music video of the year. I'd like you all to be able to walk onto the stage under your own power should they call our names, you got it?" The band and I offer an agreeable nod. It's nice to be up for two categories — but Save Me, Save You is up for three — and two out of three of them are in our categories. Stasia is already mad at me for playing a part in their record-topping songs, and if they beat us in any category, I fear what her reaction will be.

Everyone goes their own way to catch up with other friends and musicians, but as we part, I reach forward and grab Stasia's wrist. She turns over her shoulder, and for the first time all night, I get a good look at her. Her eye makeup is shades of black and green with glitter, and her contact lenses match our motif. Even her hair has hints of lime among the striking white-blonde.

"Can we talk for a minute?"

She nods then walks to a quiet area at the side of the building. As we walk away, I turn back to see if anyone's eyes are following us. There are thousands of people there, and it's highly likely any move we make is filmed or pictured, but everyone seems to be mostly preoccupied with themselves and their own red-carpet moments. As Stasia turns the corner out of sight, I take one last look back and see Ames, his height leaving him towering over most other bystanders, and for a moment, I think we make eye contact, but he turns back to the camera flashing in his face and the hundreds of fans trying to get his attention.

I turn the corner and Stasia stands there, her arms crossed and head held high. She's perfect, beautiful beyond measure and standing proud when the world is trying to break her. She doesn't bend.

"You didn't say anything to anyone about the book,…about Ames' album." I put my hands in my pockets and stare at her. I'd love to be a strong enough man to admit this is one of those moments that I'm incredibly good at eye contact, but damn it, I can't not look at her body.

"Is there a question in there?" She shakes her head and I shrug. "No, I didn't. I still don't know what's going on with you, and I'm not sure you will ever tell me, but Ames made it pretty clear if I out him about the album, it won't be his life I'm ruining."

I run my hand through the top of my hair and let out an exaggerated sigh.

"You know what?" I raise my hands at my sides then let them fall in defeat. "Ruin it. Ruin my life."

Her eyes perk up at this in a mixture of confusion, happiness, understanding and doubt.

"I don't care anymore, Stasia. I have stories, and I have secrets. I mean, who doesn't? But maybe it's just time to face it all. Regardless of what Ames tries to do to me, whatever becomes of my life…all I know is that I want you in it. So do it. Tell all my secrets."

Tears form in her eyes under her perfectly lined lids and false lashes.

"I don't want to ruin your life, Dominic," she says over a trembling bottom lip. "But I don't want to ruin mine, either. I give you my heart, and you gave it back to me every damn time. So, this is it. If you want me, here I am. But I refuse to be a part of the secret. If we're going to do this, we're going to do it right. Do you understand?"

I nod too quickly, agreeing to any parameters she gives me, then move quickly to her, placing both my hands at each side of her face and lifting so her lips face mine. We kiss in a way that's long overdue but worth the wait. The opening in her jacket and lack of anything underneath allows me to feel the heat of her skin against my fingers as I move my hands from her face to her body. I kiss her neck, and she dips her head back and whispers in my ear.

"Dom, stop," she says through a light moan.

"I'm sorry." I pull away from her. "I thought you wanted…"

"I do." She wraps her hands in mine. "I do. It's all I've wanted since I met you. But I'm performing tonight. I have to go get fitted for my mics and warm up."

Her performance with Ames.

"Right," I say, breathlessly, running both hands through my already messed up hair. "You're going to be great."

"I know," she says with a wink. She adjusts her hair and clothes and walks past me, toward a venue where all eyes will be on her, and back into a world that thinks she belongs to Ames Gaherty.

Allowing a few minutes to pass so she and I aren't seen leaving the side of the building at the same time, I follow when the coast is clear and head back to the front of the venue.

"What's got you smiling?" Blake says as he joins me at the entrance and throws his arm around me.

"Nothing in particular. I just have a feeling it's going to be a good night."

"They're all good nights, brother," he says, ruffling up my hair more so than it already is. "Any night above ground is a good one."

"Isn't that the truth."

We walk side by side into the room where our assigned seats are waiting. There's chatter around the area and the stage is brilliantly decorated with large black-and-silver curtain made from a glitter that reflects the stage lights as they move and bounce around the room.

As we arrive to the table dedicated to Consistently Inconsistent, Ames pulls Stasia's chair out for her and she takes it. He leans forward and kisses her on the forehead.

"Good luck tonight," he says. "I'll see you backstage in a bit."

She nods and her eyes find mine in a quick 'there and back again' glance. My hands ball into fists involuntarily, and I clench my jaw.

As the awards ceremony proceeds, presenters tell stories and talk, attendees laugh and cry and, overall, the night goes on as normal as possible. The performers outdo themselves, each one better than the last. With so many live viewers from all over the world, these kinds of shows pull out all the stops. The stage is set in intricate ways, the lights and effects are top notch, no expense spared.

The male and female winners of last year's Best New Artist category take the stage and start speaking. They talk about how one of the people about to take the stage was new to the scene, but taking the world by storm, and the other was a former fan favorite coming back out of the shadows to bask in his former light. My stomach turns. I know it's a performance. I know it's part of the job, but I can't see them together even one more time. I don't want to watch, but even more so than that, I know she doesn't want to be around him any more than she has to, and I can't protect her from this.

"For a performance like you've never seen before, please welcome to the stage," the perky blonde host says, "Consistently Inconsistent's Stasia, and Save Me, Save You's Ames Gaherty."

Everyone applauds as the room goes black. Three large screens are lowered over the curtains. The lights turn on as they take the stage, and just when the music usually would start, Ames adjusts his headset microphone and speaks.

"How are we all doing tonight?" His voice echoes through the area, and everyone hollers in response. "We have a very special performance planned for you."

He walks toward Stasia and takes her hand. To anyone else, it seems like she smiles and goes along with it, but I can see it in her eyes. I know her better than them. This wasn't part of the plan.

"This beautiful woman and I created something for you, and we're going to play it for you in just a moment. But there's something I need to say first."

I lean forward in my chair and bounce my knee up and down in a nervous twitch. Stasia stares at him, frozen to the stage as he speaks.

"Stasia" — a large smile grows across his face — "I'm in love with you, and I want everyone here to know it. I want the world to know that our time spent together has been some of the best days of my life. And every word we are about to sing, I dedicate to you."

The room *oohs* and *awwws* in unison. They all buy it.

"Is this kid fucking serious?" Blake says from the other side of the table. I watch as Stasia says nothing, but Ames smiles at her and I know that look. It's not a genuine smile. It's a malicious, victorious smile. *What the hell is he doing?*

Stasia smiles and stays in character, hugging Ames gently as the music starts. The screens behind them come to life. Ames opens with a powerful booming line, and the video behind him plays the music video from the original song he's covering. Then, the music shifts, and Stasia sings her line, the screen behind her plays a segment of the music video from the original run of the song she belts out. Everyone starts cheering when they realize what they're doing — they've created a mashup of popular eighties ballads, and as their chosen lyric changes, the screen behind them pays homage to the original artist and song.

It's brilliant. They're brilliant. She sells it. You'd never be able to tell she had a lot on her plate. She holds it so well. They continue their back and forth, singing together, apart, harmonizing and linking multiple songs I never would have thought to put together.

Ames takes over and stands at the front of the stage in a powerful bridge where he solos and turns a well-known, powerful ballad into a screaming, angry drum-and guitar-fueled metal style masterpiece that has everyone on their feet and clapping along. Stasia struts across the stage as he fades into the background. His contribution will be a tough act to follow, but I'm confident she's about to bring the house down all on her own.

She starts her song choice in a strong, up-tempo version of a previously slow song and hits a high note that drops the jaws of most people in attendance. Each attendant remains captivated by the show they put on and continues to clap their hands and cheer. They are musicians. We all are. They have a deep appreciation for both the acts on stage and the classic, respected artist Ames and Stasia are honoring.

Stasia stands at the front of the stage and bellows a forceful vibrato that would be an absolute showstopper...only, it's what's happening behind her that stops the show.

As she hits her note, the screen changes, but it doesn't change to reflect the clip from the song.

It changes to a video of *us*. She and I, outside the venue, not two hours before. She stands in her lime-green skirt, my mouth on hers, exploring the skin under the open jacket she wore so well with my hands. Her upper body is fully exposed on the large screens across the stage, on every available monitor around the room.

The room takes a collective gasp, and the music cuts out. She turns, slowly, and comes face to face with herself — a close-up of her kissing me in a moment that was supposed to be private but is now shared with the rest of the world.

A world that thinks she's still with Ames.

Chapter Thirty-Eight

Stasia

I stand with my back toward the crowd, watching the short clip play over and over again. I'm frozen by confusion and embarrassment, telling myself over and over again that this can't be happening. Then, someone's hand is on my arm, and I'm being pulled to the wings of the stage. Beyond the stage, the room is a mix of chatter as the screens are finally cut to a black screen and no music plays, no presenters take the stage. Ames isn't to be found.

I turn to find it's Dom who has pulled me from the stage and it all hits me at once—the turmoil, the humiliation. I collapse into him, and he keeps his arms wrapped tight around me as I hyperventilate into his chest.

"Deep breaths." He rubs my back. "We will figure this out."

"This is bad, Dom," I say in a fractured sentence.

"Maybe it's not. Maybe it won't be that bad."

No sooner than he says the words is the rest of the band stomping up the stairs, a red-faced Blake as their leader. He nudges me away from him and I step back just as Blake throws a punch that connects under Dom's eye.

"Blake! Stop!" I scream as I try to step forward toward Dominic once again, but Xander grabs me and holds me back. It's for my own good, I think. He's only doing it to keep me out of the line of fire. Blake isn't in his right mind right now. He grabs the front of Dom's shirt and throws him hard against the wall behind them. "Blake!"

"No," he says in a low growl, shaking his head. He keeps Dominic pinned, but he's talking to me.

"That's the second time in as many months that I've seen way more of you than I ever wanted to. Go put some fucking clothes on or something."

"Leave her alone, Blake." Dom steps forward, pushing against Blake to loosen the stronghold, but he pins Dom to the wall once more.

"We made it incredibly clear that my sister was off limits," Blake snarls, leaning in close to me. "You fucked up, big time."

"She's been your sister for like five minutes, Blake. I was with her long before you even knew you shared a blood line."

"*Dominic*," I snap in a way that's both angry and hurt. Yet again, Dom has this way of making me a pawn in a game. I have to give him some credit, though. He's not much of a fighter. If Blake's going to swing at him, Dominic is going to swing back, even if only with his words.

"*Not* okay," Cooper says as he joins us in the wing of the stage. He grabs the back of Blake's jacket and pulls him off Dom. "Not okay," he reiterates, inches from Blake's face.

"Take a walk." He points to Theo, Blake and Xander then points beyond the stage. "*Now.*"

The three leave and Dominic and I stand backstage as Cooper paces and rubs at his jaw.

"This is exactly what I didn't want."

"I know," Dom says, but Cooper doesn't let him speak.

"Do you?" He raises his voice. "This was a night of opportunity. It was a night where we could have highlighted every skill Stasia has and shown the world what we see in her. Do you even know what you've done here?"

Dom parts his lips but he doesn't speak. His question was mostly rhetorical, I'm sure.

"We have worked hard over the last few years to keep what we worked to build intact through all the other bullshit that tried to tear it apart. And you ruined it. Your antics, your inability to follow through on a choice you made, ruined that reputation."

For a second, I'm just a kid again, and my father is standing in front of me, wagging his finger, scolding me for not living up to his impossible expectations. Though it's Dom taking the brunt of the lecture, I feel three inches tall.

Cooper's voice finally calms, and he lifts one finger toward me, though his eyes stay fixed on Dom.

"Not only that, but you've ruined hers." He drops his hand and shakes his head. "I can't fix this one, Dominic. This is the first time this band has created a storm I can't control. I don't know how to stop this.

Because it isn't just about what the fans think of you. It's about what your *bandmates* think of you. And right now? I don't think they're exactly fans of yours, either."

He shakes his head, his eyes fill with disappointment and he walks away.

Dom turns and wraps his arms around me. I'm too stunned, too hurt to do anything but stand there with a blank expression and empty mind.

"Let's go," he whispers into my hairline, his lips lingering there before he speaks again. "Let's get out of here."

* * * *

Dom and I stay in silence in his library, lying on floor next to each other, touching, but staring at the ceiling. We left the awards show, and by the time they got back on track and continued the show, every TV, computer and radio was talking about Dom's and my cameo appearance.

This was not how I envisioned any of this happening. I want to find the silver lining — to be happy that even though everything is falling apart, I'm back here, next to him in this room — but I can't. I can't make myself be happy. I'm too confused to be sad. Numbness is all that remains.

They did, eventually, get on with the show. We sit in here with no lights on, and I know by the silence between us that he's doing the same thing I am — staring at the ceiling replaying all the events in our heads, right up until the point that Ames and Save Me, Save You cleaned up every category, including Best New Album, Best New Record and Best Music Video.

Though the sky continues to grow darker and the clock reaches its hand toward the midnight hour, there's an aggressive knock at Dom's door. I sit up straight, and the banging continues.

Chapter Thirty-Nine

Dom

"Can you stay here?" I push myself off the floor.

"Nope," she says, which I half expected, and she trails behind me. I keep one arm stretched toward her, trying to keep her at least an arm's distance away from whoever or whatever stands on the other side of that door. I've made a lot of enemies as of late, and after everything he's done up to this point, I can't say I'm not worried about what Ames might do next.

I reach for the handle and no sooner than the lock clicks does an angry Blake stomp through the door, followed by Xander and Theo. Though he's upright and not stumbling, I can tell Blake's been drinking.

"Figured you'd be here." Blake points a finger toward Stasia and shakes his head. "Let's go."

"I'm not leaving." Stasia's words are adamant and unwavering. "You should, though."

"All of us. Dominic too. Let's go." Blake starts walking down the hall and Stasia and I hesitate, looking to Xander and Theo for an answer, but Xander quietly shrugs, Theo barely looks at me and we all follow Blake down the hall and outside to a hired car. We climb into the back seats of the SUV and Blake keeps his gaze fixed out of the window.

"How's your face?" he asks without looking at me.

"Hurts, actually."

"Good."

Stasia sits directly between us. The car is filled with thick tension as Blake and I have staring contests with our own reflections.

The car pulls into the driveway of a small but well-kept and landscaped home.

"Blake," I say through an exhale that leaves fog on the window, "we don't need to bother him tonight. It's the middle of the night."

"Dom" — Blake's words sound miles away — "if we *can* fix this, and I'm not sure we can, we're doing it tonight. Right now or not at all."

He gets out of the car and heads to the house, banging on Cooper's door similar to how he beat on mine.

It's not Cooper who opens the door, though. It's a tall, thin brunette who looks familiar, only Cooper's not married and I've never seen him bring a woman around. It only takes me a few seconds of thinking back, combined with his warning that he too understood what it was like to want someone he couldn't have before I put all the pieces together and Blake confirms my intuitions.

"You've got to be fucking kidding me," Blake says. Then, he starts to laugh. It's almost intimidating, because I know nothing is funny. He's just at his breaking point.

"What? Are you going to punch me, too?" Cooper asks as he appears in the doorway.

"Are you okay?" the woman asks, gently pressing her fingers to the throbbing area under my eye. "I raised you better than that," she says, scolding Blake and narrowing her glare at him.

"Are you okay with this?" Blake turns to Xander, but their mother steers the conversation elsewhere.

"It's good to see you again, Stasia," Debbie says as she pulls her fingers away from my cheek. "Why don't we all take this inside?"

We all sit inside Cooper's living room, and Blake paces so ferociously that he might strip the hardwood of its finish. I can't decide if he's madder at me or Cooper, then again, I broke rules that were set in stone. There was never any clear instruction that Cooper couldn't date Xander and Blake's mother.

"I came here in hopes you'd do that Cooper-ish things you do," Blake says, looking more like Cooper than he ever has as he paces and figures out his next words. "You know, a lecture about *inappropriate relationships* or something."

"Blake," Debbie says in a kind and patient voice, then, in an unexpected move, changes her tune. "I owe you absolutely zero explanation. I spent my most of adult life alone and spent a lot of years putting Xander and you first. So did Cooper. It's our turn now, whether you like it or not."

Blake turns and looks at Xander with his mouth open and a classic 'Blake-in-bewilderment' look on his face. Xander nods and shrugs with a smile on his face.

"Something you want to say?" Blake asks him, and Xander laughs.

"You're not mad at Cooper, Blake. And you're not mad at Mom, either. If you're going to call us all here to express your concerns, express them. But leave Coop and Mom out of it. Let them be happy."

Blake looks lost for a moment, but ultimately sighs and looks to Cooper for advice. Cooper stands, walks toward him and places one hand on his shoulder. "I'll take this one from here, if you're done."

Blake nods and collapses into the chair where Cooper sat.

"Okay." Cooper claps his hands together and settles into his 'manager meets coach meets dad meets therapist' roll he's played for fifteen years. "What do we do now?"

Nobody looks at each other, and nobody speaks.

"We've played this game before. There have been rules and there has been consequences. This is what we didn't want. We knew having two band members together could have a bad outcome, and here we are. But we are going to sail this ship or sink it, and what happens next isn't up to me. It's up to you all."

"Xander?" Cooper asks, inviting someone to take the stage and say their piece.

"I don't know." He leans forward in his chair. "To be honest, it doesn't really bother me *yet*. Dom has never brought someone around once, and if this is what he wants, I don't really want to hold him back from that. But what happens if this doesn't work out? I mean, look at us now. While you two are together, Dom and Blake will barely look at each other. What happens if you're not?"

"That's my problem," Blake says. "If this ends badly, how do I take a side? How do I stay close to you both or cut you both out? Alternatively, how do I choose one over the other? This could end badly."

"I think…" It's Stasia who cuts through the silence. "I think none of this really matters right now. Dom and I aren't really…together. What you saw was an 'in the moment' thing. If we end up together…well, we still have a lot to figure out. So maybe we hold off on making a big deal out of this."

She looks at Blake as she speaks in fragmented, interrupted sentences.

And I'm speechless. I thought we were past this. I was under the impression that going forward, we would be together—for real, this time. Now, I don't know. I'm not sure what changed or when.

"I think our focus is in the wrong place," Theo says, leaning back into his chair. "We lost two major awards tonight. I don't know about you all, but I'm not losing another thing to Save Me, Save You. So, let's focus on this head-to-head battle of the bands, kick some ass then focus on this later."

"I agree," Cooper says. "We've lost too much this year. We haven't even made an album in a while. We're not touring this year. Save Me, Save You has taken more from us this year than any other band ever has."

"Aren't you supposed to be dating that loser or something? Talk about fueling the fire. The guy confessed his love to you on stage, and one minute later you're making out with someone else on the big screen." Blake finally makes eye contact with Stasia. "What even happened with all that?"

"No," she says, practically interrupting him. "We weren't even together when we got there tonight. I kept

L A Tavares

up appearances for the show. I'm sure Ames had something to do with the video interruption, though."

"Next time I see him—" Blake starts with a threatening expression.

"You'll do absolutely nothing," Cooper finishes his sentence for him. "You've all come too far to start something physical with this band. Beat them where it matters. This concert means more now than it did before. Let's get to planning, get to practicing and take the final win, publicly, where it matters. Let the fans decide."

They all nod and exchange awkward glances, but I am still frozen still, wondering where Stasia's head is at.

"At the end of the day, it doesn't matter what we all think," Cooper says, walking across the room and taking Debbie's hand in his. She stands at his side. "You two"—he looks at Blake then me—"need to figure your shit out or this isn't going to work. Goodnight."

They walk out of the room, hand in hand.

"We will give you two a few minutes." Xander stands and Theo follows. I know he's the next stop on my apology train. He's angry. I can feel it.

"Stasia." Xander nods toward the door, and she follows without saying anything.

"I—" I start, but he's not having it.

"No," Blake says, shaking his head. "You voted no when it came to having her in the band. You were the one most against this for this reason, and you promised, just like everyone else, this wouldn't happen."

"It wasn't supposed to happen like this—"

He stands and walks toward me, crossing his arms as he stands in front of me with disappointed eyes. "It wasn't supposed to happen at *all*." He steps past me, opens the door and stops over the threshold. "I'll play the show with you. I'll be in a band with you. I just don't know that I can trust you."

With that, he steps out and heads toward the car.

Chapter Forty

Stasia

We sit at the bar in The Rock Room and Cooper breaks down how the show will work. Both our bands' managers and PR teams made the decision to plan and perform the show quickly while the buzz and tensions are still high. As much as I'd like the dust to settle, they see it as an opportunity to turn a negative into a positive.

The plans are in motion, and the venue has been set. Tickets will be sold both for in person attendance and as an international virtual event. Buy a ticket, and get a link to access the concert of the decade.

Both bands will be set up on the same stage, with two different crew teams. We have no idea what they'll do for lights or special effects, and ours remain secret as well. We spend hours making plans and picking our set. They've already decided I should do a repeat performance of *Indecision* — violin and all. Dom looks like he's a planet away, looking off into the distance and not absorbing or contributing to the conversation.

At the end of the meeting, I walk toward the stage and sit on it, thinking back on how not too long ago, this is where it started—a simple open mic night that turned into a dream-come-true and right now is a nightmare. Pictures and videos of me still surface frequently. Parts of me that were private a few days ago are now available for public viewing. Even though that should bother me, it's not the thing that's ailing me most.

"Hey," Dom whispers as he joins me on the stage. "Got a minute?"

I nod and turn toward him.

"I've been trying to give you some time and space. I know you're going through some things right now. But what happened? We talked, and I thought we were on the same page. The band knows now. We finally have a chance to be out in the open and—"

"Not everything is out in the open, though, Dom." My words come out quiet and through an exaggerated sigh. "You still haven't told me what Ames is holding over you. Since he's now diligently trying—and succeeding—at ruining my life, too, I feel like I deserve some answers. You won't give them to me. I got lost in the idea of us for a few moments. But I've had time to think about it, and if you can't be honest with me, I can't be with you."

Dom rubs both hands across his eyebrows and down his face. He sighs and starts to speak, but rethinks his words, but doesn't say anything in full. I get up and walk away and he doesn't chase after me. In many ways, I'm relieved.

* * * *

The days are an endless cycle of talk about the show, rehearse for the show, planning the show. They're all the same and monotonous, but we have something to prove here. Though no one is saying it, we're all thinking it. It may just be time for Consistently Inconsistent to take their last bow. We're not touring. We haven't recorded an album. We're not soaring, and we're barely staying on the charts.

The music festivals were fine, and we had large crowds, but it's hard to measure success levels in weekends that have forty or more acts on the roster. We end up getting a lot of views from fans who were primarily there for another band and stuck around for our sets. The crowds were large, but smaller than what Consistently Inconsistent has accomplished in the past—and that seems to be a trend every time we've taken the stage.

This is a chance to take the musical world by storm once again—to remind them what this group can do, to hopefully give us enough fuel and motivation to go forward and turn the down-trend-arrow upright.

This show is all anyone is talking about. When I arrived today—early—there were already lengthy lines, so the general admission crowd can claim the best spots.

I lean into a mirror and apply electric-green powder to my eyelids, then spread some onto my roots for an extra pop against my white-blonde hair. In the reflection, I can see two bodies heading toward me, one from the right side of the backstage area and one from the left.

The room is an instantly darker place when Ames and Dom step in at the same time. The air is thicker, the atmosphere more tense.

"Dom, Stasia," Ames says with a chipper tone and an intimidating confidence, like nothing is wrong. "How are we doing on this fine day?"

The rest of both bands fill in the area, taking seats and leaning against walls. Ten people in one small room that seems to be getting smaller.

"What are you doing here, Ames?" Dom finally asks, his frustration seeping through the words.

"I just wanted to stop by and wish you luck, you know. The neighborly thing to do."

Blake steps forward, walking until he's about half an inch from Ames.

"Well, you did. Goodbye now." Blake places both hands at Ames' chest and shoves him backward.

"What's your problem, Mathews?" Ames pushes back.

"Do not for one second think I don't know about the role you played in the video that was shown on awards night, you worthless fu—"

"Blake—" Xander steps in. "Not even worth it."

The two separate, but the hostility stays in place.

"What do you say we make this a bit more interesting?" Ames suggests. "Raise the stakes."

"It's supposed to be for charity." I throw it out there, but the room is filled with more testosterone than tension, so my vote isn't heard.

"What'd you have in mind?" Blake asks, and though I didn't know any of these guys as teenagers, I feel like I'm getting a glimpse.

"If you win," Xander says, "and I'm confident you won't, which is the only reason I'm doing this. I'll let you cut my hair on stage—live."

The room is filled with a sound composed of surprise, laughter, encouragement and shock. Xander takes a long sip of his drink and laughs. "What do you got, Ames? What happens when we beat you?"

"You won't," he says confidentially. "But if you do…"

He thinks on it and taps his finger against his jaw. "My bass guitarist is also a tattoo artist, so I've got access to everything you need to let the band member of your choice give me the tattoo of their choice."

Once again, the mixed emotions fill the room.

.

Chapter Forty-One

Dom

Ames' eyes meet mine. Once again, he's somehow won them all over.

"What the hell is going on back here?" Cooper says as he enters the room. "Everything okay?" Cooper asks as Ames and I exchange narrowed glances. I turn toward him to answer, but Ames talks first.

"Everything's great," Ames says with an eerily believable smile on his face. "Good news, we've settled on what charity the proceeds will go to."

The bands look about as curious as I probably do, and Ames answers them.

"We settled on something near and dear to Dom's heart." He slams his palm hard against my chest in a way that almost makes me cough, but I swallow it down. "The American Heart Association."

For a moment, my mind freezes. Will they ask? But it's Theo who saves me before I have to throw in an impromptu lie.

"Because of Jackson?" he asks, and I nod. Stasia smiles and her eyes glisten.

"Yeah, because of Jackson…and the others like him."

"To Jackson, then," Xander says, lifting a glass, though it's almost empty.

"To Jackson." Everyone else follows, then the group breaks up and heads toward the wings for the show.

Ames digs his fingers hard into my shoulder as I turn toward him.

"Good luck, buddy." He winks and lets go of me, turning back toward the wings of the stage.

The crowd is likely the largest we've ever played for. Ames was right. As much as this whole charity concert is a mask to cover the fact that we're settling a personal vendetta, the turnout was unbelievable. In almost fifteen years, I've never seen anything like it. Cooper has been walking around with a giddiness like he just won the lottery. And he, too, is blinded by the glittery mirage that is Ames. The person Cooper thinks he is doesn't exist, and this version of him won't be around for long.

The setup is perfect. One band will perform a set, then the other. For the coin toss, we chose tails. When Abe turned up, Save Me, Save You chose to perform first. The crowd will use an app on their phone to rate the performance on everything from lights, to setting, to sound quality, to song choice, overall performance and more. Save Me, Save You takes the stage, and the crowd roars a thunderous welcome.

"Got a second?" The voice belongs to Blake, and I nod. "I'm sorry," he says.

I turn my head so fast that I give myself whiplash as I look up at him with a confused look.

"Look…" He places a firm hand on my shoulder. "The rest of us have all gotten a pass. We've made mistakes. I'm still going to meetings to keep me on track from last year. Xander has been forgiven a time or two. Hell, even Julian got back on stage with us once after everything he put us through. Anyway, the point is, you've never given us any trouble. I'm sorry I've made this hard on you. Call it a knee-jerk reaction."

"I should have told you." I shrug. The apology is weak. I'm not used to issuing them. "I didn't want to hurt you or the band. I didn't want to hurt her. I didn't know what choice to make."

"It's all good." He turns toward me and leans in to wrap his arm around me and pat me on the back with a hard clap. "Besides," he says as we part, "it could be worse. She could be with this freakin' scumbag." He throws one thumb toward Ames as he sings with his lips pressed to the mic, working his way across the stage. "He is good, though," Blake says, shaking his head. "Hate to admit it, but the guy does have some skill." He walks away, leaving me in the wings.

There is something about the way Ames performs that's quintessential. I can't take that away from him. No one can. It's remarkable, really, that he took this many years off. He's brilliant. He didn't need to steal my poems and turn them into songs because he *couldn't* write lyrics himself. His brain is constantly working. He could've put an album per year out over all these years if he'd wanted to. But he allowed the parts of him that used to be filled with lyrics and genius to be replaced with rage and vengeance. He chose these songs to prove a point, and he did. My life as I know it hangs in the balance. My whole life I've been my own person, until now. I am the puppet, and he pulls the strings.

* * * *

As promised, the winner of the battle of the bands walks away with bragging rights and a sizable donation to the charity of their choice. We're minutes from running onto the stage and taking over for our set and my chest tightens. My pulse increases and my breathing gets more difficult. Then I think on it. *Did I even take my medications today? Is this another episode? Or is this just nerves and anxiety, knowing how much is on the line here?*

The band starts to take the stage under the pitch-dark lights with the crowd screaming and cheering, awaiting our first beats. Stasia grabs my hand as she walks by.

"Hey...are you okay?" Her eyes, usually sharp and fierce, have been whittled down by worry.

"Stasia," I say through an exhale. But words aren't going to be enough. She knows me too well now. I place my hand at her face and she leans her cheek into it. That's all I had anticipated doing, but instead, I pull her in close and she wraps her arms around my waist. "I'm fine. I promise."

"Okay." She speaks into my chest. "I'm sorry. I know things have been weird between us, but I do care. Just because we're not a thing doesn't mean I don't care about you."

"I know." I nod then place my chin against the top of her head. "I care about you, too."

We take the stage hand in hand, cloaked by darkness in a way where the crowd can't see us, but neither can our bandmates. For the first time in weeks, months maybe, I feel like there's still a chance for me to redeem myself, to take it all back, to win her heart again. She walks to one side and our distance grows until our fingers slip out of the other's hand and we take our spots.

The crowd volume is intensified now, their yells and chants filling the air and their collective voice echoes for what must be miles. Blake fingers a twinkling, light repetition in a picked pattern and Theo adds in a series of different scales on the keyboard. And Xander? He laughs into the microphone. I'm not even sure he knows what he's laughing at, but the crowd is enamored by it. They shout at the top of their lungs over a simple, unexplained sound.

Ames is good. No one can ever take that away from him. But nobody reels a crowd in the way Xander Varro does. No one keeps them on the hook the way Consistently Inconsistent does.

I join my bandmates and force them to pick up the pace and play the song at the speed and volume it was meant to play at. Xander leans into the microphone and his voice booms across the venue. Stasia's fingers move across the frets with a fluidity that almost doesn't even make sense. She's so small, and her hands are so tiny that it shouldn't work, anatomically, but when she plays, that guitar is a part of her, and there is no note she can't reach.

She jumps in vocally and harmonizes with Xander over the chorus of our opening song. She leans in so her lips are almost against the microphone and for one moment, one beat, I'm jealous of the mic.

An energetic crowd is the world's most natural and effective medicine. As a musician, it's as if their force is contagious, and no matter how tired or how sick or how aggravated you might be, for one night they recharge you. Their electricity leaves their bodies and jumpstarts mine the way one would jump a car battery.

For these songs, for these moments where the hands spin around the clock much too fast, I feel healthy and whole.

Stasia tears the mic off its stand and crosses the front of the stage in a sultry way like she is modeling on a runway. When she reaches the center, she leans forward, reaches one hand out and connects, physically, with as many people as she can reach while connecting with the rest on an emotional level.

Ames stands in the wings of the stage, watching our performance. His focus skates back and forth between me and Stasia, then, they land on the large TV screens that are keeping a live score as the crowd votes and rates our performances — and we're just getting started.

If the crowd provides the energy that restarts the engine, the competition provides the fuel. As the song comes to a point where everyone else steps back and I solo, I attack, hard and wild at first, then pull back to a thunderous and fast-paced progression of loud booms and cymbal clashes, and just for kicks, I put in a little show within the show. I hold one hand straight in the air, stick to the sky and use the other to keep the beat. I spin the skyward drumstick between my fingers, fast and controlled in a hypnotic way, then I drop it, and though I made it look like an accident, I planned it perfectly. The stick fell straight down, bounced off the head of the snare and I grabbed it on the rebound, returning to a two handed, harder and faster-than-ever solo.

Just knowing Ames is standing there waiting for me to mess up is enough to make sure it's the best show I've ever played. And for a few songs, it is.

But then the heat I had felt earlier grows across my forehead. Sweat beads at my brow, and my vision makes it appear there are two drum sets in front of me. A sharp pain tears through my chest and this time, it's not discomfort. It's agony. The venue spins, the atmosphere quiets. I can feel myself fall from my stool to the stage floor, but I can't stop it. It's Stasia's face I can see turning toward me as the world around me starts to dim and darken, but it's not her voice I hear yelling for help.

It's Ames'.

Chapter Forty-Two

Stasia

Slow motion is the only way to describe the speed at which everything fell into place as Dom's body hits the floor.

I have never heard a venue as quiet as this one, as if the entire crowd simultaneously decided to have a moment of silence without being prompted. He's lying face-down behind his drum set, and I stand in my spot, frozen by fear.

No thoughts cross my mind. My muscles don't so much as twitch. I just stand there, watching as everyone else runs in to help.

Ames is the first one over to Dom, which only adds to my confusion.

"Call 911, Stasia," Ames yells at me as he flips Dom to his back, kneels in next to him and puts both hands against his chest, pressing down in a way I have only ever seen in movies.

Cooper is the next man in, sitting at Dom's opposite side, but Ames is still looking at me.

"Stasia, *now!*"

Still, I just stand there, frozen by panic and worry.

"Get her out of here, please," Ames yells to Blake, never ceasing his compressions. "Now. Get her the hell off this stage!"

Blake runs toward me and wraps his arms around me, trying to push me backward, but the right kind of fight kicks in and I push back, peering around his shoulder to watch what happens next.

"Xander, hand me that." Ames frees one hand only long enough to point at a box on the wall and Xander follows directions. As Cooper tears Dom's shirt upward, Ames opens the box to the Automated External Defibrillator. The machine starts speaking words through a recording, but it's hard to hear over the hustle and bustle.

"What are you doing?" I scream as Ames applies the AED's pads to Dom's chest. "You can't do that."

"He will die if I don't." Ames is all business, matter-of-fact. When the machine directs them not to touch Dom's body, nobody does. The AED delivers a shock to Dom's chest and in a way that seems almost instantaneous, Dom takes a loud, deep breath and coughs as he breathes out.

Everything happens in a whirlwind from there. The paramedics situate a stretcher near Dom. As they do, Ames stands up and walks away from him, leaving him with Cooper at his side, and Xander slides in where Ames left. I watch as he walks toward me like it was no big deal, like he didn't just play God in a venue filled with thousands of other people.

"How did you know how to do that?" I ask in a small voice.

"I've done it before." He doesn't elaborate, keeping the details buried.

Cooper stands and jogs toward us. "Ames—" he starts in a breathless way. "You—"

"Dom has been lying to you as long as you've known him, Cooper."

That's it. That's all Ames says. Cooper's breath goes from panting to nonexistent.

"Dom has a heart condition. He's had it his entire life. For years it was controlled with medications and small procedures, ablations, trials. He did well."

Cooper nodded in agreement, though the emptiness says he's not retaining the information.

"He avoids medical treatment because he doesn't want you and the band to know. His medications are failing. Today he went into an arrhythmia that an AED can fix. If he goes into full arrest, he will not come out of it."

Ames turns on his heel and walks away through the wings of the stage, not looking back.

I can feel Cooper's eyes on me, though I'm still watching Ames retreat into the darkness. Cooper wraps his arm around me in a supportive hug as the EMTs take Dom away.

* * * *

The last time we did this—this painstaking, sit around and wait for answers that may never come thing—it was Blake we were waiting for news on. As a band, they've done it several times. This is my second gloom-and-doom hang-out session, and it's not any easier.

Xander hasn't spoken in hours, which isn't really like him. Theo has paced at the windows of Xander's apartment for so long that he'll wear a path on the floor in no time. Cooper has been in and out of the room, phone call after phone call, for days.

It's not that none of us can find him. It's that he doesn't want to be found.

"How did we not know this?" Theo says as he paces, He shakes his head back and forth and has his fists balled up like he might put a hand through the glass wall that holds up Xander's apartment.

My shoulders fall and my breath cuts off. It's guilt, suddenly weighing on me. Because I knew. I always knew. Even if I didn't have all the details, I suspected. And if I'd dug, just a little more, if I'd pressed a tad harder, would he have told me? Would I have been able to help him before it got to this point?

And though I blame myself—and will for the foreseeable future—another part of me is furious with Dom. How could he be so careless? He made this choice. He hid a huge, dangerous, significant part of him from the people he's supposed to trust most, for years.

Blake swings the door open and Cooper rushes from the hallway to the kitchen.

"Any luck?" Cooper says, hanging up on whoever his call was with.

"No. But even if I could find him, none of the hospitals will tell us anything. Whichever one he's at, wherever he's at, we won't ever know."

I swear, Blake spoke a foreign language in those words. I heard them, but nothing registered.

"What the hell is that supposed to mean?" Cooper asks, surprisingly sounding more angry than worried.

"He had all this worked out, Coop. There's no one on his authorization sheets at any of the local hospitals. I'm lucky I even got that much info. They asked him to sign a release form to disclose his information. He crossed it out and signed it. All this time, he didn't put any of us on them. Not one. Not even his parents. Whatever is going on with him, he's doing his best to take it to his grave with him."

Theo storms out of the apartment and slams the door behind him. I don't blame him. For years, they shared hotel rooms and apartments, tour buses and plane rides, good times and bad, and his best friend has been lying to him for years. And I get it. It was a concrete house built on a sand foundation. It didn't matter how strong it was at the end of the build. When the tide came in and washed out the foundation, the rest crumbled, regardless.

Me? I follow him. It's all I can think to do.

Theo and I sit across from each other at Chance's on the Corner.

"Did you know?" Theo asks, his fingers wrapped around a cup of coffee he has stared at but not sipped.

"Not really."

His eyes widen in surprise then narrow in anger. I cut in before he has time to assume I was in on the secret.

"He told me he had some heart issues when he was a kid. But he said he was fine, that they had resolved. I believed him."

"He kept us all in the dark." Theo runs a hand over his forehead and into his hair.

"He told me once — and of course, now in context it makes more sense — but he told me that he didn't allow himself to get to close to anyone because every relationship ends — be it that life gets in the way or death. For a long time, I thought he was scared of getting hurt. But I don't think he was protecting himself, Theo. I think he was protecting us."

For hours there is no word, no update. We don't know where he is or how he is doing. Somehow, we ended up at my apartment. The band and Cooper find space in my cramped place to sit and stare at each other without speaking.

Xander paces back and forth. Blake seems to have picked up a cigarette habit once more and steps out to ruin his lungs what seems like every fifteen minutes. Theo stares out of the window and keeps his gaze there, never turning back in to look at the rest of us.

Over time, people leave. Blake steps out and says he's getting food, but he's more than likely getting butts and beer, because that's just how he copes. Xander goes home to check on Natalie and the baby. Cooper left with his phone to his ear, probably making every phone call under the sun until he gets the answers he's looking for.

So, it's just Theo and me. He doesn't leave, but he's not really there. He sits by the window like a statue, not even twitching in his chosen position.

"Can I get you anything?" I ask, stepping in beside him and placing my hand lightly between his shoulder blades. "Water? Beer? Anything?" He doesn't acknowledge my hand or my offer, and he remains committed to his quiet stance. I walk to the opposite side of the room and take a seat in the living room where I pick up a book — one Dom left behind. Using my thumb, I fan the pages then hold it close to me. For a moment, it's enough. It makes me feel like he's there. Like I have answers. Like everything is okay.

Then, nothing is okay.

The station on the TV flashes a bright red breaking news banner and the reporter on the screen wears a solemn expression as she starts her broadcast.

"Devastating news coming out of the music world tonight. Dominic Trudell, the drummer of Consistently Inconsistent, collapsed on stage during a recent charity event. Trudell was revived at the scene by fellow musician Ames Gaherty, but unfortunately sources have reported the drummer has died today in surgery at a local hospital. He was 33 years old."

I choke on the harsh breath I take in and turn to look for Theo at the window, but he's not there. I hadn't even realized he'd walked the length of the room and was standing at my opposite side, watching the news with empty eyes. Dom's picture flashes across the screen—a still frame where he's flashing his unreasonably perfect smile and his eyes are wide and bright. He's so handsome…so alive.

The news reporter continues on to warn about the nature of the video to follow, and soon after Dom is on stage, drumming one moment, clutching his chest the next, then, seconds later, unconscious on the floorboards of the stage. The clip continues on all the way through Ames leaning over his body, sending shocks through his chest to regulate his heart rhythm, which at the time, had been successful.

So what changed? What went wrong?

Cooper flies through my door and stops next to us at the front of the TV.

"Where are they getting this?" he asks, with considerable volume in his voice. "Who the hell are the sources?" he screams at the TV. His phone rings, and he throws it clear across the room before collapsing into a nearby chair with his head in his hands. He shakes his head back and forth, unraveling at the seams.

I'm not sure how long I'm sitting there staring at the TV, which plays the clip over and over again. Someone changes the channel, but more new stations have picked up on this hot story. We can't escape it. It's around us on the TV, the radio, social media. They speak a lot of words and say a lot of things, but they leave out the most important part, the answer to the question we've been asking for hours. How do they know before us? Which hospital messed up? No matter how big the celebrity or how big the story, he was one of us. We shouldn't find out news like this like we're some run-of-the-mill fan or follower.

This is the curse of living under the spotlight. You're not a person anymore, You're a product — a business, a name used for financial gain and 'likes' on social media. We don't get to be human. We don't get to grieve privately, because we don't get to do anything privately.

Blake and Xander are the next to bound through the door. "Cooper," Blake cries, running his hands through his hair, "how did this happen? What the hell is happening?" His words come out in a tornado of angst and confusion.

I keep my eyes shut tight. My chest rises and falls as I take deep breaths, willing myself not to break down — not to cry, not here, not in front of them. They all stand behind me yelling questions at each other that no one knows the answer to.

"Get out," I say, quietly. My demand is lost among the four of them. "I said, get *out!*" I yell, and the room goes almost silent. Their voices cut out and they stare at me, and the only sound is the news reporter in the background as the same clip plays for the twentieth time this hour. I pick up the remote and click the TV to a dead black. "Please," I whisper, and Blake, Cooper and Xander leave, no questions asked.

Theo walks toward me quietly and cautiously, like I might start throwing punches if he gets too close. He wraps his arms around me, and I allow it. His chin rests on my head.

"I always knew, you know," he whispers. "about you and Dom. I could see it in his eyes. He loved you. Even if he had himself convinced he wasn't capable of it, he loved you."

My tears run over, and a steady stream tracks my cheeks. He pulls away and gently uses his thumbs to wipe under my eyes.

He leaves and closes the door behind him, likely to go grieve in whatever way he sees fit.

For me, it's lying on my living room floor. The spot I've chosen is somewhere between the back of my couch and the start of my kitchen. There was no rhyme or reason. It's just where I ended up. None of this makes any sense.

He was there. I saw him open his eyes. I saw his chest rise and fall as he breathed when they took him away on the stretcher. He was back. He was fine.

But Dominic? He was never fine. That was the point. He's been sick for years. He's been lying for years. It was one of the first questions I'd ever asked him. *Where did the scars come from?* He told me he was fine.

Nothing is fine.

* * * *

Not that much time had passed, yet it feels like a lifetime had come and gone. *Somebody's lifetime did*. The radio and TV stations, as well as all the social media platforms, compete to be the first one to give us more information, though no one does. They mostly just regurgitate and re-report what the original broadcast did, putting their own spin on the details.

After a while of sitting there and running through my own thoughts, I turn the TV back on. I turn the radio on. I turn my computer and tablet on. I turn my phone on. I don't know why I do it. I can't tell you why someone would subject themselves to a cacophony of the words that make up someone's worst nightmare, but I can't *not* listen. Listening to it from multiple angles, multiple voices, makes it real. And I keep telling myself this isn't happening, but for those moments I allow myself a false hope to be built up that only hurts twice as much when it rebreaks. The video on my phone fades and my tablet quickly follows suit. I turn the volume down on the radio. I give my sole focus to the TV, because they are the ones that continuously show that picture of him, and that is the image I hold onto as the final pieces of my heart shatter and I sob tears like I've never cried before. I've never truly lost anyone. Not anyone who wasn't distant to begin with. This is first time I've been faced with saying a permanent goodbye to someone who was a part of me.

The one stream of thoughts I can't turn off is an endless loop wondering what his final moments were like. Was he in pain? Was he alone? Where did the surgery go wrong?

Chapter Forty-Three

Dom

My vision is blurred when I open my eyes. I blink a few times and adjust to the room, though I already know where I am. Most of my childhood was spent inside hospital walls, and there's no mistaking the beeps of the machines and the discomfort associated with thin blankets and even thinner mattresses.

Once my eyesight has focused, I can see one body sitting in the corner of the room.

"Well, you're not dead." He leans forward. "Pretty damn close this time — but not dead."

"Eloquently spoken as always." I sink my head back into the pillow and scan the rhythm strip of the heart monitor they have me on. My heart rate looks fairly normal, all things considered.

"How long have I been out?" The stiffness of my neck and joints suggest I haven't been doing much moving around.

"A few days. But you've been heavily medicated. They're trying to keep everything even and keep you regulated. Your body needed time to heal."

I keep my eyes on the even, up and down waves and points of the monitor. Though my eyes and mind are elsewhere, he keeps talking.

"The band knows, Dom."

I figured they knew at this point. You don't pass out mid-show with tens of thousands of fans watching without demanding answers. I'm not ready to think about it, let alone talk about it, so I don't respond. It hurts to know my secret no longer is one. It means my career is over. I can feel it in my heart, regardless of how damaged it may be.

He stands and starts walking toward the door.

"Hey." I turn my head toward him. "Who won?" I smile, slightly.

"You did." Ames nods and his light grin matches my own. "But I have to think there were some sympathy votes added in."

* * * *

There's one ceiling tile that's a different shade of white than the rest of them. I know because I've counted them and analyzed them repeatedly since I woke up. There's not much to do here. In a turn of events I never thought I'd see, I miss being a kid in this same situation. As a young child, there was always something on TV, and there weren't cell phones or iPads. That combined with the whole 'not being famous' thing. I purposely let my phone die because the sound it makes as it incessantly rings is worse than the sounds of the machines monitoring my every breath. I can't turn on the TV because if I see myself fall from that stool one more time, I will lose it completely. I can't ask anyone to bring me any of my books because...well...I haven't allowed anyone to visit...and I don't plan to.

It is late into the evening hours again, well past visitation times, and the hospital is about as quiet as it's going to get. There's close to nothing I can do and *almost* no one I want to see—except maybe one.

I've spent so much time on the machines that I know how to operate them flawlessly. I've watched nurses hang bags, press buttons and undo clamps for a good portion of my life. I know I can do it, and I do. In a move that's less than smart and a bit risky, I get myself unhooked and quietly slide out of bed, then dress into a pair of stylish blue hospital scrub pants.

The hallways aren't filled with foot traffic the way they are during the day. Some nurses make rounds, some machines beep, but it is about as quiet as it can be, all things considered. The elevator doors open, and I step onto them, hitting button number eight, only one floor below my own. The doors open once again and I step out to an equally vacant floor, which is perfect, since I'm breaking all the rules.

There's one person who gets me on a level no one else understands, and he doesn't even know it. I've spent years invested in his health, more than my own, and making a late-night appearance to his room— when we are both held prisoner to our disease and the walls of this hospital—is the most normal and whole I've felt in some time.

As I turn the corner and balance myself against the door frame, my smile fades. Everything fades—my waning millisecond of joy, my hope. All feeling is gone.

Jackson's room is empty. Clean. Practically sterile, as if he were never there at all. No hand-drawn pictures on the wall. No posters above the bed.

No snow globes on the windowsill.

Before stepping into the room, I double check the numbers to ensure I have the right room, though I know I do. Emotion plays tricks on us. It makes us think that maybe we made an error, like there's no way the horrible thing that's in front of us is true, and we grasp at a nonexistent hope, any kind of lifeline or error that might right all the wrongs. There's no error. This is his room.

Was his room.

My feet carry me to his bed, though I don't recall telling them to. Though it's clean and I know better, I sit on the edge and stare out of the window. I'm not sure how long I'm alone for before another body joins me in the reflection of the glass.

"They're not happy, you know," Ivy says as she leans into the doorway. "You're not supposed to be making your nurses' jobs harder, Dom. We work hard enough."

"I'm sorry." I talk to the image of her in the window in front of me rather than turning to face her. I'm not sure I can handle that. "I'll go back. I just... I didn't know..."

I turn ever so slightly and place one hand on the area of the bed where Jackson should be sitting, playing music too loud and air drumming with his sticks or any object he could get his hands on.

"I know you would have liked to have seen him, Dom. But know this. He saw you."

I turn toward her with an eyebrow raised.

"Your event was all over the news. Most people still just think dehydration or some other easy-to-assume thing. But Jackson? He knows better. He knew the minute you went down that it wasn't something simple."

Ivy crosses the room and takes a seat next to me.

"Once you were admitted to the hospital, he begged me to tell him if you were here. And I know I could lose my job for this, I know there is no one on your 'consent to release information' forms, but he needed you. So, I wheeled him up. He sat at your bedside. He caught you up on all things and told you all his stories — the same way you have done for him his entire life."

My chest hurts — and not because just a few days ago an electric shock tore through it. My eyes water, and my throat tightens.

"I never knew when the day would come that I would have to say goodbye to him. I always expected it would come, but I never knew when. And now I won't have the chance."

Ivy takes my hand in hers. "If this clinical trial works, you won't have to say goodbye at all."

My head jolts to the side to find her eyes before I realize I've moved at all. Every thought that is moving through my mind pauses, all mental traffic coming to a halt.

"Clinical trial?" I barely recognize my own voice coming from my mouth.

"Jackson left for Denver yesterday for that clinical trial we've been trying to get him in with. They accepted him. You were unconscious, so we couldn't update you real time —"

I throw my arms around her and pull her in close. "You could've led with that, you know."

"I thought you knew!" she cries, wrapping her arms around me, too, for a moment. She pulls away and leaves her hands in mine. "You have put in a decade of caring about Jackson's health, Dom. It's time to start caring about your own. Starting with getting back to bed where you belong."

* * * *

Though I'm sure the medications have something to do with it, I finally find sleep. When I wake up, Dr. Anderson sits in the chair at the corner of the room with an expression that's a mix of disappointed and stern.

"What's up, Doc?"

"I need you to be serious for five minutes, Dominic. You haven't taken this seriously enough for *years*. It's time to start."

I forfeit.

"What started out as one manageable thing has snowballed into a plethora of serious issues, Dom." He stands from the chair and walks toward me, leaning against the windowsill instead. "Your years and years of cardiac abnormalities, plus the medications, have damaged other areas of your heart. I want to put the internal defibrillator back in, but the surgery is riskier now. You're older, there's a buildup of scar tissue and your long-term medical issues seem to have caused a problem in a valve. We will bring you in for surgery tomorrow morning, but like I said, it's dangerous. Your heart is weak. It's been working too hard, incorrectly, for too long. You have to understand all the risks here."

"Damned if I do, damned if I don't, yeah?" I return my focus to the ceiling tiles.

"We can get you into surgery first thing tomorrow morning to fix the valve, if you sign the papers to do so."

As the nurses make their way through their preoperative checklist and testing, I stay silent, lost in my own head. How did it get this bad? How did I allow myself to get here?

It's the first time, I've truly had any regrets. I could've found a way to fix this years ago, I'm sure. I could've hit the pause button, taken a leave of absence, told Cooper I needed some time — but I didn't. For a few moments I allow myself to think that, then I push those thoughts away. I wouldn't be human if I didn't hesitate, if I didn't evaluate the 'what ifs' — but it's too late for that. The goal was to not just live, but to truly *live* this life. I saw hundreds of cities. I traveled. I laughed. I learned. I had successes and failures. No. *We*. My band. My family. We did all those things. And I'm not mad. I wouldn't change a thing. There isn't one of those moments that I would take back or chance missing out on.

This is the life I chose. Though there is a part of me that has a bad feeling about this, I'm content. If this doesn't go well, my life, though short, was full — mostly. I know there is one thing missing.

Chapter Forty-Four

Stasia

Looking back on it, I don't remember a lot of what I learned in school—not specifics, anyway—but as I stand there facing the windows at the far side of my room, all I can think about is my junior-year psychology teacher explaining the five stages of grief. But for us, I feel like it hasn't been steps, but more so, that each one of us has picked a bullet point that belongs to us. For Theo, its anger. At a time where we should all be there for each other, none of us have really spoken, but the few times anyone has reached out to Theo, they've been met with short, harsh answers and a large wall he refuses to let anyone over.

For Blake, it's denial. He is on a constant loop of 'This can't be happening. This doesn't make any sense'. Bargaining is Cooper's current mindset. He's living in the past, walking himself through every opportunity he ever might have had to step in. *"What if I had done this sooner…? If only I could back and say…"* Xander? Well, he's acceptance. Not in a 'I don't care' way, because he's hurting. More in a 'hug my wife and kid a little tighter, because you never know how long this life lasts' kind of way.

Then there's me…depression.

I haven't taken care of myself in days. I haven't eaten properly, and unless sitting on the floor of my tub, fully clothed, for an unreasonable amount of time while the water runs over me counts as a shower, I haven't taken one. I'm not crying anymore. I'm not sure there's any tears left to shed.

I hear my door open and steps near me, but I don't turn to look at who has joined me. People have been going in and out all day. It doesn't faze me anymore. Plus, I don't really care who it is. I turned off my 'give a damn' feature days ago.

"Fifteen years of staying invisible and now I've been front page news twice in two weeks."

I lift my head from my hands so fast that the room spins.

"Not the way I'd prefer to be recognized internationally," he continues, "but I guess it is what it is."

I want to turn around. I will myself to face him and confirm that the voice actually belongs to Dominic, that I'm not hallucinating or imagining things, but I can't. The footsteps get closer, and he steps in behind me, his chest at my back, and he places his hands on my shoulders the way he so often does. I lean back into him and inhale. It smells like him. Sounds like him. I shake my head back and forth. This must be a dream.

"Look at me." He pushes his hands against my shoulders in an attempt to turn me. I close my eyes tight and keep my feet planted. If I turn and all of this is my imagination playing tricks on me, the moment is over. If it is just a mirage, I don't want it to end.

"Stasia," he says, "look at me. I'm right here."

I turn and keep my eyes shut tight. His hand is at the side of my face, and I rest my head heavier against his palm. He runs a thumb across my cheek. I open my eyes and he's still there. I part my mouth like I'm going to speak, but no sound comes out. Confusion shuts down my mind, and none of my brain's synapses fire.

"How did this happen?" I wrap my fingers into the front of the shirt he wears, determined to keep him close to me and ensure he doesn't go anywhere. "How are you okay? How are you *here*?"

"I don't know what happened with the media, honestly. Trust me… It was a shock to me when I heard it. Someone is about to get fired, though, I can tell you that." He smiles and a light laugh escapes his lips.

"This isn't funny, Dom. None of this is funny." I step away from him, though I don't want to. I'm torn. I want to be close to him, but have I ever even *been* close to him? Beneath those gorgeous green eyes and the scars that cover his chest lies a person I don't know — and never have. My words catch in my throat but I manage a whisper.

"You scared me."

"I scared me, too."

He pulls me in close and I lean against his chest, my ear pressed to the area over where his heart beats.

"So…you're…better now?" And as the words leave my lips, I know there *is* such thing as stupid questions.

"No, I'm not."

It's likely the most honest he's ever been with me.

"How…? How are you…?" I rush the words, and they fumble and fall out of my mouth. "Your surgery…?"

"I haven't even had surgery yet." He steps toward me once again and takes my hand in his. "That's why I'm here. I was getting prepped *for* surgery when I heard the news you all heard. I'm supposed to be in surgery already. But the media released this headline, and everything was spinning out of control. I wanted to make this story right before I went into the operating room. That, and I wanted to see you again before I do."

"I…"

I'm not flattered. His grand gesture of coming to see me before he commits to surgery is not being accepted the way he likely anticipated.

"Dom…you are sick. You can't just be signing yourself out of hospitals and avoiding treatment. That's what got you in this position in the first place. If you don't go to a hospital where you belong and get the treatment that you need, the next time they report this it won't be false."

"I just needed to see you."

His words warm my heart, but the part of me that is concerned about his obvious disregard for his own health outweighs the part of me that's happy to see him.

"Ames said that this is a problem that has to be fixed immediately, and that if what happened on stage happens again, you might not come back from it."

Dom turns away from me and walks toward the door, shaking his head.

"Even in this moment, after everything I've been going through and all the stories the media is pitching—somehow his name still surfaces." His voice is cold and hardened, one that I hardly recognize coming from him.

"He saved your life."

"I didn't ask him to."

He walks away as I take a quick, sharp breath then swallow back the forming tears. I think all along I knew that the reason Dom hasn't solved this problem was because he never really wanted to. He, apparently, accepted death a long time ago.

I follow to the kitchen where he leans into the counter and stares into the granite as if he can see the reflection in it. As he stands there with his eyes downcast and fatigue seemingly setting in, a flood of emotions runs over me — the book, the songs, the secret.

"This is what he was holding over you?" It comes out in more of a yell than I meant it to, but anger sets in where sadness had once lived. All this time Ames could have said something. Instead of holding on to this secret and using it as some kind of twisted leverage, he could've saved Dom's life sooner than he did — and he chose not to. I start to wonder if Ames has any humanity left in him at all. "I want to know everything," I demand. "All of it. Every detail."

"I don't have that kind of time right now."

I can feel my eyes widen and surprise take over me.

"And neither do you," he says, his voice forming into a calm, soft tone. "I need to go back to the hospital. I'm not taking any more chances. I know now that this is what I have to do. Regardless of what that means for my future, I understand I won't have one if I don't start making the right choices now. And you? Well, I need you to round up the guys. Tell them I'm okay, and tell them I'm sorry. Can you do that for me?"

I nod a slow, light nod. I know he needs to go back to the hospital, but this is heart surgery we're talking about. I don't want to let go of his hands.

"It will be a few days before we talk again. But I'm going to change my permission forms. I do want you to know everything. I want you to be there when I open my eyes—if you want to be there, of course."

My slow nod turns into a quicker motion that almost makes me dizzy. I collapse into his chest, and he wraps his arms around me, running his hand over my hair and trying to calm me down.

"I just need you to be okay," I say through the tears, and he nods, his chin moving gently against the top of my head.

"I will be. I'm not going anywhere this time."

Chapter Forty-Five

Dom

As promised, Stasia was there when I opened my eyes, days after my successful surgery. It's not uncommon to spend time on a ventilator after a valve surgery, but that was the hardest part for Stasia. She, apparently, doesn't handle the tubes and machines well. I lost count of the days but, eventually, I was able to move from the CICU to the regular cardiac floor. There's a light knock at the door early one morning and I let my head fall to one side of the pillow, coming face to face with a tired-looking Cooper.

I turn away because looking at him hurts my chest more than the incision does.

Cooper shuffles into the room and takes a seat next to me, leaning forward into the bed.

"Are you okay?" His voice cracks as he asks, and it's the quietest I've ever heard Cooper speak.

"I will be," I whisper in a tone that matches his. He places his hand against my arm and his eyes look wet with a layer of tears.

"Fifteen years, Dominic." He shakes his head. "How the hell have you gone on like this? Kept all of this to yourself for *fifteen* years?"

I shrug but only fractionally, even the smallest motion pulls at my chest muscles in a way I'm not ready for. "I just wanted to play music, Coop. I'm a drummer. It is the biggest part of me. And I feared that if I took any time off, you all would spend more time worrying about me than enjoying this life we've been gifted. I didn't want anyone to think I couldn't do my part anymore. And the tours, the albums, it all just kept coming, and I was getting by. Then all of the sudden, I was so far in I couldn't backtrack. I didn't want to give any of this up. I wasn't ready to let any part of this lifestyle go."

"You should have told us," he says through an exhausted exhale.

"I know. I know that. How are the guys?"

Cooper lets out a light scoff. "Relieved. Angry. Happy. Pissed. Emotional."

"The usual, then." He laughs, and I do too, but only lightly, followed by a small cough, and I wince.

"They want to see you. I told them to give you some time. You'll be here a while. Heal up a bit, then we will bring the boys in. Okay?"

He grasps my hand in a firm squeeze before letting it go and leaving the room.

* * * *

Recovery is long and hard. It is part of the reason I've avoided any major medical attention for as long as I have. It will be months before I feel normal again, *if* I feel normal again. Weeks have passed, and though I'm making progress, I'm still weaker than I want to be, still moving slower than I'm used to.

I sit in the grass in front of the familiar heart-shaped stone. Fresh flowers sit at the base of it.

"I thought I might find you here." Ames' voice sounds normal in tone, but not in confidence. The sarcasm and aggression that lives in almost every word he speaks is gone, and his voice sounds miles away, like maybe whatever fight he had in him is gone, too. "How are you feeling?"

"All things considered? Really good. Healthy. Happy."

"That's good to hear." I look his direction and our glances meet. It does seem it is a genuine comment. "We have a lot to talk about."

I nod and resume staring at the words carved into Raya's headstone.

"I'm not going to apologize," Ames says, pulling his vape pen from his pocket.

"That isn't surprising—"

"I'm not going to apologize because it would be futile. It wouldn't fix anything. Dom, what I did? Anyway, an apology would be an insult."

I don't disagree. "Why did you do it?" I tried not to ask, but I need the answer. He kneels in the grass next to me, pulls a lighter from his pocket, leans forward and lights the candle. The flame flickers back and forth in the light breeze. Ames adjusts his position and sits next to me, staring forward where his little sister's name is.

"I spent years harboring this hatred toward you. Truthfully, though we were friends, I think it started long before Raya died. You got all her best moments, Dom. When she needed something, she chose you. You were more of a brother to her than I ever was. I thought, maybe, I hated you for that. I realize now that it wasn't hatred. It was jealousy."

Raya had a contagious personality. Everything about her was lovable, bright and warm. Even then, before all this, she was the opposite of Ames. The thing is, I think he suffered for it. Being the sibling of a sick child is a tough break in itself. The focus was almost always on Raya. It had to be. There were several times growing up that I watched as Ames got left behind. I'm not sure he ever truly learned how to be a child, Maybe that's why he is hardwired in resentment now.

"You got more time with her than I did," he continues in a broken voice. "I never understood how you could just not tell me she was dying. That was my sister, man. My parents…me? You sat by and looked us in the eyes and gave us no warning that she had stopped fighting."

"That's what she wanted, Ames." I turn toward him, "She begged me not to tell you. All she wanted was to live her last weeks in full. They did everything they could for her. She wasn't even a candidate for a heart transplant because her other organs were starting to take a toll. She didn't choose to die, Ames. She chose to live while she still could."

"Was she in pain?" A single tear falls, though he wipes it away quickly in hopes not to let me see him vulnerable.

"Yes."

He looks toward me and parts his lips. He takes a breath, and when he lets it out, it stays visible in the air.

"That's why I never gave you any of the details. It isn't because I didn't want you to know. It isn't because I didn't think you deserved it. Ames, it was awful. Her last moments were not good ones. I didn't want you to remember her that way. She didn't want you to remember her that way."

He is silent for a while, letting the information set in.

"My parents had the books from the library shipped over to you fairly quickly," he begins in a quiet voice that reminds me of a younger version of himself. "No one went into her room, though. For years, it sat untouched. One night when I was home in between traveling, I broke the lock on the room and I just sat on the floor against her bed, among all the things that made her *her*.

"Then I saw the book. It was sitting in a pile of her belongings the hospital had sent home. I opened up to a random page and the words were so beautiful, so carefully crafted." He looks at me for a moment, like it is causing him physical pain to finally admit the truth. "Dom, I thought they were hers. When I started this, I thought she'd written them. I found something in me I hadn't had in a long time—motivation. I wanted to perform again. I wanted to record again. For a short time, I felt like she'd left them behind for a reason. I was already two songs into recording when I opened to the back page and saw a note to her, from you, and I just... I don't know. I was so angry. It was just another reminder that you were more family to her than I was. I made a lot of bad choices out of that rage, Dom. I know that."

I have spent the better parts of the last few months carrying around a hatred and irritation toward Ames, and right now, more than ever, I don't have the strength to keep on at this level.

"I'm going to tell everyone, Dom."

I don't expect the words he spoke, but his confidence returns, and I can tell he has thought about this long and hard.

"I don't know what will happen from here or how this will play out, but I will tell the truth. You deserve it."

I stare at the stone and trace Raya's name with my eyes. She would kill us both if she saw us like this.

"Don't." I shake my head in a defeated way. "You were right. These words deserve to be shared. They were written for her, and they shouldn't be hidden away."

His expression lightens as if I can see the resentment fade away and the slate wiped clean.

"I can't just keep making money off an album I didn't write. I have gotten a little lost over the last few months, but I'm not completely soulless. Enough is enough. It has gone on too long as is."

"That's fair." I think for a few moments, then leave an offer for retribution on the table. "For years, I have donated money to the pediatric cardiology floor at the hospital. I'm not going to be able to do as much of that anymore."

Ames lights up with a small, genuine smile — one I haven't seen in years. "I'll take care of it. I couldn't think of a better place to contribute to."

I put one hand out and he takes my hand in a firm grip. There will always be troubled waters between us.

I'm not sure we will ever make our way back to friends, but not-enemies is an easier terrain to manage.

* * * *

Though I've been discharged for weeks now, I've spent a lot of time in this hospital as of late. Between appointments and trying to get the music room going strong, it's almost like I never left. The hospital had undergone several renovations since I spent many weeks at a time there in my youth. Then, the view from my window was someone else's window. The hospital was horseshoe shaped, and I was in an inner part of it. I couldn't see in the other window. There was no movement on the other side, no person waving back. When I looked out that pane, I saw the hospital I was surrounded by and my own reflection. It wasn't reassuring. I was part of the hospital, and it was part of me. I couldn't see past the hospital walls, physically or mentally.

Now, the cardiac wing is on a much higher level with a better view, where one can see the sun and the sky and know that there is a life beyond the walls. A few floors above that, where I stand now, a window within the music room I had built overlooks a park, a courtyard with grass that is so bright it appears painted and a water fountain. An ice cream truck has pulled up to the side of the courtyard and people line up, many of them in hospital gowns.

For some of those people, that ice cream might save their life. That blast of fresh air might change their whole mood. The smiles on the faces of the people keeping them company might have bought them one more day. When you're inside, listening to the same beeps, looking at the same walls, eating the same food, it's hard to stay happy. Being inpatient, for as much as it improved my physical health, damaged my mental health. I'm not the only one. I smile at the people below, though they can't see me, because I'm happy for them. They deserve the fresh air and the cool breeze. It's the little things that make the big things survivable.

A knock on the door brings me back to the music room. Xander leans into the doorway with one arm hidden by the doorframe.

"I brought you something." He throws his head over his shoulder and steps back into the hallway. I take his silent instructions and follow. Leaning against the wall is a metal sign that looks almost exactly like one I'm so familiar with, but there's a key difference.

"*The Little Rock Room.*" I read out loud as I trace every inch of it with my eyes. "It looks exactly like the one on the outside of the venue."

"That was the goal." He places a hand on my shoulder and we both stare at the piece of art. "We want to sponsor you. Sponsor this. We want to help. We can get musicians from the venue to sign up to teach lessons. Natalie and I, we want to help."

"This is perfect. Thank you."

"Let's see it then," he says, stepping away and into the music room. He looks around and smiles as does, nodding his head and *ooh*ing and *ahh*ing as he makes the rounds. "This is the smallest guitar I've ever seen."

Xander slides down the wall and takes a seat on the floor, pulls the child-size guitar against his chest and plucks a few notes. I shake my head and laugh. The body of the guitar looks like it will snap away from the neck under Xander's large frame.

"Damn it, Dom. Give me a beat." He points toward the small, electric-green drum set—a junior set that's an exact replica of the set I tour with. I take a seat on the tiny stool and join him. It's weak and light. I'm not moving with much flexibility at this point, but the beat is there. As we make noise that's a combination of the sounds from our instruments and our laughter at the ridiculousness of the whole scene, Theo and Blake join. Theo kneels in front of the keyboard and punches a few notes while Blake finds a triangle that I didn't even know we had and skips around the room, striking the instrument in a way that assures the entire floor that he's never played one.

"If only I had a camera," Stasia says as she joins us. "Oh. Wait. I do." She pulls her cell phone from her pocket and records our concert—four grown men sitting in child-sized chairs that threaten to break and playing instruments half the size of the ones we're used to.

My chest hurts, for a moment, reminding me that the reason I'm here still looms. But then, a new feeling—relief. Normalcy. These are my people. The silly, seemingly insignificant moments are the ones I realize now that I want to continue having. I want to look forward to my tomorrow's—not fear them.

"Now this is something," Cooper says as he enters the room. "If I'm being honest, this is pretty much how you all looked the very first time I met you—young, unseasoned, playing instruments that didn't fit you. But you made it. You made it big."

"We couldn't have done it without you," Xander says, and Cooper wipes a fake tear from his eye.

Stasia takes a seat on the floor near me, next to the drum kit.

"So, what are we doing here?" Cooper asks, looking at each one of us around the room.

"Marriage? Adoption? Pregnancy? It's that time of the year again, isn't it?" he says, clapping his hands together and looking at each one of us, waiting for us to offer some big news.

I clear my throat. "None of that, no," I say, and every eye is on me. "I brought you all in today because I wanted to talk to you. I know I haven't been very forthcoming about…anything. If there's anything you want to know about why I did what I did, why I kept it all in the dark, I'll answer any questions you have."

Stasia moves one hand and rests it at the back of my calf. It's concealed by the drum kit, so I'm not sure anyone else noticed. But I did. I needed her supportive touch.

"I only have one question," Theo says from across the room. I look directly at him, promising myself I will tell him anything he wants to know because he deserves it. They all do. "Where do we go from here?"

All eyes shift from him to me.

I close my eyes tight and swallow hard. Getting emotional was not in my plans. Letting them see how much pain this next statement is causing me was not something I wanted to do.

"I'm done drumming."

No one speaks. There is a hush over the room that is so silent, it's as if no one is brave enough to make the noise that breaks the quiet.

"I don't want this to be some big thing," I finally say. "I know we've always said if one quits, we all quit, that we stay true to the original crew. But change doesn't have to be bad. Look at Stasia. She has been amazing. I want you all to keep doing what you love. I just can't do it anymore — at least not full time. As much as my heart, metaphorically, is one hundred percent in it, physically it's not. I can't keep going at this speed anymore."

I'm unsure what to think. Their thoughts are unreadable, and no one is openly expressing how they feel about my departure.

"I'm done, too," Xander says, and my jaw falls open. "I want to see my kid grow up. There are days I don't want to pull myself away from her long enough to get to the studio, never mind a tour. For the first time, ever, I'm happy at home. I love playing for a crowd, but playing for my girls, at home? That's a special kind of something. I'm not ready to leave it."

Cooper nods, and to my surprise, he's smiling. He's seen every one of us at our best and at our worst. He practically raised us. In a moment when I expected some kind of push back, there is only pride.

"This is going to be good," Blake says, but there are tears in his eyes. "None of us have ever truly had the chance to discover who we are beyond the instrument we play."

"So, again, I ask," Theo says, "what happens from here?"

We all exchange looks and shrugs.

"I think we should do a final tour," he adds. "I want to say goodbye to the crowds and cities that made us what we are. Bring the wives. Bring the kids. But let's do one final go-round."

"We only do things here with a unanimous vote," Cooper says, the way he always does. "What do you say, Dom?"

I look at Stasia, and she doesn't look back at me. I can tell by the way her fingertips dig into my leg that she fears I'll say yes.

"I'll go along for the ride, so long as I'm healthy and cleared by then. But I can't drum full time. Even then, who knows where I'll be. It's not a chance I'm willing to take a second time. I can do a handful of shows. I just want to play by the rules this time, and that might mean being in the wings while you guys take the stage."

Stasia's grip loosens as I speak.

"I'd just hate to replace you with some stranger at this stage in the game." Cooper's voice cracks under emotional strain as he says the words. "It can't be just anybody."

"I agree," I say, and look around the room at my bandmates, my brothers — guys I've known since I was in high school, guys I grew up with and in many ways plan to grow old with. "If this is a final tour, if this is the last time, you know there's only one choice to fill my spot with."

Theo nods and his mouth hitches at one corner as he understands where I'm going. "A throwback to the original crew. Plus Stasia, of course."

My eyes find Xander's next. "I know it's not ideal," I say, but he holds up one hand.

"Julian is a great choice," he says. "I was honestly thinking the same thing. He can play any instrument, he knows the songs and he's an original member. It does tie the bow on the pretty final package we will be presenting to our fans."

"So that's it, then?" I say, shifting in the small drum kit stool. "It's time for the final bow?"

No one will speak the words. Not one person's lips even part. My hands shake in a way they never have before. I am a calm and stable person, but not right now. This band is all I've ever known — all any of us have ever known. In this moment, it's like a mutually exclusive break up. We still love each other. We still care. We know it's for the best and that there are other things out there. But it doesn't make it any easier. Walking away, saying it out loud, admitting that it's over, regardless of it being the right choice, is a significant kind of pain. It's a kind of loss — the kind of loss I've been avoiding my whole life.

The words aren't spoken, but they're agreed upon.

Instead of silence, instead of tears, Blake strikes his tiny triangle, and we all laugh, following up his unfortunate-sounding note with a barrage of noise and laughter.

At the end of our mini concert, we all look around the room at each other, waiting for someone to say the first goodbye, to announce their departure where everyone else will surely follow, but nobody does. Nobody budges. The room is silent and motionless as nobody wants to be the first person to break away.

"At the risk of getting punched," I say with a hitch of a smile on my lips and my eyes on Blake. "Blake, I want to be with your sister. If that means I have to ask your permission, I will." Stasia sits up straighter and whips her head around to look at me, completely unaware that I was going to do this. "I don't want to hide from anyone anymore — not the world, and definitely not you guys. I want to be with her. So, if it's okay with you, I plan to do just that."

"Very brave and bold of you, man." He smiles and shakes his head. "But it's not my permission you need to be asking. I don't get to make choices for her. But be very clear…neither do you. She's not really one to let others speak for her." He winks and I look at Stasia, who smiles and blushes.

Stasia reaches up and I take her hand in mine.

"That's sweet and all, but can we please do this in a place that has a liquor license?" Xander stands from his spot.

"I will meet you all later," I say, as they stand and collect themselves to depart. "I have a follow-up appointment in a bit."

"And he's not going to miss it," Stasia says sternly, tightening her grip on my hand.

Each band member exchanges handshakes and hugs, like it's goodbye, though we will regroup in a few hours' time. There is that lingering cloud, though. Everyone knows it is the beginning of the end.

Stasia walks to the window and stares outward over the courtyard. I step in behind her, wrapping my arms around her and settling in close.

"Are you sure you're going to be able to do this? Just...walk away from the only thing you've ever known?"

"I had a life with music, Stasia." I turn her toward me so my hands are at her waist, and she wraps her arms around my neck in a slow-dance-style sway. I press my forehead to hers. "I want a life with you." She kisses me, and her lips break into a smile against mine.

"You've said that before. You've also changed your mind," she whispers.

"I never changed my mind. Not once. I know what I said. But there was never a time, from the moment I met you, that I ever changed my mind about how I felt about you. I intend to have a future with you, Miss Marquette — if you'll have me."

"I worry about you. You've been a drummer your whole life. Giving up the magic..."

"Stasia," I whisper, and move a loose piece of hair from her face to behind her ear, "I've sat behind you for months, watching you perform and listening to you sing. I've fallen for you more every time we've taken that stage. Watching you love it, watching you excel at it, it's enough for me. Touring the cities and watching my girl perform, even if it's from the wings, is more than enough for me."

She leans up and kisses me, leaning into a spot in my chest that's still tender, but I don't stop her. The pain is also an indication that I'm healthy and healing—maybe for the first time ever.

* * * *

I pace the wings with a clipboard in my hand and a pen over my ear during the third show of our international goodbye tour. Everything came together beautifully. We invited acts that have toured with us before to tour alongside us. Openers we haven't seen in years, other bands we opened for before we were big— it's a glorious mix, old and new, and for the first time in a while, Consistently Inconsistent has sold out every show.

"Do me a favor?" I lean in to ask my new assistant for a favor. "Go run this over to Stasia." I hand an envelope down to him.

"Am I going to be responsible for passing your love notes to Stasia the whole tour?" Jackson asks. I mess up his hair with my palm.

"Probably." I shrug and Jackson runs off with a smile. Jackson and I have found new common ground. We've both been healthy with no issues for months. I always wanted to give him the chance to see the cities we toured in—and now I can.

"How are you doing, Twooper?" Xander asks, joining me at the stage. *Twooper*. The fun new nickname they stuck me with since I've started learning more about the business side of the trade. It's a compliment, though. Cooper is one of the best people I know.

"I want to ask you about something." I watch as Jackson hands the envelope to Stasia. "I need you to walk me through the adoption process."

Xander grips one hand at my shoulder and watches the same scene I do. "You're going to make it official?"

"Jackson has been living with me for months," I say.

"I'm no expert," Xander says, "but shouldn't you be living with the girl before you adopt the child?"

I point toward her and Xander and I watch as she tears the envelope and drops a key to my apartment into her hand. She looks at me in surprise, nods an enthusiastic yes and hugs Jackson before they crash onto a couch and talk as she tunes her guitar.

"She's been staying with us most nights anyway. Besides, Stasia and I aren't really known for doing things in the proper order."

"That's fair."

He smiles a rogue grin, and I back up.

"Don't you dare."

"It's tradition."

"It was tradition when I was in the band."

"You're still in the band, Dom." And with that, his hands are in my hair and he's messing up the clean-cut style I had perfect when I chose dress pants and a button-down shirt for the show. Now, my shirt is wrinkled, my hair sticks wildly out of place and I am a mix of disheveled and put together. I look over and watch as Stasia and Jackson laugh at Xander.

The band takes the stage and Jackson joins me in the wings.

"Ready, kiddo?" Julian says as he jogs toward us.

"Ready for what?" I ask, but the two are hand in hand, Jackson trailing behind half a step. Jackson takes a seat behind my electric-green drum set and the crowd goes wild. Stasia applauds at the front of the stage wearing a gorgeous, authentic smile.

Jackson whacks the sticks against the drums in a well-timed, perfectly executed pattern, the same beat I use to lead the band into the song, and the crowd screams. Julian claps his large hands together and takes over behind him, drumming wildly but guiding Jackson's hands.

It's perfect. We have health, and we have happiness. I never expected my life's Chapters to finish with me standing in the wings of the stage instead of on it. There were twists and turns, spoilers, good characters and bad and, looking back on it, I know now that in a story that could have ended with a cliff hanger and a 'The End', I'm incredibly fortunate to have a 'Happily Ever After'.

Want to see more from this author?
Here's a taster for you to enjoy!

Each and Every Summer
L A Tavares

Excerpt

The campground was quiet. Not silent, but quiet. Silence on the grounds was a rarity. Birds chirped and critters snapped twigs and crunched leaves as they ran through the abundant foliage, sounding off their small, happy-to-be-out-of-hibernation squeaks. The fire Weston Accardi kept lit continuously, day and night, crackled and popped as it chewed into the pieces of wood he fed it.

Soon the soundtrack of the campground would transform from its current nature-inspired sounds to a blend of noises that belonged to the incoming camping families. Children would run and play, shrieking at decibels specific to summertime. Their laughter and yells would echo through the plush pine trees as parents unpacked the camping gear and essentials from the overloaded trucks to prepare the site that they would call home for the duration of their stay. Music—both played through Bluetooth speakers and strummed on old guitars—would travel from the dirt driveways beneath each RV and become one with cloudless blue sky above.

Each currently bare site would have a tent or RV secured on it, and every available rental trailer or cottage would have people occupying them. *Every single one*, Weston thought as he thumbed through countless pages of reservations. He'd requested the bookings be printed and delivered to the site he'd claimed as 'The Owner's Headquarters' during the off-season renovations. The rest of the employees had WiFi access within the offices and laptops or tablets to view the information and spreadsheets, but Weston found nostalgic peace of mind by holding the printed reservations in his hand the exact way his father before him had done while sitting in the very same chair. A half-grin slid onto Weston's cheeks. He was pleased with the turnout of reservations for the grand reopening of Begoa's Point Family Campground. His father would have been too, had he been alive to see it.

Weston tucked the most recent reservation listings into the worn-out openings of the accordion-style folder and tossed it inside the door of his RV, which was situated in a wooded area well away from the hustle and bustle of the main grounds. When his parents had owned the campground more than fifteen years before, they had chosen a site at the center of the grounds directly within earshot of anything and everything going on within their property's perimeter. They'd preferred it that way—involved, hands-on. In many ways, Weston liked that too, maintaining full control, but when the sun went down, he preferred a hushed space to retreat to in order to separate himself from his work and enjoy the serene nature that surrounded him.

"Achilles." Weston followed the call with a quick, wet-lipped whistle and a pat of his palm against the thigh of his cargo shorts. He grabbed a leather leash from the picnic table with a clink as the metal clasp sounded against the tabletop. The dog's ears perked up like antennas receiving a signal. His tail picked up speed, wagging in long, swift motions that swept the sand off the patio mat that covered the land just outside the RV. "Want to go on a run?"

The dog leaped from the shaded dirt area he could usually be found in—a spot he'd claimed to hide away in from Maine's hot summer rays. He darted toward his owner and pushed his large head into Weston's hips with a force that almost knocked him over.

"I'll take that as a yes." Weston used his palm to ruffle the fur between the German Shepherd's ears. Achilles bounded around in circles with an impressive agility comparable to that of a show dog. With his energy and antics, no one would guess he was missing part of his hind leg. Then again, like pup, like owner. Most people hardly noticed that Weston was an amputee as well. He was a man who ran multiple miles per day, every day, with his dog stuck to his side. He walked all over the campground and was hardly ever seen in a golf cart unless there was an emergency that he needed to handle sooner rather than later. He maneuvered around using his left leg prosthetic as if it were his own natural limb.

Weston stretched out his back and his existing leg before clipping the dog's leash around his waist. The dog usually ran free, but the leash stayed on Weston's person in case the need arose for him to use it. Weston took off down the winding dirt path into a long trail of cookie-cutter cottages—empty now but soon to be filled with families ready to embark on their summer camping adventures. There would be some newcomers, but most of the reservation list was composed of returning families from his parents' time of owning and operating the same campground prior to its untimely closure.

He and Achilles ran uphill, turning a corner to jog past the recently updated tennis and basketball courts, as well as a newly renovated shower and bath house. A custodial worker waved as Weston came around the bend of the road and jogged past.

"Good morning, Larry!" Weston called. Larry tipped his hat in Weston's direction. Weston had made it a point to learn the name of every employee—a rule of his father's that he'd inherited and valued. He continued his journey down the pathway toward the beachfront bar and restaurant, stopping where Mark Jenson was readying the place for the upcoming grand reopening. The outdoor bar itself was a new addition, built while the cabins and sites were being remodeled, but Mark was an original employee. A longtime friend of Weston's father, Mark had run the bar and restaurant during Begoa's Point's first run and had agreed to come back to manage the new facility.

"Morning, boss." Mark moved large boxes of glasses from the ground to the bar top as the sun beat down on the tiki-themed hut while he worked. He wiped his brow on his forearm. His sweat-soaked shirt clung to his skin at his chest and back. "What are we having today?"

"The usual will be fine." Weston slowed and came to a full stop. Achilles followed suit, coming to a halt, then lying down in the small bit of shade the bar provided.

Mark grabbed a silver bowl from a below-bar cabinet and filled it with water before stepping out from the service area and coming around the bar to serve it to Begoa's Point's most prominent VIP. Mark stayed on one knee for a moment, scratching below the dog's chin. Achilles stood and started lapping water from the bowl, leaving more water on the ground in a messy puddle than he'd swallowed.

Mark returned to his position behind the counter, filled a cup with ice and water and slid it across the bar into Weston's hand.

"Where are you headed to today?" Mark leaned into the bar.

"All over the grounds, I think. The usual path." Weston paused to take a sip of the ice-cold water. "At least as far as the marina. I just want to make sure everything is ready to go for the opening."

"That's what you said yesterday." Mark raised an eyebrow. "Then again, it's what you will probably say tomorrow and the day after that too."

"I like to be prepared." Weston sent his now-empty plastic cup back across the bar.

"You will be. You are your father's son, after all. I wouldn't expect anything less."

Weston looked at Mark, analyzing the new lines that sank into his skin, but other than a few signs of aging, Mark looked almost the same as he had when Weston's parents had owned the campground before its closure, leaving Mark and many others without a job.

"Thank you for coming back, Mark. This place wouldn't be the same without you, even after all these years. I'm sorry we ever put you out of a job in the first place." Weston turned his eyes downward in sadness.

"It's not your fault, Weston—"

"It is, actually," Weston interrupted, adjusting his ballcap, with his gaze still glued to the floor. He watched the dog, if for no other reason than to avoid Mark's eyes. "You know it and so do I."

"It's not. You knock that off right now." Mark's voice teetered on scolding, and he wagged one aging finger in Weston's direction. "You know that your dad used to come down to the old bar every night for last call. *Every* night. He sat on the same barstool each time, and you know what he told me?"

Weston shook his head. He had been only seventeen when his parent's ownership had come to an end, so he'd not reached the legal drinking age where he could spend those waning nighttime hours with his dad, occupying Mark's bar stools. His 'no' wasn't an entirely honest answer to Mark's question, however. He knew what Mark was going to say — what his dad had used to say — but he wanted to hear it. If he couldn't hear it from his own father, Mark's affirmation was the next best thing.

"He said it was his dream to see you run this place. So maybe it didn't happen as he'd expected, but it's happening, and you should be proud of that. You're not a kid anymore, Weston. You've grown and should be so proud of who you've become. Your father would be."

"I remember that. He used to come down here every night but never had a sip of alcohol." Weston smiled at the seemingly small memories of his father, but they were anything but insignificant. They were everything.

"I remember watching you run around these grounds, from learning to walk all the way to chasing after the girls on the beach in your teenage years." Mark continued to speak, but Weston's mind was elsewhere, time-traveling down a winding path to his childhood.

It was a humid day, the kind where it was too sticky to do anything except sit around and complain about how hot it was.

"Give me your change," Charlie said, reaching across the table for Weston's quarters.

Weston grabbed the coins off the table and held them in his sweating palm, pulling them out of his best friend's reach. "You just had two ice creams. What do you need now?"

"Fried dough, of course. I'm just fifty cents short. Come on. I'll share it with you."

Weston handed over his quarters begrudgingly, but he couldn't resist fried dough any more than the next kid could. Charlie sprinted to the ordering window.

Charlie returned to the table, but just as he did, his mother beckoned from the beach.

"Be right back, Wes. We're number one forty-eight." The red color of his skin peeking out from the edges of his tank top led Weston to believe it was time for Charlie to reapply sunscreen.

"Numbers one forty-seven and one forty-eight," the snack bar attendant yelled from the pick-up window. Weston stood and headed toward the counter. Just as he did, a young girl with a mess of deep brown curls made her way there. The attendant handed two large, golden-brown fried doughs out of the window and they both headed toward the table where the cinnamon and sugar – the best parts – were kept.

The girl waited, rocking back and forth.

"Go ahead." Weston slid the shakers toward to her. "You ordered first."

She smiled and flipped the cinnamon shaker, brown dust falling to cover her plate. She followed with the sugar shaker, but no matter how much she tried, nothing came out. She looked at him and gave an embarrassed frown.

"It's not empty." Weston looked at the shaker. "It can be tricky, though. Sometimes the powder clogs the top. Let me try?"

She handed over the shaker. Weston tapped the container on the tabletop three times then flipped it over, hitting the side. A fractional amount of powder come out, and the girl giggled.

Weston undid the top, wiped away the excess confectionary powder with a napkin and pressed the lid back on. He picked it up once more and shook hard.

The top popped off, covering his fried dough in a small mountain of white powder. A cloud of sugar flew through the air and stuck to his black shirt and hair. The girl laughed so hard that she snorted.

Weston nodded, accepting an embarrassing defeat, then started laughing too. He picked up the fried dough and held it at an angle, allowing some of his sugary mess to fall over onto her piece.

"Thank you." She was still laughing as she walked away with her fried dough plate in hand.

Weston kept his gaze down the beach, imaging that younger version of himself as his adolescent years flashed before his eyes. He shook the memories away and returned his attention to Mark. "I was only chasing after one girl."

"Whatever happened to her, anyway?" Mark grabbed a towel to continue his cleaning.

"She got away." Weston slapped the bar top with his palm and winked before turning away and heading back to his predetermined path. Achilles bounded to his three legs, following behind him without being told.

The path came to an abrupt halt at the end of the shuffleboard courts and immediately turned to acres and acres of sandy beach at the lake's edge. Weston continued his jog, both his real foot and his prosthetic one kicking up sand as he ran down the untouched beach. Achilles kept pace, his paws stirring up a dusting of sand alongside Weston's. They ran the length of the main beach area, past the snack bar and mini-golf course, then turned left before finding a dirt pathway that led into the marina. He slowed as his feet hit the wooden dock. The structure, which extended into the lake, creaked under his weight. He kicked off his shoes, taking a seat on the edge of the dock and dipping both his feet into the water, only feeling the lake's cool temperature around his right ankle. Achilles sat next to him, proud and tall, as if the multiple-mile run had taken nothing out of him.

"We did it, Achilles." Weston wrapped his arm around the dog's shoulder blades. Achilles licked the side of Weston's face, stopping the salty sweat from dripping past his ears. The dog lay down next to Wes and inched forward, trying to reach his tongue into the rippling lake.

Weston removed his prosthetic and pushed himself off the dock, submerging in the water. He resurfaced and used one hand to balance on the wood. Achilles paced the edge of the dock, deciding between jumping in after him or remaining dry.

Weston used his free had to slap the water. "Get in here, boy!" Before he'd finished the command, Achilles dove in, splashing Weston upon entry and paddling toward him. They swam around, cooling off in the cold lake. Weston pulled himself back onto the dock then helped Achilles up next to him. The dog braced himself and shook, water spraying from the ends of his fur and further soaking Weston in the process. Achilles lay down once again at the edge of the dock, his front paws dangling over the wooden edge. Weston looked out over the unoccupied lake.

"This is what we've been waiting and working for. We counted down the moments to the grand reopening and it's finally happening." Weston stroked wet fur out of the dog's face. "Tomorrow is officially camping season, boy. Memorial Day. Best day of the year, if you ask me."

About the Author

When it comes to romance, L A doesn't have a type. Sometimes it's dark and devastating, sometimes it's soft and simple - truly, it just depends what her imaginary friends are doing at the time she starts writing about them.

L A has moved to various parts of the country over the last ten years but her heart has never left Boston. And no, the "A" does not stand for Anne.

L A loves to hear from readers. You can find her contact information, website details and author profile page at https://www.totallybound.com

Home of Erotic Romance

Sign up for our newsletter and find out about all our romance book releases, eBook sales and promotions, sneak peeks and FREE romance books!